The
LAST
MASTERPIECE

A NOVEL OF WORLD WAR II ITALY

❦

LAURA MORELLI

WILLIAM MORROW
An Imprint of HarperCollins*Publishers*

THE LAST MASTERPIECE. Copyright © 2023 by Laura Morelli. All rights reserved. Printed in the United States of America. No part of this book may be used or reproduced in any manner whatsoever without written permission except in the case of brief quotations embodied in critical articles and reviews. For information, address HarperCollins Publishers, 195 Broadway, New York, NY 10007.

HarperCollins books may be purchased for educational, business, or sales promotional use. For information, please email the Special Markets Department at SPsales@harpercollins.com.

FIRST EDITION

Map by Madeline Grubb

Library of Congress Cataloging-in-Publication Data has been applied for.

ISBN 978-0-06-320598-7

23 24 25 26 27 LBC 5 4 3 2 1

The

LAST

MASTERPIECE

FOR FLORENCE

In its beauty, all at once

complicated and simple,

fragile and mighty

The

LAST

MASTERPIECE

0 25 50 100 km

AUSTRIA

Altaussee

San Leonardo
in Passiria

Campo
Tures

Bolzano

ITALY

Modena

Poggio a
Caiano

Florence
Montagnana

Adriatic
Sea

Rome

Caserta

Naples

MEDITERRANEAN
Tyrrhenian
Sea

MEDITERRANEAN SEA

PROLOGUE

... those works of art which we owe to the genius of the Italian nation are to be returned to the open cities of Rome and Florence where they can be protected from terror-bombing and safely preserved for Europe.

—ADOLF HITLER

Use every means of transport to get all works of art out of Florence . . . saving works of art from English and Americans. . . . Get anything away you can get hold of. Heil Hitler.

—HEINRICH HIMMLER

[War in Italy is] like fighting in a goddamn museum.

—GENERAL MARK CLARK

Captured Documents of the German Kunstschutz
CATALOG ENTRY 276.

Lucas Cranach the Elder, *Adam* and *Eve*, oil on panels, 1528.
Originally from the collection of the Uffizi Galleries, Florence

This pair of vertical panels shows Adam and Eve in that fateful moment when they decide to disobey God.

Lucas Cranach, one of Germany's greatest artists, painted many versions of this subject, but this pair could be his most accomplished and beautiful example.

The figures stand against a dark background, disguising their nudity with carefully placed tree branches. Eve stands to Adam's left—the sinister side—as is customary for this subject.

The Devil, in the form of a serpent, coils down from the branches to whisper into Eve's ear, prompting her to pick a fruit from the Tree of Knowledge. She has already taken a bite of the apple. Soon, the bewildered Adam, who scratches the crown of his head in confusion, will also taste the fruit, and God will banish them from the Garden of Eden.

In these panels, Cranach captures the moment when Eve holds the fate of humanity in a single bite of forbidden fruit. When evil separates from good. The moment of an irreversible decision that will set humanity on its destructive course. The moment when a woman who has seen something beautiful—irresistible—gives in to the terrible beauty of temptation. The moment when she decides to take something that isn't hers to take.

Part I

BEFORE

SPRING 1943—SUMMER 1944

We should hope that the victor decides to leave things the way they are out of respect for our culture: that culture for which we should stand solidly, for which we should be witnesses, protectors and martyrs, if necessary.

—ROBERTO LONGHI, ART HISTORY DEPARTMENT
CHAIR, UNIVERSITY OF FLORENCE

EVA

WHEN I EMERGE FROM THE SALT MINE IN THE blinding noon, I find my brother hiding behind a boulder so no one will see him crying.

Um Gottes willen. On his sixteenth birthday.

My boots, cold and brine-covered, crunch over the gravel path leading to the woods. During the hours we've worked in the darkness below the mountain's surface, the day has turned brilliant. I remove my miner's coat, glazed with a subterranean varnish.

Gerhard hears me approaching up the grassy hillside. He swipes his sleeve across his nose and squints at me. His eyes, blue as the Alpine summer sky, betray a hint of defiance. Does he think I won't see the red around his lashes, his tender cheeks blotched and streaked?

In the past year, he's grown into a body that's gotten away from him. His faded woven shirts stretch tight across his shoulders. His ankles, white and bony, protrude beneath his trouser legs. Each month, his jaw becomes more square, his face more angular. He's already as tall as our Papa, but I doubt he will ever accomplish what every boy attempts: first, to be like his own father and then, in some way, to be bigger.

Instead, Gerhard's flushed, tear-streaked cheeks bear the memory of the boy I scolded back home in Berlin, when he tried to keep up with me running ahead with my camera but fell and battered his knees on the creek bank instead. Poor kid with a distracted older sister rather than a mother to dote on him. As much as I complain about it, I can't blame our father for bringing us to live with our Oma in the remotest part of Austria. A place you would come to only if you were trying to hide something.

"Gerhard . . ." I sling the leather strap across my body and feel the metal bulk of the folding camera bump against my hip. An old thing, no more than a wooden box with a collapsible bellows. I excavated it years ago from what was left of my mother's things. A contraption, they say, that makes the dead come alive. Only nothing brought our mother back to us.

I grasp a tree branch to hoist myself along the rise. The boulder hides a dark hole lined with moss. One of many secret entrances to the labyrinth hiding beneath our feet. Just one perforation discovered by chance generations ago, an artless entry into the mysterious, brine-encrusted universe beneath the earth.

"What is it?"

He slumps, his back sliding against the rock, until he comes to sit on the soft green carpet of moss with his bony knees under his chin. He removes his wire-rimmed glasses, wipes his nose, and blinks at me the way he used to when he was a little boy grounded for throwing pebbles at a group of boys who were taunting our German shepherd. Gerhard's always been like that: tender, sensitive. Empathetic to a fault. Willing to throw himself on a sword for any imperiled, helpless creature.

As if I've telegraphed the memory, Gerhard picks up a white pebble and dashes it to the ground. "I'm fine."

He's not. I feel it in my bones. He's scared to death. As of today, he's old enough to train for war. The truth is I am as scared as he is, but I can never show it. I have always had to appear invincible, since our mother hasn't been here to coddle us and our father wouldn't do it anyway. *Protect your little brother.* My mother's voice echoes across the years, along with a blurry image of her notepads, her raincoat, her heels clicking across the stones. The door closing behind her and my brother's wide blue baby eyes looking at me to do what our mother said.

I would switch places with him in an instant if there was any way for a girl to don a Wehrmacht uniform and fight a relentless enemy. If it meant keeping my brother from having to do it? Yes. My little Gerhard Brunner, for one, has no business shooting a gun, much less killing a man. A child who finds injured birds in the forest and nurses them back to flight, who wants nothing more than to draw in his sketchbooks and tend pea shoots in our Oma's garden? A tender old soul, our Oma says. None of us could imagine Gerhard wearing a crisp field tunic, disappearing over a snow-covered mountain pass to Linz with a pack of rations, and following in the footsteps of his older classmates who have boarded trains and have not returned for more than four years and counting.

But our Papa doesn't see it. The sight of a Hitlerjugend uniform hanging on the back of my brother's bedroom door swelled our father with pride at the same time that it unhinged me. For days, my Oma and I have only talked of baking a chocolate-apricot cake. A homemade *Sachertorte* on the table; a new uniform on a hook. *Alles Gute zum Geburtsag.* Happy birthday, young man.

I'm the one who possesses all the qualities our Papa's done his best to instill in Gerhard—hardness, resolve, a dedication to the truth. It's a stupid irony that I can't take his place. Women are as capable as men and I have eight years on Gerhard. But that possibility would never cross our father's mind when he'd just as soon send his bony-shouldered pony of a boy into the glory of battle. Cannon fodder.

"I know you're scared," I say, slumping down against the boulder beside him. "But Papa has connections in Linz. Maybe he will get you placed doing something else. Something closer to here—"

"I have to go, Eva!" Gerhard interrupts, then silence stretches between us. From our perch along the mossy rise, we watch a group of workers emerge from the stucco building that forms the mine entrance. In the warm glare, the men remove their bulky coats, rub their eyes, light cigarettes, and unpack their lunches at a wooden table in the grass. For generations, their forefathers spent their lives harvesting salt from the mines. But no one is taking anything from the bowels of the earth anymore. Instead, they are putting works of art inside for safekeeping.

It started months ago, when we began seeing trucks wind up the pass, one by one, so they wouldn't form a notable convoy. Trucks sent by museums, libraries, and churches across Austria. A coordinated, secret mission to hide away our nation's most precious paintings, sculptures, manuscripts, books, and other irreplaceable things. To keep them from the ravages of war. It's not the first time this vast, ancient labyrinth of the salt mines has been a hiding place.

Our father, both a well-regarded art historian in Berlin and a Septemberling who grew up in this Austrian backwater, must have seemed the perfect candidate to oversee this work. And so they called our Papa home from Germany. He took us away from our lives in Berlin. Away from my budding work taking pictures for our local newspaper. Away from Gerhard's school. Away from our friends, our lives, our futures. Toward what? Toward our Oma with her cuckoo clocks and chattering hens, toward work in the dark mine shafts, toward looming hours of waiting for a glimpse of a priceless masterpiece before it's tucked away in the bowels of the earth.

Papa says he relies on Gerhard for his physical strength and on me for my photography skills. That's because the miners' numbers have dwindled in recent months. Every able-bodied man in Altaussee has gone to Poland, Russia, France, the Low Lands, or even to Italy, where Papa says Benito Mussolini seems our only ally in a sea of enemies. Only those workers too young, old, or sick to go to war remain in our village, a place shut off from the rest of civilization by a formidable range of craggy, snow-covered peaks. Gerhard would die of embarrassment if any of the old men eating at the picnic table spied him hiding behind the rock, a crying sixteen-year-old who's suddenly supposed to be a man.

"Anyway," Gerhard continues, his voice now resigned, "you know I don't want to go. But what choice do I have?" We're both thinking of his older classmates who've received orders and will never come back here. We've been at war long enough for there to be no illusions about that now.

"Then talk to him." I gesture with my chin toward the entrance to the mine. "Don't keep it trapped inside. Come now. It's better if you speak your mind."

He hesitates. I grasp his sleeve and try to pull him from the ground. He brushes my hand away, pulls himself to standing, and shrugs on his stiff miner's coat. Gerhard squares his shoulders and walks down the hill. I follow, cradling my mother's old accordion camera in the crook of my arm. I don't go anywhere without a camera. There's no newspaper in this hinterland, of course, but I take pictures of weddings, festivals, oddities. And now it's mostly photographs of all the paintings. Of altarpieces, sculptures, and books, displayed for a moment in the light before they disappear into the darkness, a mile or more deep into a network of tunnels and chambers. Safe from calamity. I've taught myself to develop pictures in a makeshift darkroom fashioned from my Oma's garden storage shed. For what else am I to do? I can hardly fulfill our Führer's vision of being a dutiful babymaker, what with only sick and old men left in our village. And with all the world in confusion right now, taking a picture seems the only way to tell the truth.

At the door to a large stucco building that marks the mine entrance, we leave behind the staggering vista of gray and green mountain peaks. We step into the shadows, down the first set of stairs, and then into the familiar abyss. Each time we enter is a shock to the system: the thin, cold air that tastes and smells of brine. The beautiful pink of the rugged tunnels where salt, one of nature's most precious gifts, has been extracted since the Middle Ages. Lights extinguished, there is only darkness blacker than a moonless sky.

At the top of a dim staircase, I grab a safety lantern by its metal hook. We descend farther, down the wooden stairs, past the mud-splattered pit dogs on their squeaking metal wheels, full of fresh lumber pulled from Alpine forests. We move through passages so tight we have to bend over, knocking our helmets on the ceiling. Along the way, the other workers greet us by name. We are one family here. A narrow passage opens to the Saint Barbara chapel, a sacred, candlelit space the miners carved out centuries ago, which probably gave people the idea to store paintings down here in the first place. As always, we quickly bow and cross ourselves in front of the altarpiece and a painted sculpture of our patron saint of miners.

After more than a half hour of following the familiar path through the ever-descending passages, we arrive at an open cavern. We find our father overseeing the construction of wooden scaffolding, directing three old men with hammers and a room full of raw lumber. Twelve thousand paintings. That's how many the men are planning for, our Papa has said. Already, there are dozens of oil paintings in shimmering, gilded frames, stacked haphazardly in the shadows. This complicated system of rooms, tunnels, and chambers is the perfect place to protect every masterpiece in the world from destruction at the hands of the Americans and British, he says, thanks to its stable temperature and location more than a hundred meters below the surface of the earth. So far, the men have fashioned dozens of wooden shelves to store the treasures of churches across Austria—large sculptures of the Madonna and Child hundreds of years old. Ornate altarpieces disassembled into separate panels. Crates of valuable manuscripts and books. All of them held here for safekeeping until we've declared ourselves victors of this relentless war and then everything can go to the new museum our Führer is building in Linz.

My father has done his best to corral whomever he can into this effort of sawing and nailing lumber. Injured soldiers returned home. Carpenters and pensioners from nearby villages. My scrawny sixteen-year-old brother. And even me, with my mother's camera, the only tool I know how to wield. My thumb brushes the cable release, an old habit that feels as comfortable as cuddling a blanket.

Even before we left Berlin for Austria, I tried to convince my father that I could be useful, that I could do *something* with my photography skills, even if he will never allow me to follow the path that took my mother from us. Even if it's the one thing I want to do most. A big, looming truth between us, unspoken after all these years.

Taking pictures of paintings under the earth? Safe enough for a girl.

My brother's sniffle echoes in the sonorous underground chamber. Gerhard straightens his back and finds his voice. "Papa." Standing behind him, I see his shoulders squared. "I've decided. I'm not going to Linz . . ."

A tired exhale. Papa is already shaking his head, his bushy mustache twitching.

The twitching mustache is enough to silence Gerhard. His mouth hangs open, but no more words come forth. Going to war is the one thing Gerhard could do to earn our father's approval. The one thing he is the least qualified for; the one thing he can't admit. And the one thing I can't let him do.

"Papa." I step in. "Surely you have some authority to say where he goes." The men stop their hammering. "Let him stay. Let him keep working here." Keep him out of the line of fire, I almost say. But I don't want to humiliate the poor boy in front of the old men. *I* could do something important, something that matters. Like our mother did. But I don't say that out loud, either.

My father seems to think about this for a long moment, his forehead wrinkling. But before he can formulate a response, I butt in again.

"Let me go instead."

2

JOSIE

❧

THERE'S BLOOD ON ONE OF MY MOTHER'S HANDKER-
chiefs. A little swipe. A dried, rust-colored streak across the white
linen and frayed stitching. Maybe she didn't intend for me to see it,
but it's Tuesday. My turn to do the washing.

The sink is stained orange from the tap. I fill our big copper pot
and drag it to the narrow gas range, water sloshing. Strike a match,
coax the blue flame, then look at the handkerchief again. Did she
cut herself in the kitchen? My mother is usually careful about such
things. Meticulous. A bloody nose? I don't know if it will come out.
I open a blue box of Lux soap and tap it on the counter to loosen the
lumps. Then I gather a few worn garments into the hamper. I pick
up the two chipped, dirty dinner plates on the counter and put them
in the sink.

The apartment is tired beyond its years, peeled wallpaper marred
by decades of grease crackling from our stove, but the radiators work
and it's rent-controlled. "Try to find anything in New Haven, Connecticut, that don't cost a packet," my mother always says. But one
cruel comment spread around the school playground from a third-
grade classmate I'd invited home was all it took for me to learn my
lesson, and I never invited anyone again.

The old clock mounted on the kitchen wall reads 8:15. The rest of
the washing will have to wait if I want to get to my job early. I turn

off the flame. I leave the hamper bag in the dark kitchen hallway, turn down the heat on the radiator—as low as it will go without making the pipes freeze—and push my arms into my old tweed coat. I fumble with the keys and pull the front door shut behind me.

Along the sidewalk, lavender and green weeds pry through the cracks, seeking the frail light. In recent weeks, reddish buds on the trees lining the park have turned to fuzzy pink. The interminable New England gray sky has brightened. Before long, I won't need my coat. I turn onto York Street, past the foul-smelling dry cleaners and the five-and-dime, where the apartment buildings loom grander as they reach the edge of the Yale campus.

A lucky break, working as a typist at the university art gallery. A step up from the custodial job my mother's been shackled to for the better part of three decades. "Gotta get by, Josephine," my mother says as she scans the *Register*, pointing out a want ad for laundresses at the dry cleaners, and another for line cooks in one of the dining halls. I couldn't find the heart to tell her that instead I wanted to find a clerical job that not only feels like a step up, but will put food on our table until I find a husband. If I could accomplish both—a typing job and a husband—I reckon it means I won't turn out like her: a woman who spends her days scrubbing toilets and raising a child all by herself with no explanation for a father. An embarrassment.

Just one problem: there aren't many potential husbands around here. Jobs for women have opened only because the men are leaving. The academic year has been cut short for most of the Yale boys, what with mandatory conscriptions, not to mention those who sign up voluntarily. Even old Mr. Worley in the museum's curatorial department got himself shipped off to the Philippines. And the *Register* says more boys will be called up to Europe soon.

"Mouse! There you are!"

I recognize the voice immediately, feel it down to my core, as if it came from inside my own head. There's only one person who still calls me by this childish nickname, earned on that same cruel elementary school playground. Dot is home for her college break.

Dot is a burst of light on the dingy sidewalk. She is tall, blond, and beautiful, the sum of a handsome Yale anthropology professor plus a New York City socialite. Too shiny for her own good in a tailored pink suit with a matching handbag. The crowd parts as if a Hollywood starlet has touched down on York Street.

"Dot!" I can't suppress my stupid grin.

Dot and I are both only children, but that's where the comparison ends. Dot's parents raised their perfect daughter in the galleries of the Metropolitan Museum of Art and in the cities of Europe. Whipsmart. The kind of girl who should be sitting in the Yale lecture halls with the boys, if the university would let her. Instead, her parents have sent her off to Wellesley College to learn even more about Michelangelos and Leonardo da Vincis. Just a year left, and I expect she herself will be working at the Met. Dot knows me better than I know myself, except I'll never understand why she wanted me as her friend. Mousy little Josephine Evans, who doesn't know the first thing about art and wouldn't have a snowball's chance in hell of going to college.

"Get a soda with me, doll!" Dot pulls me into a tight squeeze, kisses both my cheeks loudly, then flashes her winning smile. Her aroma overwhelms me: the familiar, heady concoction of expensive perfume, shampoo, and setting lotion that forms her blond pin curls in neat patterns to frame her face.

I plant a light peck on each of her cheeks in return. "I'm on my way to work, thanks to you."

She slaps my hand playfully. "I'm sure they can get on just fine without you for ten minutes. Come on! I haven't seen you since Christmas."

"Well . . ." Dot's father helped get me this job as a typist at the Yale Art Gallery, and I'm ever so grateful. If not for his support, I might be cleaning toilets in the dormitories like my ma. "Alright. Anyway, I don't have to be there for another half hour."

I loop my arm through Dot's and we make our way down the sidewalk. I, Josie Evans, aka Mouse, drawn to Dot's bright light like a moth to a flame. We brush past the clusters of Yale men left on campus. They rush by in striped ties, off to their next lectures, secret-society meetings, or pre-military training. We continue past the whoosh and ding of the trolleys on Church Street, then push through the door of the soda fountain everybody calls Nickel Charlie's.

"How's your ma?" Dot asks as we settle ourselves on slippery barstools at the edge of a cracked linoleum counter. The soda fountain hop, a burly man with thick black hair on his arms, a stiff white shirt, and a paper hat, slides two vanilla milkshakes with cherries and long-handled spoons across the linoleum. The kind of breakfast only Dot could command without saying a word.

"She's . . ." I shrug. For a second, the memory of the stained kitchen sink, the ammonia smell in the hallway, and the bloody handkerchief flickers through my mind like a rattling newsreel. *Gotta get by, Josephine.* "Swell. Same as always. And your folks?"

Dot shakes her head. "Also the same." She rolls her eyes. "Impossible. Mother asks after you."

"Priscilla Melbourne Nichols asked about me? You lie." I take a deep slurp of the creamy, sweet coldness. Dot's ma never approved of her Dorothea socializing with Josephine Evans, daughter of a Yale cleaning lady. I imagine Dot's mother, her platinum-blond hair coiffed and sprayed hard as a helmet, looking me over with her false eyelashes, carefully painted lips, and curious, icky grin, as if her daughter had brought home an actual mouse instead of a girlfriend who resembles one.

While my mother urged me to invite Dot to our drab apartment, I never dared to, for fear of losing her friendship altogether. And I've only once stepped inside Dot's parents' home on the edge of campus—filled with books, pipe smoke, and wood paneling—and never to her mother's Upper East Side apartment, just a short train ride away. Once, Dot paid for my train and museum ticket to bring me to the Metropolitan Museum of Art. I stood in awe at the still faces of the Egyptian mummies and considered the beautiful and puzzling paintings from centuries past. She tried to explain everything to me, but it all remained as mysterious and out of reach as sitting in a Yale classroom. I've lived vicariously through Dot, since living a life like hers seems as likely to me as flying to the moon.

In the intervening time, Dot and I have grown up together in the campus quads, inserting ourselves in the boys' impromptu football games, pelting them with snowballs through the winter, or sneaking into the library reading rooms around campus to lounge in the plush chairs before the librarians shooed us out of the building. Girls. It didn't matter that one of us was the daughter of a maid, the other the daughter of an esteemed professor. They just knew we had no business there.

"It's true!" Dot insists. "Mother said she was happy you got that job at the art gallery. How is it?"

"I like it," I say. "It's just typing. But at least I have something to help pay the bills. My ma works so hard," I say. "And you? I suppose you're not going on some grand adventure this year."

"I'm going to Europe."

"Right, Dot. In case you haven't heard, Europe has been at war for the past three years."

"I know. But I'm enlisting in the Women's Army Corps."

I nearly spit out a mouthful of vanilla foam. "Horsefeathers! Now I know you're lying. Your mother would die before she sent you into a war, Dorothea Nichols."

Dot takes a long drag of the straw until the bubbles run dry, making a loud, spattering noise that turns heads at the counter. "She doesn't know."

"What!? You're off the cob."

"Only way for me to get back overseas." She puckers her lips around the straw and sucks one last time before giving up.

Every year, Dot returns to New Haven to tell me about the summer parties she's attended in Paris, her hours spent looking at pictures in the Uffizi Galleries in Florence, the fancy restaurants she's been to in London. She shows me a silk scarf she found at a shop in France and a sparkling gold bracelet she bought on the Ponte Vecchio. I've traveled vicariously through her stories, so much that I feel I've been there myself. I'm grateful, since it's the only way I could ever dream of going to such a place. But I cannot for the life of me imagine Dot in uniform.

"No offense, but what in the world use are *you* to the army?"

"The president's signed a bill," Dot says excitedly. "We don't have to be nurses or even auxiliary. If we pass basic training, we're going not as Women's Army Auxiliary Corps but as full-fledged soldiers! They're taking out the word 'auxiliary' altogether. We'll just be WACs. Women's Army Corps." She gives me a smug smile.

"You? A soldier? Dot! For heaven's sake."

"Why not? We're just as capable as any man. And you've lived around campus long enough to know that half of these guys are full of wind—or worse." She slaps my arm with the back of her soft leather glove. "Mouse!" she exclaims. "You'd make an ideal WAC! They're looking for smart single women with clerical skills. You fit the description perfectly." When I huff in disbelief, she continues. "Come on! What are you going to do, sit at home and knit socks for the boys? Where's your sense of adventure, ambition? We can do anything they do. Let those boys stay home and knit sweaters for *us*—we look better in them anyway. You should come with me. Sign up. Let's do it together. Why not?"

"I for one have nothing to contribute to a war," I say. "I'm just trying to help my ma."

She clasps my shoulder. "Oh, your ma will be fine. Jeepers, Mouse. What's keeping you in New Haven, Connecticut? The chance to sit at a typewriter all day?"

I poke my spoon into the depths of my shake and consider the fact that sitting at a typewriter already seemed a step up for me. An image of my mother bent over her mop fills my head. When I was little, my mother was my North Star. I tried to copy her expressions, the flip of her brown hair, the way she danced with her broom even though she was exhausted from the hours of mopping dining hall floors and wiping sinks in a dormitory full of spoiled boys who wouldn't have the slightest idea how to do it themselves.

But as I grew into a teenager, all it took was a few comments from my schoolmates, the sons and daughters of Yale faculty, to realize I shouldn't hold my mother in such high esteem. A college campus cleaning lady with a daughter but no husband in sight. That maybe even I should feel ashamed of her. It didn't stop me from loving her, of course. But it meant I spent the rest of my teenage years trying to be as different from her as possible. What's keeping me in New Haven? I meet Dot's gaze and tell her the truth. "Nothing, I guess."

Dot grins, self-satisfied, as if she knows better what's for my own good.

"But the Women's Army Corps!" I shake my head and shove my shoulder against hers before lowering my voice. "I've heard those gals are on active duty in more ways than one."

Dot looks serious for a moment, then her face lights up and she bursts out laughing. "Well, I hope so! I'm banking on it. Hey, let's get out of this dump," Dot says. "You need an adventure worse than I do." She pushes her empty glass toward the barman. "You're the best, darling," she says to him. He winks at Dot, grabs our empty glasses, and clinks them into the tiny bar sink.

Another short walk down the sidewalk and before I know it, Dot pulls me by my sleeve into the army enlisting office on Chapel Street.

Through the dust motes suspended in the frail morning light, I look out my bedroom window to the street. Behind me, my canvas duffel bag rests on the worn, frilly, little-girl bedspread. My shelves hold a sad-looking cluster of familiar things: a droopy ceramic pot I made in junior high, a stack of tattered romance novels bought at a library sale, a few flat pansies collected from the park and pressed between the pages of a book. For a long moment frozen in time, I watch the deserted, buckled-up sidewalk below the budding oak tree in front of our apartment and wonder if this is all a huge mistake.

Perhaps I was too rash in following Dot out of the soda fountain and to that enlistment center. And if I don't show up at the Union Station platform an hour from now—she also with her duffel bag headed to basic training in Florida—surely she would leave without me. Maybe I could write to her in Daytona Beach. Maybe she would even understand.

Instead, I could decide to peel off the layers—the wool skirt, the thick pantyhose, the girdle. The pin with a profile of Pallas Athena, the symbol of the WACs. I could unpack my spare uniform, my hat, an Italian phrase book, the pile of sanitary napkins and belt, the pressed handkerchiefs—and just return to my typewriter at the museum at nine a.m. I should go to the kitchen and tell ma I've decided to stay in New Haven.

Some say it won't be long till this war is over and the Yale men are back. Staying here is my best chance to find a husband and a better life for myself. At least that's what my mother and her sister, my aunt Betty, have always told me. Just stick around campus until you meet the son of a lawyer or a doctor who will change your life for the better. A man who will provide for you and your future children.

Instead, I signed up for basic training and an army experiment. Out from under Dot's dazzling spell, I see more clearly now. And what I see is I got nothing to contribute to a war.

Plus, for all those reasons, and because I'm my mother's only child, I expected she might have refused to let me go. Or at least that she would have broken down crying at the news that not only did her only daughter want to not just get by but wanted to leave her altogether. Of all things, she wanted to *join the army*. And that joining the army might be another of those things in life that's as far out of reach for me as going to college or affording one of Dot's mink stoles.

But she doesn't say any of that. Instead, my ma surprises me.

When I come out of my room, she grasps my shoulders and looks at me standing there in my pressed uniform. I see my mother as I always do these days: a skinny, drawn woman in a ragged housecoat, prematurely aged, with thin hair fading around the temples and deep circles under her eyes. I take in the distinct smell of her—a mixture of lavender soap, cigarettes, rose-scented hand lotion, and Glo-Coat floor polish. All the things that make me feel ashamed of her, as much as I love her all the same. A wave of guilt washes over me.

She squeezes my shoulders and takes a deep breath. She looks at me, awe-struck, as if seeing me for the first time. Right in the eyes. "You have always made your mother proud, Josephine."

After that, it feels too late to change my mind.

3

EVA

DURING THE OVERNIGHT TRAIN RIDE TO FLORENCE, I attempt to study the slim Italian phrase book my Oma pulled from a dusty shelf and slipped into my camera bag. I flip through its thin pages and try my best to ingest the words, this language that sounds like music on the wireless. *Com'è si chiama? Dov'è la stazione? Potete aiutarmi, per favore?* Ever since the train brakes squealed from the steep heights of the Alpine rails, I have browsed its pages, lingering on the phrases I will need for a stay in Italy. The train sways and tugs, a slow crawl through the black mountain tunnels, and then back into the flashing summer light. *Un bicchiere di vino rosso. Vorrei un caffè, per favore.*

But the words don't stick. That's because I've not been able to rid myself of the image in my head: the way my father looked at me for a long time. Silent. Pensive. Weighing. His wiry mustache shifting while he regarded me in the harsh, artificial light of the mine, as if he were seeing me for the first time. A daughter instead of a son who wants to go to war. Who could blame him? Look what happened last time he let a woman he loved go off to do something that mattered.

I close the phrase book and unwrap the cloth from the slice of apple cake Oma packed in my bag. I pull apart its spongy crust and savor its familiar sweetness as I watch the landscape clip by outside the window as the noon sun sears everything bright.

Italy.

For hours after our descent from the mountains, the scene outside the train has been a vast, flat plain of lonely farms and swaying stalks of wheat, with an occasional ruined building or a convoy of German panzers rumbling along in the distance. But as the day grows long, the monotony of the agricultural landscape transforms into a rolling panorama of tall, skinny cypress trees and hills like a great blanket unfurled. A flashing patchwork of ruddy, blond, and green.

I run my hand down the leather strap around my neck and pull the lens cap from my old Leica. I pick up the camera and squint through the viewfinder as the countryside rattles by. Such a moving panorama would come out blurry and anyway, it would be impossible to convey the rich palette of green and gold. A waste of valuable film. Whenever I pick up a camera, I always look to see if I could capture an image that could make someone else see something they've never seen before. That could make them see the truth. If not, I don't press the shutter release.

Of course, I was surprised my father agreed to my proposal to use my camera for a good cause. But it didn't take long for him to arrange it. The world of Austrian and German art history is small, and Papa is well connected. It only took a letter to a colleague in Berlin, and a phone call placed over static lines with the help of operators pushing plugs into a switchboard to connect him to Munich. But it was a brief telegram to one of his old classmates, Friedrich Kriegbaum, that sealed my fate. Soon enough, I packed my scuffed leather suitcase and organized my camera lenses and film for transport. I pulled Gerhard's lean frame so tight that I could smell the sticky perspiration on the back of his neck. *Stay safe, brother. Stay home.*

An exchange of sorts, my father conceded. Gerhard stays in the mines. Eva goes to Florence and puts her skills toward the service of art rather than journalism. A photography project for an esteemed German academic institution, my father explained. Something a young woman can do. Something respectable. And out of the line of fire. Friedrich Kriegbaum is one of the most upstanding members of the German art history community, my father told me before handing my worn leather suitcase up to me from the train platform. An eminent scholar and the director of the German Art History Institute in Florence. An honorable man who needs help with preparing glass plates that will be reproduced in his latest books on Italian Renaissance sculpture.

Slowly, the panorama of the Tuscan countryside gives way to a more populated area with apartments and laundry strung across balconies along the train and tram lines. I stand and open the window, letting the fresh, warm air blow my hair away from my face.

It was a hedge, of course. My father arranged for me to go to a place where the risk is lower than anywhere else. Italy. Our ally. Perhaps he knew that if he didn't arrange it, I might go off on my own. I'm old enough to make my own decisions, after all. And he must know that at my age, my mother's example might be powerful enough to draw me somewhere more dangerous. But if this exchange has bought Gerhard even one day out of the battlefield, then for me, it would have been worth it.

The train slows, its metal wheels emitting a high-pitched squeal as the conductor walks through the train car, announcing Santa Maria Novella. Several other Deutsche Reichsbahn trains stand waiting on the nearby tracks. I lift my worn suitcase, sling my heavy camera and tripod bags over my shoulders, then push through the crowded aisle. I step down from the train into a crushing crowd of Italians. The language of my phrase book comes to life, wafting into the air around me like a complicated song, amid pigeon feathers and dust captured in the stifling, sun-streaked air. Now I wish I had studied the phrases more closely.

"Fräulein Brunner."

I spy a hulking man in a shabby tweed suit jacket and crooked tie. He is in his thirties, the size of an ox, with a broad brow and hunched shoulders. He pushes his way through the crowd toward me. How did he recognize me? I can only imagine I look as out of place as he does in this chaotic tangle of pushing, talking, gesturing train passengers.

"*Wilkommen*," he says, taking the handle of my suitcase. "I'm Horst Schutz. From the Kunsthistorisches Institut. They sent me to fetch you. Stay close."

In the wake of this lumbering giant, the crowd parts. I follow Horst's broad back, among the dust-filled light and the sound of huffing trains. Long red banners flutter from the upper reaches of the station, with their familiar black swastikas on white circles. German soldiers, neat in their uniforms, patrol the entrance to the train tracks, watching the crowd. The sound of Italian on a loudspeaker wafts and echoes into the space. We thread our way out of the chaotic throng and into the sunlight of a large city square.

"It's a bit of a walk to the institute," he says. "Palazzo Guadagni is on the other side of the river."

I hoist my camera bag on my hip. "I've been sitting for hours on the train."

Horst steps out into the street, holding my heavy leather suitcase and tripod bag as if they weigh nothing. He raises his hand and several cars stop and let us jog across the street. On the sidewalk, a group of young men sing loudly, their arms slung around one another's necks.

On one side of the square is a beautiful church façade made up of multicolored marble slabs in geometric patterns. My fingers are itching for my camera, but I don't dare to stop to open my bag amid the traffic. I catch up with Horst. He turns down a narrow street, taking up the sidewalk with his broad back. Along the road, I perceive a blur of small shops—a butcher, a fruit seller, a man selling hats. Men in suits and women and children holding hands weave around us, just a step away from bicycles and small delivery trucks. A pair of German motorcycles patrols the streets. We hear the *putt-putt* of their engines as they slow to a crawl, sending pedestrians bustling out of the way. The soldiers watch inhabitants from under their turtle-shaped helmets.

"What do you do at the Kunsthistorisches Institut?" I say.

Horst turns toward me. "I'm the press officer. But mostly Herr Director Kriegbaum's assistant," he says, blotting the sweat from his brow with a wrinkled handkerchief. "He was my dissertation advisor in Munich." He gives me an assessing look from head to toe. "And I heard you are a lady photographer?"

"I'm here to take pictures for Professor Kriegbaum, yes," I say, pulling my sweater more tightly over my chest, even though the air is oppressive.

At last, the crowded street opens to a circular piazza lined with centuries-old buildings decorated with life-sized stone figures. I stop in my tracks and gasp at the sight. Horst gives me a sideways grin, revealing a sizable gap between his front teeth. "There will be plenty of time for sightseeing. To see something important and beautiful, all you have to do is take a walk. *Florenz*," he says with a strong Bavarian accent, "is a living museum."

"You've been in the city for a long time?"

"Since 'thirty-seven," he says. "I was with Professor Kriegbaum when he escorted the Führer and Il Duce together on a tour of the city," he says, puffing out his broad chest. "Our Führer was enchanted with the artistic treasures of Florence, especially those in the Uffizi. He promised to protect the city in the name of the Reich."

"Professor Kriegbaum is an old classmate of my father's." I sidestep a cluster of Italian women, petite and neat in their flowered dresses.

But Horst doesn't seem to hear me. He continues recounting his 1937 visit with Hitler and Mussolini. "We walked together through the Vasari Corridor—the upper level of the Ponte Vecchio. See?" Along the quayside, a jumble of medieval houses and towers lines the river. Many of the stone houses project out over the rushing waters, a pleasant pastiche of centuries as the dark warren of streets opens to the expanse of the Arno.

"We're not far now," Horst says. "The Kunsthistorisches Institut is just on the other side of the bridge."

Before me, a panorama of sparkling water, stone towers, and a series of bridges unfolds. From this vantage point, I admire the old bridge Horst indicates—the Ponte Vecchio—a two-story bridge bustling with people, with houses and shops right on the bridge itself. Beyond, the Tuscan hills appear gray and distant, like the background of a painting by Leonardo da Vinci. I feel my lungs fill with the damp air, and I feel the promise of adventure flow through me like the torrent of the river.

Another group of young people is coming across the bridge toward us, cheering and singing. "Is there some kind of celebration or are Italians always like this?" I ask.

Horst raises his eyebrows. "You didn't hear the broadcast?"

"What broadcast?"

His brow creases. "The Italians have surrendered to the Anglo-Americans. Badoglio announced the armistice on the wireless last night."

I stop walking. "You mean the war is over?"

Horst stops walking, too. His face darkens and he shrugs, his huge shoulders nearly reaching his ears.

From the third-floor loggia of the Palazzo Guadagni, I raise the Leica to my face and wonder if my father would have agreed to let me come here if he had known the Italians were about to switch sides.

I set the elegant façade of Santo Spirito in the viewfinder. The loggia is a beautiful Renaissance terrace that has been repurposed as a boardinghouse bar. Through the columns and arches, there is a scenic view of the Piazza Santo Spirito, the rooftops and church domes, and the gray-blue Tuscan hills in the distance. I lean over the stone railing for a better vantage point. I peer into the black square that frames my vision. I search the church's circular window, its three wooden doors, and the scrolls, all beautifully stark in their simplicity. The stucco is the color of butter.

"Fräulein . . ." Horst's voice behind me.

But I don't turn right away. Instead, I center the church's small round window in the middle of the view and hold my breath.

Snap.

The aperture closes shut for a split second, its kaleidoscopic folds spiraling together until—for a fraction of a second—everything turns black before opening back up to the light and the simple geometry of the church façade.

"You found your room to your liking?"

Finally, I turn. "Yes, thank you. Just taking a few pictures of the church." I let the box camera fall to my waist from its thick leather strap.

He nods, then leans out over the stone ledge next to me. He overlooks the church and the square below. For a moment, it seems I have made him see the building with fresh eyes. That's our job as photographers, to make people see things they wouldn't see otherwise. To see the truth of the matter.

"One of the city's most beautiful churches, in my view," he says finally, then displays a broad smile that reveals the gaping hole between his two front teeth. "That's saying something, in a city of churches. Of course, if you go inside, you'll find it empty." The smile disappears and a fleeting darkness passes over his face. "All the paintings, the altarpieces, the crucifix Michelangelo made when he was still very young . . . The Italians have taken them out of the city for safekeeping." He turns away from the ledge and gestures to the stairwell. "We're all going to the *caffè* for a bite. I will introduce you to Professor Kriegbaum—and the others."

I replace the lens cap. I take one more look at the beautiful square, then leave behind the golden light of the upper-floor loggia, with its neat tables and chairs. I follow Horst into the shadows of the once-elegant, now shabby Renaissance mansion that's been repurposed into the Kunsthistorisches Institut, a center for German scholarly research that's been in operation since the Age of Enlightenment brought people to Italy to turn them into connoisseurs.

"I'll get a new roll of film and meet you downstairs," I say. I climb the narrow stone stairwell to the top floor of the building, where I've been assigned a sparse bedroom that's part of a *pensione* run by three aging Italian sisters. Once part of the mansion's servant quarters on the upper floor, the Pensione Bandini now houses some of the staff of the Kunsthistorisches Institut, as well as visiting artists and scholars. My small room contains a narrow bed with a thin mattress, a scratched wooden desk, and an unstable chair squeezed into the last remaining space. A tiny square window is a portal to an ancient tiled roof with pigeon droppings and an interior courtyard. Under the bed, I've arranged my meager belongings packed as neatly as a soldier's—worn leather shoes, newly polished. A few pressed and folded skirts and blouses. A wool coat. A notebook and pens.

In the hallway, I've stored my photography equipment in a large wooden armoire pushed against the wall. I've organized metal canisters of film procured from my favorite photo laboratory near Salzburg. A pair of tripods. A telephoto lens. The old box camera that belonged to my mother, back when she was writing for the *Berliner Morgenpost* in her hometown in Germany.

Horst is waiting for me. At the foot of the staircase, a handsome Italian man is repairing a door lock, pulling tools from a worn leather bag at his feet. "*Buongiorno, signori!*" he greets us enthusiastically, his deep voice echoing in the stairwell. His black hair is slicked with pomade, and his belted brown trousers and shined shoes seem too formal for a laborer. Horst ignores the man completely, moving toward the door with his quick, lumbering gait. "*Signorina,*" the Italian man says more quietly, addressing me with a dazzling smile of straight white teeth. I am not yet skilled in Italian, so I just return his smile, then rush to keep up with Horst.

I shield my eyes from the wash of bright sunlight as we exit the Palazzo Guadagni. Across the square, a small bar bustles with a handful of people—a man in a suit unfolding a newspaper, a waitress in an apron serving espresso to a man and woman huddled at a table. A faded wooden sign announces Caffè Firenze. From here, the church of Santo Spirito portrays a different aspect. Now its looming wall of butter-colored stucco is cloaked in stark shadows. Along the bottom half of the façade, sandbags lie dusty and sagging in tall stacks.

At my waist, my thumb finds the shutter of the camera instinctively, but Horst is already far ahead, striding across the cobblestones. I finger the pair of film canisters in my dress pocket to make sure they're there. I follow Horst down a few narrow streets. He slows now to walk alongside me. "The Oltrarno," Horst says. "It used to be the artisan quarter of the city. Not very fancy. Mostly poor people. But there are some nice shops here." We pass a *tabacchi* selling cigarettes, stamps, and newspapers in rotating metal racks. I spy a few German titles among them.

At the corner, a pair of German soldiers stand chatting, their weapons slack. One of the soldiers looks no older than Gerhard, with fat red cheeks and a boyish face. I feel a pang and then relief that my brother is still safe in our remote village tucked into the mountains. Horst greets one of the soldiers and the other one gives him a brief salute as we pass. "They have some partisans locked up near here," Horst tells me. "Near the Piazza del Carmine." He gestures with his thick thumb toward the next street.

"Partisans . . ."

"*Partigiani*," he says in a thick German accent. "Italians who have broken ranks from the Fascists. There are more of them now than before, especially in this neighborhood. You won't read about them in the papers, but I can tell you they are everywhere. You can't trust Italians. If no one has warned you about that already, let me be the first."

Horst turns down a small street overhung with washing lines, a ragged zigzag of flapping socks, handkerchiefs, and undergarments above our heads. The sound of an Italian radio broadcast emanates from an open window with a broom handle and a wet rag visible on the sill. He wends his way expertly among the chaos of pedestrians, cyclists, careening cars, a horse and buggy.

Horst stops before a cluster of neatly arranged outdoor tables, a trimmed hedge, and a wooden lattice barrier that occupies most of the cobblestoned street. A tangle of rusty bicycles lies propped against the wall. An espresso machine whirs to life and spoons clink against cups and saucers.

"Professor!" Horst calls toward a cluster of chairs around a table, unstable and leaning on the cobbles.

The Institut's director, Friedrich Kriegbaum, lean and elegant in a dark suit, stands and pulls out a chair for me. "Fräulein Brunner," he says. "Welcome. Or *benvenuta*, as we say here. Gentlemen," he announces to the group, "I present our new photographer. Freshly arrived on the train from Austria this morning. Her father was a classmate of mine in Berlin."

Still achingly tired from the clattering overnight train into Santa Maria Novella, I heave myself gratefully into the chair. Suddenly, I realize I'm famished. Professor Kriegbaum makes introductions as I settle among the cluster of tall, fair-haired men—librarians, archivists, visiting art historians. They introduce me to Rudolf Levy, a balding man with thick glasses whom Professor Kriegbaum tells me is an important painter who has exhibited across Europe. I fear I won't remember all their names. A young woman with an apron tied at her narrow waist puts a plate of noodles in front of me. I stare down at the pile of pasta.

Across the table is the only other woman. "Paloma Innocenti," Kriegbaum says. "She is an assistant in our archives." Paloma is a neat, prim-looking woman with dark hair pulled back from her face in a bun. She stretches out her hand in greeting. "*Piacere.*"

"You are Hans Brunner's daughter." A tall man with hunched shoulders leans into me. I turn to see fleshy jowls and clear blue eyes.

"Yes." I lean back from the rush of his breath, a combination of coffee, cigarette smoke, and lazy hygiene.

He nods and grins tightly, as if I have given the correct answer to a trick question. "I knew him in Berlin." He lowers his voice and talks to me behind his hand. "Your father is doing good work at the salt mines; highly secretive, of course. Rightly so. Best we move Italian artworks into the mines, too, if you ask me. They will be protected there. And better sooner rather than later, now that the Anglo-Americans have landed in Italy. But I'm surprised he let his young daughter out of his sight." I squirm in my seat. My hands clasp the camera in my lap, as if it could provide some defense against his scrutiny.

"Fräulein Brunner will assist our photography efforts now that we have renewed support from our government for new art-related projects." Kriegbaum leans forward, shielding me from the old man's uncomfortable gaze and acid breath. "As you know, photographing our activities—and damage caused by others—is more important than ever.

"We've been working with the Italian superintendents to protect as much as we can from bombardment," Kriegbaum tells me. "Not only here in Florence. In every Italian city, movable works like paintings, sculptures, and altarpieces have been taken to the countryside. Villas. Monasteries. Castles far outside the cities. We have also overseen the evacuation of archives and libraries with valuable historical documents and manuscripts."

"Seems like a complicated undertaking."

"Very much so. But it's part of our job."

I quickly clean the plate of noodles, warm and delicious. Our server clears the tables with a clatter of ceramic and metal, then brings everyone at the table a shot of bitter espresso. "*Ecco ci, Herren—und Damen*," she says in heavily accented German, a serious expression on her face. The men push back and cup their hands around freshly lit cigarettes. I turn my attention across the table to Paloma.

"You are the only Italian here—and the only woman?"

She smiles. "No. There are other women in the institute—in the library, in the archives, secretaries in the director's office. And there are a few other Italians employed by the institute. They need us to translate, to help work through the city and regional bureaucracy."

"Your German is perfect," I say.

"*Danke*. I'm good at languages. That's how I got a job at the Kunsthistorisches Institut."

"And you have also been involved in moving the works of art to safety?" I ask.

"Only indirectly," she says. "The Italian museums and regional art superintendents moved most of the artistic treasures out of the city several years ago, at the beginning of the conflict. That is to say, anything portable—paintings, smaller sculptures, antiquities, works of metal and ceramic. Most of our great institutions—the Uffizi, the Bargello, the Pitti Palace, many smaller collections, even churches—have been closed, empty, since 'thirty-eight."

An image of the Altaussee salt mine crosses my mind. I can't imagine they have such natural resources here. "Where have all the works gone?"

"Into the countryside." She lifts her tiny cup to her lips. "There are depots outside of Florence. Several dozen of them in Tuscany alone. Private residences, historic villas, old castles. There are art officials keeping them safe there. Italians," she adds.

"But why have the Italians taken everything out of the city? I thought Florence was protected; that Hitler assured it would be so. You think the city is in danger?" Surely my father wouldn't have sent me here if he thought I was in peril. An art institute inside a protected city must have seemed like a safe bet.

Professor Kriegbaum interjects. "Up to now, yes. But the Italians have moved most of the pictures out to various depots in the countryside to avoid having all of them in one place. That way, if the Americans bomb, it won't destroy everything. And now that the Italians have aligned themselves with the other side . . ."

The archivist butts in. "Certain things are not movable, of course.

They've walled up Michelangelo's sculpture of the *David* inside a brick enclosure that looks like a giant beehive. Many of the monuments in the city have been sandbagged; I'm sure you have seen that already."

"You think the Brits and Americans will really bomb Florence?" I ask.

"They already have." An archivist sitting across the table leans forward in his seat.

"Yes," Paloma says. "We have shelters across the city—and we've had to use them."

Professor Kriegbaum leans into the table and addresses me directly. "We have a few more private collections to photograph and evacuate from the city. You'll see."

At last. A real purpose. A proper job. I've done it. I've convinced my father that I can do something useful, something important. Even in a city that is more at risk than he might have imagined.

"It's our job to save them, to protect them for our future," he says. "Every last masterpiece."

Then Professor Kriegbaum takes a swift drag on his cigarette and we watch the smoke loop upward toward the streak of light breaking over the tiled rooftops.

4

JOSIE

DOT HAS CLAIMED THE TOP BUNK, OF COURSE.
The clumsy, slow ocean liner has barely untied from the Newport News naval docks, but Dot's already spread her things across the thin mattress—a messy scattering of a hand mirror, lipstick tubes, a comb, hairbrush, and new pens from her favorite stationer on the Upper East Side. I slide my duffel across the floor, under the creaky springs of the lower bunk. The deep reverberation of the ship's horn shudders through my bones. I've never been on a boat before, even a small one. For the first time in my life, I teeter in the destabilizing sensation of the solid earth falling away.

Dot's disappeared with a clutch of uniformed women to explore the ship's plush, faded glory. The army has repurposed SS *Empress of Scotland* as troop transport bound for the coast of North Africa. I hear their excited voices and laughter in the narrow corridors. Dot must feel right at home among this luxurious conglomeration of purple velvet permeated with cigar smoke, grand pianos, staterooms, thick carpets, and seaside balconies. One heck of a way to send dozens of women into war, if you ask me.

From the start, Dot and I vowed to stay together. It's the only way I'd agreed to sign up for this supposed adventure. And during our weeks of basic training, Dot and I did stick together like peanut butter and jelly. At Daytona Beach, Dot and I held each other's feet to the ground for sit-ups, answered the psychologists' repeated questions, and recited the army ranks from private to brigadier general until we could spew them in our sleep. We learned the proper form for a salute, how to line-dry our girdles and stockings out of view of the boys, how to sew on our insignia, how to wear a gas mask. In our advanced training at Camp Polk, Louisiana—hotter than any place I've ever imagined—we endured billeting in a desolate former POW camp, little more than a gaggle of exhausted girls in our slips crowded around the cracked mirror next to the men's urinals.

We survived. And we did it all together, Dot and I.

But in the face of our continued promises to stick together, as soon as we board SS *Empress of Scotland*, we're separated. That's because, for all her first-class Wellesley education, Dot has the ugliest penmanship and the poor girl can't type for all the money in the world. So they've assigned her to a rolling chair before a giant telephone switchboard plugged with a tangle of cords and headsets. Other girls have trained to bandage wounds, to turn out trays of biscuits and salt pork, to load rolls of paper inside the complicated teletype machines.

As for me, I guess stenography was the most natural fit. I was a quick study when it came to the typewriter and my boss at the art gallery told me I was good with language. I've filled up dozens of lined steno pads with the strange Gregg shorthand that looks more like those Egyptian hieroglyphs in the museum than a series of words. My fingers have begun to move faster across the clunky metal stenotype keyboard. I'm nowhere near the three hundred words per minute they promised, but I'll get there.

"Come on, Josie! They're feeding us—finally!" Ruby Stevens, another stenographer, calls to me from the hallway. Ruby and I have been competing to see who can type faster on the teletype, an unspoken race I'm pretty sure I can win.

"Coming . . ." I push the loose strap of my duffel under the bunk and follow a group of excited girls down the narrow ship's corridor, which tips slightly. I press my hand to the wall. Sea legs.

We file into a plush dining room transformed into a mess hall. I bring my tray to a long table to find a seat among my new friends, all of us embarking on this unlikely adventure together. Instinctively, I search for Dot. At one end of the table, Dot's found a place near Staff Sergeant Everette Barnes, a strapping, middle-aged woman who looks like she's been waiting her whole life to wear the Pallas Athena insignia. Another stenographer, a fair-haired Minnesotan named Margaret Olson, has taken a seat next to Dot. I keep walking down the line of chattering women in pressed uniforms. I sit next to Private Lollie Dee Grange, a tough-looking, tan-skinned girl who tells me she'd never been out of Mississippi before she went to Basic. A few other stenographers gather around us. I dig into the salty meat and soggy green beans.

"Ladies!" Miss Barnes—Sergeant Barnes—stands at the head of the table. The excited babbling in the room falls to a din. "You know by now this is the first time the United States Army has integrated women into tactical field units, just the same as men," she says. Sergeant Barnes begins to pace back and forth as we drag bites of pork chop into the watery applesauce. "Soon enough, we'll be traveling along with the Fifth Army headquarters as they advance. Just a few miles behind the front lines."

"She means we're an experiment," Ruby says behind her hand to me. I've heard this enough—the fact that we're the army's guinea pigs—to believe it.

"Now that our troops are pushing the Huns across Sicily, we're well on our way to forcing them back to the confines of Germany. If you're on this ship," Sergeant Barnes says, "it means you're just as qualified and well-trained as any male soldier who's been assigned overseas. Don't let anyone lead you to believe otherwise.

"All of us will be tested," she continues, her face turning serious. "Those of you on the switchboards will have to get through complicated communications networks to reach commanding officers in minutes—whatever General Clark wants. Clerks, you will have to track movements of troops, equipment, and our critical supplies. I can't promise you creature comforts, recognition for your efforts, or that you'll be treated fairly by your male counterparts. The only thing I can promise you is long hours of work in far from ideal conditions. And all I ask is that you make whomever you left back home proud."

Most of the women have already made their families proud, I think as I push another piece of pork across the plate. Lollie Dee's shown me the faded clipping her parents placed in her local newspaper back in rural Mississippi.

> *The youngest daughter of Floyd and Ethel Grange has enlisted in the Women's Army Corps and is en route to Mostaganem, Algeria. Miss Grange is believed to be the first young woman from Lamar County to enlist in the WAC.*

I imagine Floyd Grange as an aging farmer in faded overalls, putting his daughter on a train. Might have been just as dumbfounded, and just as proud, as my own mother. Parents who never could have envisioned their children spinning out of the ruts of the well-worn road they had laid for them.

I suppose it's lucky I didn't have a father to convince. I don't even know my father's name. When I was about six years old, I asked my mother where he was and her only response was "Gone." I never knew if that meant left or dead. I asked again when I was a teenager. This time, she said she had no idea where he was. And something in her expression kept me from asking again.

It seems everyone has left behind parents, siblings, boyfriends, even husbands. I've only left behind my mother. In my mind, I see her, skinny and smiling, standing on the noisy train platform in New Haven and blowing me a kiss. Trying to look brave while she says goodbye. All alone in her ragged coat.

"They don't want us here," Lollie Dee says as the chatter resumes.

"The boys. They want us at home, minding their children, keeping their houses clean. They only see us keeping everything in order back home while they're over here doing men's work."

"And they don't want us taking their jobs, either," Ruby chimes in.

"Nothing wrong with working—or taking a husband," I say. "Gotta do whatever it takes to get by."

"If all you want to do is settle down." Ruby looks down her nose.

"I'll bet none of the boys could imagine any one of us a war hero," Lollie Dee says. "And they won't be very glad to see us when we land."

"I should think they will be happy to see girls at all." I smile at her and push my tray away as I brace myself against another great roll of the ship.

In the darkness, I lie awake in my bunk and worry about my mother. Images from home flood my mind—our peeling wallpaper, my walk to work among the crisp, fallen leaves, the black afternoons in New Haven as winter approaches. My mother's tiny, lone shape on the train platform. Around me, there is the soft sound of snoring and shifting on the creaking bunks. And the ever-present feeling of floating. Even after a few days at sea, I'm not sure I'll ever get used to it.

"You up, Josie?" Lollie Dee's whisper from the bunk beside mine.

I turn to face her in the dark. Stretch out my arm toward her.

She squeezes my hand. "I can't sleep," she whispers in her peculiar drawl that to my New England ear sounds like "ah caint." Now I can see her outline, the whites of her eyes. "All my life, I wanted to travel and see strange sights. And here I am, so I have no right to complain," she whispers. "And I know we trained for this. But now . . . I just keep thinkin' about the U-boats them boys talked about. Under the water . . ." Her voice trails off, but I feel her fear like an electrical current crackling between her thin mattress and mine.

"Nothing will happen to us," I say. "They keep the women behind the front lines, remember?"

But I've spent some time thinking about those German subs, too, their hulking shapes under the rippling surface like a shiver of sharks. And now, Lollie Dee has given words to the fear. There's at least another hour before the sun rises, but no chance of going back to sleep now. I sit up on the edge of the thin mattress. "Wanna come up on deck?"

Lollie Dee shakes her head and turns her back to me. She puts her palms together and tucks them under her cheek. She looks like she's praying. I pull on my skirt and my carefully shined shoes that still reek of polish. I grasp the handrails along the steep metal ladder to the top deck.

The ship's three giant smokestacks are looming black shadows. The *Empress of Scotland*, we're told, has ferried laughing, dancing, champagne-clinking passengers across the seas of the world. Now it only carries troops back and forth between the east coast of North America and war zones abroad. I stand on the deck alone and watch the sky meet the rolling sea the color of shale.

Soon, the dawn will appear as a thin line of yellow on the horizon. For now, the moon makes wavering reflections on the surface. I watch the timeless ebb and flow, the mighty force of the water that might be calm one moment, or might thunder as our ocean liner-turned-warship slashes through the waves. Threats from above and below.

Lollie Dee is worried about the subs under the rolling surface; I suppose I should be scared, too. I grasp the metal railing and look down into the relentless swells of glinting black. Below the impenetrable sky, it's easy to imagine how small this giant ocean liner might appear from the air, in the sights of a German plane. I am little more than a speck in an endless sea, the hulking ship little more than a tiny piece of metal that could be smashed or sunk in a second, tipping and creaking until it's upended, disappearing under the slick surface as if it was never there. I imagine my ma as another tiny speck on the other side of the world, pushing her mop into the bottom of a dirty bucket.

I've marked the days in a fresh steno pad. A few ticks of my pen and they begin to blur together. Nine so far. Soon we'll be traveling across the desert into the heart of Algeria. I don't know if I've made the right choice, but there's no going back now.

When I begin to think I may never see land again, the sun rises and the coast of Algeria comes into view across the stretch of sea. We disembark, a swarm of women soldiers in drab skirts, neat hats, and duffel bags. We find our land legs on the docks, where the heat bears down as if someone has opened an oven door and pressed our heads inside.

Once we've left the ocean liner behind, Dot and I are reunited. This time, we sit next to each other in an open boxcar with our legs dangling over the side, swilling warm water from our canteens and peeling back the metal covers on our C-rations. Rattling across the desert leaves our bodies wrung out and parched. Our friends prop themselves on the piles of duffels, trading secrets or napping in the heat. Shaking in the train, Dot attempts to put lipstick on her dry lips, which makes me giggle.

The sun, a wavering ball of orange, drops below the horizon. As the night falls, I think that in one day, we've seen sights that most people don't see in their lifetimes: camels, people eking out a living in the dirt, warplanes circling in formation above the sands. New Haven, Connecticut, seems more than a lifetime and a vast ocean away; it could be on another planet. Our future feels utterly unknown, as fractured and elusive as a mirage.

But as we watch the sands of the Algerian desert shift and swirl while the train rattles eastward in the darkness, I realize we are in this together. From the outside, no one would know if one of us was the daughter of a socialite or a campus janitor. We all have the same uniform, the same pack filled with the same supplies. The army is a great leveler. For the first time in my life, I'm just like everyone else. Even Dot.

Through the hot autumn, I write to my mother nearly every day. So much to tell. How I've grown accustomed to Algerian latrines, little more than holes in the ground. How I've come to appreciate the spicy tang of round peas and soft flatbread. That I've learned some Italian phrases because soon we will leave this god-forsaken heat bowl for Italy, now that Prime Minister Badoglio and King Victor Emmanuel have signed an armistice with the Allies. How I've gotten so fast at Gregg shorthand that Sergeant Barnes has promised me a good assignment once we get there.

But then I think about my ma with her sunken cheeks and her broom, stuck between our worn little apartment and campus, never having left Connecticut in her life. How could she visualize everything I've shared in my letters? In turn, I receive almost weightless sheaves of V-mail, a cost-saving, all-in-one piece of stationery that's censored, microfilmed, flown across the ocean on an army plane, and printed back to paper before it's delivered to us. The Yale campus, Ma tells me, has been practically converted to an Air Force training center and the trainees have taken over half the student dormitories. A friend's son has gone missing in the South Pacific. Another friend has left her job in the Yale dining halls and is now working in a munitions factory in Bridgeport. From the depths of a small care package, I unfold a *New Haven Register* newspaper clipping, whose main subject is the two girdles and three brassieres the army issues to WACs, and policies on those who fall pregnant while on duty.

"My ma must think they issued us packs of rubbers along with our helmets," I say to Ruby, who is completing her evening routine one hundred strokes of the hairbrush through her brown pin curls.

She bursts out laughing. "They should have. Some of us are more Khaki Wacky than others." She looks pointedly at Dot.

Dot returns the smug smile. She's got at least a dozen boys wrapped around her little finger. She could have her pick of them if only she would say the word. From her cot next to mine, Lollie Dee's face turns bright red. "I don't know about y'all, but I want to go home from here with a husband. Sleeping around sure don't seem the way to get one."

For a moment, I feel outraged to think that my mother might hear these rumors, might think I'm carousing over here instead of working harder than I ever have in my life. I've gotten fast at taking dictation on my steno pad, using only a series of strokes and curves. A short upward curve to make a K sound, a little longer for G. A bottom curve for an L sound. A short horizontal stroke for N. I spend the day typing twice as fast as anyone can speak; I can follow multiple conversations at once. Every day, Ruby and I are locked in an unspoken competition to see who can go the fastest. I'm annoyed when she brags to Sergeant Barnes about her scores. I don't do that, even when I come out ahead.

And to be fair, Dot is doing a lot more than carousing. She tells me the switchboard is second nature for her now. The switchboard girls in their mobile trailer have helped get supplies to Sicily, have intercepted several important messages, and have gotten critical ammunition to the front lines. Meanwhile, many more WACs have arrived from the U.S. to join our ranks in Algeria. We hear about a group arriving with the SOS headquarters at Oran. Another signal company arrives in Algiers. Every day, more women are breaking code, typing, operating radios, cutting tape in radio rooms, taking notes, translating African dialects. Together, we work as a machine to get engines, supplies, and ammunition to the front lines. In this way, we let the boys go to the front.

I set down my mother's letter and walk to the second-floor balcony of the crumbling stucco building where we're lodged. I look through my field binoculars toward the distant sea. Below the window, clusters of leaning palm trees and a shallow reflecting pool seem something straight out of the Arabian Nights. The large building was once used as a rug-making school, with onion-shaped arches and open arcades. Years ago, under the tiled arches, Algerian craftsmen sat cross-legged on the floor and wove colorful woolen threads. Now barren, the great hall is a cool respite from the oven-like heat outside. It serves as the place where we do everything—eat, play cards, write letters, chat with the boys. Upstairs, the sixty of us are divided ten women to a room, on army cots, living from the contents of our barracks bags. Our time to socialize is squeezed into moments in the canteen or whispering to one another from our cots after our bosses have had to tell us to stop working. Before the lights go out, I thumb through a slim guide with Italian phrases. If nothing else, maybe I can learn a few words before the abyss of exhaustion lures me to sleep each night.

From the window of our room, it seems I can see forever, the vast, spangled, sparkling surface of the ocean beyond a ribbon of sand. Along the horizon line are a couple of dots, warships far out at sea. Hot breezes bring whiffs of dry salt air. It would be a peaceful scene if it weren't for the black shapes in the sky, like insects against the incessant glare. They are far away, yet we hear the distant buzz of patrolling aircraft.

Each morning in the courtyard, we line up across from one another as if we are about to do the Virginia reel—boys on one side, girls on the other. A perfectly aligned row of army jeeps stands at attention behind us. The men, clean-shaven and neat in their newly issued uniforms, watch us in our starched skirts and hats. Lieutenant Hamm, a sturdy man from Georgia, ogles the women openly, his eyes scanning the line from one WAC to the next. I can't help myself; my own eyes rest on Private Dante Ruggero, a dreamboat from Buffalo with thick black hair. Waiting in the mess line, he's told me he already would've been running his family's plumbing business by now if he hadn't gotten drafted. My gaze lingers there for a moment too long. He catches my eye and winks. I look down at the toes of my shined shoes.

Dot's elbow jabs my side. "And you thought they didn't want us here," she whispers behind her hand.

After the morning's drills, we assemble in the hall for the daily briefing. Captain Rand Thomas, a sculptor who teaches at a college in New Hampshire, is the day's speaker. He's a strapping man with wide, square teeth and graying hair whose uniform buttons threaten to pop across his bulging midsection. I've seen him working in a tent, alone, with a rickety table and stacks of books and maps, but I never knew what his job was until now.

"Italy is richer than most countries in its artistic heritage," Captain Thomas tells us as we shift in our chairs. He points to a large map of the boot-shaped peninsula tacked to the wall. "It is hard to put into words the vastness, the density of human achievement. Rome as the capital of the ancient world. Florence as the capital of the Renaissance. Venice as a jewel unlike any other in the world. Countless churches, towers, villages of inestimable value to our heritage as human beings.

"What happens, then, gentlemen—and ladies," he continues, "when this dense landscape of human excellence—so carefully preserved through the centuries—lies in the crosshairs of modern warfare whose like has never been seen in human history? How do we ensure these treasures will endure for future generations? This is why the U.S. government established the Roberts Commission. There are artists like me, plus scholars and curators, all of us embedded with army units like this one. The job of the Monuments officers is to protect cultural treasures in war zones."

"Pretty dang sure of himself, ain't he?" Ruby whispers from the seat beside me.

"I'll say."

Captain Thomas continues, spreading his legs out wide as he leans against a table at the front of the room. "The Brits have their own version, which is controlled by the War Office in London. We've been creating maps and exhaustive lists showing the location of important monuments and art collections up and down the peninsula so that we don't accidentally destroy something important. Earlier this summer," he continues, "our troops went to hit German targets—bridges and railways—near the archaeological site at Pompeii. Instead, they accidentally hit the archaeological museum and some of the most important remains of the ancient city. An unfortunate mistake and a press nightmare. We want to make sure that doesn't happen again."

Captain Henry, a tall, skinny career officer from Iowa, steps in. "For now," he says, "our flying fortresses have been focused on targets in the northern part of the country where there is more industry and economic strength. Milan. Turin. Genoa. The Germans are no longer friends to the Italians. They are occupying enemies. But the Huns will try to hold their positions and I won't sugarcoat it. We're looking at a brutal fight up the boot of Italy."

At a table on the edge of the camp, Sergeant Barnes signs us out on a wooden clipboard for our biweekly day off. She rattles off the obligatory reminder of the rules, especially the one about no fraternizing between enlisted women and officers. "And you're not the paid entertainment, even if someone tells you otherwise," she says. She gives us a tight salute as we leave behind the camp for the sliver of white beach. "Have fun, ladies."

I follow a group of soldiers and WACs down the meandering trail to an ocean-side park leading to a stretch of beach. The pathways are lined with tall date palms, their big fronds reaching up to the sky as if in supplication. In the distance, the town of Mostaganem splays out along the crescent beach where the desert meets the vast, spangled ocean.

I find Private Ruggero walking with several other men who are talking about Captain Thomas's morning briefing.

"I don't get it," I say, catching up with them. "All the resources put behind this Roberts Commission. Isn't it better to protect people's lives than to save some old pile of stones?"

"Hey, didn't you work in an art museum back home?" Private Ruggero laughs.

"It was a typing job. I was just trying to help my ma keep the lights on."

"I'd say you're selling yourself short, Evans," he says, surveying me until I feel my face turn hot. "I heard you're the U.S. Army's best stenographer. I wouldn't have the first idea how to use that machine."

As much as we thought the boys wouldn't want us here, if anyone had any doubts that we could do our jobs well and work hard, they must now remain silent. If a soldier says anything disparaging about our work ethic, the other men jump to our defense. They know we have worked as hard as any of them.

"It's not so hard when you get the hang of it," I say as we reach the beach. We stop and remove our shoes, feeling the soft sand between our toes. "Instead of typing letters, like on a typewriter, we can make a whole word with just one or two strokes. To type a word like 'calendar,' we make a chord using three keys. That's how I can write or type faster than you can talk. My stenotype can go twice the speed of a typewriter . . ."

But Private Ruggero is not listening. Have I bored him with my talk of the stenotype? No. Of course. Dot has just walked by and suddenly I have disappeared into the scenery. Happens all the time. I watch his gaze follow the sway of her hips and her blond hair. She removes her hat and shoes, and continues down the park pathway that unfurls toward the sand, with several other men in tow. Behind them, Lollie Dee has caught up with Private Brunson, a handsome

insurance man who's left a wife and three kids back home in Little
Rock. They walk in step together, ahead of us. When Dot stops and
turns to see if we are following, Private Ruggero fans out his elbows.
Dot and I each grab an arm. I lean on his hard forearm as we continue down the beach.

"Look!" Dot says.

In the distance, there is an enormous convoy of some fifty or sixty
ships—vessels similar to the *Empress of Scotland* that brought us to
this strange place all the way from Newport News. Their metal bows
glint in the waning sunlight. Along the horizon line are a couple of
dots, warships far out at sea. It would be a peaceful scene if it weren't
for these black shapes in the sky, like insects in the incessant glare.
They are far away, yet we hear the distant buzz.

"They're ours," Brunson says, motioning to the ships. "Allied, I
mean. Probably British."

For a while, we stop to watch the fleet of ships, which must hold
hundreds if not thousands of navy personnel, heading eastward
along the coast.

"What do you think they're doing?" Lollie Dee asks.

"Probably shipping ammunition and other supplies," Brunson
says. "You see how the destroyers are surrounding the other ships
like a belt. They are carrying something valuable."

The drone of engines grows louder. I tent my hand over my eyes
and the silhouettes of black planes come into focus. The sounds ac-
celerate, and suddenly they form a great flock of planes as if from
nowhere.

"Those ain't ours," Lollie Dee says.

The planes dip lower. From the decks of two of the ships, we see
colored tracer bullets stream up into the darkening sky. For a long,
suspended moment, it looks like a Fourth of July fireworks display is
getting underway.

But then, the low-flying planes open their bellies. Torpedoes drop
like deadweights. Immediately, two large ships burst into flames. An

explosion lights up the sky and one boat shatters into a black cloud in the water.

"Get down!" Brunson cries. We dive together against a low stucco wall that lines the beach. For what seems an eternity, there is only the sound of explosions and droning planes. I dare to move my hands from my face long enough to witness a scene of pure hell. Two broken planes floating in the sea. Several ships are on fire, others nothing more than shattered metal remnants. Others appear to be intact. One is listing, rolling on its side. Another ship is lowering its lifeboats, and we see men climbing onto them like ants as the sun sinks below the horizon and the sky turns gold and deep blue. Within minutes, it will be dark. My heart plummets to imagine how any of these men will be found.

The next morning, we get orders to board naval transport ships bound for Italy.

5

EVA

✧

A PURPOSE. A CHANCE TO DO SOMETHING THAT matters at last. It's all I wanted, all I asked for, and I'm still surprised that my father allowed me to come here.

I walk in step with Herr Doctor Kriegbaum, elegant in his dark suit and narrow tie, his thinning hair slicked back from his high forehead. Along the Arno, armored German vehicles roll by in a rush of grinding engines. An Italian woman in a flowered dress yanks her small son's hand to pull him from the vehicles' path. The midday sun illuminates the Ponte Vecchio as a ragged, beautiful patchwork of colored stucco, wood, and stone.

"You will like Doctor Planiscig," Kriegbaum says to me. "He's an Austrian like you."

I'm only half-Austrian, thanks to my father, I start to say. Growing up in Berlin, I always considered myself German, like my mother. But talking about my mother is a long, complicated story and I'd rather not explain myself to Professor Kriegbaum, upon whom I want to make a most professional impression on my first assignment outside of filing catalog cards in the institute's Phototek.

I shift the heavy camera bag to my other hand. Inside is one of the institute's finest cameras, a wooden box with an accordion-like center that folds up into a leather case, a contraption much nicer than any camera I've ever owned. Professor Kriegbaum carries the tripods in another bag. He tells me he will have me take pictures that will be used as illustrations in his art history books. Serious pictures that will produce large-format negatives, with beautifully defined lines of silver and black that will transform in the darkroom. Magic every time. The camera bag becomes heavy and my back aches, but I don't dare complain.

"The bridges are beautiful," I say as we walk across one of the many elegant spans of stone that connect the north and south sides of the Arno.

"Indeed. I've written extensively about the Ponte Santa Trinità," he says. "It was built in the 1550s by Bartolomeo Ammanati, probably advised by Michelangelo."

Ever since Italy signed the armistice with the Anglo-Americans earlier in the month, there is more urgency than ever for us to go around the city and photograph everything, Professor Kriegbaum has told me. He is especially keen to photograph the private collections that remain in the city. At last, he tells me, he's convinced Leo Planiscig that he must pack up his fine collection of Renaissance bronzes for safekeeping and move them out of the city.

We pass through the Piazza della Signoria in the blazing heat. Horst was right; walking through Florence is like walking through a living museum. Standing in the middle of the square is dazzling and disconcerting, as you hardly know whether to focus your attention on the loggia full of Renaissance sculptures, the medieval town hall with its imposing battlements and its tall, skinny watchtower, or the elegant buildings. But today, three German tanks command the view instead. A soldier sits on top of one of them, a machine gun balanced on his lap. A few Florentines dart furtively across the square.

"There was an enormous equestrian statue there," Kriegbaum says, pointing to where one of the panzers is parked. "Cosimo I de Medici. Giambologna made it in the sixteenth century. We helped the Italian authorities disassemble it and move it by ox-drawn cart to one of the depots in the countryside."

We leave the square and head down a side street. "What's Doctor Planiscig doing here in Florence?"

"He's been here for many years. A connoisseur. Italian Renaissance bronzes are his specialty. He's written some important scholarly works on the subject. And since he's been in Italy, he's amassed quite a collection. I convinced him we should photograph everything before he crates the works for transport. That's where you come in." Professor Kriegbaum and I turn down a street, where a pair of German soldiers stand on a corner, watching a group of girls in their school uniforms, all white collars and plaid.

"I've received a telegram from the High Command," he tells me. "The government has announced the reactivation of the Kunstschutz," he says. "The same art protection unit they used during the Great War."

"An art protection unit. What does that mean for the institute—for us?"

"It means we may have more German and Austrian art professionals joining us here. Curators. Other art historians. Specialists. But mainly, it means they will allocate more resources to us. Fuel. Laborers. Transportation. Probably they will have us hire more Italian laborers to build protective structures around some of the historic monuments and other works of art."

"I thought the contents of the Florentine museums have already been taken to the countryside?"

"The ones that could be moved easily, yes." We press our backs to a crumbling stucco wall as a German motorcycle putts by in a rush of dust and gasoline odor. "The contents of the museums were mostly evacuated to the countryside many months ago. A massive undertaking. But there are many smaller museums and private collections still to be protected. Now that the Italians have capitulated, we have to move quickly to get the works to safety. You and I will have enough to keep us busy for a long time, I expect. The photography of the works will be of critical use to our mission."

I feel excited, filled with purpose. My camera bag is full of new film cartridges, thanks to the help of the staff of the institute's Phototek. I have already planned the letter I will write home, telling Oma, Papa, and Gerhard about the hundreds of drawers and archival boxes in the institute's rooms, the dozens of fine cameras at my disposal. A photographer's dream.

"I can't imagine what it must have taken to move everything out of a huge museum like the Uffizi."

"Indeed. It was strange to see those pictures loaded into the backs of trucks and headed out of the city. I got the privilege of seeing many German paintings up close. Masterpieces like Lucas Cranach's sixteenth-century panels of *Adam* and *Eve*."

Cranach. German pictures. I stop to process the information. I have seen thousands of works of German and Austrian art, carefully dismantled and transported to the salt mine at Altaussee. And our father has described the wholesale destruction of many other works considered "degenerate," those that have burned in Berlin and Munich years before the more valuable works were transported to the mines. In this way, our father has said, we ensure the future of the best of our culture.

"But paintings by Lucas Cranach are *not* works of Italian genius or patrimony," I say. "They are German. Surely they belong in Germany—not in Italy?"

"Many Germans share your sentiment," he says, and I feel embarrassed to have asked such a naïve question. "But the Cranachs were in the hands of the Medici from 1688 as part of Cosimo III's private collection. They've been part of an important Italian collection for a long time—as have many other works of Germanic origin. They've become part of Italian cultural heritage, too. At least that is how most Italian art experts we've collaborated with over the past few years see it. I have come to appreciate that point of view."

I let the idea of a German art protection unit in Italy sink in as we make our way toward the quarter of the city that adjoins Florence's train marshaling yards. "It seems overwhelming. Almost undoable. There is so much here to preserve."

"Yes. No other nation has so many art treasures as Italy. And no city more than Florence."

"Horst says you led the Führer and Il Duce through the Uffizi."

Kriegbaum nods, but I perceive a shadow cross his thin face. "Seems like a long time ago now. The Führer has stated that he would ensure the safety of the city. At least from our side." He shrugs. "We can only hope the Americans and British will also see the importance of preserving it."

Near the Campo di Marte train yard, we turn onto the via Masaccio and Professor Kriegbaum stops outside a brick gate leading to a handsome home from centuries past, its upper-story windows framed with stone. "I've been trying to get Doctor Planiscig to move his collection outside the city for months." He lowers his voice. "An incredible mind. But a bit stubborn." He smiles and rings the bell.

Suddenly, there is the sound of a distant plane engine in the air. Professor Kriegbaum and I look up. The whirring noise continues, but then our attention is distracted as the front door opens. An Italian woman, perhaps a housekeeper, lets us into the entrance hall and closes the door behind us.

"*Un momento, signori.*" She wipes her hands on her apron and disappears up the stairs. "*Dottore!*"

The noise continues and gets louder, even though we are inside Doctor Planiscig's grand entrance hall. We look up as if we could see the planes from inside. My eyes scan the ornate furniture, the inlaid marble floor patterns, and a bronze figure of a man with a boar near the front door. As the engine noise grows, I watch the bronze figure shudder, then teeter on its pedestal.

"*Professore.*" A short, bald man with large round glasses appears at the top of the stairs. "Welcome."

We can't hear the next words out of Doctor Planiscig's mouth, as suddenly there is a high-pitched, shrill whistle. The housekeeper stops and grips the stair railing. The Renaissance bronze rattles on its pedestal and the crystal chandelier begins to jingle. All of us pause and look up at the coffered ceiling and the frail light coming through a skylight above the stairwell. I freeze as the sound of the whistle grows louder, more like a whine, and then finally, more like a shriek.

For a split second, everything falls silent. The servant woman and I meet each other's gaze. Then there is a burst, an ear-splitting crash, and a rain of shattering tiles and stucco.

"Professor!" Acting on instinct, I push my weight into Professor Kriegbaum and we crouch under an arch. But at that very moment, the arch crumbles. The explosion blows the wall open, propelling shards of stucco debris and plaster rattling across the tiles. All at once, there is another relentless shower of tiles. I throw my arms over my head and feel the stabbing of a thousand broken shards over my hands and wrists as the world disappears into a cloud of ash. Then I am knocked to the floor and feel myself sprawl across the tiles. Only my camera bag stops me from hitting my face on the floor. Then a stabbing, excruciating pain shoots through my right arm. I feel the cold floor under my cheek and stare out across the patterned tile. Dust and ash float weightlessly through the air. A stream of light floods the house, illuminating from a new hole struck through the roof.

I don't know how long I lie there in Doctor Planiscig's shattered entrance hall. Time is suspended. The sound of an engine outside the house rouses me. Where is the servant woman? I no longer see her at the bottom of the stairs.

Professor Kriegbaum. I try to push myself up, but my right arm collapses beneath me. I use my left arm to pull it to my body, but it won't go. It's hanging at a horrible angle, akimbo. I feel dizzy and disoriented, having lost my bearings.

I pull myself up to standing using my left arm, then stagger toward what's left of the arch.

"Professor!"

But there is only a muffled roar in my ears and dust-flecked sunlight. Even the sound of planes has vanished. I drag myself forward, pushing my hand against my nose and mouth, trying to block the choking dust. A fruitless effort.

"Are you alright, sir?" But I see only his feet, protruding from a tangled pile of tiles and stone.

The front door is hanging from a single hinge. I step out into the daylight and retch into the rubble at the doorstep, then look at the surreal sight of the buildings that stood next to Doctor Planiscig's house only moments ago. They are nothing but brick pilings, and an arch left standing, silhouetted by the bright blue sky. My mind cannot comprehend how I have walked out of such a place.

A Kübelwagen rumbles across the littered street in front of us, soldiers with rifles hanging to the sides, rushing toward the train yard. Two motorcycles follow, gray with ash, maneuvering through the fallen stones. Horns blare through the streets.

I stagger toward the sidewalk.

"*Hilf.* Help . . ." My voice aims toward the vehicles. It comes out in a dry crack. Futile. Creaky. The Kübelwagen and motorcycles have already disappeared into the dust.

Another attempt. Louder this time.

"*Aiuto!*"

But my voice is drowned by the sudden burst of an air-raid siren, which only now, too late, sounds its lonesome wail.

6

JOSIE

WHEN WE BOARDED THE *EMPRESS OF SCOTLAND* just four months ago, one of the soldiers snapped our picture. In that photograph, we are smiling, giddy even, like we were off to cut a rug at some damn party instead of a war. Back then, the girls and I traversed the Atlantic on the promise of adventure, of gainful employment, of the fun of the uniform, of the glamour of being a trailblazer. Compelled by the power of Dot's certainty. By the audacity to do something my mother never dreamed.

I think back to how silly we were, rushing from the staterooms and ballrooms of the tired ocean liner, filled with excitement and commitment to our cause. We landed on the coast of North Africa, naïve, as if we were on some fantastic transatlantic cruise. That picture was even published in the American newspapers. Looking back, it seems little more than a publicity stunt.

And now, another ocean crossing.

This time, our minds are filled instead with images of spectacular, deadly explosions and those ships slipping under the water. All those lives lost. The ships lost along the Algerian coast, we now know, were part of a British convoy carrying ammunition and explosives. We have seen firsthand that any of us might be plucked out at any moment. The exploding ships have torn away any veil of illusion. When my mother told me she was proud of me all those months ago, did she understand I might be centered in the cross-hairs of a German gunner?

We sit on the hard, narrow benches of the USS *James O'Hara*. Everything on this attack transport is a gloomy shade of gray—the benches, the hard bunks. We get hot showers and even listen to piped-in music in the dining hall. But we keep our life belts on. We are gray, too. A cloud has descended over our unit. We've seen the explosions, the dramatic collision of water and fire, the sudden, senseless, and devastating loss of life. This time, we know what can happen.

Even Dot is subdued in her lifejacket, examining her bare fingernails. She is a plainer, softer version of herself, still beautiful. The raw elegance of someone of her social class. Ruby has gotten a telegram that her brother has been killed in action in the Philippines. Even though she has irritated me with her silent competition at the steno machines, my heart goes out to her. When I asked if she wanted to go home, she only shook her head.

Three days ago, our platoon loaded into trucks for the long, cold ride to Mers el Kabir, where the looming shadow of the *James O'Hara* awaited us. For three days, the naval warship cut noiselessly through the water. We hugged the Algerian coast just out of view of Mostaganem, where we have worked harder than we ever have in our lives. In the same waters where we saw the Allied convoy blown into the sky.

And so we wait for our landing in Naples—Dot and nine other telephone operators, a half dozen clerks, and two dozen or so typists and stenographers, Lollie Dee and the other cooks. And me. All of us stone-faced.

Sergeant Barnes tells us we should be proud; with the exception of a nursing unit that's already landed at Salerno, we'll be the first American women to set foot in war-torn Europe. And she has told us we'll be billeted in a palace beyond Naples, a building so large and overwhelming that it'll make our old Algerian rug factory look like the slums. But it's impossible to imagine from here. "I, for one, think we deserve to stay in a palace," Sergeant Barnes joked after we boarded the ship, trying to cheer us.

"Look!" Lollie Dee calls, turning around on her bench to the window blurred with rain and fog. "We're here!" We abandon our hard metal benches and rush for our first look at the Italian coast.

We step out onto the decks and into a shroud of fog. Cold rain spits across the metal, glinting and slick. I press myself under the protection of a narrow stretch of overhang so I don't get soaked. The coastline is a dark mass on the flat horizon. We make out only a few shapes.

Suddenly, an opening breaks in the clouds. "Capri!" Dot cries. "I told you, Mouse. Italy's the most beautiful place I've ever seen. And the harbor of Naples . . ."

I move to her side and squint. And as the fog lifts, I begin to see through Dot's eyes: a dramatic, green cliff, then another, rising out of the sea. From the tops of the cliffs, ancient stucco villas perch on the sides, draped with vines. Surreal, as if it's emerged from the edges of a dream.

Then another hulking shape. The reality of it hits me like a kick in my side: a giant warship, lying on its side, its hull like a beached whale. As we drift into the harbor of Naples, there are more. Ships with bottoms up. Broken mastheads. Other ships lying on their sides or with the sterns sticking up out of the water.

"Looks like we could be in Pearl Harbor," Ruby says.

We disembark, wet and cold, carrying our packs and splashing through the muddy puddles and muck. The fog lifts and I see Naples for the first time: a mass of crumbling, ornate façades, battened and splintered shutters, tumble-down elegance. A chaotic tangle of people, broken buildings, vehicles, horses, and buggies. Warehouses, little more than twisted steel, skeletons with windows blown out, roofs caved.

Then, wave after wave of American boys. The troop ships come into the harbor, heaving with the weight of their human cargo. But in the gloomy destruction, all we see are their smiling faces. They come off the boats singing, full of hope, some already having gone off to battle, others going to war for the first time. We stand around in the mud and watch them disembark.

"Hey look!" they call. "American girls! Gee, it's good to see someone from home. What are you doing here? How long have you been here? Where are you from? Are you going where we're going? When will we see you again? Will you come visit us?" Question after question. How could they be so cheerful? I've never been so popular in my life. For a wallflower like me, it's a revelation, a strange bluster to feel the center of attention.

A vast number of American troop trucks await at the harbor. One by one, we climb in, women and men alike. I huddle in next to Lollie Dee and Dot. Several American soldiers, laughing, launch a mock battle to see who will get a seat next to us.

"What are you smiling about?" Dot presses against me.

"*You're* used to having to beat boys away with sticks." I press her back. "But I'm not."

The troop transport trucks move off through mud a foot thick. My feet are soaked and freezing. Only as the vehicle leaves the chaotic tangle of the harbor does the winter sun break through the clouds. We climb into the hills above the city, which lies at the bottom of a great basin, a beach filled with smooth, dark pebbles. Beyond, there are hills with swaying grass, and a steep embankment from the emerald sea. The Bay of Naples comes into view. From a distance, it appears not as a wrecked harbor but as a beautiful curve of blue sea with umbrella pines, the curve of a sandy coastline, and verdant mountains. In the distance, Vesuvius, the great volcano, rises dramatically from the coastline.

Next to Dot, a boy no older than eighteen is staring at her like he's never seen a woman before. "And what are you looking at?" she says.

A dumb, giddy smile breaks across his face. "I'm just glad to talk to an American girl."

Even if our own soldiers believe we women are here for their entertainment, our experience in Algeria has already given us the confidence to know better.

In the back of the rattling troop transport, the boys' initial excitement of traveling alongside newly found American girls subsides as the reality of the Italian countryside unfolds around us. Heading toward the palace of Caserta, we pass desolate villages with desperate-looking old people and scrawny children with haunted eyes. In a village, I see an old man standing in a doorway, his bent legs spread wide like an arch, his gray hair lying limp around his empty eyes and speckled jowls. His blue shirt is ironed and neat though, tucked into baggy pants hiked high on his torso and cinched with a belt. He raises his shaking hand ever so slowly to wave as we pass. What horrors and deprivation have these innocent people suffered during the German occupation? I feel their suffering in the pit of my stomach. It gives me a small injection of resolve that our mission is important, after all. We men and women are in this together.

Climbing farther out of the city, we move into a beautiful landscape of verdant hills populated only with sheep and giant cattle. Outside a dilapidated village, we pass through a bivouac for American and English soldiers, men sleeping in pup tents on the cold, muddy ground. Instantly, I feel guilty for despairing on the ship to Naples, when we are so much better off than they are and somehow, the men remain cheerful through it all.

At last, the transport truck squeaks to a halt. "Allied HQ!" one of the men shouts from the back of an adjacent truck.

We unload. I tug on the elastic waist of my pantyhose and tighten the strap on my helmet, an awkward turtle shell made for a man's head. I grab my canvas roll and adjust the straps on my pack. We hand down our supplies to the women on the ground. My shoes, so shiny when we boarded in Algeria, are now covered in mud. The rain has stopped and the sun shines on the most incredible sight I've ever seen: a palace grander than anything I could have imagined: a vast, pink palace of a thousand windows, like a mirage on the horizon. From here, war seems impossible.

7

EVA

WHEN I STAGGER ACROSS THE THRESHOLD OF PA-
lazzo Guadagni, holding my limp and horribly placed arm, the Italian carpenter drops his hammer and comes running.

I stand frozen, my brain reeling, searching for words—whether
German or Italian—about Doctor Planiscig's house on the via Masaccio, about the planes, about the explosion, about my arm and
the shooting pain, about Professor Kriegbaum and his shiny shoes
motionless under the stones.

But the Italian carpenter says nothing. Instead, he scoops me up
in his arms as if I were a toddler. Then he runs into the Piazza Santo
Spirito.

In the streets, the sirens continue to wail. The butter-colored
church façade passes in a blur. The carpenter speaks to me, a sudden
stream of Italian, but my ears are ringing and I only catch one or two
words. He rushes with me down a side street, as dark as a tunnel.
With my good arm, I hang on to his firm, broad shoulder.

At the corner, a Red Cross sign comes into view. He runs through
the door yelling, "*Aiuto! Dottore!*" He doesn't let me go. Around us,
injured people collect in the dark courtyard of an old building. A
wailing mother. A little boy with a crooked leg. A woman holding a
baby, half her face covered in blood.

"*Come si chiama?*" I manage to say. Something pulled magically from my phrase book.

"Enzo."

"Enzo," I murmur into the warmth of his pulsing neck. "I can't do this."

I say it in German and I have no idea if he's understood me.

Then a Red Cross nurse rushes over to us. Enzo sets me gently on the ground. The nurse kneels and cuts off the sleeve of my ash-coated blouse with a large pair of scissors.

It's hours later before I dare to look myself in the face.

In a faded mirror in the old boardinghouse bathroom in Palazzo Guadagni, the ghostlike specter of my face comes into focus. The harsh light of a single bulb in a metal cage reflects off the cracked marble tile. A fine layer of gray ash coats my hair. The ash fills the creases across my brow and the hollows of my eyes. I look like I feel—as though I've aged fifty years in a day. Only the sling supporting my right arm shines white and new in its gauze wrapping under my ragged, cut-off sleeve.

The fingers of my left hand fumble awkwardly with the buttons of my skirt while the right arm lies helpless in its sling. I struggle with my shoelaces and step out of my stockings, letting them fall to a cloud of filth on the tiles next to my ash-coated leather camera case. I stand and look at my pale, naked body for a minute—the familiar birdlike, skinny legs, the bony clavicles, the white, puffy stomach and small breasts. The numb, slightly throbbing arm resting L-shaped in its wrapping.

Shivering, I step into the claw-footed bathtub and pull the chain. A blast of cold water sprays out from the nozzle above my head, knocking the breath out of me. I turn my head into the stream and let the water turn my hair into a funnel of gray ash, dirty rivulets across the stained basin and into the drain. I hold my broken arm and its wrapping out of the water. I turn my body to let the cold water wash the filth of the bombing from my feet and ankles.

Only now do I see the rusty traces of dried blood swirl across the tub's worn basin, then disappear into the metal slots. Whose blood? The sling smells faintly of sulfa powder, and for a moment, I feel I will retch into the drain.

How am I standing? How did I avoid the same fate as the others?

I close my eyes and the stream of images barrels toward me like a wave—the growing roar of the British planes, the whine of the projectile and the second of silence before the crash, the shattering clash of exploding ceiling tiles, the cries of despair from the street, the sight of Professor Kriegbaum's twisted legs just inches away. The kindness of the Italian carpenter—Enzo. That patient Italian doctor who instructed me, in halting German, not to get my arm wet. *Kein Wasser, kein Wasser, signorina.* I gasp, a shock of remembrance in the ice-cold water, and open my eyes again to the stark bathroom light as the wave of images recedes.

Perhaps that doctor was right; I should have stayed at the clinic long enough for him to check the wrapping. But how could I wait there and watch the stream of people in much more wretched states than my own—those disfigured who threw themselves at the mercy of that poor doctor's patience and skill?

I'm not that brave. And I couldn't stay in that darkened clinic corridor smelling of sulfa, sweat, and death for one more minute. The echoing pleas in Italian, the crying, the interminable suffering of those who were indiscriminately disfigured by a random projectile dropped from the air. As soon as the nurse finished wrapping my arm and told me to wait in a chair in the corridor so the doctor could check the dressing once more, I walked back out into the street.

Enzo had been waiting for me, pacing on the sidewalk with a cigarette. We walked back to Palazzo Guadagni together. I smelled fire, saw black clouds in the air. Florentines hurried through the streets and our soldiers paced, surveying the street corners while others rushed by on low-slung motorcycles as the cacophonous sound of ambulance and bomb sirens wailed.

"I feel terrible," I had said to Enzo in German, with an Italian word or two thrown in. "I'm the one who pushed him under that arch. The professor." I'm not sure he knew what I was saying. He only continued to talk to me, a stream of Italian. I didn't understand every word, just that I was safe. Things would be alright. He had not hesitated to carry me all the way to the Red Cross clinic; but he then grew suddenly shy, as if trying his best not to touch me at all. As if I were breakable.

I step out of the tub, shivering. I hold the rough, stiff towel in my one good hand and dry my stomach and legs. Maybe I should pack up and catch a train to Salzburg. Back to the salt mines and the world I know. I was stupid to think I was cut out for war.

Would Professor Kriegbaum have found his task of saving works of art so worthy as to lose his life? Was he prepared to put his own existence on the line for a few bronze figurines? And how was I the one left with only a broken arm? I pick up my dust-covered leather camera case and attempt to cover my nakedness with the little towel, long enough to slip down the dark hallway to my room.

From the top of the stairwell, I hear someone cry out in anguish and I know I have to face the rest of the institute's people. I run the towel over my wet hair and put on a clean skirt and blouse.

I descend the narrow stairwell to a small reading room of the *pensione* where the staff has begun to gather. There is Horst and that Jewish painter, Rudolf Levy. There is Paloma, the photography curator, the Bandini sisters who own the *pensione*, and the others. Enzo leans against the wall behind the group, his cheeks haggard. I don't want to face them but I can't hide. Soon enough, they'll know the inescapable truth. That their director is gone. And that I'm the reason Professor Kriegbaum was put in harm's way.

For days after the Anglo-American bombing attack that took Professor Kriegbaum's life, I attempt to write a letter home. Each time, I fail. The wastebasket is full of false starts, crumpled wads of paper piling up one by one. I want a cigarette, but smoking is not allowed among the archival boxes in the Phototek. Paloma has promised to try to get a telephone line through to Austria for me. Most of the communication lines have been cut in recent weeks; even telegrams fail to reach their recipients.

I sit at an ancient table surrounded by archival boxes that reach from floor to ceiling, each containing documentary photographs of works of art in and around Florence. Shelves contain hundreds of bound volumes in German on photography, Florentine art, and the city's history. All of Professor Kriegbaum's writings on Michelangelo and other Renaissance sculptors are collected there. Weak light comes through small windows near the ceiling. I can hear institute staff and visitors going up and down in the stairwell, but I have the Phototek to myself, a bastion of quiet so I might find the words to tell my father. The building is awash with shuffles and echoes, stifling in an autumn heatwave. People are idle, working in whispered continuity while we await further instructions, and until a new director can be found.

Words have never come easy for me on the page. I tell stories through my camera instead. Black and white. Good and bad. Easy to understand in a single instant. One picture, a thousand words. And only the truth. My right arm stiff in its bandage, I twirl the pen between the fingers of my left hand, as foreign as if the hand belonged to another person.

And what could I possibly say? That Gerhard had every right to be afraid of going to war? That I was the one arrogant enough to think I could contribute something, that I would be braver than everyone else? That because of me, the director of the German Art History Institute has been retrieved from the rubble and buried in a Protestant cemetery outside Florence? That saving a work of art might mean sacrificing a life? Did they know that?

The main thing I should tell them, I guess, is that I'm coming home like a dog with my tail tucked between my legs. I wasn't cut out for wartime work. And with my arm in a sling, I can hardly take a picture. I'm of no use here. How could I put into words what it was like to feel the earth shaking, to feel the roof tiles fall over us with their ruddy shards?

"Eva."

Paloma, the archival assistant, appears at the door to the Phototek. "They got through to Austria for you. Hurry, before the line drops again."

I go to the main floor and pick up the black phone in the back hallway. I press the receiver to my cheek.

My Oma's house in Altaussee comes rushing back in a flow of images, as if flicking rapidly through an old family photo album. I imagine the flowery cloth on my Oma's kitchen table. The firepit in the garden. The little painted scene of Vienna hanging on the wall. My father sitting in the iron chairs in the garden with a newspaper in front of his face. I listen to the static, then a series of distant pops between shrill, pulsing rings.

At last, I hear my father's voice, faint and crackling on the other end of the line. "Brunner. *Hallo?*"

"Papa," I begin. It takes everything in me to gulp down the lump in my throat and keep the crack from my voice.

"Eva! You're well."

I attempt to swallow. "I'm alright," I manage to breathe. "I wanted to tell you I've decided that—"

But he interrupts.

"I received a letter last week from Herr Doctor Kriegbaum," he says. "You're doing good work in Italy. Important work."

I raise my finger and trace a ragged crack in the stucco wall. "About that . . ." I say, knowing I will never find the words to describe what I've already seen and experienced.

"And now that they are reactivating the Kunstchutz," he says, "you are there at a good time. He's told me of your photography project. They have big plans for you. I am proud of you, Eva."

He continues going on about new paintings and boxes of archives being brought into the mine, but I don't hear anything else. Instead, I feel my eyes glaze over with hot tears until everything goes fuzzy and out of focus. It's the first time in my life my father has said he was proud of me.

8

JOSIE

SIXTY WOMEN SPREAD OUT, GIDDY, CARRYING OUR
packs up the impossibly ornate staircases of what was once the largest private residence in the world. Our voices echo off the patterned
marble floors, the endless corridors, the dizzying gilded walls and
painted vaults. For a moment, a vision of our dreary apartment in
New Haven surfaces in my mind, and I know I'll never find the
words to describe all of this to my mother in a letter.

We grow accustomed to the bright light streaming through tall
windows with views to the sweeping, tiered gardens with gurgling
fountains. Dot and I claim two cots alongside each other. We open
our change purses and spill out the strange coins, trying to imagine
what they're worth, with so many zeros. At night, we lie with our
heads side by side, looking up at the little angels who peer down at
us from the edges of the ornate ceiling. "They're not angels, they're
putti," Dot informs me.

Our commanders waste no time in handing out assignments. To
my surprise, Sergeant Barnes assigns me to support Rand Thomas,
the Monuments officer who, back in Algeria, told us about the role of
the Roberts Commission in protecting historic buildings and works
of art. I watch Ruby's face sour as she slinks off to the palace under-
belly, where she's been assigned to a lieutenant in the postal office.

In a jewelry box of pink marble, mirrored doors, and crystal chandeliers, the strapping sculptor from New Hampshire has repurposed a pair of the castle's fanciest gilded chairs alongside a folding army field table with one short leg. His office consists of a few pens, a portable field typewriter, and some tattered Michelin guidebooks that look as though they've already been through a war. In this makeshift office, I spend hours taking dictation on my steno machine and typing reports and letters to our troop command. I type countless memos to Washington, asking for more men, resources, gasoline, and transportation. Anything to support Captain Thomas, who is otherwise working alone.

"Take a gander at this." From across the rickety table, he pushes a page of the *New York Times*. In a small column, under an ad for shaving cream, the article reads, "Unique Collection of Art Treasures Taken Away by Germans in Italy." The journalist has included a statement from Professor Amedeo Maiuri, curator of the Museo Nazionale in Naples. "The responsibility of the Germans before the whole civilized world," the article says, "will be multiplied beyond all their previous responsibility for devastations, sacking and lootings. I weep not only for Italy, but for the things that are the heritage of the world of culture."

"You must be worried about what you'll find once you get into Naples."

Thomas rubs his lined forehead, but then points a finger at me and says, "You bet your sweet cheeks."

So far, I only know a little about Captain Thomas: he's a strapping man who looks like he's handled marble, bronze, and metal for years. Grew up in Iowa. Divorced. Left behind a little boy with the mother. Teaches art at a women's college in New Hampshire. Red cheeks. A man who enjoys a hot dog and a beer. But beyond the sketchy details and rough exterior, I've lived around an Ivy League institution long enough to recognize his type. Rich parents. A confidence with women that seems beyond justification. A way to make you believe he's got things all figured out. A surefire answer to anything you ask.

"And," he says, "we just got an intelligence report that a panzer unit set fire to a villa south of here. It was a temporary storage depot for the Filangieri Museum and the state archives in Naples. Burned up more than forty paintings by Botticelli. Van Eyck. Andrea del Sarto. Pontormo . . ."

At the mention of these names, my hand hesitates over the steno pad as the familiar feeling of being outside looking in washes over me. It's the same feeling I got the first time I stepped into the Metropolitan Museum of Art with Dot. Like there was a whole world I didn't know the first thing about, and maybe never would. "I should tell you up front, sir . . . I don't know much about art. And I've only picked up a few Italian words. Just what I learned in the phrase books while we were in Algeria."

"You go to college? Secretarial school?"

I shake my head. "I grew up around Yale. But I don't suppose that counts."

"Well, maybe you'll get the chance someday."

I can't help but huff out a small laugh. "I don't think so, sir. My ma never had that kind of money and . . . we just get by. You know?"

"The army is its own kind of education," he says. "And they're paying you big bucks to type, doll, not be an art expert." He gives me a wide, square-toothed smile, self-satisfied about his own joke. "Anyway, like I was saying, the Italians think there were more than eighty-five thousand manuscripts in that museum in Naples. Just like that," he says, snapping his figures. "Poof. Up in smoke."

"You think the Germans took some of the things with them, before they started the fire?"

He shrugs, running his eyes over me. Assessing. "Depends if you believe those brutes know what they're looking at. And if you ask me, *they're* the ones who don't know anything about art. But whether they do or don't, they seem hell-bent on despoiling Italy of all her treasures. You've already seen what they done to this place," he says, looking around the room. The men tell us they found the palace of Caserta stripped of its furnishings. That the Nazis ripped paintings with bayonets and left behind piles of human waste in the glittering hallways.

I think all of this would make Dot cry; I debate whether to share this news with her. "Don't they have better things to do? They have taken something more important than a few pictures. They have taken lives."

"You're right about that, doll," he says, turning in his rickety chair and slicking his hair back with both hands. He ogles me openly until I feel the hairs on the back of my neck tingle and I feel my heart sink a little. I want to be on his side, but I see a man who's all too familiar; one used to showing off his education and erudition in front of a classroom full of girls infatuated with him. He's used to it. He feels he has every right to ogle me, as if he knows I won't be able to find a reason to say no to him, especially when my grade in the class depends on saying yes. Full of confidence in his own brand of leering charisma. I wonder how many more professors like him are at his women's college in New Hampshire. He seems to sense his upper hand, and he grins before he finally turns his attention back to the newspaper article.

"But if these monuments are accidentally bombed, then we lose part of the world's heritage for future generations. Someone's got to care about it. The Huns have spread the word that *we're* the ones who are going to burn up all the monuments out of spite. That we are going to load paintings onto our naval ships and bring them back to American museums."

I gasp. "But that's not true! As if we needed something else that would convince us to make them our sworn enemies."

"You see the problem, then, Miss Evans," he says, standing. "Our biggest job is educating people. On all sides. And don't worry. You'll pick it up along the way, too, sweet cakes." He chucks me under the chin with his knuckle. I cringe but he doesn't seem to notice. "Anyway, tomorrow, we head into Naples to see what we can find out. We get an early start. See you at O Six Hundred."

I close the latches on my stenotype case with two loud taps that echo through the otherwise empty palace room. "I'll be here. Goodnight, sir."

I leave the makeshift office to find my friends for dinner, threading my way through a palace that's like a city unto itself. As the Allied headquarters, Caserta contains everything we need. There are men and WACs sorting mail in a post office. There is a communications wing where Dot sits with her British and Australian counterparts at the switchboards, under an elaborately carved ceiling and white marble. There is a hospital section, where injured boys lie in their beds, talking to English and American nurses who read them mail while they look up into the painted vaults as if they are in heaven. Some of the women complain about the cold showers, the crowded conditions, or the erratic heaters. From here, it feels impossible to imagine our tight little apartment in New Haven, with its peeling wallpaper and linoleum floor that crackles under my feet, all of which would fit inside one of the little storage rooms in this vast palace. "How could anyone complain about being here?" Lollie Dee says as we line up with our trays, the smell of meatloaf and mashed potatoes wafting into the hallway. "They'll have to drag me out kicking and screaming."

After dinner, the winter darkness falls quickly. The stars are absent and only the moon, a dim copper orb, illuminates the outlines of the palace. I step out onto a marble terrace and look into the blackness, my breath gathering into clouds. In the distance, searchlights scan for planes like moths in the beam of a flashlight. It's remarkable, I think, how quickly I've become used to this, the sound of planes in the sky, the constant unease and scanning for bombs that could be dropped at any moment. I stretch my fingers, a respite from the force required to push the keys of the steno machine down over the long hours at work.

Suddenly, from the black, I make out the bulky outline of Lieutenant Hamm, the tip of his cigarette a pinpoint of orange light in the darkness.

"Evenin', Mouse," he says.

"*Buonasera*, Lieutenant Hamm."

He pulls another cigarette from his shirt pocket, brings it to his face to light it from his own, then hands it to me. "You speak Eyetalian now?"

"*Un poquino*," I say, taking a small drag and then blowing a stream of smoke into the cold air.

"Wowser, you're good! I didn't know you could speak it."

"Neither did I." I laugh. I take another puff of the cigarette, trying not to cough. "I'm practicing."

"Why you spending your time on that, doll?" he says. "That ain't your job."

"Oh really?"

"Nope. Your job is to keep up morale," he says, dragging out the word "morale" as if poking fun at it. "To keep us happy, so to speak." A sly, lopsided grin.

I stare into the bright arc of the searchlight, but don't answer. He continues. "Ain't that why you WACs are here? To support us in every way? Keep us happy?"

"Is that so?"

He nods. "You want to keep us happy? I can show you how." I feel his fingers at my waist, a slow, claw-like grip. His sickly sweet tobacco breath on my neck. I slap his hand away, which only seems to make him more eager. He cackles quietly and takes another step toward me, pulling at the waistband of my skirt.

"Stop it right now!" I slap his hand away again as he lurches toward me.

"Beat it, Hamm. Leave her alone." Dante Ruggero steps through the door onto the terrace. "Last thing she wants is your grubby mitts on her."

My first thought is that Private Ruggero has just committed a terrible error—an enlisted man reprimanding an officer. I brace myself. But Lieutenant Hamm takes two steps back and shrugs. "What? We're having some fun. Ain't we, Evans? Mouse?" Another sly grin. He flicks the butt of the cigarette on the stones at Ruggero's feet, where it flickers, then goes black. In the doorway, he and Ruggero stand chest to chest, like roosters. "That's what WACs are here for, right? Keeping our *morale* up? She's doing her job."

"Take your morale somewhere else," Ruggero says. At last, Hamm slinks back into the building.

"He hurt you?"

I shake my head, stubbing out the cigarette on the stone railing of the ornate parapet. "You were brave to stand up to him. I know his kind. He'd never agree for his sister or girlfriend to be a WAC. Doesn't get it. Doesn't think we can do anything of value."

"And what about your father . . . or brothers?" He leans against the parapet and considers me with raised eyebrows. "What'd they think about you joining up?"

For a long stretch of seconds, nothing comes out. How could I begin to explain that I don't know the first thing about the man who made my ma in a family way, all those years ago? I wonder if I could write Ma to ask about him now, if somehow the years and the vast ocean might be the thing that closes the chasm between us. Might make me brave enough at last to ask the questions buried inside. But whatever I might say about my so-called pa to Dante Ruggero might only serve to push him away, to illuminate my shame as if in the bright circle of a searchlight.

"I'm an only child." I lean against the parapet next to Dante and look into the black sky.

"Well." He clears his throat. "If anyone could change Hamm's mind about WACs, it's you."

He is beautiful, I think, his thick black hair a mass of swirls, his boyish face. I imagine his nose must have been covered in freckles when he was younger. A handsome plumber ready to take over his father's business when he gets back home. "Type of fella you'll want to wear lipstick for," my ma would say.

"Anyway," he says, "I've heard you say who cares about some damn paintings when we might get blown up any minute. And I agree with you."

I shake my head. "All those buildings in Captain Thomas's guide-books. The pages of churches. Museums. Paintings. Sculptures. It's overwhelming. Seems impossible to think a couple of soldiers sitting at a desk could save it all anyway."

He smiles, his dimples deep in his cheeks. Immediately, my face feels hot. I'm not used to a man looking at me that way. But I've seen the way he looks at Dot, just like every man does, swayed by her blond wavy hair, her dogged self-confidence that comes with a lifetime of Manhattan party invitations. Who wouldn't be dazzled by her glow? I've seen how men gaze at her with open desire, how they flatter her. Women are drawn to her, too, like bees around their queen. I, too, have been under her spell. Ruby would crush me to be near Dot.

"Yeah. All those paintings. Sculptures and stuff. But I reckon you're right for trying. Fighting a good fight. I'd say you're a smart girl."

Never have I been the center of attention, the focus of a man's ad-oration. Above all, never considered myself smart. Not smart enough or rich enough to go to night school, much less college—a place re-served for men and women like Dot. But here on this dark terrace, in this magical palace, for a moment, Dante Ruggero makes me believe what I'm doing is at least worthy. And that I might be worthy, too.

9

EVA

I STAY IN FLORENCE.

It's the place where I will earn my father's pride. The place where I can use my skills and talents, even though I've had to learn to use my left hand to pick up the camera and my right arm to bend enough to adjust the focus. It's also the place that's given me a purpose. And there's no leaving Italy now, anyway. In the weeks following Professor Kriegbaum's death and the airstrikes on Florence, most of the train lines over the Alps have been cut.

I follow Paloma, Horst, and Enzo through the snaking streets of the Oltrarno. Paloma carries a stack of sturdy signs, Horst a list on a wooden clipboard, Enzo a hammer and a leather pouch full of metal tacks. I follow with my small Leica in my left hand, a bag of film cartridges slung over my shoulder.

Paloma and Enzo walk ahead of us, speaking quietly in Italian. They are cousins, I've learned, along with a few other pieces of their lives. Paloma has secured the job for Enzo as a carpenter and handyman at the Kunsthistorisches Institut. She's studied languages at the university. The family owns a multigenerational tailor shop and textile business in a section called Por Santa Maria. Along with her work at the institute, Paloma lives with her extended family and helps care for her aging mother and her sister's children.

The alley opens to the broad Piazza del Carmine. The façade of

Santa Maria del Carmine is a mass of rough-hewn stone, unfinished like so many Florentine churches. The bottom half is hidden under scaffolding and sandbags. Paloma and Enzo stop at a large pair of carved wooden doors.

"*Ecco ci*," Paloma says, peeling a sign from her stack. I watch Enzo put a few tacks between his lips, then nail the sign to the hulking wooden door.

MIT SEINER GESAMTEN AUSSTATTUNG STEHT ALS KUNST-EDENKMAL UNTER DEUTSCHEM SCHUTZ! BELEGUNG VER-BOTEN.

THIS BUILDING WITH ALL ITS FURNISHINGS IS UNDER GERMAN PROTECTION AS AN ART MONUMENT! OCCUPANCY PROHIBITED.

The notice bears Generalfeldmarschall Kesselring's signature, and we nail them up all over the city—at churches, monuments, and historic buildings. There is something solemn and quiet about our task, and after a while, I realize why. We're continuing the work of Professor Kriegbaum, who, before his untimely death, instructed us to mark all the monuments in the city that might be misused—by Germans, Italians, or anyone.

Horst flips through his clipboard and marks off the church. I jog into the middle of the square and raise my Leica to frame the three of them standing at the church door with the newly placed sign. There they are in black-and-white precision: Paloma with her hair pulled into a neat bun secured with a wooden pencil. Horst, giant next to her petite frame. And Enzo, cupping his hand to light a cigarette, then smiling at me. Snap. The aperture swirls, flits. A record of a fleeting second.

Through the afternoon, we fall into a rhythm of work, checking off one monument at a time. Paloma and Enzo lead the way through their city, explaining the signs in Italian to locals who stop to ask or read them. The cousins know shortcuts through the alleys that suddenly open to piazzas with church façades, trees, and benches, and children kicking a ball from one end to the other.

We pass the Duomo with its bright costume of candy-striped marble. The portals are filled with sandbags. Where Lorenzo Ghiberti's famous bronze doors of the Baptistery once stood, there are more stacks of sandbags. I wonder where the doors have gone for safekeeping, and what a project it must have been to dismantle them and take them away. Nearby is Giotto's tall, defiant bell tower in its equally patterned, colorful glory. At the corner, a knot of German soldiers scan the square. One of the men grinds a cigarette under the heel of his boot then sets off, his rifle across his back.

I can't help but remember Professor Kriegbaum's words, that these signs are as much for the German soldiers as for the Florentine public. For the most part, he told us, the German guards aren't educated about art history and cultural heritage. They won't hesitate to use a historical monument for barracks or a latrine. Some may even stash a small object away in their bags as a souvenir.

As we make our way around town, there are new posters showing handsome German soldiers alongside Fascist ones, with captions in Italian stating that we are friends, that we are working together for the same goal. I wonder how many Italians believe this, now that so many of them side with the Anglo-Americans.

Our supply of signs runs thin. Shadows lengthen down the alleys, casting one side into darkness, and drawing deep crevices between the cobblestones. We walk past a man removing beautiful leather bags from his sidewalk display with a hook on a long handle. The aroma of leather fills the street. We turn onto the riverside to take in the last of daylight. I have heard about it, this famous light of Italy. The Golden Hour. *L'ora dorata.* The moment when the sun hits just the right angle to turn everything to a burnished shade of gold.

I raise my Leica and aim it toward the ragged patchwork of the

Ponte Vecchio, with its projecting windows, tile roofs, and agglomerations of centuries. Even in the winter, the light is perfect. I adjust the F-stop and snap a series of images, trying to capture the beauty of the medieval houses along the riversides, with their narrow windows and turrets. Turn and snap. Turn and snap. Take as many pictures as you can of the monuments, Professor Kriegbaum had told me. You never know when we might need them.

My father was right. I must stay in Italy. The important work is here. The work of documenting what we are doing to preserve these monuments for future generations—to save them from destruction at the hands of the Americans, British, and Australians who seem to want to blow everything apart. The aura of winter sunlight rakes across the top of my camera, and I see the fine layer of persistent dust from the bombing that killed Professor Kriegbaum. No amount of cleaning will remove it.

Horst comes to stand next to me. For a moment, we watch the golden light shimmer on the river. A single rower drags a V through the water in the refracted light. After a stretch of silence, Horst says, "It wasn't your fault, Eva."

They've all said it to me. Paloma. Enzo. The staff of the art history institute.

I nod. I do try to believe them.

"It was a bomb," he says. "There was nothing you could do to stop it."

Now we know it was British aircraft that aimed their strike on the train marshaling yards at Campo di Marte. But they killed innocent people in the surrounding neighborhoods instead. Now the marshaling yards are nothing but a graveyard of twisted metal train carcasses in a basin of cratered homes. I hear that Dr. Planiscig miraculously survived the bombing, but has abandoned Florence and returned to Austria. Part of me still believes I should have, too.

Instead, I raise the Leica and press the shutter release. It seems the smallest, yet best—and perhaps the only—way I can atone for that day, by continuing Professor Kriegbaum's mission to document Florence and its monuments, to do my part to protect the cultural heritage of the city he loved. And to consider the Anglo-Americans our sworn enemies.

I lift my camera and frame the old bridge. "I know." Then I squint one eye and do what I always do. I hide myself behind the camera.

In Palazzo Guadagni's ancient wine cellar, I've fashioned a darkroom. Cobwebs hang like silvery mesh in the darkened corners of the eaves between the vaults. An old tap on the wall releases water at just the right temperature to dilute the developer solution, acetic acid, and fixing bath measured out into metal trays. Two assistants from the Phototek help me move the yellow lights and negative printer with its fragile bulbs to the lower level. A stack of photographic paper and a drying rack improvised with a long string and clothespins will work just fine, even better than my old darkroom in Oma's converted garden shed.

I pin the latest pictures from our sign-posting campaign to dry on the line. The image of Horst, Enzo, and Paloma comes out darker than I would like, its black details overexposed. I'll have to reprint it. But now, I see for the first time how Enzo was watching me that day, cupping his hand around a cigarette while observing me as if assessing my intent.

I check the old clock on the wall. Cocktail hour. The time when all the important work of the institute happens. I wipe my hands on a rag, remove my canvas apron, and shut off the yellow light. Then I pull myself up the four flights of stairs to the top floor of Palazzo Guadagni, where everyone will be assembling for an *aperitivo*.

As I climb the steep stairwell, the ceilings get higher and the proportions grander. I pass the darkened doorway of the institute's library, its shelves packed with thick art history books in German and Italian, presided over by a librarian with a long, gray beard. There is a large lecture hall and the institute's collection of photography, with its thousands of archival cartons, and the offices of the two dozen or more German, Austrian, and Italian staff.

Through the weeks, we have watched Professor Kriegbaum's predictions come true. The Kunstschutz has brought more art professionals in armored cars from Berlin, Munich, Vienna—historians, curators, critics, artists—but only those who are party loyalists. Some are lodged with us in the Pensione Sorelle Bandini in the upper floors of the Palazzo Guadagni; others are housed among collectors and dealers across the city. There is much talk of the Führer's grand new museum in Linz, designed to house all the world's masterpieces under one roof.

At the reception area of the *pensione*, one of the petite Bandini sisters presides over the desk. She is stooped and beady-eyed, examining me cautiously as I pass. I see the other institute staff collecting on the upper-floor loggia bar. I step through the doorway, feeling a cool breeze waft across the terrace. Every afternoon, it's the place we do the important work of the institute. And where our new director receives visitors. The elder Bandini sister, a sharp-eyed, stooped woman, hands each of us a glass of bubbly prosecco.

From the door, I watch Ludwig Heydenreich, our newly appointed director of the Kunsthistorisches Institut. At first glance, it would seem the Nazi-led art protection organization has stamped out a carbon copy of Professor Kriegbaum: our new director is in his early forties and graying, dressed in an Italian-tailored suit. He shares a similar pedigree to Kriegbaum, having taught art history at the University of Berlin, spent years studying in Italy, and written several books about Leonardo da Vinci. But that's where the comparison ends. Where Professor Kriegbaum had a softness, a gentle demeanor, the new director is stone-faced, unreadable. He has rearranged the furniture in the director's office and has set out new procedures in the Phototek that we are trying our best to digest. All of us pay close attention, as each of us is learning what he expects of us.

The men have arranged their chairs around Heydenreich. When Paloma sees me at the door to the loggia, she pulls up another chair and the two of us squeeze our places between the men. Three Florentine men from the Uffizi Galleries lean forward. The Italians are at the same time refined and haggard-looking, their eyes ringed in shadows. They look as though they have been wearing the same finely tailored suits for weeks. They regard the new director warily.

"We need to request fuel to bring more works to Monte Oliveto," says the oldest-looking man, who is introduced as Giovanni Poggi, the director of the Uffizi.

"And travel permissions, of course," says the younger man, Cesare Fasola, the museum's librarian. He says this in broken German.

Professor Heydenreich responds in what sounds to me like impeccable Italian. "Of course. We will need a copy of the inventories showing everything that is being moved."

Poggi sets down his drink and tents his fingers. "We have more sculpture than painting this time, so the transport is of course more delicate."

"But Professor Heydenreich," the institute's archivist interrupts in German, "I thought our High Command wanted all the works from the Tuscan depots to be sent to the Borromean Islands in the lakes region. Now that the Anglo-Americans are moving up the peninsula . . ."

Poggi has understood enough. His face turns white. "No!" he says, standing. He flips back to a scrambled mix of Italian and heavily accented German. "Everything must stay here. If not in Florence, then in Tuscany. It is not right that our treasures be taken far away."

"But . . ." the archivist reacts, surprised, "surely we could care for them better, north of here—far from the violence."

"We have agreements," the third man says. Filippo Rossi, head of the Florentine Galleries, is a slim, middle-aged man with an intelligent face. "The General Direction of the Arts and Colonel Langsdorff's office . . . We have already agreed not to remove anything unless there is some imminent danger. And only then, we would return them to Florence. Not across the Apennines." Rossi speaks calmly, but his face seems to have lost its color. Beads of sweat appear along his receding hairline even in the cool breeze. Around the circle, men take small sips of their prosecco within a long stretch of awkward silence.

Horst interjects, leaning his huge bulk forward into the circle. "But Herr Professor," he says, "I thought the Kunstschutz was planning to bring everything from the countryside depots to Rome. That Vatican City will stay neutral." I try to imagine the massive effort to empty more than fifty historic buildings across Tuscany. To transport priceless works of art by Michelangelo, Botticelli, and other famous Italian artists, all to the protective confines of the papal enclave. "Has the Holy See not agreed to safeguard everything?"

Poggi begins to pace behind our chairs. He switches back to Italian and I struggle to follow. "You must understand, *signori*. Our artistic patrimony must be defended in the same way as families, houses, and land. These masterpieces . . . They are the pride of our people. If they left the confines of Tuscany, well. It would be a kind of defeat, and just when we need to be most confident. I tell you, we will lose hope. For what are we without our history? You cannot leave us here in a cultural wasteland. Not after everything we have been through." Beside me, Paloma's fingers fidget in her lap.

Heydenreich calmly raises his hand and Poggi stops talking. "For now," he says, crossing his legs in his elegant suit, "things are uncertain. So everything must stay in the depots." He turns to Fasola. "And we'll do even better than fuel and permissions. We'll provide you with an armed escort to Monte Oliveto."

"*Bene*," Poggi says, sinking back into his chair. "*La ringrazio, direttore.*"

"My office will ensure you have it in the morning," Heydenreich says, taking a sip of his cocktail.

"But . . ." The obvious question is burning inside me and I can't let it lie dormant any longer. "I don't understand why we don't transport everything to the salt—to the safe places—in Germany and Austria," I interject. Suddenly, all the men's attention is on me. I shift my camera in my lap.

"Only for a while," I say. "Then everything could be brought back here. When it's safe again. Trust me. I have spent many hours there myself. And I can say for certain that it's the only place in the world where nothing will happen to them."

Rossi's face blanches again. "No," he says. "They must not leave Italy. Not at any cost."

Beyond Florence, the countryside unfurls like a golden blanket over rolling hills. There are lush vineyards, lone chapels, deserted medieval villages, and rows of cypress trees. The fields lie fallow in the wan light. The air is heavy with the scent of decaying haystacks and abandonment.

From the back seat of an elegant Mercedes, my view consists of Horst looming in the passenger seat alongside a diminutive Italian driver. Kicking up dust onto our windshield is the armored transport vehicle Heydenreich promised. Behind us, a third vehicle transports Poggi, another Italian superintendent, Paloma, and Enzo, who will be tasked with making wooden crates. Behind them, two trucks containing sculptures from Florence rattle along the pitted, winding roads.

Horst turns his bulk toward Professor Heydenreich, who sits next to me and my camera bag in the back seat. "If you ask me," Horst says, "it doesn't matter where the paintings and sculptures are— Rome, the Borromean Islands, the Tuscan countryside—as long as they are guarded. Otherwise, they might end up in a soldier's bag."

"Yes or the Italians . . ." Heydenreich says. "We don't know what they will do. Poggi, Rossi, Fasola, the others . . . They seem to have good intentions. But before any of the works move from here, we need to check their condition and review the inventories ourselves. And of course, photograph everything for our records." I watch his eyes flit to the Italian driver, but the placid man doesn't seem to understand our German conversation.

The armored escort slows and our driver turns into a long, dusty gravel path that winds up a hillside. We pass a shepherd with a ragged herd, the sound of the bells clanging around their necks, their shredded, matted wool, and their shaky, trebled bleating. Bristly cypress trees lined up like a regiment. Before us lies a perfectly proportioned medieval castle façade, complete with crenellated battlements and a small arched doorway. We step out of the vehicle into the quiet.

I'm unprepared for the relief I feel in leaving Florence, where the tensions have risen slowly, silently in recent weeks like a pot on the verge of boiling. Across the city, there are more SS troops in the streets and *caffès*. More panzers in the deserted squares. Gestapo banging on front doors and barking orders through ground-floor windows. Jewish families packing up their belongings in horse-drawn carts or on their backs. Only German heard in the restaurants.

Italians emerge from their homes quietly, furtively, only long enough to line up outside the corner bakeries and grocers for meager supplies. More posters on the doors depict American soldiers as gorillas or Jewish thieves. But here in the countryside, things unfurl in a slow, eternal pace, as if nothing bad has ever happened in history and where nothing could disturb it again.

Poggi exits his vehicle first, and we follow. At the entrance to a cavernous hall, another Italian official stands waiting. He shakes Poggi's and Heydenreich's hands and introduces us to a motley array of assistants and laborers loitering under the arcades of an interior courtyard. There is a flurry of slamming car doors alongside German and Italian niceties.

Under the arcades, the caretakers have already lined up several works of art for us to inspect. A pair of panels comes into view, tall and narrow. I back up, trying to frame them in the camera view-finder while the men begin to examine the other works.

All at once, I recognize the pair of nearly life-sized figures. It's Lucas Cranach's *Adam* and *Eve*, the same pictures Professor Krieg-baum and I discussed the day of the bombing. Masterpieces of German patrimony, locked within the confines of Italy. Eve stands to Adam's left. Their bodies are serpentine, pendants to each other against their dark backgrounds. Each figure is nude, holding small branches over their groins. Eve holds the apple in her palm while the serpent coils down to her from the branches of the Tree of Knowledge.

I adjust the bellows on the box camera to frame the figures, ar-chetypes of blind innocence and irresistible temptation. I focus on Eve with her fine, red curls and even features, a woman who holds the fate of humanity in the palm of her hand. And Adam, scratch-ing the back of his head in consternation. Cranach has captured the moment of decision, the moment to obey the rules or give in to the urge to taste the sweetness of forbidden fruit.

I sense Paloma's petite frame standing next to me. "What do you think of it?" she asks in German.

I look from the camera to her. "I think the woman always seems the wrongdoer in these pictures. But plenty of men make bad choices that affect the future of humanity, too."

She stifles a laugh with her hand. "You are right," she says. "Come. They are bringing out more pictures."

Under the arcades of the courtyard, they bring more paintings into the light as the men mill around, discussing them. I begin to get a sense of the scale of this operation. Monte Oliveto is just one of some fifty safe places across the Italian peninsula, Professor Hey-denreich has told us. Thirty-eight in Tuscany alone. Inside castles, private villas, wine cellars, and other historic buildings, thousands of priceless paintings from museums and private collections are tucked away. Instead of hiding everything away inside a single salt mine like Altaussee, the Italians have instead scattered their treasures across dozens of hiding places.

After a morning filled with taking photographs and double-checking the Italians' inventories, we proceed into the cavernous kitchen, where a pair of local women have prepared hand-rolled *picci* and bland bread with salty pork and cheese. I watch Enzo and several other Italian laborers fill their metal canteens with Chianti wine and walk off with them to sit in the grass. The sound of the women's lively voices mingles with the clatter of pots and pans.

I pile my plate with the soft noodles and move outside to a grassy area in view of tangled vines spilling out of the eaves of the castle, alongside a fountain spitting water so cold it hurts to touch. Professor Heydenreich, Horst, and the Italian caretakers find seats at a wobbly table in the gravel.

From the dilapidated wooden door of a stone outbuilding, a child darts out. Then another. They soon become a group of children chasing one another into the field beyond the castle. "Refugees," the castle caretaker tells us. "They have filled up the servants' quarters, all the outbuildings. Even our underground wine cellar. Many have come up from the South." For a moment, I feel gratitude for my narrow bed in Palazzo Guadagni. A change of clothes. And food to eat.

"Having the refugees mingled here with the artwork . . . It's a risk," Heydenreich says.

The caretaker shrugs. "What else are we to do? We are outnumbered. And they don't harm the paintings."

The afternoon consists of more hours of pulling out paintings from the dark halls and bedchambers of the castle. Double-checking the inventories. Photographing everything. By the time the light wanes, we have counted more than three hundred pictures. After hours of squinting through my viewfinder, wrangling my tripod, and hunching over my camera, my body feels wrung-out and exhausted.

I step out onto the terrace and catch my breath at the sight of the Tuscan panorama bathed in golden light. Thousands of hectares spread out in every direction, as if someone had unfurled a green and burnished patchwork quilt across swells of the sea. A ribbon of road snakes through the landscape, bordered by tall, skinny cedar trees lined up like soldiers. In the distance, a small farm consists of an ancient stone house with a red tile roof, a goat pen, a neat orchard, and neglected, overgrown rows of grape vines cascading down a hillside.

I find Enzo sitting on the edge of a stone wall overlooking this panorama of golden, rolling hills and sparse trees. As the light wanes, the landscape turns vivid and lustrous. There is no way to capture its fleeting beauty in a black-and-white photograph. All the same, I raise my camera from the strap around my neck and take a shot.

We've developed a crude way of communicating, he using the maximum number of German words he knows, and I, using what I've picked up listening intently to what I hear on the streets, and from the workers and superintendents around us. How beautiful the words that roll off his tongue. Like a song. Whereas my own words feel cold and brutish. Ugly.

"Cigarette?" I ask this in Italian. That, at least, sounds like a similar word in both languages.

He fiddles in his shirt pocket with his rough hands scarred by years of manual labor, then pulls out two long cigarettes and puts both between his lips. He strikes a match and lights both while I gather my skirt under me and sit beside him, our legs dangling over the edge of the wall. Then he hands me one. I put the cigarette in my mouth and feel the deep, burning sweetness of the tobacco mingled with his particular scent of shave cream.

For a moment, we sit in silence, contemplating the indescribable beauty of the countryside. He looks unfazed, having known nothing other than being surrounded by this landscape. I inhale the scent of dried hay and clean air. From here, it's impossible to imagine that, just a few hours' drive south of here, there is nothing but bloodshed.

"*Sei fotogiornalista,*" he says, gesturing to my camera.

"A photojournalist? Me?" I laugh. "That sounds a bit too important, but well . . . I guess I've taken a few pictures for the newspapers." This makes me think of my mother and all I want to do is
change the subject. "They say our enemies are coming up from the
south . . ." I gesture toward the landscape.

He takes a quick drag on his cigarette and nods. "*Americani.
Inglesi. Sud-Africani. Australiani.*"

"So . . . You think those paintings are better off here in the country? Or in Florence or Rome?" I watch his reaction closely. "Or perhaps north of the Alps instead?" I remain unconvinced the pictures
are safer here than in the Austrian salt mines.

He doesn't respond right away. Instead, he blows smoke in the air
and studies me intently with his deep brown eyes. He seems completely unaware of how beautiful he is to behold, as carelessly,
effortlessly lovely as the vista before us. "Depends on what you think
happens in the end, *cara*."

"And what do you imagine, Enzo, when you think of the future
of Italy?"

He struggles to find the words. His hands move in the air for a
moment, as if the gestures themselves will cause words to come forth.
Smoke from the stub of his cigarette swirls into the air. Then, in a
mixture of Italian with a few German words thrown in, he tells me a
story about how the last war devastated his country, how he lost his
own father in the chaos. How, ever since, they have struggled to find
work; how, in the factories, there are only strikes. How his cousins
in the countryside had their land seized, how the Italian government
could not address these problems, and how Il Duce promised to provide them protection from these crises. I have seen Paloma, her face
a twist of worry, listen to the nightly Fascist broadcast from Salò,
where Il Duce now has his headquarters. I begin to piece together
the complicated story of what the Italians have endured over the last
generation.

"It's not that we want another war," he says. "We just want back everything they have taken from us. *Vedi?* Too many stand by and do nothing," he says, tossing the butt of his cigarette into the void with a violent flick of the wrist; but the fire still burns behind his brown eyes. "But I won't stand by and do nothing."

For a moment, his face hardens. A fleeting darkness.

"Meh . . ." He shrugs finally, and his face turns soft again. "But we work together, no?" He grins now, and dimples form deep crevices in his cheeks. "*Italiani. Tedeschi.* Together." I feel something like prosecco bubble up inside my veins, and I think I may have had too much of it in recent weeks.

"*Fräulein!*"

From the top of the rise, Horst is looking down at us sitting on the wall, his eyes slits, as if he has caught us doing something naughty.

"The trucks are waiting. We're trying to get back to Florence before dark."

Enzo offers his hand to help me up from the wall. He pulls me to my feet with an earnestness that makes me lose my balance and for a second, I fall into him, feeling his hard chest against my palms. I laugh, stepping back and dusting off my skirt.

On the rise, Horst shakes his head slowly, like a disapproving parent. Without a word, he turns toward the trucks. We follow his ox-like back and leave behind the idyll of the countryside and the hundreds of beautiful paintings hidden in the castle.

We return to Palazzo Guadagni to find that the artist Rudolf Levy has returned. For the past few months, he's been sheltering with Italian collectors in the countryside, far from the emptied synagogues and Jewish homes across Florence. Levy has told us that in Germany, his work is considered "degenerate" and has already been removed from museums in Cologne, Berlin, and Hamburg. Now he's completely reliant on dealers and collectors who continue to support him. As for Heydenreich and the other staff, they appear to ignore the fact of Levy's Jewishness; his acclaim as an artist speaks for itself and they welcome him to the loggia along with our other colleagues.

In the breakfast room of the *pensione*, Levy has displayed some of his latest work on easels, a series of expressionistic portraits and landscapes, full of color and life. One of the Bandini sisters is sweeping bread crumbs from the floor. She stops sweeping long enough to admire a picture Levy has painted of the loggia right here in the Palazzo Guadagni; in a few black strokes of his brush, he's depicted her arranging flowers in a vase.

We collect as usual on the upper loggia of the building, where the Bandini sisters hand out tiny cups of espresso. "There are some dealers coming to see my work." Rudolf Levy sits near me, stirring a packet of sugar into a small shot of thick espresso. He looks happy, I think. Time in the countryside outside of the increasingly tense atmosphere of the city. "I will bring them up to see some of my pictures." Nearby, Horst and two of the archivists are drinking their coffee and shuffling a deck of cards.

"Levy!" the archival assistant calls from the door. "The men want you to come downstairs to meet them." The artist gets up, leaving his empty espresso cup on the table between us.

After a few minutes, we hear a ruckus in the square below—a combination of a car engine and simultaneous yelling in Italian and German. All of us in the loggia spring up and lean over the stone railing to see a large German police truck. We watch a small group of men in gray uniforms, SS officers, grasp Levy and put him in handcuffs. I see the top of his bald head disappear into the truck, then the metal door slams shut, and the vehicle rolls over the cobblestones. Just like that, he's gone.

All of us from the loggia run down four flights of stairs to the street, but it's too late. The square stands in silent desolation. All of us stand in stunned silence, watching dried leaves swirl across the cobblestones. What recourse do we have to get him back? None at all.

We return to the upper floors, where Levy's paintings stand, bold and abandoned, in the breakfast room. When Signora Bandini picks up his empty espresso cup, it rattles against the saucer. She wipes her cheeks with her cleaning rag and hurries into the shadows of the boardinghouse kitchen.

10

JOSIE

BEFORE AN ORNATE CHURCH FAÇADE SO RUINED IT could be a sandcastle, a cluster of barefoot children are picking through a mountain of jagged, broken stones. Captain Thomas eases the dusty jeep into the square. The children spy us, stop what they're doing, and come running. Their hair is filthy, their ragged clothing covered in gray dust, their faces smudged with black. They are pure energy, all squeals of excitement and jumbled words. The only word I can make out is *americani*!

But Captain Thomas pays little attention to this ragtag welcoming committee. Instead, he looks at the church and groans. I follow his gaze. The façade, surely once of indescribable beauty, is riddled by blasts. Sandbags that might have shored up the centuries-old carved portals have tumbled to the ground, where a little boy clambers over them. The church door is a gaping black hole. In the alleys snaking away from the square, crumbled balconies overlook the rubble-strewn paths and laundry flaps in rows of dirty flags, abandoned and covered in dust.

Captain Thomas reaches under the squeaking springs of the driver's seat and produces the file full of signs we've prepared back at Caserta. I've studied them at length, careful to memorize the English and Italian words that instruct people not to enter, not to requisition, and not to take anything out of the building. That this is a historic building protected under Allied authority.

In my own accordion file, I have lists of all the historic buildings in Naples that Captain Thomas—from his desk in faraway Algeria— managed to prepare based on an old Italian Touring Club guide. I've stayed up late on my cot, running my penlight over the pages full of Italian place names. Trying to commit them to memory, struggling to understand. Looking up words in my phrase book.

"San Filippo Neri," Captain Thomas announces. He steps out of the jeep and hikes up his pants, adjusting his crotch. I have never understood why men do this so openly and in plain view of whoever may be present. A woman would never do such a thing. I avert my gaze and focus intently on the typewritten list of Neapolitan monuments in my lap. There. San Filippo Neri. I press the point of my pen next to the name.

But Captain Thomas has no time to say anything more, because he drowns among the excited children who buzz around him like a swarm of bees. There are kids of all ages, one no older than five, jumping up from the dust, chattering, thrusting their hands in his pockets, smiling, demanding, foisting their little bodies on him. Captain Thomas is nonplussed. Another cluster of children runs around to the passenger side. I don't dare to step out.

"*Signorina!*" a boy calls to me. His eyes are huge and as brown as milk chocolate. "Cigarette?" His friend, a boy no older than seven, is smoking a cigarette pulled from a shiny new pack of Marlboros in his shirt pocket.

"*Dov'e trova?*" I attempt my rusty Italian, but I know it's wrong— where you find?— I know I sound ridiculous and he doesn't seem to understand me anyway. But I don't understand how Captain Thomas can turn away from these dirt-caked children and their miserable circumstances. How could a building possibly matter in the face of such devastation?

Captain Thomas swats his way through the swarm of pesky children and steps over the debris toward the church façade with a hammer and one of the signs. The boys scamper after him as if he is the pied piper. Alone at last, I step out of the jeep with my steno pad and pen. Captain Thomas nails the sign on a busted piece of wooden door, then disappears into the black portal of the church. At last, accepting his complete nonresponse, the boys dash down an alley alongside the church.

Stepping into the church is like stepping into an exploded cave. Ragged chunks of the once-carved and gilded ceiling are all that are left. The roof has all but caved in. Carefully, I step through the shattered pieces of wood and everything coated in ash. I follow the gritty, marred columns toward the altar, where streaks of dust-filled light stream through a gash on the side of a high dome. A dove flies through the cleft, its wings making a shuddering sound.

Captain Thomas is nailing up another sign near the altar. "San Filippo Neri," he announces without turning toward me, his voice echoing in the ruined space. "One of the most significant monumental complexes of Naples." I scramble to turn to a fresh page on my steno pad as he continues. "Attached to one of the largest historic libraries in Italy. Portable altarpieces by Tuscan and Neapolitan masters missing; location to be sought among the regional superintendency. Roof bombed. Sculptures damaged by bullet holes. Vaults partially collapsed."

I capture his words with a few hatch marks to type up later.

"Damn," he says, then he cups his hand around a cigarette and a small blue flame jumps from his lighter.

We return to the royal palace of Caserta as the sun makes its dramatic finale behind the silhouette of hills. In the glow, the palace appears like an impenetrable mountain of coral-colored stone. The jeep crunches across the long gravel approach. Captain Thomas and I remain silent, numbed, emptied of every ounce of wherewithal we left with in the morning. We part ways with a few mumbled words and I heave myself, dead tired and covered in dust, up the marble staircase.

I long for a bath even though I know I'll be lucky to draw hot water. We all complained about it before. But after seeing the way thousands of people are eking out a harrowing existence in the makeshift
slums of Naples, I can't bring myself to complain. I feel I'll never
complain about anything again.

But as I turn down an ornate corridor toward our bunk room, the
sound of giggling fills the cavernous space. I pause in the doorway
of a gilded ballroom, where I find the girls decorating for Christmas
as if it's a normal day in America. In the whirlwind of our strange
existence here at Caserta, I've completely forgotten that we are in the
midst of the holiday season. That Christmas is just a few days away.

The girls have found jumbled decorations somewhere in the vast
maze of palace storage rooms. Ruby has collected cards families have
mailed to us in recent weeks, and has hung them on a string across
the vast stone hearth. They have pushed the chairs back against the
wall to make a dance floor of patterned marble. Someone has set up
a phonograph. Private Simpson is mixing drinks, stirring a clinking
spoon in a glass. A few of the boys have begun to collect on the terrace at the far doors.

"Mouse, jeepers!" Lollie Dee says, spying me at the door. She gig-
gles, appraising me from head to toe. "Did Captain Thomas dump
you out in a ditch?"

For the first time, I look down at the state of my mud-caked skirt
and shoes. "It's . . ." But I don't know what else to say. For how could
I begin to describe how Captain Thomas and I came to be covered in
filth? How we spent the day making our way through the ruined city,
observing the hollow, defeated eyes of Neapolitan parents, as their hungry children ran through the rubble seeking candy and cigarettes? How
women eke out food at giant cauldrons in hovels near the wrecked
harbor where we landed weeks ago, still a jumble of overturned ships
like a vision of the apocalypse? How the human toll of this war is more
individual, more personal than any of us could fathom? Over weeks,
we've grown accustomed to explosions that light up the night sky, to

searchlights and droning planes, to bangs that shake the foundations of even this impenetrable building. But all of that pales to the human toll I've witnessed in a single day in Naples.

Instead of trying to explain, I pull my exhausted body up the stairs. I remove my filthy shoes and feel the cool marble under the soles of my feet. On my cot, someone has left a small box. I recognize my mother's crude handwriting, everything in small, ragged capital letters. I tear open the tape and remove an Almond Joy and a few pieces of Bazooka bubble gum. My favorite. My mind fills with the dinging trolleys on Chapel Street, snow on the Yale quads, the slurp of a milkshake at Nickel Charlie's, and I feel homesick to the pit of my stomach. I press the Almond Joy into a pocket of my field jacket. Next time Captain Thomas and I drive into Naples, I'll bring the candy bar along and gladly pass it on to one of the kids.

I unfold a wrinkled piece of Yale stationery, undoubtedly pulled from a campus waste bin, and run my eyes over my mother's crude handwriting. There are fewer students on campus, she tells me, and many more cadets. Many of the university's female employees have left to work in factories across New Haven and Bridgeport. And the art museums have closed. *Just as well that you left New Haven when you did*, Ma says. *There's nothing for you here now, Josephine.*

I am covered in shame. In all the time since we've been in Caserta, I have barely written home and New Haven seems a world away. I want to write her, to tell my ma about everything—the friendships, the beautiful and the ugly, the honorable and horrible, how Italy is all enchantment and devastation, palaces and poverty. I want to tell her about the enormous, looming volcano that smolders and smokes, and the many parts of Italian life that are hard to fathom. That Captain Thomas has us working toward a goal that seems unattainable, maybe even futile. That I wonder if what we do even matters in the face of such human misery.

I hardly know where to begin to say all of this. The crooning voice of Bing Crosby lures me from the marble stairwell, so I put down my pen and head to the bath. Dressed again in a clean uniform, I make my way back to the ballroom, where the Christmas party is in full swing. The sun has set and twinkling candlelight turns the ballroom into a place of magic.

"Come on, Mouse! The party's just getting started!" A glimpse of the old Dot flits by, a blur of blond pin curls and red fingernails. Even Lollie Dee has put on lipstick. From across the room, I spy Margaret Olson swaying with Staff Sergeant William Pierce, their hands locked and her head resting easily in the crook of his neck. The two of them have been inseparable ever since we set foot in the palace.

"Mouse!" Lollie Dee cries. "Private Simpson said he would take us to Pompeii tomorrow! Come with us!" In recent weeks, Lollie Dee has discovered that her homemade apple pie is a valuable currency to exchange for rides to the beach or into the countryside on our off days.

Ruby rolls her eyes. "Our time is theirs, not ours."

"Take advantage of it," Dot says. "Might be our last chance for time off before we leave Caserta. When are you ever going to get another chance to see a place like Pompeii?"

"Lollie Dee!" I whisper, pulling her to the edge of the dance floor, where everyone is swaying to the last refrains of the "White Cliffs of Dover." "Why are you flirting with Simpson? I thought you were looking for a husband."

She twists the button on the front of her blouse. "We're just having some fun, Mouse. It's nothing. Come on." She pulls me onto the dance floor. But I see a sparkle in her eye.

"Come on, Mouse!" Dot echoes as Bing Crosby's voice begins to croon the lyrics to "Santa Claus Is Coming to Town." "Don't be a drip! Ruggero's turned this place into a juke joint!" Across the room, I spy Dante Ruggero's smiling face at the phonograph. I let Dot pull me across the floor, while Lollie Dee's married private spins her around until she falls into him, laughing.

11

EVA

I'VE NEVER BEEN AWAY FROM HOME FOR CHRIST-
mas, so I follow the lead of the other institute employees who have
been in Florence for years. In an ancient wine cellar turned *tratto-
ria*, a dozen bulbous, straw-wrapped Chianti bottles and dirty plates
lie empty along the long wooden table. The men from the Kunsthistorisches Institut have pushed back their chairs and lit cigarettes.
Loud German conversations and laughter echo off the vaulted brick
ceiling. In the background, Italian servers keep their heads down
and hastily clear cutlery, trying to escape notice. They speak softly to
Paloma—the only Italian at the table with us. As we make our way
to the door, it's not hard to read the relief on their faces.

"*Grazie. Buonasera, signori!*" the restaurant owner calls as he wipes
down the bar counter with a rag. Professor Heydenreich passes a wad
of Italian lire to the owner's wife, who remains stone-faced as she
swipes it into the pocket of her stained apron. We climb the stone
stairwell and head out into the street.

I fall into step with Paloma. "It will be strange to have a few days
off," I say to her. We've been working untold hours in the days leading up to this evening and it hardly seems like Christmas.

"Yes, strange. Normally, the city should be full of light. Now there
is only darkness."

The men walk ahead of us in the dark streets, talking loudly in

German. Above our heads, a woman opens her shutter, glares down at us, then clatters it closed again. Florentines seem accustomed to the blackouts, covering their windows with shutters and dark cloths.

We pass the Mercato Nuovo, an open market space that stands vacant, a small trickle of water collecting in a fountain beneath a bronze sculpture of a pig. "Have you rubbed the *porcellino*'s nose?" Paloma asks. She reaches her hand to the boar's nose, just above the tusks, where the bronze looks like thousands of hands have rubbed it, resulting in a rich, golden patina.

I reach out my hand and run my palm over the smooth, cool metal. "What does it mean?"

"It's a tradition. During normal times, our visitors rub the *porcellino*'s nose for good luck—and to guarantee they will return to Florence."

We walk faster to catch up with the others. "What is Christmas like here—in normal times?" I ask. For a moment, my heart is back home, in the snow-covered mountains far from this place of musical language and golden light. I am transported to the alleys of Salzburg and its Christmas markets full of mulled wine, carved wooden toys, and honey cakes. In my Oma's kitchen, where the smell of apples and homemade crust fills the snug space.

"Normally, there is an enormous tree in front of the cathedral façade," she says. "And candles in every window. People put garlands with lemons and oranges above their doors."

"It sounds wonderful," I say.

Eventually, the street opens to the Piazza Ognissanti, where a doorman paces before the elegant entry to the Hotel Excelsior. Inside, we glimpse the bar lit with candles, full of Nazi officers huddled around tables piled with food. Italian servers in tuxedos pour wine and clear empty plates, trying to make themselves invisible.

"But we can't risk the lights and decorations now," Paloma says. "Well, this is where I leave you. Merry Christmas." She pulls away, turning down a narrow street. Before I can respond, Horst falls into step beside me. He clears his throat, seems uncomfortable.

"Eva . . . Maybe we could find a bar open that will serve us a drink? Or maybe more noodles?" For a moment, he looks helpless, sheepish. Like a little boy. Is he asking for a date? I heard one of the archivists say he left a fiancée back in Munich.

"I would, Horst, but . . ." How to let him down easy? The last thing he'll want to hear is that I'm looking for Enzo. Sometimes Enzo disappears for days and I don't know where he goes. Then he turns up again with no explanation. "But I . . . I promised Paloma I would help her with something." I gesture to Paloma, a small, curvy figure in a flowered dress, hurrying ahead down the sidewalk. The other staff begin to cross the Ponte alla Carraia, heading toward Palazzo Guadagni. "I'll see you later?"

Horst's shoulders fall, and for a moment, I pity him. But he only nods. "Alright then. I guess I'll see you back at the institute." Without waiting for my response, he heaves off in the opposite direction, a great shadow on the bridge moving toward the Oltrarno. For a moment, I feel exposed. Vulnerable. As much as I don't want to go for a drink with Horst, he is, after all, something of a natural bodyguard in the dark streets. I jog to catch up with Paloma.

"So . . . Where is your cousin tonight?"

Before a battened-down door, she is fumbling with an ancient-looking key pulled from her dress pocket. She puts it in a lock, turns it, then bends over. With one hand and a terrible clatter, she lifts the metal shutter to reveal a tailor shop. Then she opens the shopfront door and steps inside, switching on the light.

"Enzo?" Her eyebrows fly up and she purses her lips as if she's sucked on a lemon. "Who could keep up with him?"

I hesitate in the doorway. As light illuminates the space, no bigger than a closet, I see an ancient sewing machine on a counter, and hundreds of garments and threads stacked high on shelves from floor to ceiling.

A small boy bursts through the door at the back of the shop, excited by the clatter and ruckus of the unlocked shutter. "*Zia!*" he cries, pulling at Paloma's dress. He jumps up and down, displaying his missing two front teeth.

"*Ciao, amore.*" She bends and grasps the boy's cheeks, planting a kiss on top of his head.

Through the doorway, I see a small, ragged Christmas tree decorated with a few ornaments, and a sagging armchair covered in worn, floral upholstery. The smell of roasting onions fills the space. My mouth waters. I catch sight of a gray-haired woman wiping her hands on an apron and hear the scratchy sound of static and an Italian radio announcer. A man walks through the door, ducking his head.

"This is my brother, Corrado," Paloma says. "Corrado, this is Eva. From the institute."

"*Piacere.*" Paloma's brother is a handsome man with a tanned face, thick curls, and large brown eyes. Grave and self-assured. He looks as if he could have come to life from one of Masaccio's frescoes, walled up behind a brick enclosure and sandbags at the church of Santa Maria del Carmine. He looks at me in the same way the Italian servers look at us Germans in the *caffès* and restaurants, with a sense of wary politeness.

Two more small children burst through the back door into the shop, chattering so fast that I cannot make out the words. One of the children pulls at Paloma's hand.

"*Aspetta. Aspetta!*" She swats the children away as if they were flies. "I lock the door."

"And those are my sister's children," Paloma says to me, growing ever more uncomfortable as her family members appear. "*Bene*, Eva," she says, hesitating. An almost imperceptible waver in her smile. Then she puts her hand on the lock. "See you Monday?"

I won't be invited into the warm, tiny apartment, the closest thing to a home I've seen since I left Austria. I back through the shop doorway toward the sidewalk.

"*Buon natale*," she says, pushing the door closed.

"Yes. Monday. *Gute Nacht*. And . . . *buon natale*."

The children jabber more loudly as I turn to leave. Paloma pulls the shutter closed behind me with another loud clatter and turn of the lock. Behind the metal barrier, I hear one of the children cry something about a *signora tedesca*. Paloma shushing them.

For a moment I stand in the darkness, listening to the muffled chatter and radio announcer on the other side of the battened-down shop. Then I make my way back through the dark, empty streets to the Kunsthistorisches Institut alone.

I'm pouring acetic acid into the metal fixing bath when Horst opens the door to my darkroom and floods it with light. He doesn't knock.

"Close the door!" I cry, nearly knocking over a large jar of precious developer solution in my rush to slam it. "You'll ruin everything!"

He only shrugs, then closes the latch as the dank underground room returns to the dim glow of yellow light.

"Don't you knock? It's a darkroom."

His eyes scan the space, thick with cobwebs and dust-covered, unlabeled wine bottles abandoned long ago. "Looks like a wine cellar to me."

"Tsk." I walk over to a shallow metal tray where I'm developing my shots of the bridges. "The light will ruin it." I stare at the quivering surface of the liquid and then remove the print from the tray with a pair of tongs.

Slowly, the picture emerges: the long, elegant span of the arches between the piers of the Santa Trinità bridge. Michelangelo's vision of perfect symmetry. The epitome of Renaissance harmony. The four seasons, like beacons at the four corners, personified as women, announcing the cycle of the year. An eternal rhythm of death and rebirth. The statues look as if they have been there for all time.

It's become a sort of personal project, taking pictures of the beautiful bridges and the medieval towers lining the Arno. I open a clothespin and attach the print to the line, leaning in to see where it might have been overexposed when Horst opened the door.

I feel Horst standing at my shoulder now, his peculiar labored breathing at my ear. He runs his wide finger along the edge of the fixing bath tray. The surface of the liquid quivers with the disturbance.

"What is it?" I continue to stare down into the pan, where another image of the Ponte alle Grazie is surely ruined. At least overexposed.

"I'm not trying to ruin your pictures," he says. "It's just . . . I wanted to catch you alone. And that's kind of hard. That skinny Italian is always trailing you."

"You mean Enzo? He's trailing us because the institute has hired him to help us. Remember?"

He hesitates. "Professor Heydenreich says we are going to Rome. The superintendents are emptying some of the depots north of here. As far as Venice. They are bringing everything to the Vatican. There will be press coverage about what we are doing to protect the museum collections. I'm sure they will want you to take pictures. We'll be there for a couple of days."

"You think it's the right decision to bring the works of art south?" I ask into the darkness.

"In my opinion? It's better than having them in the countryside. You can't trust the Italians. They are not like us. Not like you and me." I feel his thick index finger on my shoulder. "Those Blackshirts give the illusion they are after the same things as we are. But as soon as the Yanks came, you saw how fast they changed their story. If you trust them, you are foolish. They will turn on us at any moment."

For a while, I'm silent, swishing the second photo of the bridge around in the solution with my tongs. "You don't know him," I say. "Enzo. He's a supporter of Mussolini. He told me that. I think you have more in common than you believe."

Horst turns his body now, leaning up against the developing table. His hulking silhouette blocks the yellow light like a boulder. "You need to be careful," he says, looking at me pointedly.

"Me? Aren't you working with him, too?"

"We all have to work with macaroni eaters here." Horst smiles, displaying the gap between his front teeth in full glory. "But it doesn't mean we have to trust them. They told us they were on our side. But now look at them. As soon as their Duce was removed, see how quickly they turned." The word "Duce" comes out in a sarcastic tone.

He narrows his eyes and his thin, red lips purse as if he is coming up with another insult. But now I feel angry. And I can't take his overpowering presence any more. I push open the door of the darkroom, feeling his eyes on me as I climb the spiral stone stairs. At this point, my pictures of the bridges are all but ruined. I'll have to start over tomorrow.

"And that skinny Italian is not the only one!" Horst calls after me from the darkroom doorway.

I climb up to the entry of the Palazzo Guadagni and exit the building, squinting into the blinding noon light. The *caffè* and restaurants disappear into the aching rays of sun.

I wonder about Enzo and if he can be trusted, but my judgment is as sun-streaked as my vision. So bright that I can't see anything clearly anymore.

As my eyes adjust, I head across the square, where the Caffè Firenze stands quiet. A short woman with a broom lingers in the doorway, peering out at the sun making stark streaks of light and shadow across the façade of Santo Spirito.

I find Enzo standing at the counter, chatting with the barman and tearing a narrow paper packet of sugar. Stirs it into a shot of espresso as thick as honey. When he spies me at the door, I see his face soften.

"*Un caffè ristretto, per favore,*" I say to the barman in my best, most confident Italian.

"*Caffè ristretto!*" the barman exclaims. A tiny cup, saucer, and spoon clatter on the countertop before me and the cappuccino machine begins to hum. I sidle up to Enzo.

"*Brava.*" He nods, then gives me a dazzling smile.

From the back seat of a Mercedes, I look through the camera lens and frame the crenellated stone façade of the Palazzo Venezia. It was Benito Mussolini's residence and headquarters before his arrest six months ago. In any other setting, this rose-colored medieval fortress would be the main attraction. But in Rome, where every street corner boasts an impressive monument, Il Duce's former headquarters fades into the backdrop, competing with the ancient Roman Forum and the imposing Altare della Patria, the white-columned building that Mussolini remade as a symbol of his new Roman empire. Dozens of armored vehicles with flapping swastikas line up before it.

Our group from the Kunsthistorisches Institut rolls behind an armored escort, arriving in the Eternal City to the thundering sound of German boots in unison, to the sight of dozens of soldiers in helmets and long coats, lined up in perfect symmetry in the Piazza Venezia. Professor Heydenreich has ensured my camera bags are filled with fresh rolls of film, and I do my best to document each significant step in our journey to the ceremony centered around the safeguarded paintings.

Through the crosshairs in my camera lens, I can see that Rome is not like Florence at all. The city is vast and intimidating, grand on a scale that is hard to put into words. Where Florence feels intimate and cozy with its narrow streets and piazzas, Rome with its oversized ancient monuments makes me want to sink down in the back seat of the Mercedes. Insignificant. And almost unable to take in such a city so ancient and yet still so alive.

"Six hundred crates," says Professor Heydenreich, smart in a suit and tie. "All of them filled with paintings. That's what's inside all those trucks. And it's a fraction of what remains in the hiding places across the countryside." The car doors open and we pile out. Now I have a better view of some three dozen Nazi cargo trucks from the Hermann Göring Division with their hulking, curved hoods lined up like toys in a children's game. Beneath their drab canvas covers, hundreds of wooden crates are stacked in the truck beds.

And there's another reason to feel anxious: the Anglo-Americans, they say, have made it as far north as Naples, just a short train ride away from here. I cup my palm over my brow and search for planes. Nothing. The sky is overcast and dull, perfect for taking a picture.

Behind the neatly arranged trucks, dozens of press vehicles and journalists have assembled. I admire the parade of giant still and film reel cameras on tripods, and hanging from the necks of journalists who have traveled to see some of Italy's treasures—among the crown jewels of its churches, museums, and galleries—that have been hidden away in countryside depots for the last four years. They are coming to deliver their masterpieces to the promised peaceful haven of Vatican City. And so many German newspapers, radio stations, and film reel producers are here to report it. Dozens of Italian women and men collect along the sidewalks to watch us.

I follow Professor Heydenreich and Horst toward a palace side entrance, where Italian and German guards with machine guns check our papers and let us through. Around me are dozens of German and Austrian journalists with fancier cameras than even the best ones of the institute's collection. I tuck myself into the group and peer through the viewfinder of my box camera while we wait for the ceremony to begin. I frame an image with four large German soldiers standing at attention alongside a truck bed. I set up the shot and press the shutter release. Snap.

"Good shot," a photographer next to me says in German.

"Thanks."

"I'm Wolf," he says. He flashes the press card hanging around his neck. *Berliner Morgenpost*, it says.

"My mother wrote for them. Many years ago." It comes out before

I have a chance to think about it. I don't tell him it's the same newspaper that sent her on the assignment that took her life. "Eva. From the Kunsthistorisches Institut in Florence."

My comment about my mother seems to confer some credibility—surely undeserved. But Wolf gestures for me to follow him. We move through the arcades of the palace courtyard and the news photographers fan out, peering through their viewfinders to scout the best vantage point and light to capture the dozens of wooden crates coming off the trucks. Wolf seems to know what he's doing, his professional-looking vest pockets full of lenses, his press credentials now tucked into his hatband. In the shadows of the arcades, it is easy to recognize the Italian regional superintendents who have come to see their works delivered to the Vatican. Haggard-looking men in dark suits, pacing.

A German official approaches the podium. He talks about the treasures of Naples being saved from the enemy, about the hundreds of precious books saved from the important monastic library at Monte Cassino. Thanks to the German people's commitment to preserving the artistic patrimony of Italy, he says, we are here today to witness this great event. He wraps up his speech and steps down from the podium.

At the head of a line of soldiers, one man barks out a series of orders and they respond in unison, with their hands outstretched with palms down. Then, in formation, they march to one of the crates, which is upended. Another soldier opens the crate, and they pull away the piece of wood. A giant oil on canvas appears, showing dozens of elegantly dressed nobles before a classical building. Dozens of flash bulbs go off and the sound of hundreds of shutters closing fills the space. I raise my camera to my eye and take as many pictures as I can before the men replace the wood on the crate.

"That one's from Capodimonte, but most of them are from Monte Cassino," Wolf leans in to tell me. "We got the bulk of the library and archives just before Christmas. Got here just in time. That abbey has stood there for eight hundred years. And now the Americans have blown it away. I heard it's completely destroyed."

I feel a pang in my gut. How could someone blow up an eight-hundred-year-old abbey full of art treasures, books, and peaceful monks? And we've already heard about the atrocities in Naples. If the Americans were willing to do that, would they be ready to blow up Florence, too?

The official speeches ended, the soldiers begin unloading the many crates from the trucks. Now the Italian officials snub out their cigarettes and get to work. They open their own inventories and begin scribbling madly. I snap a few more pictures.

"You think they're on their way here next?" I ask Wolf. "The Anglo-Americans."

"If you ask me, it's only a matter of time. They want to take everything and give it all to the Jews in America anyway." He lights a cigarette and then turns his head to blow it away from me. He holds out his crumpled package of Sturms, but I decline.

"There are two trucks missing," Horst says behind us, filing through his inventory pages. On the other side of the courtyard, the Italian superintendents ruffle through their own set of pages.

"I heard they got delayed on a pass in the Apennines," one of the German journalists says. "A tough stretch through there with enemy fire."

"*Quinidici cartoni*," one of the Italian men says, a tinge of panic in his voice. Fifteen crates.

Wolf laughs. "You believe that?" he says softly to me. "Funny how things get lost in transit."

"What does that mean?"

"You think they're coming back to Rome, dear?" He grins at me in a way that I'm not sure if he's trying to endear me or make fun of me. "They're not even coming back to Italy. They're probably already in Berlin by now. Göring's birthday's coming up." He lets the cigarette drop to the ground and grinds it with his heel. Then he moves off to take a photo from a different angle, leaving me standing there wondering if this is true. If the soldiers have made off for Germany with the pictures instead.

It's a relief to return to Florence, to leave behind the oppressive, heavy air of Rome and return to the now-familiar warren of streets in the Oltrarno, to the sound of clinking spoons and espresso machines in the Piazza Santo Spirito.

But since our return to Florence, the city lies enshrouded in fog, its buildings shuttered, its streets empty of all but the occasional lone figure on an inevitable errand. At all the city's monuments, laborers are throwing heavy sandbags into fresh sacks. They pile up before the portals of the cathedral, sending up dusty clouds along the pink and green marble slabs of its flanks.

The octagonal baptistery, with its matching medieval marble patchwork, is surrounded by sacks of sand. Sheets of plywood cover the gaping holes where Lorenzo Ghiberti's famous bronze doors should be. Professor Heydenreich tells me the bronze doors have been removed to a railroad tunnel in the countryside for safety from Allied bombs.

I lift my little Leica and frame one of the Italian laborers in the viewfinder. The skinny young man lifts a sandbag and tosses it into the stack, the muscles of his forearms twitching.

Snap. Snap. Snap.

I capture several frames, the fluid movement of the man's body and the black-and-white pillows of the sandbags in motion. I lower my camera and check the aperture settings, watching my breath make puffs of vapor in the air.

Ever since I arrived in Florence months ago, I've assumed what everyone has told me to be true. That we are on a noble quest. That our efforts will protect, safeguard the masterpieces in our care. That if it were not for the efforts of German and Austrian art officials, the entire artistic patrimony of the Italian nation would be in peril. That I myself signed up to join this cause, a minor and unsung cog in a giant wheel.

Was I wrong to assume such a thing?

Is it true that a regiment of German soldiers might steal a truck-load of paintings right out from under the noses of the Italian custodians whose job it is to protect them?

Outside Rudolf Levy's room at the Pensione Bandini, I find the sisters removing his belongings to the hallway. I put my cameras away in the armoire on the stair landing, and watch the sisters bring out a battered suitcase, a leather waist belt full of stained paintbrushes, and a few white, rolled canvases to the hallway like a pile of refuse to be gathered and discarded.

It was a trap. The Gestapo lured Levy down to the street, where they could arrest and deport him. We all thought he was part of our group, just an organization of Germans working together for the greater good. For art.

Before, I assumed so many things. But I don't know what to believe anymore.

JOSIE

IN THE DEAD OF WINTER, OUR WAC UNIT SPLITS into a forward and rear echelon, and heads north from Naples to the front lines. There is no going back to the splendor and challenge of palace life at Caserta. No more exploring the ruined wonders of Pompeii or Herculaneum in exchange for one of Lollie Dee's apple pies. In the palace hospital wing, the number of injured men has dwindled as the troops begin moving toward Rome. Hundreds of British and American officers have left behind their palace rooms-turned-offices. Piles of V-mail stand quiet and abandoned in the mailroom. Finally, Captain Thomas has told me, the wait is over and our real work can begin.

Packing up our cots in the WAC billet, we exchange our pressed skirts and stockings for trousers, laced boots, and oversized men's wool shirts tucked in at the waist. We press a new stash of bulky sanitary napkins and belts that are an inconvenient reality for us and take up so much room in our packs. We leave behind care package boxes, letters, even small souvenirs collected from Naples and the villages beyond. We carry only the few necessities that can be moved with us from the palace and into field camps. Dot gives away her set of hair rollers but tucks one tube of red lipstick in her pack. "Only

the important stuff." She smiles. All of us now wear the green neck-
erchief of the Fifth Army, same as the men. We are part of them, and
anyone who still believes we don't belong here keeps it to himself.

Sergeant Barnes, more herself than ever in field trousers and an
oversized shirt tied at her bulky midsection, reads our orders. Lollie
Dee and I will form part of a forward echelon that will move toward
Rome with the front lines. Ruby, Dot, and a few other operators will
work the mobile switchboard trailers as part of a rear echelon that
will head to the western coastline of Italy. Our breath swirling in the
frosty air, Dot and I squeeze each other for a few long seconds. "God,
I'm going to miss you, Mouse," she says.

"You won't," I say. I think instead she'll miss Private Ruggero, who
unfortunately has caught Dot's eye, but who has been assigned to my
echelon instead of hers. I can't say that I'm sorry, but of course I don't
say this aloud.

"Stay safe," she says in my ear. "I'll try to call you from the switchboard trailer."

"It's the least you can do. You got me into this," I tease her, giving
her one last squeeze before letting her go.

At the top of a marble staircase, I look through an enormous glass
pane to the rigid geometry of the palace gardens. In one of the fountains, an army chaplain is baptizing a dozen men. I watch him circle
a man's slim shoulders in his arm, bordered by spilling fountains
and elaborately carved grottos. The soldier pinches his nose, and
the chaplain dunks him under the dark water, mouthing a string of
words that are silent to me.

A cluster of women stream past me, lugging their heavy packs.
One woman wears a metal helmet on her head, the straps flapping.
Their voices echo in the hallway. But I am frozen at the window,
watching the men's bodies disappear one after the other under the
surface, then come up ready to board the armored trucks and head
off to the battlefields north of here. Headed off into God knows
what. They come up from the black water drenched and full of hope

for their souls in case they run out in a flash of bravery and don't return. I watch the last man get dunked, the poor guy hanging on to the promise of eternal life in the face of death. The chaplain climbs out of the fountain and dries himself with a towel. Then I haul my barracks bag over my shoulder and follow the women down the marble stairs.

I find Captain Thomas's new quarters at the edge of our bivouac camp. He's set up a makeshift office, a small canvas tent leaning precariously toward the ditch. Beyond a fallow field, a medieval village appears as if it might tumble down the hillside at any moment—an impossible jumble of dirt-colored homes with tile roofs clinging to the cliffside, alleys snaking along the edge, barking dogs, and laundry on lines sagging from window to window.

I push aside the tent flap to find a table littered with a Michelin guide, the tattered Touring Club volume, Shinnie maps showing protected monuments overlaid on photographed terrain, and stacks of handwritten notes. He's pinned a map of Italy to one canvas wall. The map is a complicated mess of red circles, lines, crosshairs, and marginal notes. Captain Thomas is absent but the tent reeks of stale cigarette smoke, sweat, and amaretto.

On a second rickety table, I excavate an empty spot among the pile of handwritten lists of churches and pictures that look like they've been cut out of textbooks. I unpack my steno machine. I pick up an old tourist brochure to Rome that looks like it's passed through many hands. I peruse the pictures of the Colosseum and try to make sense of the Italian words at the same time that Italian voices grow louder outside the tent.

A group of villagers has come down the hillside, helping to finish digging latrines, along with deep trenches for us to leap into in case of a direct hit on the camp. In the field beyond, the nursing unit has set up the medical tent. I watch Private Ruggero follow a group of officers from an area where men sleep on the cold ground. I feel sad for them, having to sleep on the hard dirt under an open sky while we women are housed in a modest communal tent where at least we have cots and a roof over our heads.

The villagers look much the same as the Neapolitans—like they've been through hell—women and men in ragged woolen layers, their faces etched with deep ridges. They stare at us as if we've just landed from a faraway planet. From the dirt road comes a trio of women carrying large, straw-covered jugs on their heads. They appear like Greek statues, erect and lean, their bodies the color of ripe olives even in winter. What a strange sight, we in our men's repurposed army drab on one side of the road, these elegant creatures on the other.

I spot Captain Thomas's lumbering silhouette on the horizon as the sun sinks. He paces back and forth, smoking. I know he's awaiting the cessation of the air raids, of the explosions that make the hills rumble and set off the night sky in orange, just long enough that we can load into the jeeps and get to the nearby villages. I know he is on edge, filled with trepidation about searching the villages as soon as it's safe. He's anxious to put to use all those Shinnie maps and lists he's compiled. To finally check on the monuments and masterpieces he can't stop talking about. To see at last what the Germans have done.

Before dawn each day, the men leave our camp for the front lines. Quiet. Full of resolve. They come back in waves, black and bloody. We meet them inside the largest tent, which doubles as our mess hall and community center. It's become the heart of our temporary home, where we gather for lukewarm coffee, cigarettes, card games, and news from the battlefield and back home. Thanks to Lollie Dee's wizardry, the tent smells of chicken soup, banana pudding, and va-nilla wafers. In a short stretch, she has become a wondrous combi-nation of the most nurturing grandma and the strictest French chef, bossing everyone around her kitchen while turning out exactly what we need to feel at home.

I bring a stack of Captain Thomas's notes on Rome to the communal tent. I inhale the steam from another cup of tea while I pore over a copy of the Italian Touring Club guide. I pick up phrases, passages describing the wonders of Rome's triumphal arches, its magnificent forum and temples that have survived centuries of turmoil. "Did you know people in the Middle Ages lived inside the Colosseum because it was safer than anyplace else?" I ask Lollie Dee. "How many wars do you think it's seen over two thousand years?"

"Jeepers, Mouse, you've learned a lot about this stuff."

"I don't know anything." I set down my cup. "You know how it is. People like us don't get the kind of education Captain Thomas got. But reading about it, looking at the pictures, well . . . I want to see it now, at least."

"Let's hope it's still there." Lollie Dee brings another cup of coffee to one of the nurses who's come to sit awhile. The nurses take quick turns in the communal tent, tending a second or third cup of coffee, clinging to as much comfort as they can muster. We see the dark rings under their eyes, feel their weariness in the pits of our stomachs. We become accustomed to the incessant roar of planes, the fire and rattle just over the horizon. The action is closer than ever before. The men trickle back to camp, and even if they refuse to speak about it, their faces tell a thousand grim stories.

Private Simpson tells us we are fighting a war of terrain. "Every damn bridge is blown," he says, heaving himself into a teetering camp chair. "Between here and Rome, there must be a thousand rivers." And he tells us of the Bailey bridges they've erected, one after the other. He tells us how the Germans have placed explosives at the base of every bridge leading northward. That this scenic heart of Italy is a terrain of rocky, rough hills, thousands of rivers and streams, and once-bridges now little more than rubble. From here, he says, it's nothing more than a slow, bloody fight up the boot of Italy.

Suddenly, a small band of Italian men push back the flap and walk into our communal tent. I nearly turn over my cup of tea, startled. The other women and men in the tent stand.

But it's clear they mean no harm. They are ragged and covered in dust. One of the men is injured, his arm bloody and hanging askew. One of the nurses rushes to his side and leads him back out toward the medic's tent.

The other men sit while Lollie Dee brings them water. They only speak Italian. They begin to talk, all of them at once, trying their best through words and gestures to explain what's happened. Their words are rapid and animated, but I begin to capture some of the meaning, as if grasping for a leaflet dropped from a plane. They were soldiers, they tell us. But they never really wanted to fight for the Fascists. Now they say they want to do whatever they can to help the Allies.

"They are partisans," I say.

"*Sì*," says the man who seems to be their leader, a brusque-looking, middle-aged fellow with intelligent eyes. "*Partigiani.*"

After a short while, the injured Italian man pushes back the tent flap and smiles as his friends cheer his return. His arm is now wrapped in a sling. He talks excitedly, and all at once, I understand. I burst out laughing.

"What did he say?" Lollie Dee asks.

"He said that if he had known American nurses were so beautiful, he would have gotten himself injured a long time ago."

"I didn't know you could speak Italian, Mouse," Simpson says.

I shrug. "Neither did I. But I understood enough."

"Morning, sir." I salute Captain Thomas as I enter his sagging work tent, then flip open the metal hinges of my steno case.

"At ease, baby doll." He spins around on his chair and hands me a typed page marked up in red pen.

For two days, we've been working on an official letter to his superiors. It's gone through four drafts so far. Captain Thomas is searching for the right words, the right angle to get us the support we need—transportation, authorizations, supplies, gasoline. More than anything, his dictation focuses on educating the higher-ups about why it's so important to protect Italian monuments and works of art. And on the support we need to keep the soldiers out of the historic buildings.

From his worktable, I pick up one of the pictures he's cut out of an art history textbook and attached to a page of notes with a paper clip. It shows a group of men in colorful robes against a panorama of architecture and rugged hills. The caption reads, *Brancacci Chapel, Santa Maria del Carmine, Florence.*

"Masaccio's *Tribute Money*," Thomas says without lifting his pen from paper. "A masterpiece of Renaissance fresco."

I examine the fine details of drapery, hair, haloes. "Must be a million of these."

"Yep," he says, turning toward me, his legs splayed. For a moment, his eyes scan me from top to bottom. "At least one priceless masterpiece in every damn church in Italy." He pushes back in his camp chair and lights a cigarette, ogling me openly now. "You've seen enough already to have understood the magnitude of it. And we're not even to Rome yet."

I turn away so he's forced to look at my back instead. "How many church treasures do you think the Germans have taken?" I clear my throat and say over my shoulder. I insert a roll of paper into the machine.

"The last war taught us to expect anything," he says before turning back to dictation.

"After the Great War," he says, pacing, "international conventions that didn't exist before were put in place to protect cultural heritage." My fingers fly across the keys of my steno machine, as familiar to me now as any typewriter. "National arts organizations and governments across Europe put in place measures like the widespread preparation of inventories of works of art. Also, some cities of great importance were to be considered demilitarized—cities like Venice, Florence, Rome, Bruges, Oxford, Paris."

I stop typing and for a moment, I sit there numb. I think about the cities far beyond here, far beyond Italy. And all the works of art and important buildings there must be. France. Poland. The Netherlands and Belgium. England. Beyond.

"But in today's warfare," Captain Thomas continues, "the bombs don't hit just military targets. They can kill innocent people, of course, but also historical monuments and works of art."

"Like we saw in Pompeii," I say over my shoulder, "where our planes accidentally hit some of the ancient city."

He stops pacing and addresses me directly. "Yep. And back in September, there was a British air raid on Florence. They were targeting the marshaling yards, but they missed. There were a lot of civilian casualties. A tragedy, of course. But I must admit that my first thought was relief that they didn't hit Brunelleschi's dome or Michelangelo's *David*."

"Surely the Allies wouldn't bomb those kinds of historic sites on purpose."

His face turns grim. "No. But I can only hope the Italian superintendents had the sense to move everything out of Rome and Florence. We won't know until we get there."

"But where would the works go? The whole countryside is a battlefield."

"For the most part," he says, "villas, churches, private homes. We've seen the same thing across Europe. The entire collection of the Louvre in Paris has gone into hiding. Thousands of works of art. Even the *Mona Lisa*."

For the first time, I realize that this effort to save monuments, paintings, sculpture . . . It's much bigger than what we are doing in this little corner of Italy. We're just one cog in a giant wheel. And I wonder how many people like Captain Thomas—even people like me who don't know the first thing about art—have been corralled into this effort.

"But sometimes," he says, "I feel we are shouting into the void. We're the only ones who are telling the higher-ups about this. We don't really have much authority, or any resources. Right here in this part of Italy, it's just me and you, sweetheart." He strikes a match and cups his hand around a cigarette. "We're it. The whole team. That's why this letter has to be good." He taps his marked-up page.

"You think they will listen?"

"Off the record?" He shrugs. He rolls his cigarette between his fingers and stares at it. Sits with his legs spread wide. "As far as I know, all this stuff could already be in Germany by now."

We haven't even gotten to any of the places on Captain Thomas's list yet. What will we find there, I wonder, when so much remains unknown? The camp lantern on the desk flickers, then flares and goes dark. My eyes adjust to the dimness. I stare up at the wavering ceiling of the tent and think about all that is hidden from us.

In an otherwise deserted medieval village, we find a priest who looks like he's all but given up. The black rings under his eyes match his dusty cassock. His shoes are coming apart, the leather barely attached to the soles. Captain Thomas and I follow him into the dark, tired church, little more than an empty shell, past tombs, pulpits, and fonts covered haphazardly with sandbags and tarps. Before a bricked-up wall, he stops.

"*Vedete*," the skinny priest tells us, his voice weary and slow. "We have put air holes in the protective wall. The superintendents told us it was important to allow air circulation to prevent mold from developing on the surface of the fresco."

I scratch shorthand notes on my steno pad.

"You get that?" Captain Thomas asks.

"I understood some. Maybe half?"

"Good," he says. "Be sure to note they have taken their trecento altarpiece to a repository near Rome."

Trecento. I know what that means. Made in the 1300s.

In fact, as long as I can sidestep Captain Thomas's more objectionable behavior, the more I realize he has to teach me. That's because he has begun to show me how to see, to *really* see what's around us in Italy. As we make our way from village to village, he's taught me how to tell from the windows and portals if a medieval building was built in the *dugento*, *trecento*, or *quattrocento*. How the towers protected the villagers from invaders so many centuries before there were such things as artillery and panzers. How to tell the difference between Etruscan, Roman, and medieval layers of city walls. I begin to see that these tumbledown villages are part of a long stretch of conflicts over the centuries, that these monuments have endured hundreds of injustices over the years as people battled for this rugged land while the locals did their best to raise their families, to work their purpose, to live another day. How life springs from death, then springs again. How art and human creation is a testimony to those who would otherwise remain silent. An eternal cycle.

"We also put a few paintings and an altarpiece in there with the fresco," the priest says. "Behind the wall."

"You kept the pictures here? In the church?" Captain Thomas says in fluid Italian, patting the wall with the palm of his hand. "Why didn't you evacuate them from the village?"

The priest thinks about this for a moment, then only shrugs. "This is their home, no?" When Captain Thomas furrows his brow, the priest tries to explain. "If the people in the village saw us taking their beloved paintings out of the church and driving down the hill to some unknown place, they would lose hope. And we can't afford that, especially now. If we lose hope, *capitano*, we have lost everything. You understand?"

Standing inside the lonely church, I think about what must be thousands of others just like it, in every corner of Europe. Where untold numbers of humble priests, mayors, museum staff, and other brave individuals must have hastily hidden away or covered up the things they treasure, all the objects that give them hope.

Captain Thomas reaches out and squeezes the priest's skinny shoulder, speaking to him in what sounds to my ear like slow Italian with a heavy American accent. "Alright, Padre. Don't take anything out of the church at this point. Hopefully the *tedeschi* are done here," he says, gesturing to the door where, outside, several town blocks smolder in the ruins of German shelling. "As soon as we have the resources, we'll try to send you some men to guard what's here and make sure it stays safe."

We say our goodbyes and return to the square in front of the church. Beyond the smoldering buildings, the rest of the village seems empty.

"Where is everyone?"

Captain Thomas puts his clipboard under his arm and looks at the vista before us. "Probably Rome. Maybe they believe the city will be more secure. Oh, Jesus." He walks to the edge of one of the church portals and runs his hand over the stone. I walk closer to see what he sees. With a knife or a nail, some G.I. has scratched JAMES BUCEY WAS HERE TO SAVE THE DAY. "The Germans are only half our problem," he says. "Our own men will make the propaganda come true."

We return to the jeep and rumble down the winding road out of the village to the main road, which we find cratered and filled with debris.

"So who is responsible for hiding or covering all these works?"

"Ultimately, the Italian regional governments," Captain Thomas says, as we teeter over the rocky landscape. "All the treasures of Italy fall under the protection of the Superintendencies of Monuments and Galleries. There are fifty or so of those. They all come under the General Direction of Fine Arts, which is part of the Italian Ministry of Public Instruction. The churches, I might add, also fall under the government's protection, at least since the Italian State was organized in the last century."

"Sounds complicated. Bureaucratic."

"Very," he says, his eyebrows flying up. "But generally, they are a competent group of people—art historians, restorers, architects—people who care about art and would do anything to preserve it. It's their national heritage. It's part of their own personal identity. It's who they are. In the U.S., most of our museums are private corporations."

I have never thought about this, the fact that we do not have the legacy of ducal courts or royal collections in America.

"You'd think the locals—like that priest—would want to get the works out of here," I say. "Get them to safety."

"I guess," he says, leaning forward in the driver's seat. "But the people have looked at these pictures in their churches for their entire lives. They see them as part of themselves, part of their own identity. Like a family member. If they are gone, then what? They have lost their soul."

I worry about Lollie Dee. She's spending more time with Private Simpson. I watch them through a second-floor window, in a former schoolhouse the army has repurposed as a women's barracks. It's the latest in a string of temporary schools, town halls, and inns requisitioned for a few days at a time while we crawl through the winter landscape toward Rome.

Through the dusty glass pane, I can't hear their conversation. I can only see them standing close together outside the cafeteria where we play cards, read months-old, ragged copies of *American Soldier* and *Yank* magazines, and drink chicory coffee. I watch him bring his palm to Lollie Dee's cheek. Then they disappear behind the rise of a hill.

She is playing with fire. It can't end well for either of them.

I think of Dot, whose echelon has gone out toward the coast near Pisa. Whenever she can, she connects to our switchboard, and I go out to the mobile trailer to talk with her. Often, I find Private Ruggero there, too, talking to Dot through the switchboard mouthpiece. I have no more illusions that he will seek me out, even though we are in the same place.

I step into the shower stall. Such a welcome occurrence, to take a real shower indoors. I close my eyes to the flickering light of a failing bulb and let the tepid water wash away days of dust and ash from traveling over rutted roads and makeshift Bailey bridges. Days of collapsing our cots, rolling up our bedrolls, and rolling them out again. Mostly, we stay in camps, freezing. But sometimes we women are lucky enough to get a billet in a schoolhouse, a barracks, or a town hall. And every once in a while, I get a bath.

Afterward, the sun sets over the fallow fields and olive grove beyond the schoolhouse and the men's tents. A cluster of soldiers deal cards and laugh around the fire. Beyond, there is a wrecked German tank abandoned in the hard dirt under the gnarled branches of an ancient tree. I spot Captain Thomas sitting alone in a folding chair under its silvery leaves, his fists on the top of his head. He grasps his stubby hair as if he will pull it out from the roots. For the first time, I see his grandiose self-confidence waver. One of the enlisted men plays taps on his trumpet, a silhouette against a harsh field lamp.

Every time we move is another opportunity for Captain Thomas and me to judge the state of churches and historical monuments, and to search for anyone who can give us an account of what has happened to portable works of art. I stand in awe of Captain Thomas's ability to speak Italian. I catch twenty percent, then thirty, then maybe half. Every day, I learn more. I order a chicory coffee if I can find it. I talk to women selling meager supplies from rolling carts in town squares. I ask for the bathroom. I begin to understand more and more each day.

But the days of making slow progress from village to village have taken a toll on both of us. We find caretakers and superintendents in deserted churches and historic buildings who show us the cursory, handwritten receipts they've gotten in exchange for tucking away irreplaceable masterpieces in villas, castles, and wine cellars. Others tell us they can't part with their pictures, their beloved sculptures. That they will stand and face the Germans themselves to protect them, even though all the other men in town have gone—off fighting, taken prisoner, taken to the woods, or defected. In many villages, we find a woman on a bike, hanging laundry, or pulling weeds from winter gardens. We hear only the wind or the creak of a well pump, the occasional putter of an old Fiat alongside horse and buggies, along with a distant sound of artillery fire or the rumbling of an American tank.

And we have a bigger problem. Allied soldiers *have* made the Nazi propaganda come true. They've used church pews as makeshift billets. They've made the corner of a sweeping marble staircase a latrine. They've taken "souvenirs" out of churches and ancient buildings.

I doubt Captain Thomas would admit it, but I, for one, can't see how we could ever put things back together again. Looking at the man tugging on the roots of his hair, I taste his fear, his frustration. A man who has studied and loved this country for decades, one who understands these works of art that to me, remain a wondrous mystery.

In the gathering darkness, I walk to the communal tent, careful not to let my foot slip into the trench outside it. The cold is stark and biting. Silent. The darkening sky transforms into a carpet of twinkling lights. The camp is far from the pink marble of Caserta, but it's somehow better.

I sit in a camp chair and shine my light on the tattered pages of the *Touring Guide* in Italian. My body is dead with fatigue, but I thumb through its pages again. The Italian words begin to come together, little snippets that tell the story of a long, unbroken history of human creativity, of human passion, of a will to live. The names jump out. Botticelli. Cimabue. Caravaggio. Michelangelo. If it's just

Captain Thomas and me responsible for stopping the American military from destroying a bunch of these irreplaceable works of human achievement, I figure I need to get myself educated. I read the Michelin and Touring Club guides from cover to cover. I pore over the things I've typed for Captain Thomas, looking at the carbon copies we've filed away. I read what Italian I can.

In another corner of the tent, a group of men and women have started a round of poker. Sergeant Barnes hefts her bulk into the middle and deals a hand of cards. The men would stay there all evening if they could, exhausted and hungry for female attention. Even Lieutenant Hamm seems to have fallen into a state of begrudging acceptance. He pulls up a camp chair and leans into the circle, dog tags jingling. To my relief, Lollie Dee is there, too, making tuna crackers for everyone. She's layered a set of too-big men's fatigues over her issued uniform.

But I don't want to join them now, because someone has delivered another care package from my mother. I tear open the tape to find a pair of gloves, which I sorely need, a hat, and more candy. *Don't worry about me, Josephine*, she's written in jagged capital letters. *I'm fine. And I'm proud of you.* I'm reminded of the blood and then I feel guilty for how long it's been since I thought of it.

I think about everything I could say to my ma in a letter. About how we are searching for treasures unseen and about how our troops have almost made it to Rome. About my work with Captain Thomas, who has helped me find indescribable beauty amid the horrors of the complicated, wrecked villages. I want to tell Ma of how, in a war, it's possible to see signs of despair and resilience all at once—*bruto e bello* in a single view. And that it's important to save monuments and works of art because—as Captain Thomas says—it helps people remember who they are. If it's destroyed, they lose their identity. They lose hope. They lose themselves.

Suddenly, the familiar drone of plane engines grows in the distance.

"Douse the light!" Lieutenant Hamm nearly knocks over the poker table. Beyond the tent, the sky turns orange with artillery fire and the earth shudders.

I turn off my flashlight and the tent falls into darkness. My mother's familiar handwriting disappears in the blackness. I fold the thin paper in my hand and press it to my waist. I don't know how I'll find the words to describe all of this, to make her understand my adventure in a way to make her see why I have left her all alone back home.

The next afternoon, I hear Captain Thomas's whoop of excitement. At last, after weeks of waiting, weeks of traveling northward, ever more slowly toward Rome, he gets the response he's been waiting for. He opens the tent flap, waving a page in the air. "Look!" He hands me a memo printed from the teletype machine.

To: All Commanders

Today we are fighting in a country which has contributed a great deal to our cultural inheritance, a country rich in monuments which by their creation helped and now in their old age illustrate the growth of the civilization which is ours. We are bound to respect those monuments so far as war allows.

If we have to choose between destroying a famous building and sacrificing our own men, then our men's lives count infinitely more and the building must go. But the choice is not always so clearcut as that. In many cases the monuments can be spared without any detriment to operational needs. Nothing can stand against the argument of military necessity. That is an accepted principle. But the phrase "military necessity" is sometimes used where it would be more truthful to speak of military convenience or even of personal convenience. I do not want it to cloak slackness or indifference.

It is a responsibility of higher commanders to determine through

A.M.G. Officers the locations of historical monuments whether they be immediately ahead of our front lines or in areas occupied by us. This information passed to lower echelons through normal channels places the responsibility of all Commanders of complying with the spirit of this letter.

Dwight D. Eisenhower
General U.S. Army,
Commander-in-Chief

Next is an order from Headquarters Allied Armies in Italy forbidding occupation of any monument on the list outside of certain limited conditions. Attached to that is an alphabetical list of the towns, their geographical coordinates keyed to the military maps, and all their principal buildings and art collections.

"Ha!" he exclaims, shaking the papers at me. "It's what we needed. We'll make sure these get into the hands of every battalion commander so their troops don't accidentally ransack something important."

An immense relief washes over me. They listened to us.

Captain Thomas grasps my shoulders and plants a loud, wet kiss on my cheek. "We did it, doll!"

I pull away and wipe the uninvited overture from my cheek. Then I look at the general's memo again and can't help but smile.

I'm helping Lollie Dee lock up a newly arrived set of rations in a troop trailer when we see a ragged group of our men walking toward the camp from the back of one of the troop transport trucks. They are covered in mud, their helmets askew.

"Where's Simpson?" Lollie Dee says to me. A silent moment passes as if in slow motion while we scan the familiar faces in the squadron. "Where's Simpson?" she says more loudly, walking to the men, her tone more demanding as she reaches them.

"Lollie Dee!" I call to her. She ignores me. Instead, her eyes are on Private Ruggero, who stretches out his hands to her. The men's hunched shoulders, their slow walk toward us, tell us everything we need to know. Ruggero bows his head and says something out of earshot.

Then I hear Lollie Dee's cry of anguish as she puts her face in her hands and Private Ruggero pulls her to his chest.

They don't say anything, but they don't have to.

We all know Simpson is not coming back.

13

EVA

I'M PACKING UP MY CAMERA EQUIPMENT IN FRONT of the colorful marble cathedral when there is the distant, then growing buzz of a plane engine. Instinctively, I duck into the hollow of one of the sandbagged portals. In the square, a group of boys is kicking a ball, their high-pitched voices echoing. The boys stop their game and scamper into a nearby street.

It's the same sound I remember from that horrible day when Professor Kriegbaum lost his life. I feel the back of my neck prickle and I have a sudden urge to rub my right arm, which is now fully healed. I press myself into the hefty, soft bulk of the sandbags and look to the sky.

Suddenly, a plane shudders by, frighteningly low. Its birdlike silhouette makes a brief, oppressive, whooshing shadow across the square. I squeeze my eyes shut and brace for impact, thinking of Brunelleschi's centuries-old, one-of-a-kind terracotta dome just above my head.

But there are no bombs, and as soon as it appeared, the plane is gone. Quiet returns to the square and I open my eyes.

There is only the sound of gentle fluttering as the plane engine goes silent, and all at once white leaflets tumble from the sky like snowflakes. They dance and fall, like delicate butterflies plunging to their death on the rough cobblestones. The leaflets spin and whirl as the breeze picks them up and tosses them against the dirty façades, then down the nearby alleyways.

I step out from the sandbags. The boys run back into the square, snatching up the leaflets as if they were lire. Money from heaven. They squeal with excitement.

I hurry out into the square and pick up one of the white papers that's lodged itself against the great marble slabs of the Baptistery. I struggle to make out the Italian. It takes me a few tries.

URGENT MESSAGE TO THE INHABITANTS OF FLORENCE. STAY INSIDE WITH THE SHUTTERS AND DOORS CLOSED. STAY AWAY FROM THE WINDOWS. THIS IS FOR YOUR OWN SAFETY.

Will the Americans and English drop another bomb on Florence? If they did, anything could be destroyed. Innocent lives, yes. And also some of the greatest treasures ever made.

I gather up a bunch of leaflets and stuff them into a side pocket of my camera bag. Then I hurry back over the Ponte Santa Trinità to Palazzo Guadagni.

I climb the stairs to find that everyone has gathered in the library reading room. Professor Heydenreich is nervously straightening one of the many stacks of books perched on one of the ample desks. Horst's shadow blocks the light from the high window. There is Paloma, along with the gray-bearded librarian, and a handful of other staff members shifting in the room. Enzo appears, leaning against the doorjamb as if he isn't sure if he's allowed to cross the threshold.

"I'll get to the point," Professor Heydenreich says, rubbing his forehead. "We have orders to evacuate the institute."

Around the room, gasps of horror. Nods of knowing. A breath of relief. "We're leaving Florence?" the librarian asks.

"It's not yet decided who will stay and who will go." The professor removes his thick, black-rimmed glasses and presses the bridge of his nose. "For now, everything in this building has to be packed up and loaded onto a train. I don't need to tell you what an undertaking that will be."

Another round of gasps and mumbling. "It's for the best," I hear someone whisper.

"I'm sorry, but there is no choice," Heydenreich continues. Now that he's delivered the pent-up news, he slouches down on the edge of a nearby desk. "It's the only way to protect our books and archives. Our photographs. The Yanks are just south of Rome and they are moving north fast. The Kunstschutz central office has ordered that we pack up and remove the contents of the Kunsthistorisches Institut as quickly as we are able."

"Where are we taking it?" I ask.

"Everything portable inside this building is going to Germany," he says. "Our archives, our photographs, all the books." He gestures to a shelf that houses his own titles about Leonardo da Vinci as well as Professor Kriegbaum's books on Michelangelo. "It's all going to the salt mines near Heilbronn."

At the mention of the mines, the flickering images, like an old newsreel, unravel in my head. The hundreds of altarpieces, oil paintings shimmering in the harsh underground light, the wooden crates full of church treasures, priceless manuscripts, and small, precious objects. The pang in my gut is like a magnetic pull, a force that lures me back to the Alps. But then, a glance around the room and I feel my gut flop in the other direction.

As if he can read my mind, Professor Heydenreich says in Italian, "Enzo! You and your helpers will make sure we have enough crates for everything. If they don't exist, you'll need to make them with your own hands."

He nods. "*Certo. Senz'altro, direttore.*"

"Horst, you will work with me to oversee the logistics."

Horst nods, his expression shadowed and grave.

"And the library staff will pack up all the books and archives. Eva, you will work with Paloma to make sure the photographic collection is properly documented, then packed for transport."

"Of course," I say. Beside me, Paloma nods and I feel relieved she is on my side.

Heydenreich hesitates, but I can see there is more. After a few long, silent moments, finally, he continues.

"We've also been ordered to stop packaging up works in Florence and taking them out to the countryside depots. In fact, some of the works from the Tuscan depots are on their way back to us right now."

Around the room, there are gasps of surprise and dismay.

"But," the librarian protests, "that's madness! If the Allies end up taking Florence, those paintings will be halfway to America before we can even think of getting them back!"

Professor Heydenreich nods, his jaw pulsing. "I'm as concerned as you are, of course. You know I would rather the works stay in the depots than go anywhere else. But what can I do? We have our orders."

I think about all those works of art we photographed as they were unloaded in Rome months ago. All the treasures tucked away in the countryside. And the historic core of Florence, which now seems so very fragile as the battlefront races toward us like an unrelenting tide.

I am packing an archival box from a shelf in the Phototek when a newspaper page flutters to the floor. I pick it up off the tiles and turn it over. *Berliner Morgenpost*, it says in the upper register. Placed between an article about rising wheat prices and an advertisement for men's shaving lotion is my mother's name. Elisabeth Brunner. Black and white. A witness that she existed, after all.

Through the dim light, I read the headline. CHANCELLOR HERMANN MÜLLER FORCED TO RESIGN. I scan the article, but it's just the facts about a political resignation. Nothing that would reveal anything about my mother's personality. About her dreams. About her love for us. About what she believed. And no picture. I check the date of the newspaper. March 28, 1930. Two weeks before the automobile crash, while on assignment outside of Berlin, that claimed her life. A tragic accident that left its mark on us forever. I wish that instead, she had written about what led her to follow her passion to write about the world around her. Her commitment to the truth. Did she believe her actions made a difference in the end? Was it worth her life in exchange? I've never needed an answer to these questions like I need it now.

I only have a vague memory of what my mother looked like. Gerhard not at all. He was just a baby. She stays remote for me, like a grainy, out-of-focus photograph that came out overexposed. And my father was in such a state that he got rid of everything when we left Berlin for Austria, where our Oma would paint a completely different picture of a woman for me. A woman who raised children and chickens, who spent her days honing her skills making apple tarts and hanging sheets on the line.

Now with some distance, I see that Papa accepted I couldn't stop my urge to work with the camera; it was irrefutable. And I understand why he discouraged me from working for the newspapers. And why he pressed me into working in the field of art history instead. A much safer bet. Isn't it?

"What is that?" Paloma says, coming to stand beside me and looking over my shoulder.

"It's nothing." I return the article to the folder where it belongs, then pack the box inside the crate for transport.

The next time I hear the drone of a distant plane, I am walking with Enzo from the Piazza Santo Spirito toward the Palazzo Pitti, I with my camera and he with his constant banter in Italian. He is off duty, and my heart lightens to think he would choose to spend his free hours walking around the city with me and my camera.

"And so, this group of men came up to Florence from Rome to tell us about how they were organized," he explains. "There were lots of Blackshirts in Rome back then, very close to Il Duce. A few of my friends and I began to meet with them in an apartment near the Signoria."

My Italian has gotten better in the months since my arrival in Florence, but we still communicate in a comical combination of Italian, German, and expressive hand gestures. I understand more than I can say in return, but it's surprising how effectively we are able to make ourselves understood.

I raise my Leica to my face, framing the mountain of stone that composes the Renaissance palace, the Palazzo Pitti. It is impossible to capture the building in a single image. But listening to Enzo's beautiful language while I take pictures turns work into pleasure. It is hard to believe Horst's adamant warning that I can't trust Enzo or any of the Italians. The distant drone of the plane grows louder.

"My aunt and uncle and my cousin Corrado lived in France for years," he continues, ignoring the buzz in the sky. "But the French didn't trust us. They pushed all the Italians out of their country. My aunt and uncle lost their jobs in the garment factories in Paris. My cousin lost his textile business. They had no choice but to return here, but they have had trouble getting back on their feet. That's why they live with Paloma. She's the responsible one in our family." I think of Paloma in her small house, trying to care for her aging parents, her sister and her children, and her brother returned home from France to pick up the pieces of his life.

At the edge of the square, I squat down to reload my camera with a fresh roll of film. I pull out the old roll and place it back into its metal canister, then replace it in my leather satchel, which Enzo has graciously offered to carry for me. Now he looks up to scan the gray sky. "I think we should move from here," he says.

At the portal to the Pitti Palace, we watch a haggard-looking mother collecting her small children around her skirt. In recent weeks, hundreds of refugees have gathered, judging the city safer than their homes in the countryside. And many of the apartments of the city have been abandoned by those who believe instead that it is safer to flee Florence for their relatives' homes far away from the city. No one seems to know which idea is correct. Around the city, the last remaining leaflets cartwheel in the courtyards and dusty corners. The windows of the abandoned apartments are shuttered. The Pitti Palace looks big enough to hold thousands. Yet people spill out of the doors as if the building will burst. Men in neat-looking suits and ties. Women in fashionable dresses, children running around, grandmas in black, shrieking babies.

The sound of plane engines grows louder, then the air raid sirens begin their horrible wail. "*Dio*," Enzo says, taking my hand. I don't ask. I just let him pull me through the streets. We run toward the river as anyone left on the narrow sidewalks dives into buildings and shuts their doors. Arriving at the Ponte Vecchio, we descend an ancient stone staircase that leads to the lazily moving waters of the Arno. He pulls me under the hulking span of the ancient bridge. Too late, I think of all the reports of bridges blown and I doubt it's the best place for us to seek cover.

Enzo pulls me down to the grass under the shadows of the bridge. As the roar of the planes grows louder, to my surprise, he covers me with his body. He is gentle, but I feel the weight of his body press me into the grass. From here, we smell the damp, hear the slap of the water against a wooden boat roped to a metal ring. I feel his lean, hard chest, the bony protrusions of his hips. His hot breath on my neck.

"*Non ti sposta*," he whispers. *Don't move.*

I don't move. Instead, I inhale the scent of his hair oil, the sweat of his neck and behind his ear. It takes me by surprise. I gasp, and even though shot through with white fear, I can't help it. I feel the stirrings of desire.

Then I open my eyes and look up into the heavy sky beyond the curve of the bridge's span. And wait. The droning fills the air with a high-pitched buzzing. A row of lumbering planes, like a formation of giant insects, appears in the gray sky.

I close my eyes again and pray that from high in the air, those British and American pilots will look down on Florence with its river snaking through the ancient city. That they will see the great egg-shaped dome of the cathedral, the other spires and domes across the city. The defiant, strong towers of the Palazzo Vecchio, Giotto's *campanile*, that would dare anyone to challenge the sovereignty, the self-assured independence of Florence that has endured for centuries. That they will be so struck by its beauty, by its significance, that they will decide not to drop their payload after all. That a young soldier from so far away might look into his sights and count, then stop before getting to one. That those pilots, just boys hardly older than Gerhard, would report back to their superiors that the city was a clear target, but that they would not attack it. That they had decided not to destroy one of the most beautiful cities on earth. That they will bank and head back south to their airstrips.

But none of this happens.

Instead, there is only continued droning and at last, the sound of metal, the whine of the drop. Worst of all, that interminable, terrible second of silence before the blast. After that, I see a spray of smoke and spewing earth and a litter of sprays in a row. There is a flash of light, then the orange glow of crackling fire. Yelling in the distance.

I burrow into the protection of Enzo's hard, lean lines as the sky turns to a blazing flash and under our hips, I feel the earth rumble and shatter.

Dear Father, Oma, and Gerhard,

First of all, I am safe.
You may have heard about the latest bombing of Florence. If you did, I'm sure you're worried.

Some of the institute staff are leaving for Berlin, but Professor Heydenreich has asked me to stay. He says Alexander Langsdorff has been assigned as the head of the Kunstschutz in Italy, and there will be important photography projects to document the damage the Anglo-Americans have done. I'm staying put in the pensione with the old Italian sisters.

The conditions in the city are poor. The air reeks with the stench of rotting garbage, spoiled food, and broken sewer lines. That part is hard to get used to. There is still smoke and occasional fires break out in the rubble. Thankfully, we still have running water in the Palazzo Guadagni.

The Kunstschutz and the Italian superintendents are cooperating well together. Most of the treasures of the Uffizi Galleries and the other museums were evacuated to depots in the countryside months ago. We all know they would be safest, well, you know where. But of course I have no say in such matters. And the Italians are adamant about keeping everything within the confines of Tuscany, for better or for worse.

I will have many pictures to show you when I get home. I'll write again soon. Don't worry about me.

Yours,
Eva

At the Santa Maria Novella rail station, we watch Italian laborers load the last of the wooden crates containing the contents of the Kunsthistorisches Institut into the dusty train cars. Over weeks, we have done little more than pack up thousands of documents, photographs, and small objects, testament to a century of German scholarship in Florence. Paloma and I have spent countless hours checking the contents of archival cartons and dusty old cameras held in the hands of photographers before me. I've watched Enzo craft dozens of wooden crates from a pile of raw lumber in the inner courtyard.

Now Palazzo Guadagni stands bare and stark, only empty shelves and abandoned rooms.

In the filtered light, smoke and steam mingle with the flutter of pigeon wings. The station is full of SS soldiers, pacing back and forth in their greatcoats, their rifles slung across their backs. There are no more bustling, pressing Italian passengers.

Now the few of us who remain—the Italian workers, Professor Heydenreich, Horst, and I—stand on the platform and wave good-bye to the rest of the staff who are heading to the German Institute in Milan or returning to Germany. I don't know if I'll see these friendly people again—the dozens of archivists, librarians, researchers, and administrative staff—who have made me feel welcome here, a little slice of home in a foreign city. I am alone on the upper floor of Palazzo Guadagni now, in my little room filled with my meager belongings and a wall decorated with photographs of Florentine monuments I've developed in the darkroom.

Everything loaded, the train huffs and squeals under the heft of its cargo, headed to the salt mines near Heilbronn. We feel the shudder and churn of the train under our feet as it starts.

I think about the day I arrived in this very train station some eight months ago, under the illusion my father had handed me some consolation prize. A safe bet. How naïve I was. I wonder if I shouldn't be on that train, too, headed back home. I think of the briny, cold air of the mine; my dog with his typical German shepherd smile; my brother and his red, tear-streaked cheeks. It all seems very far away.

The chug of the train grows distant, and I turn to see Enzo wipe his sweaty brow. His shirt is damp from the exertion of loading the crates. He grins at me, all hardness and dimples. A mysterious paradox that lies just out of my grasp, like an Italian phrase I only half understand. I feel heat rise to my cheeks.

No. My work is here now. Here in this beautiful, complicated place. Even if we are on the brink of something terrible. Even though the city seems a hollow shell of itself, scarred buildings and bridges, its population of shifting loyalties battened down and holding its breath. Even if the future, the next moment, is scary and unknowable. There is no denying that Florence has stolen my heart and now, the last thing I want to do is get on a train and leave it behind.

14

JOSIE

BUOYED BY GENERAL EISENHOWER'S BLESSING, Captain Thomas and I return to the villages with new resolve. We spend weeks arranging labor, clearing sculpture from rubble, excavating books and documents buried under wreckage, and posting signs. We begin to draft slender, pocket handbooks with lists of protected monuments, which we plan to hand out to troop commanders as we head north.

But as we near Rome, the roads are clogged with automobiles, bicycles, carts, horses, people on foot carrying bags and crates. Children's wagons. Hundreds of people moving forward in little clusters, covered in dust, carrying whatever they can. We make our way around an old white Fiat with a flat tire and dust-covered leather bags strapped precariously on top. Weary children, a bird in a cage, and a dog watch from the window. The fields beyond are crushed flat under the traffic of people banking on the safety of the city. On the dusty road, a dozen white leaflets flutter and spin. I reach down and unfold one of them, reading the Italian aloud to Captain Thomas.

"An announcement from General Alexander's headquarters to the Italian people," it reads. "Looks like they're trying to explain why they need to come through the city. To push back the Germans."

Farther ahead, we pass a makeshift Allied cemetery, little more than a wheat field sprouting hundreds of dirt mounds and white crosses. Captain Thomas and I fall silent. We're both thinking about

Private Simpson, just one of so many forever torn away from their families. From home.

When the earliest tender blooms begin to emerge from the cold ground outside our camp, my fellow stenographer, Margaret Olson, marries Staff Sergeant William Pierce.

"I tried to talk him into waiting until we got back home," Margaret says, her cheeks glowing. "But he didn't want to wait. Things could change at any moment, after all. And life is short." I squeeze her hands but say nothing. For what could be said when we have lost Private Simpson and many other men in the prime of youth.

They've scrounged up a decrepit Italian man to perform the ceremony, the only Protestant minister they could find among a sea of available Catholic priests. A dozen of us walk into a nearby village to bear witness to their little ceremony in the town hall. Private Ruggero and I may be the only ones who understand a word of the quick ceremony. The bride and groom don't seem to care. They are beyond elated to be bound together for life.

One of the teletype operators has fashioned the most incredible wedding dress out of a parachute. "It didn't open," Ruby whispers to me as we listen to the minister continue to drone. "I'm not sure that's good luck."

"Nothing could separate them," I say, smiling and clapping as the newly married couple kiss and run out into the square.

Back at the WAC camp, the senior officers have set up makeshift decorations in the communal tent. Lollie Dee, still a pale shadow of herself, has not been able to come to the ceremony at the town hall, but she's baked a delicious vanilla cake. I squeeze her shoulders and she takes my hand, letting me know without a word that she will be alright. After the short reception, the senior officers send Margaret and William off in one of their own jeeps to a hotel in Rome, where they will spend their wedding night. And then they'll have seven days of R & R on Capri.

After we wave the couple on their way, we return to the camp to find some of the girls setting up for a dance. They've found the phonograph, set up some lights, and cleared the area for a dance floor. Someone puts the needle on the record and the voices of the Andrews Sisters fill the tent. Lollie Dee and I sit on the sidelines and watch our friends dance. It seems we're the only ones who aren't paired up, but I'm not sweating it. I've given up on finding love here.

As if reading my mind, Lieutenant Hamm darts across the dance floor and takes my hand. I don't worry about him anymore since I don't need to prove my worth to him or anyone else. He smiles and spins me around like a top until I am dizzy.

"Next stop, Rome, doll," he says.

"No more sleeping on the wet, cold ground for you, I suppose." I feel my skirt twirl out as he spins me.

"You gonna see some famous pictures there?"

"I expect Captain Thomas will take me to see something incredible. He always does."

As the evening draws late, I say goodnight and step outside into the light of a bright crescent moon. The drone of a distant fighter, the music of the outdoor movie, and the familiar sounds of the girls bent on doing a few more chores around their tents fill the air. I fall on my cot. But just as I am drifting into the oblivion of sleep, I hear Ruby's voice in an urgent whisper.

"Girls! Come outside! Look!"

Reluctantly, I push my tired feet back into my worn shoes. We step out into the blackness, careful not to trip over into the trenches that lie just beyond the tent flaps.

Suddenly, there is a twinkle. Then dozens of twinkles. Fireflies in the utter darkness. It's as if we've stepped into a fairy tale. Twinkling lights in the firmament. They buzz slowly. I reach out my hand and catch one easily. I curl my fingers and watch the light, see my skin look transparent and golden as it flashes. Lollie Dee comes to stand by me.

"It's like magic," I say. For a minute, I feel like everything will be alright.

I feel Lollie Dee's slight form next to me. I unfurl my hand and the twinkling fly lifts up and away. The two of us watch the insect free itself, lift higher and higher, this single light in the vast darkness that has the power to transform into something bigger. Brighter.

"Mouse, can I tell you something? But you have to swear you won't tell anyone. I just don't know what else to do."

"Sure."

She whispers, "I missed my period."

Long after midnight, I retreat to my cot, still reeling from Lollie Dee's revelation. A letter is waiting on my pillow. Ruby is snoring loudly. I move the kerosene lamp closer and pick up the lightweight piece of V-mail. At first, I don't recognize the return address and I think someone's made a mistake and it's not for me. But then I recognize my aunt Betty's address in Bridgeport. My mother's sister works in a munitions factory while her husband and son are fighting in the Pacific.

Your mother probably won't tell you, I read in the dim light. *I've been taking the train up to go with her to the doctor. They say her cancer has progressed. I don't want to worry you but I thought you should know.*

Cancer? My mother has cancer? My mind flashes with her sunken eyes and sallow skin, the blood in the handkerchief. A quick gasp, then the truth settles somewhere in my bones, where some part of me sensed it already. A deep place of knowing. The place where primal fears are born. Where instinct propels us far away from the painful truth. Where we take flight. All the way to Europe.

In the cot next to mine, Ruby stirs. "Everything OK, Mouse?" she whispers.

"It's my ma," I say, sitting on the edge of my cot. "She's . . . sick."

"You said your ma was tough as nails," she mumbles.

I flop back on my cot and stare at the wavering ceiling of the canvas tent. Between us, the little flame in the field lamp shudders.

In Rome, our front and rear echelons reconvene. I am thrilled to see Dot after so many months and I run to embrace her. I long for the comfort of the one person who's known me the longest, a flighty, blond-haired American girl who I need more than ever to stand in for me, to give me a deep breath of home. The one person who will understand everything in Aunt Betty's letter, who will let me hang on to her and cry.

There. A quick, familiar squeeze. But before I have a chance to share news of my ma, Dot's eyes are searching the crowd for Dante Ruggero. He picks Dot up off the ground and twirls her around before planting a long, slow kiss that makes me look away. The months of talking to each other in the telephone trailer have only served to fuel their fire, the kind of heat I have given up hope of finding for myself. Part of me feels a certain satisfaction for Dot; I was deluded for thinking I could compete with her for Ruggero's attention. Sergeant Barnes calls for us to form up, and my moment to share my news with Dot is gone.

In an impressive square in view of an immense, white-columned monument, we line up, the forward echelon on one side and the rear on the other. I take a deep breath and blink away tears as I fall into position. We've changed back into our most ladylike uniforms, freshly pressed skirts and hats, as General Mark Clark himself walks between the lines where Lollie Dee and Sergeant Barnes stand honor guard.

In his speech, the general recognizes the WACs' long hours, loyalty, dedication, and discomfort. He tells us the Fifth Army WACs have left no doubt in the minds of Americans that women are considered valuable members of the U.S. Army. Then he presents a Women's Army Corps Service Medal to Sergeant Barnes, which makes her face beam as if illuminated from inside. Afterward, another officer reads a list of WACs and their specific contributions. The women in

Dot's telephone unit earn awards for communicating classified information, for getting crucial supplies to the front, and for jamming German supply lines at Anzio. A few other women earn awards for developing new methods for processing quartermaster requisitions.

Then, to my surprise, I hear him say, "To Private Josephine Evans, a Legion of Merit, for exceptionally meritorious conduct in the performance of her duties supporting the mission of our Monuments officers."

"Mouse!" I feel Ruby push me forward to shake the officer's hand and receive the award. I search the lineup for Captain Thomas's face, knowing that if I were to get such an accolade, he would be the one to nominate me.

After the ceremony, Dot and I meet up under an umbrella-like canopy of pine trees within view of the Roman Colosseum. We congratulate each other on our awards, and I share the news of my mother.

"Your ma is strong as a horse," Dot tells me, giving me a squeeze. "Don't you worry, Mouse. She's going to be fine."

"I hope you're right."

"Sure I am. She'll be back to herself in no time, darling."

I don't know if Dot is right, but I hang on to this fleeting moment, this small attempt to bring home close for the first time since we boarded the train in New Haven all those months ago. To console myself with someone who knows who I really am, and loves me anyway.

In the afternoon, Captain Thomas insists on bringing me along to meet the director of the American Academy in Rome and the local Italian superintendents. Along with Lieutenant Hamm and several other officers, we travel to the Castel Sant'Angelo in clean, comfortable U.S. Army vehicles that seem a luxury as the convoy crawls through the crowded city. From the window, I marvel at the vast, intimidating panorama of the Eternal City, with its ancient buildings that have stood the test of time, its streets clogged with people, cars, and bicycles. Even more, I marvel that the Germans did not easily destroy these important monuments.

"Thank you for my award," I say sheepishly.

"I didn't give it to you, doll face," he says, but then he looks sheep-ish himself. "You earned it."

Under the arcades of the Castel Sant'Angelo, the Italian officials tell us the Hermann Göring division has made off with some fif-teen crates of priceless paintings. Then they recount the story of how the Germans made a show of bringing masterpieces to Rome from across the Italian peninsula. "They brought many journalists and photographers here to portray the idea they were doing some-thing noble."

One of the superintendents adds, "We were opposed initially to bringing all the works to the Vatican. What would the victors of this war decide about all these works—a huge percentage of Italy's cultural patrimony? In the event of a treaty, what would happen? We would hope that the Germans—or the Allies—would leave these works in Italy out of respect for our culture but who could be sure? I suppose we're lucky only a small percentage of the works went missing."

"Well," Captain Thomas says, "*we* don't have any plans to bring these works out of Italy."

"But we cannot say the same for the Germans," one of the officials from the American Academy says. "We have reports of widespread Nazi art looting north of here. And all of the works of Tuscany—just think of it. The treasures of the Uffizi, the Pitti Palace, the Bargello . . . We don't know what their status is."

Captain Thomas's face turns grim. From all my evenings reading his battered guidebooks in my tent, I know that every region of Italy is rich in artistic treasures, but no other region is as rich as Tuscany, with Florence as its crown jewel. The birthplace of the Renaissance.

"I only wish I were going there to see it," Captain Thomas says.

"We're not going to Florence?" I say.

"*I'm* not going to Florence. From here, our commander is shifting the responsibilities of the Monuments officers. I'm being assigned to the western coast."

"Sounds like Florence is Foster's problem, then," the American Academy director says.

Foster? I have no idea who he's talking about.

"I'm being reassigned," Captain Thomas says again, and this time it sinks in, takes my breath away. What will I do next? Now that I've learned a little something about the history of art, I can't wait to get to Florence. "But you know Foster," he continues. "That crumb wasn't going to let anyone else have it."

"Who's Foster?" I ask.

"Wallace Foster. Another Monuments officer. Art historian from Cornell," Captain Thomas says. "Thinks he's a big cheese. I can't guarantee it, but I've recommended you be assigned to support him when your WAC unit gets to Tuscany."

"Mouse . . . Evans worked at the Yale Art Gallery," Lieutenant Hamm tells Captain Thomas before turning to me. "You'd be perfect," he says, rapping my arm with the back of his hand.

"And an award-winning WAC," Captain Thomas says, pointing to my new medal.

"I'm just a stenographer," I say, feeling heat rise to my cheeks.

"I'll warn you. Foster . . . He won't want any help," Thomas says. "Thinks he can do everything himself. We've had our disagreements in the past, but we have the same mission. There's no one who knows the Florentine collections better than him. Not even me. But I won't say that to his face." He gives me a smug grin.

"Ever since I've been working with you, I've heard and read so much about Florence. I'd be honored, sir."

Hamm hands me a small pamphlet with a red cover and a medieval soldier on it. "Here you go," he says. "Just got these hot off the presses."

A Soldier's Guide to Florence.

"Thanks." I thumb the thin pages as a flock of screeching swifts lunges and spirals, like a mad carousel, above the high battlements of the ancient fortress.

EVA

A LITTLE GIRL WITH BARE FEET AND A FADED print dress wants to hold my camera. I feel the leather strap bear into the back of my neck as she grasps the device and pulls it between her palms.

"*Aspetta*," I say, having gotten comfortable with this useful Italian word. Wait. I pull the strap over my head and squat down to show her how to look through the viewfinder. She presses the box to her face and squints, one side of her lip curling up to reveal missing front teeth. From this vantage point, I peer into the depths of her matted hair, where I can see two pests milling about.

With the camera on her face, the girl pivots to take in the scene before us: two open-bed trucks with wooden slats along the sides. A quiet hilltop called Montagnana. A looming villa, just a square stucco box with a tiled roof and small windows with closed shutters. Professor Heydenreich, neat in his suit and tie, his arms crossed. Horst and Paloma, comparing their inventories of some three hundred Italian Renaissance paintings hidden inside. Enzo, handsome in his gray trousers and his white shirtsleeves rolled to his elbows, his thick curls falling over his forehead. A few additional Italian laborers engaged to help load some of the paintings from this Tuscan villa, the Villa Bossi-Pucci, into the trucks.

In recent weeks, we've joined the mad scramble to return as many paintings, sculptures, and other art objects as possible from the Tuscan countryside to the city. In the evenings, we crowd around the wireless, listening to German and Fascist reports of widespread artillery fire and American and British looting as they make their way northward.

After much debate among the Italian superintendents and the Kunstschutz officials, Heydenreich says the idea that the precious treasures of Tuscany will be safer in Florence has prevailed. The Kunstschutz has arranged for laborers and a small fleet of German trucks to dispatch to the countryside depots, where they have cleared the roads of mines, at least for now. It has taken all our remaining staff, plus many local Italian laborers, to load the pictures and return them to museum storage in the city.

Now there are more refugees than ever, countless desperate people having fled their homes. They seek refuge in the Pitti Palace in Florence and in the countryside villas—large stone and stucco buildings that appear like they might be impenetrable.

The girl pokes and presses at the shutter. "*Perchè non fonziona?*" she whines.

I take the camera, cock the advance lever, and hand it back to her. "*Guarda?*" I say. "Pretend the camera is another set of eyes." She peers through it now with great concentration.

She presses her half-scrunched face against the metal and aims it at the Villa Bossi-Pucci. All morning, I have taken photographs of the hundreds of paintings inside. A close-up of Mary Magdalen's sorrowful face in a *Pietà* by Bronzino. A strange-looking centaur painted by Botticelli. A fat, sleeping cupid that Caravaggio depicted in the glow of a bright beam of light. Jacopo Bassano, grave-looking in his self-portrait as an old man. Any one of these pictures, I think, would warrant an entire gallery in a museum. The girl presses the shutter release with a loud click.

Suddenly, a group of planes materializes in the sky, as if the girl's loud click of the shutter has made them appear. They move in formation like crosses against the clouds. One of the laborers holds a hand over his brow and looks up. In the distance, I hear the relentless rattle of the antiaircraft guns. In a single second, a nearby hilltop explodes into a rain of dirt and debris as the shriek of the antiaircraft guns responds. Suddenly, there is chaos. All of us run into the building, among screaming, crying, billowing smoke. I slip in the mud and catch my balance.

"Francesca!" The little girl's mother appears from nowhere, a full-grown double of her daughter in her own faded dress. She scoops up the girl under her arm and my camera drops into the weeds. She runs toward the villa. I see Professor Heydenreich running, too, his tie flailing. Suddenly, Enzo is by my side. I pick up my camera, he takes my hand, and we run toward the villa.

We wind our way down a steep, grassy slope, where there is a pair of wooden double doors opening to the villa's wine and root cellar. The other refugees join us there—men, women, children, an elderly woman carrying a patchwork cat. A little girl clutches a ragged doll. On one wall, there are hundreds, maybe thousands, of unlabeled glass bottles full of blood-colored wine and covered in dust. Abandoned cans and vegetables in glass jars. Everyone huddles together in the dark. The air is rank with body odors. With fear. A little boy hacks, a raspy, unending string of coughs. His mother rubs his back.

Above our heads, a narrow window offers a dirty view to a sliver of grass and the blue sky beyond. Fine, gray dust shakes loose from the ceiling and rains on us. A rusty metal shelf stacked with pottery clatters like ice cubes in a glass. The old lady clutches her cat as if for dear life and it widens its round, glossy eyes.

The planes open their bays and release their fury. An explosive lands nearby and the building shudders. Dust and rubble rain down the stairwell. A woman chants a series of Hail Marys while babies cry and fathers shield their families with their bodies. People crowd in close together under the stone stairwell, among the smell of mold, damp, and sweat. I press my body tight to the inner wall and pray that the stairwell doesn't collapse. For a moment, I feel the horror of pushing Professor Kriegbaum under the arch, moments before it crashed to the floor.

A little boy starts crying and pleading with his mother. "*Voglio andare a casa, mamma!*" He repeats, pleading and crying unceasingly. Poor thing just wants to go home.

"*Zito!*" Make the kid stop, someone says. His mother wraps him closer and brushes his long black bangs away from his forehead.

At last, silence. Fine white dust falls around us. As abruptly as chaos arrived, it's over. The mumblings begin, the sniffling, the frenzied whispers. People shift. Stand. Brush the dust off their ragged clothes. Someone cracks open one of the rugged wooden doors. A few venture out of the wine cellar and into the light. I step outside.

All at once, the little boy crying in the dark root cellar is running through the tall grass with the girl who peered through my camera, the attack long forgotten. The other children emerge, laughing, running, and pushing one another into the weeds.

We spend an hour or so walking through the villa, checking everything to make sure there is no damage to it or to the paintings. "Nothing was hit," Professor Heydenreich says. "But we can't travel these roads with truckloads of pictures right now. It's too risky."

In the afternoon, when the rumble of the planes is no more and the sound of birdsong returns to the countryside, we make our way in the empty trucks to a lone train tunnel in the crook of a hillside.

Still shaking and lightheaded from the bombing near the Villa Bossi-Pucci at Montagnana, I try to steady my hand and take a few pictures of the fleet of cranes and trucks that have assembled outside the train tunnel, a black arch lodged into a craggy hill. We step from the wan spring light into the cold tunnel.

In the darkness, Lorenzo Ghiberti's fifteenth-century doors, the entrances to the Florence Baptistery, glow like flickering candlelight. I've read about the famous doors that took Ghiberti more than twenty-five years to complete, so magnificent that Michelangelo himself called them the Gates of Paradise. For as long as I've been in Florence, the entrances have been covered in wood and sandbags. Even in the darkness, I can appreciate their beauty and importance, and can understand why they've been protected here in this place where no one would expect to find them.

"We have to get the doors out of there," Heydenreich told us on the way, in the cab of the rattling, empty truck. "Without a doubt, the Allies will target the tunnel."

At the entrance, a group of important-looking men has collected. I recognize Signor Poggi from the Uffizi, and a man who can only be Colonel Alexander Langsdorff. I hang back and observe the tall, severe-looking man, the front of his uniform covered in metal. In my mind, I review what Professor Heydenreich has told us about Langsdorff. That he spent two formative years as a prisoner in France during the Great War. An archaeologist of great renown who has overseen important archaeological digs in Egypt and Iran. A curator at the Berlin State History Museum. A Septemberling who joined Hitler's movement in 1933, the same as General Wolff, who now oversees all of Italy. A personal assistant to Heinrich Himmler.

And yet, Heydenreich has told us, Colonel Langsdorff is complimentary of his Anglo-American colleagues who, he claims, have the same goals of protecting precious works of art from destruction in war. He also speaks fluent Italian and is a lover of Italian culture; even owns an apartment near Piazzale Michelangelo, with a view of San Miniato al Monte.

I raise my camera and take a few shots as a large crane raises Ghiberti's sparkling doors, five centuries old, out of the tunnel and into the weak light. I take a picture of Langsdorff, Heydenreich, and Horst standing, hands behind their backs, watching the doors teeter and spin in the air. The men say that the doors won't go back to the Baptistery right away. They'll go to the upper floors of the Pitti Palace, away from the refugees who spill into its courtyard.

After the sparkling doors are loaded at last into the back of the trucks, the men walk down the hill to where I am standing, feeding a new roll of film into the back of the camera. Heydenreich makes the introduction. "This is Eva Brunner, Colonel. Her father heads up the mines at Altaussee. She worked as a photojournalist back home." I am surprised on both counts—to hear Heydenreich mention the word "Altaussee," which is supposed to stay a secret but no doubt Langsdorff is well aware of it already; and secondly, that he has called me a photojournalist. "She is very good with the camera and her pictures have been important for our work."

"*Fräulein Fotografin,*" he says, giving me a tight smile that looks more like a grimace. Langsdorff seems to file this information about the "lady photographer" away while he watches me press the tiny holes of the film into the camera. Appraising, as if I am a work of art to be valued, judged. "Pleased to know you." Something in his scrutiny of me makes my skin prickle. Once the doors are finally loaded into the trucks and the colonel in his armored sedan, I feel relieved to be out from under his gaze.

To my sister:

Since you went to Italy last year, there are many more treasures collected here—things not only from Austria but from all across Europe. I wish I could make a complete list of everything but I fear this letter would never reach you. We have many new guards now. And so many crates in our Saint Barbara chapel that you can hardly see the altar anymore.

Father asks after you.

I'm including a drawing of Michelangelo's Madonna *from Bruges. Let me know if you like it?*

Your loving brother,
Gerhard

On a Sunday afternoon, Enzo and I walk up to the hillside church of San Miniato al Monte. The air has turned warmer but the sky is still a sea of gray, pressing down on the tile rooftops. Everything is quiet, eerily still. I press my hands into my skirt pockets and finger my brother's brief letter. I smile to think of his beautiful, elegant drawing, his re-creation of a centuries-old masterpiece conveyed with just a few strokes of black ink. I try to imagine it, thousands of works of art inside the labyrinthine passages of our salt mine. The men unpacking Michelangelo's *Bruges Madonna* so Gerhard can sketch it. More and more wooden scaffolding, all of it bursting with thousands of pictures. Our father, overseeing it all.

Below us, the bridges splay out over the sparkling river. As the sun sinks on the horizon, we watch the river turn to copper. The dome of the cathedral towers over a sea of red tile, jagged rooftops around it. From here, the city seems eternal, as if it has always been like this. As if nothing could ever change it.

At a stone retaining wall at the top of the hill, Enzo points at a long row of old buildings on the north side of the river. "That's where I live," he says. "Just beyond the Vasari Corridor. It was my grandmother's apartment. An old building."

"You don't live with Paloma?"

"She won't have me." He laughs. "No. Just me. I can't really afford to keep the place up. And there's no running water or electricity. But it suits me."

"Paloma says she got you the job at the Kunsthistorisches Institut."

He nods. "She says it's smarter to work with the Nazis instead of against you." Then he purses his lips, as if he's slipped up, perhaps revealed something he shouldn't.

For a few silent moments, we survey the city's medieval defenders, Giotto's *campanile*, the fortified prison called the Bargello, the tall, skinny watchtower of the Palazzo Vecchio. They must have seemed so strong, all those centuries ago. Long before bombers could easily release their fury from the sky. Now the low-lying city seems vulnerable.

I wonder if we have made a tremendous mistake, moving some of the treasures back to Florence. Surely it would have been a better decision to take the trucks north rather than south, where the Allies are sure to find them. I can picture it easily in my mind. The trucks in a convoy, a caravan of vehicles in front and behind, rolling across the Austrian countryside, through the Alps and down the valley to Salzburg. And in my mind, I can see them disappearing into the mines, the doors closing behind them, the entrance sealed with an impenetrable steel door designed for this very purpose.

Enzo perches on the wall overlooking his city. From here, he seems one with his birthplace, as if he himself has stepped out of one of those shimmering Italian Renaissance portraits, a picture of ideal beauty and human achievement with his city glowing behind him in the golden light.

"Smile."

Enzo turns his body to look at me. He smirks, one side of his mouth curling, his brown eyes studying me. I snap the release and for a moment, his face disappears behind the swirl of the aperture, breaking the spell. When I lower my camera, he's stood up from his perch on the wall.

"I wish there was a way to move all the Tuscan and Florentine masterpieces north," I say. "Surely they would be safer. But I have no say. And Professor Heydenreich and the others . . . They think it's the right decision to move as much as possible back to Florence."

"A calculated bet," he says.

"I hope it's the right one."

We miscalculate.

The warmer air brings a new glow to the city. Across from Palazzo Guadagni, the Caffè Firenze opens its shuttered door and a few residents dart out from their own battened-down homes to chat with the barman and drink a coffee. A few stirrings of life after months of stifling, suffocating quiet.

But even after all the assurances of Florence as an open city, it also brings the Allied planes back. The tired wail and moan of the air raid sirens fill the air. And the promise of compromise feels empty. Like it was a lie all along.

I'm on my way back from photographing Allied damage near Santa Maria Novella when I hear the siren and the plane engines, and then the inevitable whistling of the payload as it hurls toward the earth. The familiar sense of dread coils in the pit of my stomach. I duck into a doorway along a narrow street, where an exhausted-looking shopkeeper is yanking down the rattling metal shutter over his door.

The planes' bellies open. I squeeze my eyes shut against the tremble of stone buildings that have endured centuries of injustice. Against flares that fizzle and die, then the eerie, drawn-out silence before the next mortar shells land and the thunderous roar shakes the ground. The flashes of light. The erupting, spewing debris. It is hard to imagine that I have grown accustomed to such atrocity.

In a stretch of quiet, I run back to the Kunsthistorisches Institut, camera in hand. I find the last few of us remaining at Palazzo Guadagni in the inner courtyard. Professor Heydenreich paces back and forth, his arms crossed.

"Eva!" he calls. "I was worried we might have to send a search party for you."

"The lights are out," Horst says by way of greeting. He gestures toward the upper floors, where the Bandini sisters are dusting the stair railings as if it were any other day. "And be forewarned. There's no more running water in the lavatories."

Signor Poggi, once so neat and elegant, stands haggard in the same suit he's worn every time he's come to call. He leans against an arch, smoking. Months ago, Professor Kriegbaum told me the arch is one of the most stable structures in all of architecture. But that turned out to be a lie, too.

"We're waiting for word from our colleagues at the Uffizi and the Pitti," Heydenreich says.

Everyone is worried about what has been brought back to the city. Over weeks, works of art and important archives from the countryside depots have gone to the Vatican or been returned to Florence. And still, according to our tattered inventories, much remains in the countryside. Professor Heydenreich has done everything possible to support Poggi and the other Italian superintendents, but it is little consolation.

"The Uffizi, the Pitti . . . Those buildings have been here since the days of the Medici," I say half-heartedly. "Surely they will still be standing now and long into the centuries to come. I'm sure everything is safe."

"We thought it was best to bring everything back to the city," Professor Heydenreich says. "Now . . ." He shrugs. "I just don't know."

"No," Poggi says, his face haggard and his eyes rimmed in bags as if he hasn't slept in weeks. "Now we don't have the ability to bring anything more back to Florence, even if we wanted to."

"The depots are in the line of fire and anyway, the roads are all mined," Horst says.

"You have done everything you can," Poggi says. "But we can't get any more transportation or gasoline—neither from you *tedeschi* nor from our own Fascist leaders." He only shakes his bald head. "No. At this point, we can't go anywhere and we can't bring anything back. It's too late now."

In the weeks following the latest air raid, the city seems unable to recover like before. The air is foul with the stench of rot, open sewers, and death. Ragged craters in the ground fill with fetid water. On top of the daily miseries, the June air has turned stifling, as if someone has opened a great oven door on the city. At the grocers', a few skinny housewives queue to see what meager rations are left. They stand in a ragged line, sweating, whispering to one another, fanning themselves with ration cards made up of squares to cross off for oil, butter, sugar, and soap. They do not make eye contact with anyone they hear speaking German.

From our wireless in Palazzo Guadagni, we hear the scratchy broadcast announcing that the Allies have taken Rome. I think of those hundreds of pictures unloaded in the courtyard at Palazzo Venezia—the ceremony, the speeches, the rows of German trucks as far as the eye could see. The cameras flashing, the great reels and the pomp around the return of the masterpieces, our military's efforts to protect and save them within the walls of Vatican City.

Have the Americans and English already discovered these crates? Have they already loaded them on their own trucks, their own destroyers, leaving the ports and headed to America? Will they be moved to Jewish collectors, wringing their hands with delight, just like we see on the posters tacked to wooden doors all over town?

And the heavy, important question that no one is asking out loud: Are the Anglo-Americans coming for Florence next?

Two weeks later, Professor Heydenreich utters the words I feared most.

"We're leaving Florence," he says, pacing among the small tables and chairs on the upper-floor loggia, seeking the slightest waft of breeze. "There's nothing I can do; we have orders. And moving works of art from the countryside to Florence is to be stopped." Beads of sweat collect on his forehead.

"As if we could get to it now," Horst says.

"But the Americans—won't they take it?" I ask.

"And won't they be here before we know it?" Horst says.

"Of course we are all worried about the fate of the works in the depots," Heydenreich says. "But we have to think about human lives at this point. We've already seen what the Allies can do from the air. With forces on the ground, well . . . We can't stop them. The only thing we can do is slow them down. And the only way to do that is to blow the bridges." He leans against the edge of a table.

"Blow the bridges? Surely not!" I say.

Horst heaves himself into a chair. "The destruction of all the bridges in Florence. Unfortunately, I think it's inevitable at this point."

"Except for the Ponte Vecchio," Heydenreich says. "We can only hope."

I sink down in a chair, too, my blouse sticky and hot on my back. I fiddle with the knobs on the Leica in my lap. Would our troops really destroy the historic bridges? Our own forces? If they would steal two truckloads of priceless paintings, then perhaps the answer is yes. Professor Kriegbaum, rest his soul, took the Führer through the Uffizi himself, walked him through the Vasari Corridor on the upper floor of the Ponte Vecchio. Did the Führer look out the windows at the Ponte Santa Trinità and imagine that just a few years later, he would give the order to have it destroyed?

"It could happen, if Kesselring gives his approval," Horst says.

"But I thought the supreme headquarters—even the Führer himself—promised Florence would be spared," I say. "As you've said many times, Florence is the jewel of the Renaissance." When

Heydenreich stays silent, only rubs his forehead, I say, "But you don't believe the agreement will be respected."

Horst blurts, "The Allies have already made it abundantly clear they don't respect it! How many times have we nearly been blown off the street in the past three months, right here in the 'jewel of Renaissance'?"

Heydenreich's face remains shadowed, drawn. "The Florentines and German authorities have met about this many times, have written proclamations. Everyone agreed that Florence would remain an open city and spared as much as possible. But now, I don't know. Whatever the case," he says, "it's time for us to pack up."

I stare down at the camera in my lap, where my fingers are shaking. If I leave now, then what do I have to go home for? A chance to say I made a mistake? That I couldn't make a contribution to a war, like I led my father and everyone else to believe? Besides, I'm invested in our mission to safeguard the works of art now. At least that's what I've told Enzo. I put the camera to my face and frame the blue hills in the distance, masking the hot tears stinging my eyes.

16

JOSIE

ON A HOT, CRATERED ROAD NORTH OF ROME, I PULL
the slim copy of *A Soldier's Guide to Florence* from my pack. The
women in the back of the troop transport truck are silent. Lollie Dee
is sleeping, slumped over on Big Nellie's hefty shoulder. Ruby stares
out at the lone farms and umbrella pines, beleaguered, brown hair
whipping her cheeks.

The booklet fits in the palm of my hand, its pages thin and crisp
as I thumb through the text and black-and-white plates.

The Six Bridges
Six bridges cross the Arno into Florence. The most famous is the
PONTE VECCHIO, in existence in the 10th century and rebuilt
in the 14th century after it had been damaged by a great flood. Its
characteristic feature from earliest times is the row of shops which
cover the entire bridge. Downstream from the Ponte Vecchio are the
PONTE A S. TRINITÀ, leading into the via Tornabuoni, rebuilt
in the 16th century by Ammannati and decorated with statues rep-
resenting the Seasons of the year; the PONTE ALLA CARRAIA,
also rebuilt by Ammannati, leading into the piazza Goldoni; and
the PONTE DELLA VITTORIA, a modern bridge leading into
the Cascine park. Upstream from the Ponte Vecchio are: THE

PONTE ALLE GRAZIE, a 14th-century bridge leading into the via dei Benci, and the PONTE DI FERRO S. NICCOLÒ, a modern bridge leading into the Viale Duca di Genova.

I close the pamphlet against the wind and think about how much Captain Thomas has been dying to get to Florence for so many months, all the way from Algeria. I feel sorry he won't get to see the treasures he cares so deeply about. And if I am honest, I will miss working with him. As much as I disliked his leering, swaggering demeanor, he taught me a lot about art. His award and his uncomfortable questions have made me see that maybe I have more to offer to this mission than I might have thought.

Outside the truck, the umbrella pines begin to give way to tall, pencil-like cypresses. Before us lies a dramatic landscape with a patchwork of fields; it's easy to imagine they were carefully cultivated before their sudden abandon. A striking panorama unfolds: tall trees with thick white trunks and dense green bristles. Winding dirt roads leading the eye to distant, secluded farmsteads. The sun turns everything into a warm glow, illuminating hilltop villages like a heavenly spotlight, light reflecting off the tile roofs and rugged stone structures perched high above sloping vineyards. The hills rise and dip into gullies and small rises over a landscape unfurling with green and gold. From the back of the troop trucks, we fall silent, taking in the indescribable beauty. I adjust my helmet. Beyond a zigzag row of cypress trees, medieval abbeys and small villages come into view. For a few moments, the war feels far distant, as if this magical landscape is untouched by the evil devastation that the Nazi regime has unleashed. That there are no mines left in the fields or bridges blown to stumped fragments. Farther on, giant rolls of hay lie abandoned. A cratered village is a heavy reminder of why we're here, of what damage has been done.

I turn back to the page inside the front cover.

—*A Soldier's Guide to Florence*, published by the United States Army to assist the servicemen in their quest for information concerning the famed places which are being liberated. This guide has been passed by the United States censor and may be mailed home.

Mailed home. If I sent this little booklet all the way to New Haven, would it be enough to convey to my ma what I am doing here? Why I have to stay? Would it be enough of an excuse for why I can't come home? For why I can't face her illness?

On the front of the slim booklet is a sculpted saint who looks like a warrior. I return the booklet to my pack and breathe the warm air tinged with the scent of artillery smoke and rotting haystacks long abandoned.

I meet Captain Foster—my new boss—as soon as we begin setting up camp in the hills south of Florence.

Beyond the nearest horizon of burnished green hills, we hear the rattle of gunfire. The air is heavy with moisture, sweat, and the smell of distant fires. Our commander has prepared us that we'll be closer to the fighting here than anywhere we've set up camp so far. In the midst of this cacophony of shelling and smoke, we unload from the trucks and begin our familiar routine of setting up camp.

I catch sight of Captain Foster's rusty, dilapidated jeep as it rumbles into camp. The name GEORGETTE is scrawled across the hood in black paint. The jeep stops, and a tall man with wire-rimmed glasses steps out. Our commander appears from behind a tent flap to greet him. Captain Foster is skinny as a rail, his belt ratcheted tight around his waist. He strides confidently across the caked ground, a clipboard under his arm.

"I've been waiting in Orvieto for a few weeks," the lean captain says as he shakes our commander's hand. "Thankfully, the old part of the city is intact. I've been using it as a headquarters until I could get here. But I've been angling to get to Florence ever since I landed in Sicily. The suspense has been almost intolerable."

"We've also been waiting for months to get into Florence," our commander says. "It'll be a great moment when we get to liberate the city—second only to Rome."

Captain Foster joins a group of officers at a table set up under an olive tree. All of us, women and men in the camp, gather around to listen.

"Cup o' mud?" Lollie Dee smiles and pours a stream of hot coffee into his metal cup. Captain Foster is well-spoken and intelligent-looking, light-colored eyes behind small, circular glasses. His fair hair, cropped a quarter of an inch, swirls around the crown of his head. His hands are long and elegant, curved around the tin cup. At first glance, he's the opposite of Captain Thomas, with his crude, swaggering bulk. I catch a glimpse of why they might have locked horns in their academic circles back home.

After a while, I pull up a chair among them. Everyone knows I've been reassigned to work with this new Monuments officer and no man in our camp would dare ask me to leave the table. "Hello, sir. Allow me to—"

But Captain Foster ignores my arrival. "I haven't been able to reach Fifth Army communications in weeks," he continues talking to the men at the table. "The phone is impossible. And I haven't been getting reports from any of the other Monuments officers."

Our commander says, "I can tell you we've heard Siena is intact, as well as a lot of towns across southern Tuscany. And Hitler has declared Florence an open city, so hopefully that means that it, too, will stay out of harm's way."

"The entire city of Florence could be considered a work of art," Captain Foster says. "But to be honest, I'm anxious about what we might find."

Captain Foster takes a sip of coffee, and in the silence, I say, "Captain Foster, I'm Josephine Evans."

His face is blank until Big Nellie comes to my aid. "Private First Class Josie Evans. Captain Thomas assigned her as your assistant, sir."

He looks up at me now, surprised. His sharp blue eyes look me straight in the face.

"Pleased to meet you, sir," I say, standing and saluting.

For a moment, he looks disconcerted, then seems to remember his manners. He stands and shakes my hand with a quick, firm grip. But he hesitates, as if he's unsure if he should pull out the chair for me. "Ah, I see . . ." He scratches the crown of his head where the hair swirls. "Yes. Captain Thomas wrote to me about you."

"Captain Thomas and I have traveled from Algeria together," I say. "Have been all the way up from Caserta. I can show you the—"

"Yes. Well. He has his way of doing things. I, on the other hand, I've done everything myself. Ever since Sicily." He looks around nervously. "Thank you, miss, but I'm afraid I don't need an assistant."

Smarting from Captain Foster's rejection, I march to the WAC tent to clear my head. During the time I've been listening to him, the girls have set up our billet.

Freshly laundered undergarments dangle from the tent poles. Ruby has tucked mosquito nets around our cots and fogged the tent with insect repellant so the whole place reeks as sharply as tear gas. "They say the mosquitoes are deadly around this area," she says. One of our nurses has already distributed anti-malaria tablets in our packs. After the fog of the foul-smelling spray recedes, I push back the net around my cot to find a small box from my mother.

I've been to the doctor who is looking at my lungs. I'm taking a little time off work to heal up. Betty has come up from Bridgeport.

I didn't want you to be concerned but she says she already wrote to you. Please don't worry about me. I'll be fine.

I sit on my cot and put my face in my hands.

Ruby reaches her hand through the mosquito net and puts it on my back. "Maybe you could ask to go home, Mouse," she says quietly.

"I'll be damned if I'm going home now," I snap. "Don't they see we have important work to do here?"

"Sorry, Mouse. I was just trying to . . ."

"Forget it," I say, swatting her hand away.

I sit on the edge of my cot, remove my shoes, and rub my feet. I think back to when I signed up for WAC duty. I knew none of these things then. Nothing about the long history of art and what it means to people, to entire cultures. How dare Captain Foster dismiss me so summarily, when I have learned so much? When I am the most qualified of any of the girls to go into Florence with him?

I pick up the booklet about Florence from my side table and decide to mail it home to my mother. Maybe if she reads it, she will get a small glimpse of what I'm doing here and why it matters. Of how her own daughter might have something to contribute after all. If only I can figure out a way to convince Captain Foster to let me continue. I fish a pen and a blank slip of V-mail from my pack.

It might be hard for you to understand, I write, *but know that I've never before had the feeling of satisfaction of worthwhile accomplishment that I get from my present work. And I doubt that I shall ever be inspired to put such wholehearted energy and effort into anything which my life after the war will demand of me. If anyone here doubts my ability, they are mistaken.*

It's the truth, but it feels like an excuse. An excuse for why I'm not there to care for her. An excuse for why I felt ashamed of her, for why my life in New Haven wasn't enough. An excuse for why I am too afraid to face her disease, to face the fact that each of us is alone in our grief.

To my surprise, it's Ruby who comes to my aid.

"After you left the table, I told him how you worked at the Yale Art Gallery," she says with a bit of New England matter-of-factness. "He seemed surprised, but it's a small world. He said he worked there too for a short bit, before he went to teach in upstate New York. Lucky for you, I guess. He said for you to meet him in his 'office'— over in that olive grove."

I give Ruby's broad shoulder a squeeze but she only shrugs, then heads off to the switchboard trailer to deliver a message to the half dozen women sweating in there.

I find Captain Foster at a makeshift table, in front of a stack of paper held with rocks covered in ruddy earth to keep it from blowing away.

"I hear you worked at the Yale Art Gallery," he says, not turning around.

"Yes." I almost tell him I was just a typist, but I stop myself.

"I did, too, for a bit, before I went to New York. And then I came to Italy to learn." He pulls out a chair for me with his foot. "I've been preparing lists of monuments in Florence," he says, jumping in without further explanation or apology. He looks at me at last. "Captain Thomas tells me you've been doing the same."

I look at the papers. One handwritten list names the buildings in the city that should not be used under any circumstances. Another names structures that could potentially be used for Allied offices or other purposes. The length and detail of the lists is staggering. Much longer than anything Captain Thomas and I managed to cobble together from our tattered guidebooks.

"Yes we have," I say, sitting down in the chair. "But I'd be embarrassed to show you ours, now that I see what you've put together." I muster a smile.

My flattery seems to have an effect on him. He softens a little, pressing back in his chair and squinting into the shifting shadows of the olive branches, the shimmering, silvery leaves on the underside of deep green. The warm streaks of sunlight. "I spent a lot of time sitting under a tree at an Eighth Army camp compiling that," he says proudly. "With my guidebooks . . . and my memory." He taps his temple with a long, elegant finger.

"You must know Florence well."

He nods. "*Firenze*. Did my graduate studies there."

"You went to college here in Italy?"

He nods. "I spent several years studying in Florence. Still have friends there. Most wonderful place on earth if you love art and history. An art history paradise of sorts."

"So, where do we start?"

"Well. I don't know how long it will take before we can get into the city. For now, we have to keep troops and residents out of the historical buildings nearby . . . They might do damage by accident or on purpose. Our troops, they . . ."

"I know. Captain Thomas and I have spent untold hours doing that already. We put up signs and ran soldiers out of hundreds of buildings in Naples."

This brings a tight grin to his otherwise bristly demeanor. "Then I suppose I should be glad to have you, Miss Evans," he says, looking at the name embroidered on my field tunic. He raises his hand in a quick salute. Then he picks up a stack of handwritten inventories and puts it in front of me.

We have barely completed setting up camp in the hills outside Florence when Italian partisans come to find us.

They are a ragged but determined-looking group of men and

women, dressed in heavy layers of clothing and weapons, tanned and sweating in the oppressive air. And when Captain Foster hears that many of them are Florentines, he nearly knocks over his stacks of papers to get to them.

I am impressed to hear the fluent, singsong quality of Captain Foster's Italian, which, to my ear at least, sounds like native quality. He peppers the partisans with questions, and eventually, a handful of their leaders settle around Captain Foster's rickety table in the olive grove. The American officers come out of their tents to join us.

The leader of this group is a sturdy, lean Italian man with a lively energy, a sort of internal spark that I have observed in so many Italians. He is handsome and strong-looking, with muscular, tanned forearms, straight white teeth, and eyes the color of milk chocolate. Like his fellow partisans, he wears his worn, black clothes in a kind of effortless formality, just a dusty shirt and trousers, but he looks as if he is wearing something beautiful and expensive.

Captain Foster turns to the group of American commanders. "Many of them are from the Oltrarno," he translates quickly. "That's the southern side of the river in Florence. They are saying there is a large cell of partisans there." With further translation assistance from Captain Foster, we learn that Florence is more or less intact but there is widespread damage and hardship. It has been many weeks since they have had clean water, electricity, and working sewers. There are thousands of refugees overflowing the Palazzo Pitti. And anyone who has stayed in the city is confined to their home. That the Germans have ransacked many of the homes and businesses on the southern bank.

Captain Foster asks where the art from the Uffizi and the Pitti is—and if those buildings are secure—but none of the Florentine men has a good answer. From the looks of this ragtag group, I suspect they've been trying to sleep, eat, find weapons and cash. Paintings aren't as high on their priority list as they are for Captain Foster.

"All I know," I understand from their leader, "is we've seen truck-loads of paintings coming from the countryside back into the city."

Captain Foster stands and paces. "So they're in the city!" he exclaims. "That's a relief—I think—but where did they go? I guess we won't know till we get there."

"I don't know. I have just heard the superintendents say they don't care who is in charge—Germans, English, Fascists, partisans—whoever. They just want to save those treasures for the future. And we want our city back. Whatever it takes."

Before the partisans leave our group, Captain Foster shakes the handsome leader's hand vigorously. "Thank you, thank you for coming to find us. For sharing this important information."

The leader nods and then catches my eye before turning away.

"Wait!" Captain Foster says. "Please tell me your name."

"Corrado Innocenti."

Just about the time I think we will die of heatstroke or malaria, or that Captain Foster will explode from the suspense of getting to Florence, at the end of July, a BBC reporter sends Captain Foster a tip. A hoard of Italian masterpieces has been discovered in the countryside. And it's not far from our camp.

"It's a place called Santa Lucia," I tell Ruby as I scramble for my steno pads and helmet in the shadows of the sagging tent. Outside, Captain Foster has pulled up in his dusty jeep. "The report said there are paintings by Raphael, Botticelli, Cimabue, Giotto . . ." Ruby looks at me like I'm speaking a language she's never heard. "Some of the greatest masterpieces of the Uffizi Galleries in Florence." I can't take the time to explain. I roll up my bedroll.

"Well then, good luck, Mouse!" She waves as I exit the tent.

I toss my steno case, a few steno pads, and my bedroll into the back of the jeep alongside Captain Foster's rifle and a metal box that carries his precious inventories and lists. I pull myself into the passenger seat and hold on to my helmet as the jeep rumbles out of the encampment. I latch the helmet under my chin and unfold the field map.

Beyond the camp, we rattle across the rough roads, over hills that stretch out like a vast patchwork in the waning light. It is nearing eight o'clock but still daylight, the sun casting its suffocating heat across the green and yellow fields. A flock of sheep grazes lazily in the golden light, as if pulled from the background of a painting. A lone chapel stands on a rise, where the road snakes down to a cluster of farm buildings.

"I thought the partisans said they saw paintings returned to Florence from the countryside?"

"So did I." Captain Foster shakes his head as his hands steady the steering wheel. "So now I'm alarmed. It means the works could be scattered. Maybe unguarded. And Santa Lucia has been in the heart of the battle. I don't know . . . I haven't been able to get any information about what's happening." His mouth draws to a thin, determined line and he falls silent, concentrating on the winding dirt road ahead of us. For a while, we don't speak. We circumnavigate the ruins of a desolate, ruined village, continuing on through the landscape. He slows and steers the jeep around a giant crater in the middle of the road.

"You've been driving this thing all over Italy?"

"Georgette." He pats the dashboard, sending up a puff of filth. "Got her in North Africa. She got a little roughed up in Sicily." The windshield is a web of hairline cracks, the tires worn bald. The suspension squeaks like springs in an old mattress. There are no side or rearview mirrors.

Suddenly, over the rise of the next hill, the sky lights up with an orange glow and there is shelling like the sound of thunder, then a rain of artillery fire. Captain Foster slams the brakes and we pull over alongside the ditch. I stare at the map, unfolding it again between my shaking fingers. "They said this road was clear," I say, thinking back to the instructions we received from our commanders.

"Well, they were damned mistaken," he says, tightening his helmet strap as another explosion lights up the rise of the hill, making the jeep shudder. I register the disappointment on Captain Foster's face. "We're not far from the Eighth Army press camp. We'll stop there."

I'm relieved to hear we won't be going forward. I need to find a latrine, but I don't dare say so. Foster turns his beloved Georgette around. We continue across the arid landscape, the chug of the tires blowing dry dust around us. I press a handkerchief to my nose and mouth. The blaze and thunder of artillery fire recedes in the distance.

The explosions fall away as the sun sinks below the hills. Sundown brings cooler air and a clear, navy-blue sky. The crescent moon rises high. The landscape is dark, and we cut our lights, making our way along the dirt roads, up and down the hills of Tuscany, with the cypress trees making tall, ragged silhouettes against the dark. The silent, deserted ruins of a village open to a wide vista of blues and black, a mournful yet beautiful scene. At last, we see a distant encampment of sagging tents tucked beyond a village.

We rattle across one of the now-familiar Bailey bridges the Allies have constructed. "There was a medieval bridge here," Foster laments, then falls silent again. He presses the squeaking brakes and we roll into the center of a small encampment on the edge of an olive grove. A few men sit under the trees, drinking from metal cups. One of the men waves as Foster cuts Georgette's engine.

"Foster!" the man calls out in a clipped British accent. He slaps Captain Foster on the back as he steps out of the jeep. "Greetings, my friend."

We follow the man into an enclave of leaning tents, where we are introduced to a motley group consisting of a BBC correspondent, two British newspaper reporters, and a slight man who says he's a novelist and that he was living in the hills outside Florence for many months before the Germans chased him off. There is also an intelligent-looking, middle-aged woman who says she's an archivist at the British Institute, and has been reporting from the press camp.

In the darkness, they relay the incredible story of how they stumbled upon Santa Lucia.

"There was an Italian man from the Uffizi there. He told us there are works from the Uffizi scattered all over the countryside near here," one of the BBC men says as Captain Foster hangs on his every word. "They weren't returned to Florence like we thought. They're still in these hilltop refuges, maybe churches, villas . . . God knows where."

The British group tells us they've seen four of the deposits—at Santa Lucia, the Villa Bossi-Pucci at Montagnana, the Villa Guicciardini, and the Castello Guidi at Poppiano. I rely on my newly acquired Italian pronunciation to scratch out these place names along with the other testimonies on my steno pad.

"They are all close together, then," Foster says, pushing back in his rickety chair.

"You mean those paintings are hiding on people's private property?" I struggle to imagine all the priceless masterpieces I've seen in Captain Thomas's books and lists hiding away in the countryside.

"Yes, and right in the middle of hell," one of the journalists says. "They've blown everything up in that area. You should stay the night. We have a place for you, Miss Evans."

"Whatever the case, we won't know the full state of things until we can get into Florence," Captain Foster says.

"Hopefully it won't be long," the archivist says. "The whole city is a work of art."

Very late, in complete darkness, the woman from the British Institute leads me farther into the shadows of the olive grove. "It's so hot that I've been sleeping on the ground," she says, holding up a kerosene lamp. "I'm sorry we can't offer you better lodging."

"It's alright," I say. "I've been camping out for months now. I'm used to it. It's just important that we women stick together in this chaos." I unroll my bedroll on the red, parched earth. I lie there in the darkness and stare at the gnarled branches of an olive tree and the moon above, which make garish, shifting shadows on the ground.

The next morning, we depart the press camp and make a second run for Santa Lucia. The sun awakes in a harsh and punishing mood, illuminating a striking landscape of neatly arranged cypress trees casting long shadows along a winding gravel road. Captain Foster's mouth is a thin line of determination as he leans forward in his squeaking seat and guides Georgette onto a dimpled road. Already, there is the sound of gunfire and shelling in the distance. Up ahead, the sun shines through the ruined roof of an ancient church.

Captain Foster steers the jeep up a winding hill, seeming to know the way by heart. At last, we arrive at a cluster of buildings among the thickly planted, pointy trees. On the hillside, a wide stair leads to a cream-colored building with a pair of ornately carved wooden doors. A small watchtower presides over the quiet landscape. A feeling of grave anticipation washes over me. "You really think there are paintings in there?" I whisper to Captain Foster, but he remains silent.

We exit the jeep and climb the stairs to find a surreal vision of Indian sentries guarding the door to the villa, neat in their uniforms. They scan us with their dark eyes, and at last, one of the sentries takes note of our uniforms and he breaks his vigil. He opens the doors and gestures to enter a large, open courtyard. An elegant Italian in a suit comes out to greet us.

The balding man introduces himself as Cesare Fasola, librarian of the Uffizi. He grasps Captain Foster's right hand in both of his. Captain Foster makes the introductions—Miss Josephine Evans, his trusted assistant who has worked in an art museum at Yale University. "Ah!" The man nods in recognition and immediately I feel an impostor, for surely I am nothing of what might be in his head. But I don't dare correct him. I'm here, after all. And anyhow, this mission seems too important to bring attention to myself.

We step across the threshold into a spacious Renaissance courtyard. Around the space, more Indian sentries stand in formation,
at the same time relaxed yet on high alert. Dottore Fasola produces
an ancient iron keyring from his pocket. We follow him to a pair of
doors on the other side of the courtyard.

A whoosh of cool air rushes out of the darkness and into the heat
of the courtyard. At first, I see nothing. Fasola steps into the room.
I hear a clatter of wood and then a streak of light comes through an
open shutter. Fasola opens two more shutters and the space begins to
reveal the silhouette of dozens of pictures stacked against the walls.
Captain Foster and I step forward over the stone threshold and into
the room.

The sun's rays streak into the space. I hear Captain Foster's gasp
and I see the outline of an enormous painting with beautiful light
colors. In the middle is a woman with red waving hair standing in
a lush, green garden bursting with fruit trees and flowers. A blind-
folded, winged cherub flies above her head, and she is surrounded
by dancing women in flowing drapery, and two male figures. The
painting is so elaborate, so refined, that I have never imagined such a
thing of beauty existed in the world.

Fasola continues to open more shutters. More paintings come
into the light. There are dozens of them, two and three deep, stacked
against the walls of the room. An overwhelming jumble of gilded
picture frames, faces of angels, colorful flowers, still lifes, Madonnas.
It is impossible to take it all in, in a single glance.

I want to see Captain Foster's reaction at this sight, but at first I
don't see him. Then I look down. Before the enormous painting of
the dancing women, on the terracotta tiles, I find Captain Foster on
his knees.

"I came up on foot," Fasola tells us after Captain Foster's initial shock
has worn off and he is standing again. Both of us are beginning to

absorb the sight of dozens of priceless masterpieces stacked all around us in the villa's dark room. "I left Florence as soon as I could. I didn't have a German travel permit but at that point, the *tedeschi* were focused on patrolling the river and they didn't stop me. I moved as well as I could through the hills. *Dio*, there were mines and shelling everywhere. Now I can hardly believe I am still in one piece," he says, gesturing broadly at his body with his large hands. He says all this in Italian, and I find myself following the gist of the conversation now.

"Good Lord," says Captain Foster in English. He begins to pick through the pictures. He stops to look at an Annunciation with an angel gazing down at the Madonna, and a tranquil landscape that looks as if it could be pulled from what's outside these very windows. "Andrea del Sarto," he says. "And Giotto." He smiles, gesturing to an enormous enthroned Madonna radiating from a mass of shimmering gold.

Fasola leads us out of the room and down a dark corridor with the overwhelming stench of urine. "The Germans were using this as a latrine." He leads us to another large salon, where we find Botticelli's *Coronation of the Virgin* lying flat on a large table. Captain Foster sputters, a mixture of incredulity and relief. Along the walls are dozens of Madonnas, Crucifixions taller than Captain Foster and me put together, saints, huge altarpieces of gilded wood. All of them lay sideways and stacked against the wall like discarded chattel.

Over the next hour, Fasola continues to unlock doors and lead us through room after room. With each turn of a doorknob, Captain Foster's shock turns to excitement. "It will take us a while to inventory everything," he tells me in English, then asks Fasola in Italian, "You have a list of everything here?"

Fasola shrugs, one of those Italian shrugs that involves the entire body. "*Sì*," he says, "but . . . we don't know yet how closely what is here will follow the lists. Or if things have been taken."

We move into a room where a large, circular *Adoration of the Magi* lies on a table. "The Germans were using this as a beer table," Fasola tells us.

"A Ghirlandaio!" Captain Foster exclaims as I struggle to capture the words in shorthand. "Good God," he says, running his hand across a great rip piercing the canvas.

None of the pictures are wrapped, crated, or covered. "Did they travel across the countryside like this, with no protection?" I ask.

"For the most part, yes," he says. "What choice did we have? We had to move everything quickly."

"Who owns this building?" Foster asks.

"Sir Harwell. But they flushed him out of Italy along with all the other British expatriates. His Italian driver deserves all the credit. He has been single-handedly responsible for the safety of all these works."

After Fasola leads us through the last rooms full of pictures, we step outside to a high terrace overlooking the Tuscan countryside on a picture-perfect summer day. For a moment, the shelling is quiet and we glimpse life in normal times. Behind us, an Indian guard stands at the door, looking out at a landscape of cypresses, birdsong, and roads winding lazily through the hills. It's impossible to imagine that explosions and brutal fighting might be a second away, just over the rise.

"You see why the Germans wanted to stay here," Fasola tells us. "We can see almost to Florence from here."

"This building holds the entire history of Italian painting," Captain Foster huffs.

"How did this happen?" I ask.

"For a time," Fasola says, "the Germans were helping us. There is a German Art History Institute in Florence, you may know. They have specialists who know the historical importance and value of these works. And at first, everyone obeyed the OFF LIMITS signs signed by their generals."

"But then," Fasola continues, "as you Americans, British started to arrive, things turned. I fear that the closer the Allies are to winning, the more in danger these works are. There is looting everywhere. They won't hesitate to throw everything into their trucks, or even to set it all on fire on their way out of town."

A little boy runs into our field of view. He is ragged, seeming to have come somehow from beneath the villa. After a moment, another boy and a girl run after him.

"Refugees," Fasola tells us. "There are hundreds of them, wretched people living in the wine cellar. They were here already when the Germans came. They are lucky they still have their lives. We've had to maintain order as best we can under these conditions." For a moment, his entire body seems to deflate. "I protected the pictures as best I could."

Captain Foster lays a hand on the man's shoulder.

Beyond the terrace wall, we watch the boys start an improvised game of splashing one another from a gurgling spigot, squealing in the cold water.

Sandro Botticelli, *Primavera*
Giotto di Bondone, *Ognissanti Madonna*
Diego Velasquez, *Equestrian Portrait of Phillip IV*
Andrea del Sarto's *Annunciation* from the Pitti Palace
Giotto di Bondone's *Madonna* from the Uffizi
Cimabue, *Madonna*
Pontormo, *Supper at Emmaus*
Rubens, *Nymphs and Satyrs*
Sandro Botticelli, *Enthroned Madonna*
Paolo Uccello, *Battle of San Romano*
Raphael, *Madonna del Baldacchino*, from the Pitti
Perugino and Filippo Lippi, *Descent from the Cross*, from the Uffizi

Botticelli, *Coronation of the Virgin*
Ghirlandaio, *Adoration of the Magi*
Dugento crosses from the Accademia
Rucellai Madonna from Santa Maria Novella

Our lists grow long. Over the next two days, with a mixture of relief and worry about what else may lie hidden in the battered countryside beyond Santa Lucia, Captain Foster and I make our own inventories of the 246 priceless works of art from Florentine museums in this single repository. We compare them with the handwritten lists and slips of receipts Fasola has brought from the Uffizi. In the orange glow of a sunset amplified by intense shelling over the hillside, I flip through my steno pad and transfer some of the pages to Foster's field typewriter so we can send a report to our commanders about what has been found.

After months of working with the Monuments officers, now I understand why Captain Foster has been so desperate to find these works. For if not for this handful of dedicated art professionals, who would account for them? And if they were erased from history, how much poorer we might be. I feel sorry now that Captain Thomas hasn't had the same benefit of discovering these hidden masterpieces, the ones he so desperately cataloged from our sagging tent south of Rome.

In the end, it is only a few pages. A list of names, subjects—little more. Words that fail to describe the beauty, value, and importance of these works—in and of themselves, to the Italian people, and to the cultural heritage of the world. Most of all, I don't know how to begin to describe the miracle that the works are still here, that the Germans didn't make off with them in the backs of their trucks. I am left to wonder if the German art professionals have their own inventories, their own detailed catalogs that they pore over, wishing and desperately tracking where they will go next.

• • •

Over the following days, Captain Foster and I make our way across the rutted roads to other countryside depots, dodging the ever-shifting heat of rattling gunfire and explosions. We follow a trail of scattered breadcrumbs spread by the Italian superintendents, brave villagers who have remained in place, even refugees. They share ragged pieces of information that lead us to unassuming hilltop villages, to dark wine cellars, to the dusty attics of Renaissance villas. One after the other, we find priceless Florentine treasures waiting. Safe.

On a hot afternoon, we rumble up a steep hill to Poppiano, a five-minute jeep ride from Santa Lucia, where a medieval castle with a tall tower overlooks the ragged countryside. In the intense heat of the noon sun, we arrive to find one side of the old residence of the counts of Guicciardini crumbled from shelling.

Inside the cool darkness of the medieval castle, we discover that Pontormo's *Visitation* from Carmignano has been knocked to the floor in the shelling. And the New Zealanders who are assigned to guard it have not been as careful as the Indian troops at Santa Lucia. They have trampled over the giant panel painting with their boots, grinding plaster and brick dust into the fifteenth-century surface.

"It's a wonder anything is left." Captain Foster directs a team of guards to lift the altarpiece upright.

"Can it be restored?" I ask.

His nose an inch away from the deep gouges on the surface, Captain Foster examines the ground-in dirt over the varnish of blue pigments.

"It could be that the damage is only on the surface," he says. "We won't know until the day comes when we can get this to the restoration studio—the Gabinetto Resaturi—in Florence. It's the best in the world."

In the same room, we prop up Rosso Fiorentino's *Descent from the Cross*, an enormous, colorful altarpiece transported from a church in Volterra. "When I inspected Volterra, I noticed it was missing. Thank goodness," Foster says, running his fingertips over the scratched and dusty surface. We find another work by Pontormo, a *Deposition*, which Foster tells me comes from Santa Felicità in Florence. The grief-stricken figures rise from rose-colored and green shadows, their horrified faces seeming to encapsulate perfectly how we feel.

While we are examining the *Deposition*, Captain Roberson, a grave-looking British military police officer, comes to meet us. "You are best advised to remove these pictures at once," he tells us. "We are under fire and the main tower of this castle is being used as an observation post for an artillery battalion of the New Zealand division. From the tower, we can see the entire countryside. That means we are in their crosshairs. As soon as the Huns discover we are directing all fire from this building, they will plaster us."

"Will you provide us with transportation to remove the works?" Foster asks.

The officer scratches his head. "Even if we could get trucks and men," he says, "you can't use the roads; we are under attack and expecting more this evening."

Foster only gestures to two small canvases that the New Zealanders have slashed with their knives. "Then with all due respect, sir, you need to post more guards until we can get these works back to Uffizi," Foster says. "Surely you recognize that our own men might do as much damage as the Germans."

Until we can get into Florence, Captain Foster decides to set up a makeshift headquarters at Santa Lucia, giving us easier access to the nearby depots. And I am certain he wants to stay close to the Botticellis and the other masterpieces that brought him to his knees.

Captain Foster chooses a large bedroom with a giant four-poster bed, a space that lies directly above the room with some of the largest and most impressive of his beloved pictures. There is no light and no running water. Sir Harwell's driver, a sturdy man who remains the villa's unsung protector, helps us locate candles. He recruits a hefty woman from among the villa's refugees to cook for us. Everywhere she goes, a cat and two geese follow behind as if trusted assistants.

I find a quiet bedroom that seems an unwarranted luxury after months of living in the WAC camp, with its constant rotation of dust, cold, heat, ruin, mosquitoes, and shellfire. I feel guilty, watching the refugees who collect in the dark cellars and around the building. I stare out the window and think about my friends in our camp. I wonder about the guys and gals who have become like family to me. As I listen to the distant fire and trembling of the earth, some part of me wishes I was there with them.

In the presence of the masterpieces, I set my steno machine and typewriter on a large wooden table across from Captain Foster. We spend the next week writing letters and meeting with officials to try to secure responsible guards for all the depots. My hands are numb from scratching marks on my pads and pressing the metal keys of the steno machine. I grow accustomed to the sight of the masterful images, the bright colors, the artistic achievement, and long span of history.

"We probably only know about some of the depots," Captain Foster says, pacing back and forth as I take dictation for a letter to Eighth Army commander General Leese. "Sir," he says, stopping before the *Primavera* by Botticelli, "the list of important works of art in the depots is more extensive and precious than I expected. It is imperative that we post guards not only for the liberated depots but also those that might be found along the way. With this letter, we enclose a map with references." In closing, Captain Foster pleads his own case to be assigned to the Tuscan depots, to be the first to arrive, to set guards, to take any measures for safekeeping.

"Maybe we should invite the commanding officers to come see for themselves," I suggest.

"Good idea!" Captain Foster says. Soon enough, our telegram prompts the arrival of a string of guests at Santa Lucia. General Alexander, driving his own open jeep, comes to see us, and leaves promising to do everything in his power to help the American Monuments officers. Our friends from the British press camp return, as well as an English lieutenant general who brings us a new set of guards after sending the Indian unit closer to Florence.

Captain Foster and I lead each new visitor around the villa to show them these masterpieces, just a small fraction of the Tuscan collections' treasures. Foster's enthusiasm never wanes no matter how many times he points out that Botticelli has painted a landscape as lush as a tapestry in his *Primavera*, and that art historians have identified dozens of plant species in the picture, how certainly it was made for the Medici family but the allegorical meaning remains somewhat mysterious. He explains how Giotto was the father of the Italian Renaissance, how his *Madonna* stands at the fulcrum of the medieval world and the modern one. He knows details of each artist's life, so much that you believe he either knew them in person or made them up. I find myself stopping my shorthand to just listen, to see, enraptured by the stories in the pictures. Two hours pass as if five minutes.

One afternoon, I find Captain Foster sitting at the iron table on the upper terrace, sketching the outline of Botticelli's *Enthroned Madonna* from memory. With just a few strokes of his pencil, he's captured the tilt of her head and the Christ Child's outstretched hands.

"That's lovely," I say. "You're good!"

"Thanks," he says sheepishly, then folds it.

"Who are you sending it to?"

"Helen. My wife."

The small mention of home is like a knife-wrench to my gut. I've been so immersed in the discovery of the paintings that my ma and her cancer have retreated again to the shadowy corners of my mind. Captain Foster—all of us—have left loved ones back home, fending for themselves while we battle our way forward, doing this work that feels so important yet so difficult to explain to those who might struggle to understand how we have left them to continue on without us.

• • •

I don't understand how, but the partisans know where to find us. From a second-story window, I see the small group of men in their black clothes and rifles walking up the steep stairway to the villa's great wooden doors. I recognize their leader, Corrado Innocenti, at the front of the group. I smooth my skirt and quickly apply some lipstick before heading downstairs.

I find them settled on the terrace in the midday heat while Signora Donati, our now beloved cook and her feline and goose assistants, bring us small cups of thick espresso. As I arrive, the *partigiani* are recounting to Captain Foster a horrible story of a massacre in Piazza Tasso, the heart of the Oltrarno district of Florence.

"Four men and an eight-year-old boy," Corrado says. "Gone." His face is drawn, his eyes ringed with darkness. "I don't believe they were targeting any specific person," he says. "The *tedeschi* just drove through the square with their machine guns and cut down anyone they saw. They seem to know now that our groups are clustered on the south side of the river. A message for everyone in the quarter.

"We got a little more information about the works of art," he continues. Foster and I both lean forward. "It seems that the Germans and the superintendents were able to bring some of the works of art back to the Uffizi and the Pitti in recent weeks," he says. "The doors to the Baptistery are stored in the upper floors of the Pitti Palace," he says. "They were hiding in a train tunnel. But I understand there are many more works still in the countryside. I'm sorry. I wish I could tell you more."

The men stay for the afternoon, and Captain Foster takes them on his usual tour of his beloved pictures. This time he recounts the stories in Italian, and I follow along, learning more words each day. When we reach Ghirlandaio's circular *Adoration*, I ask Captain Foster to tell the men the story of how the Germans used it as a tabletop. But I ask it in halting Italian.

Corrado's thick eyebrows fly up. "You've been keeping a secret from us, Signorina Evans!" he says in Italian. "Your *italiano* is good."

"No it's not," I say in English. I feel heat rush to my cheeks.

"*Ma dai*," he says, then gives me a lovely smile that makes dimples emerge on his tanned cheeks.

"You can call me Mouse," I say. "Everyone does." For a fleeting second, I am back on the school playground in New Haven, bouncing my rubber ball away from the cluster of kids talking about what their fathers do for a living.

"Signorina Topolina!" he exclaims, and the rhyming, singsong tone of his voice makes me laugh. "But why? You don't look like a mouse at all to me."

"It's an old name," I say, and for a moment, I imagine old Mouse back there in New Haven, as if I left her on the docks before I steamed across the ocean.

We say goodbye on the front stairs of the villa. The men promise to keep us abreast of what news they can from Florence.

Captain Foster shakes Corrado's hand. "Thank you. Every morning, I awake with the hope we will get into the city at last."

But the Germans hold Florence and we stay at Santa Lucia for weeks.

17

EVA

THEY DON'T SEND ME HOME TO AUSTRIA, OR EVEN to Germany.

Instead, to my utter surprise and nervous relief, as much as I wanted to weasel out from under his penetrating gaze, Colonel Langsdorff has taken note of me and has asked me to stay in Florence. He's asked Horst as well. The two of us are the last of the institute's staff to remain in Florence. We will move out of the Palazzo Guadagni, out from the duties of the Kunshistorisches Institut. We will transfer to the payroll of the Kunstschutz, I as a press photographer and Horst as a press officer.

I'll be the last thing my father wished me to be. A journalist.

"Your pictures will be valuable to show what we are doing to preserve the city and on the other side, what damage the Allies have caused," Professor Heydenreich tells us before he gets into a Mercedes that pulls up in front of Palazzo Guadagni. The train lines cut, he will relocate to the German Institute in Milan by car. "They need stories from Florence for German radio and newspapers."

I open the creaking doors to the wooden armoire at the top of the stairs in the sisters' *pensione*. Palazzo Guadagni has been my home in Florence. I feel a sense of profound regret and nostalgia as I unload my cameras, film, and tripods from the armoire. I pack up my meager belongings in the tiny, monkish room and my darkroom supplies in the dusty, cold wine cellar. I say goodbye to the Bandini sisters. The oldest one nods, broom in hand, as we leave the empty building behind.

The Kunstschutz has granted us a vehicle, an old Kübelwagen with rusted fenders. Horst fills its little space. He rolls up in front of the Palazzo Guadagni and loads my suitcase and photography bags into the back. "Hop in," he says, baring his silly smile, seemingly giddy at the prospect of escorting a lady across town. Slowly, we make our way through the hot, deserted streets. It's the first time I've seen Florence as a passenger in a vehicle. We cross the Ponte Santa Trinità and I feel as if we have traveled to another city altogether.

Ahead of us, in the Piazza Ognissanti, stands the Hotel Excelsior, a grand, elegant nineteenth-century mansion with an imposing façade lining an expansive, empty square with a view over the Arno and the Ponte Vecchio beyond. The new Nazi headquarters in Florence. Horst lugs our suitcases through the front doors and into a lobby covered in patterned marble floors. I follow behind with my camera bags. Through copper-colored marble columns, the hotel bar hangs heavy with smoke, conversation, and clinking glasses from two dozen men in SS uniforms sitting in plush chairs. Behind the reception desk is a grand salon with a stained glass ceiling and a broad, sweeping staircase.

"Signorina?" A bellman, short and neat in his uniform, his too-large hat askew, hands me a room key attached to a heavy brass fob. Then he gives me a nearly weightless envelope with Austrian stamps, addressed in care of the Kunstschutz, Florence. "Your room is ready. And there is a letter waiting for you."

Dear Eva,

Father and Oma didn't want me to write to you, but I thought it only fair that you should know. I got my conscription papers.
I'm leaving from Salzburg soon.

Please don't worry about me. We both know it was inevitable.
I would like to send you a list of everything we are holding, well,
you know where. But if I did, this letter might never reach you.
I will try to write to you from my new location.

Your brother,
Gerhard

One afternoon, in a street near her family's tailor shop, Paloma appears with a long loaf of bread sticking out of a small sack. I am relieved to see a familiar face. "Where's Enzo?" Immediately I regret these first words out of my mouth. I should have told her the truth, that it is a relief to see her smiling, familiar face in a city that's become oppressive and desolate in recent weeks. That she's the closest thing I have to a female friend here. That she's the one person I feel I could share news and sadness of my brother without appearing weak. She seems to understand the unshakable bonds of family, after all.

She only shrugs. "*Caffè*?" she says, with the now-familiar hand gesture that looks like lifting a small cup with the pinkie finger outstretched. We duck into a quiet bar, where the solemn-faced barman fires up his machine and clinks two small cups in front of us while I lay our list of buildings on the bar. I tell Paloma about how Horst and I have spent the past weeks—ever since we moved from Palazzo Guadagni to the Hotel Excelsior—with maps and a growing list of historic buildings that have sustained damage from the Allied raids. Horst with his notebooks and I with my camera, we compile detailed reports of the damage to feed to the German-language newspapers and radio. As Paloma listens to my story, her face grows shadowed and grave.

When I finish my story, she asks, "Something else bothering you?" She stirs a heaping spoonful of sugar into her thick espresso.

"It's my brother," I say, letting out the breath I didn't know I was holding. "I thought I could protect him from being sent into battle, but he got his conscription papers anyway. He's seventeen."

Paloma reaches out and squeezes my shoulder as if I am one of her nieces.

A small gesture, but it brings me comfort. Throughout the months in Florence, with all its beautiful and harrowing moments, Paloma has been a fellow woman on a mission to do the right thing: to protect the monuments and works of art under our care.

But she sips her coffee and says nothing, only looks out the bar window to the otherwise deserted street.

The Kunstschutz has arranged to have my photos developed at a local photography studio run by Blackshirts. I hand off my rolls of film at the end of each day to a stern-looking woman at the counter. I could do a better job with the processing myself, but what choice do I have? My makeshift darkroom in the old wine cellar at Palazzo Guadagni seems far away now. A few days later, I pick up the prints and bring them back to my luxurious hotel room, with its thick rug, soft bed, and ponderous drapes. I lay the prints out on my silky bedspread and decide which ones I will bring to the censor.

Every few days, I meet Colonel Langsdorff's censor in the bar of the Hotel Excelsior. The barman, neat in his white jacket, pours us a Negroni the color of blood. I watch the skinny censor peer through thick eyeglasses and run his claw-like fingers over the photographs. He examines my pictures of crumbled walls, toppled Madonnas, scattered debris, and the many notices Enzo has nailed on doors across the city. He considers each image, then sets aside the ones that tell the most brutal story. He puts them together with Horst's carefully edited press releases. Later, Horst and I will gather with the SS officers around the wireless in the hotel bar and listen to our news from Florence on the nightly German broadcast.

It is strange, I think. We began as photographers, as art historians, as people concerned with the preservation of all that is important to the cultural history of humanity. And yet we have become war correspondents instead, because art has somehow become the center of this war.

"Very well," the censor says, regarding me through his glasses, as thick as the bottoms of the liquor bottles lined up in rows behind the barman. "Colonel Langsdorff is arriving in Florence this evening. I'm sure he will want to review the reports."

As evening falls, I step out of my plush hotel room onto the narrow balcony. I raise the small Leica to my face but it's impossible to capture in black and white the shades of gold, umber, and green that fall on the shimmering waters of the Arno, with its medieval tower houses and the colorful expanse of the Ponte Vecchio.

I hear a shifting, shuffling nearby. I feel the tiny hairs on the back of my neck prickle and rise, the same as they did that day when we removed Ghiberti's doors from the dark train tunnel. As if I've just been locked in the sights of a weapon I cannot see, can only sense from a distance. Slowly, I turn my head to see Colonel Langsdorff leaning over an adjacent balcony. From the plush hotel room right next to mine, he, too, is regarding the spectacular sight of the Golden Hour making its nightly pass over the riverside vista. His profile is visible as a dark silhouette with slick hair and a hooked nose, a shadow framed by the gilded light.

Langsdorff turns his head, and I recoil. As imperceptibly as possible, I back into my room and close the doors, turning the latch. I close the heavy curtains against the brilliant golden light, casting the room into darkness and stifling air.

The next day, I arrive at the hotel bar to meet the censor, only to find a contingent of Horst, other Germans, and Italian superintendents in-

cluding Signor Poggi from the Uffizi. In their midst is Colonel Langsdorff himself, hard-looking in his uniform hanging with medals.

Before I can slip away unnoticed, Langsdorff catches my eye.

"Join us, Fräulein Brunner," he says.

The men are already full of drinks and cigarettes. And yet, the
atmosphere is no longer jovial. A tense feeling hangs in the air, as
if trapped in the cloud of cigarette smoke that materializes over the
group. Reluctantly, I slide into a slippery leather chair and unloop
the camera strap from my neck.

Poggi looks agitated. "With all due respect, Colonel, we couldn't
return the works from the countryside depots back to Florence at
this point, even if we wanted to. Your lieutenants have made it clear
that they can't provide trucks or gasoline. And as you know, it has
been many months since the Fascist government has provided us
with anything at all." He scratches his bald head.

"Of course," Langsdorff says, slickly. "All our resources are needed
at the front lines now. I'm sure you understand."

"But sir," Poggi says, "someone from your Kommandantur called
me and asked if there were any important works in the depot at
Montagnana. I told him yes, there were many important works—
you know yourself we moved a significant number of pictures there.
Works by Caravaggio, Bronzino . . . I feel certain that he intended
to take the rest of the pictures somewhere in northern Italy—outside
the bounds of Tuscany." Under the raking light of the Belle Époque
fixtures in the bar, I see small beads of sweat have formed across
Poggi's forehead.

"I see," says Colonel Langsdorff, who, by contrast, appears calm
and coldly self-assured, observing everyone else at the table with an
icy, intelligent gaze. "No one from my office agreed for the works to
leave. All of us thought they would be safer in the Tuscan depots or
returning to Florence."

"Good," Poggi says, and I see relief wash over him as he leans back

in his chair. "Yes. I reminded the kind counselor of the agreements between your office and the General Direction of Fine Arts, that nothing
was to be removed from the deposits except in the case of dire danger."
He becomes agitated again. "I said we would accept their assistance if
they intended to move the works back to Florence. But nowhere else.
And certainly not northward of the Apennines. That's why I immediately informed General Consul Wolff about this."

"Yes, of course," Langsdorff says. "You were right to do so. And
that's why Wolff asked me to come. You have our assurance. We
agree that nothing more should be removed from the countryside
depots. We have no intention of taking anything to northern Italy."

"Thank you, sir," Poggi says, rubbing his sweaty forehead with a
bar napkin.

"Very good," Langsdorff says, standing. All the others follow suit,
crushing out cigarette butts and taking a last swill of their glasses.
"You will provide me with an updated inventory of everything at
Montagnana and the other Tuscan depots. I will take personal responsibility for them."

The men shake hands. Seeing an opportunity, I frame Langsdorff
and Poggi in the viewfinder, clasping palms, but the censor extends
his arm in front of my camera. "No pictures."

As soon as the Italians leave, I find Horst in the stairwell, observing his bulky frame in an ornate mirror.

"Horst," I whisper, "you know damn well some of those pictures
have already left the repositories."

He remains silent. Pensive.

"And you've already seen the order from the Fascist ministry for
all the principal works of art to be transferred to northern Italy—"

He interrupts. "And that's why General Wolff insisted Langsdorff
come down from Verona," he whispers, "to sort out this mess."

"Then why did he tell Poggi those works are still in the depots?
You know he is lying."

I begin to suggest we should tell Poggi and the other Italians, but I take a deep breath and think better of it. It might put them at risk and I don't want to be responsible for endangering our Italian colleagues after everything we have done to work together so far. But in spite of Langsdorff's assurances, the meeting has set me on edge. Something in the balance of power has shifted, but what it is remains as smoky, as obfuscated as the cloud of cigar smoke that hangs in the hotel bar. I take a deep breath and resolve to wait before saying something that might put our Italian friends—or myself—at risk.

Less than a year ago, I stepped out of the Santa Maria Novella train station and found a city full of life. The sound of the melodious Italian language filled the streets. Butchers, hat makers, leather artisans, and grocers lined the streets, continuing the trades of their ancestors. The streets were filled with people on foot, bicycles, horses and buggies, tiny cars. You couldn't get lost; just follow the flow of the Arno or look for the dome of the cathedral through a slit between the buildings, a giant terracotta egg in the sky. At any time, you could step into a doorway for a coffee or a plate of pasta, joining people living a vibrant life even as war raged around the globe.

But now, as I walk through the vacant alleys near the Duomo with my Leica around my neck, I find all the windows shuttered or covered in fluttering black drapes. The inhabitants have either fled the city for the countryside or are battened down inside, ducking away from the oppressive heat, hiding from view of the German soldiers patrolling the streets, ducking from the putter of a German motorcycle, the clatter of a Kübelwagen with small swastika flags flapping from its hood. The soldiers move through the empty streets, watching for anything out of order, scanning the upper floors of the centuries-old *palazzi* for partisan meetings or snipers. Now you can taste fear in the air. German soldiers have begun to post edicts on all the doors. No one is allowed in the buildings along the river. Women and children have to show a pass to leave their houses once a day to seek food. But there isn't any. Many of the stores are shuttered, their owners having fled to the countryside.

In a few months, Florence seems to have lost its very essence, its soul. A tense, oppressive atmosphere mingles with the summer heat. Something looming and unknowable feels upon us, just out of reach, like a predator waiting in the tall grass.

I cross an empty Piazza della Signoria, where months ago, the tall, skinny watchtower seemed the embodiment of Florentine defiance, independence, and strength. Snaking toward the hotel, I find warnings and directives, written in Italian language with German script, posted on the doors, admonishing people to stay in their homes.

At the Hotel Excelsior, a Red Cross ambulance is standing at the front door. It seems out of place in a square full of sleek Mercedes sedans for transporting the officers. I wonder if someone has been injured.

I make my way up the grand staircase to my room facing the river. Turning into the corridor, I hesitate. The door to Colonel Langsdorff's hotel room is open, and two bellmen are hefting tall, rectangular packages wrapped in paper, the height of a man.

Paintings.

I move past them quickly, not wishing to draw Langsdorff's attention. I turn the key to my room and dart inside. The air is stifling, the heavy drapes blocking the light. I cross the room and turn the bolt of the enormous balcony door to allow in a waft of air, then dare to poke my head through the opening. The adjacent balcony is quiet, the heavy drapes closed. Against the still, hot air, I strip down to my slip and secure my hair off my neck with a pencil. Then I press my ear to the wall and listen to the bustling, shifting sounds, and the murmur of men's voices in the room next door.

Early the next morning, Horst and I are called to the Piazza San Marco, where we find a convoy of three open-bed trucks loaded with a jumble of wooden crates and paintings. Around the large square, bars and newsstands are battened shut, and all the windows facing the square are shuttered. Several pigeons parade across the cobbles; otherwise, the square is quiet and mercifully cool in the morning air.

We find Signor Poggi pacing the square, watching a small group of Italian laborers and German officers unloading paintings from the trucks. Some of them are unwrapped, open to the elements in the backs of the trucks. "The German consulate asked me to be here," Poggi tells us as we approach; he holds a clipboard with tattered pages marked up in red ink. "They said there was heavy fighting around the depot at Oliveto. They decided to transport everything here at once for safekeeping." He looks haggard and stressed, as if he hasn't slept in days.

We watch the men open the doors to the church of San Marco, an unassuming entrance to a vast medieval monastery, once one of the most important historical institutions in the city. As safe a haven as could be found in Florence. The men unload two dozen crates and a handful of paintings, one by one. I watch two Italian laborers strain under the heft of a large wooden crate. I frame the picture in my viewfinder and take several shots of the men bringing the paintings inside the monastery. It will tell a good story for the press, I think, how the Germans are helping shelter these important treasures in the line of fire.

When I remove the camera from my face, I find Signor Poggi standing next to me, ruffling through his pages. "I don't understand," he says. "The custodian from Oliveto told me that Lucas Cranach's *Adam* and *Eve* were coming to us in the back of an ambulance," he says. "But the panels are not here." He sighs, exasperated, and marches back to a small cluster of Italian laborers, rustling his inventory pages and speaking so rapidly that I can no longer follow the conversation.

I am left standing in the midst of the pigeons, when I remember the ambulance parked outside the Excelsior Hotel.

• • •

The next time I see Signor Poggi, he bursts into the lobby of the Excelsior, where I am sitting with the censor, shuffling through prints showing the men unloading the trucks at the monastery of San Marco.

"But Colonel Langsdorff . . ." I hear Poggi speaking loudly in Italian to the man at the front desk. "He asked me to meet him here. To bring him my inventories . . ." His voice grows more agitated. "He assured me he would help track down everything from Montagnana. And an important pair of panels from Oliveto . . ."

The inside of the hotel lobby is dark and hot. There is no more electricity in the city. At night, we are cast into a darkness like I've never experienced. They say our troops have blown the power plants so the Americans won't be able to do anything if they do make it as far as Florence.

"I am sorry, Signor Poggi," the man at the front desk says, "but Colonel Langsdorff has already checked out of the hotel."

I stand, speechless, as the pieces fall into place in my mind. The Cranachs have left Florence in the back of an ambulance. And now, Colonel Langsdorff has left Florence, too. If there was something I could say to help Signor Poggi, I would say it, but the truth is I have no idea where they have gone. The only certainty is that I was right not to trust the colonel.

There is only one person I can think of who might be able to shed some light on this confusing sequence of events. Paloma. Ever since my arrival in Florence, she has been steady. Reliable. A voice of reason. The closest thing to a friend I have here. If I can find her inside her home at the tailor shop, if I can tell her about the missing works at Montagnana, about the parcels in Langsdorff's hotel room, about the pictures unloaded at San Marco and Poggi's increasing desperation . . . Perhaps she will pour me a coffee, squeeze my shoulder, and tell me everything will be alright. That's all I need right now.

I leave the hotel and walk toward Paloma's family tailor shop, to find new notices posted on the buildings near the river.

INHABITANTS ALONG THE ARNO ARE TO EVACUATE BY 12:00 NOON ON JULY 30, 1944. THE GERMAN COMMAND RECOGNIZES FLORENCE AS AN OPEN CITY, BUT THE ENEMY HAS NOT DECLARED FLORENCE OPEN. THESE MEASURES ARE MEANT TO SPARE CIVILIAN LIVES. THE REMOVAL OF PERSONAL POSSESSIONS IS NOT NECESSARY.

Ahead in the street, there is a nervous flurry of activity as a few haggard residents latch their doors and carry their belongings in loosely tied sacks. A skinny man grasps the hands of two small children. They make their way down the sidewalk in the direction of the Pitti Palace, where thousands of refugees are now huddled within its fortifications.

I find Paloma's family tailor shop. The street is deserted, each door with posted signs. One of the signs has come loose from its doorway, tumbling over the cobblestones. I struggle to recognize which of the shuttered doorways is hers. At last, I find it. Everything is covered up, including the windows. Perhaps I've arrived too late. Perhaps her family has already fled the city. I rap firmly on the metal.

To my surprise, after a few moments, the shutter clatters open. Paloma is standing there, the same as always, neat in a patterned dress. She has let her hair out of its usual bun at the nape of her neck and it falls, dark and lush, around her shoulders.

"Eva!" Her brown eyes grow wide. "What are you doing here?" The words come out in a rush of Italian, then she gathers herself and switches to German. "You need help with something?"

"I . . . I didn't know where else to go . . ."

But I hesitate. Behind her there is a group of men filling the dark space of the tailor shop, their chairs clustered together in a circle. One by one, the men push back their chairs and stand. They are rough and dusty, as if they have been living outside for many weeks. Several rifles are slung across the backs of the chairs on their straps. They are intimidating in their neck scarves, their drawn cheeks. Has Paloma been ambushed by this rough group of men? Is she being held against her will?

"Are you alright?" I whisper. "Do *you* need help?"

But then, one of the men pushes to the front of the group, and I recognize Paloma's brother. Corrado. He's one of them. Corrado is a *partigiano*. One of the Florentines Horst warned me about. Working with the other side. It takes a few moments for the truth to settle, to spread in my mind like spilled honey.

"You . . ." I stare into Paloma's face, seeing her for the first time. "You're helping them!" My eyes flit back and forth between Paloma and the men collecting behind her.

"Eva," she begins, her forehead a mass of lines.

"Oh," I gasp. "Oh!" I back up onto the sidewalk.

"Let me explain," she says. "You know we want to do whatever we can to keep the paintings, the buildings, the other treasures safe. My brother and his friends . . . They are working in a different way than you are, but . . ."

My mind reels, trying to make sense of how different things are than the way I thought. "But I thought . . . I thought you and I were working together. You were helping us at the institute . . . I didn't know . . . Your brother and those men . . . They are in contact with the Americans?"

Paloma hesitates. "The Americans are not going to steal or destroy the paintings. We have the same goal, Eva, just different means. Surely you can see . . . ?"

But I don't see. I only feel a fool for trusting that the Italians would be on our side. For not seeing that Horst was right about them all along.

"And Enzo . . ." I don't know what to ask.

"Enzo is not involved in this," she says. "He . . . he's confused. Wait . . ." She reaches out but I back away from her small hand, away from her doorway. I turn and walk quickly down the sidewalk, away from the tailor shop, my mind reeling. "Eva!" Paloma's voice echoes down the empty street.

As I near the Arno, the pain of loss spreads out like a thick pool in the pit of my stomach. It's not about the art, I realize. It's that I have lost the city I've come to love, along with the one person I thought I could trust. Everything I thought was good and bad, black and white, is all mixed up and nothing was what I thought and I have only myself to blame for being so naïve. I turn out of the dark street and run toward the river.

To my surprise, I find Enzo waiting for me in an alley alongside the Hotel Excelsior. He stands with his back against a stone wall, one knee cocked, smoking a cigarette. Just out of view of the hotel doorman, who doesn't seem to know he's just a few meters away. Nearly invisible in his dark clothing, blending into the shadows.

For a moment, I stop walking. Hesitate. For months, Enzo has been a compelling, if mysterious, presence. One minute there, one minute gone, but a magnetic pull for me all the same. A protective force. A humble carpenter willing to set down his hammer, pick me up, and carry me in his arms like a baby to safety without a moment's hesitation. A man who covered me with his own body as bombs fell from the sky.

Have I got that wrong, too? Have I misunderstood who Enzo is as well? Is he a *partigiano*, just like Paloma's brother and his friends, working silently, furtively, against the Germans, who they pretend to help at the same time? I don't trust myself anymore to recognize the truth. All the same, at the sight of him, I feel the inexorable pull, like a tide to the sands of the beach.

He catches sight of me, drops the butt of his cigarette, and crushes it under the heel of his dusty leather boot.

He walks toward me, his dark eyes glowing. "Take a walk with me, *cara*?"

I am frozen in place. "To where?"

One side of his mouth rises in a half smile. "One of the best places in the city."

I hesitate, but I look at his steady, deep-brown eyes, his sideways grin. He extends his hand. Against my better judgment, I put my hand in his. And I follow.

I walk with Enzo through the dark warren of streets until he unlatches a small, unassuming wooden door and I follow him up a narrow, dark staircase. When we emerge into the light, I am surprised to see that we find ourselves inside the Vasari Corridor, the upper level of the Ponte Vecchio. The long, private passage once allowed the Medici family to pass safely across the river from their residence in the Pitti Palace to their offices in the Uffizi to the north. Afternoon light makes jagged patterns through the broken glass shards. The Arno moves relentlessly below us. It stretches out to the medieval houses along the riverside. From here, there is a view toward the Hotel Excelsior. I can see the balcony of my hotel room, along with dozens of others above and below it.

"*Abbassa la testa!*" he says, pressing my head away from the window. "They will fire on us if they see us on the bridge."

"Who will fire?" I ask, squatting down below the sill. I think of Paloma amid the rough-looking men in the tailor shop and the German patrols on the streets. Germans. Partisans. Blackshirts. I don't know who I'm supposed to fear anymore. Or who to trust.

I follow Enzo's hunched form as we move through the corridor. A pang in my stomach, I look at the empty walls and realize that not long ago, there were dozens of paintings hung along this wall. Self-portraits by Rembrandt, Velazquez, Filippo Lippi. Just a few years ago, Horst followed Hitler and Mussolini on their official visit here. Our Führer looked out the windows of this narrow passage to admire the expanse of the river and the jumbled, singular cityscape of Florence. Resolved to preserve it. Now there are only bare hooks and the sun-burnished rectangular outlines on the wall where the paintings used to hang.

We arrive at the arch of the via de Bardi and look toward the Borgo San Jacopo, on the southern side of the city. Enzo stands now and looks through a window into the heart of the Oltrarno. It's the first time I've been on the south side of the river in weeks, ever since the day we had to leave Palazzo Guadagni and relocate to the Hotel Excelsior. We look down at the medieval houses below us. When I arrived in Florence, the riverbed was lined with a view of medieval houses, their upper floors projecting over the riverbed with the colorful patchwork of centuries of construction. A medieval jumble of windows, shutters, open loggias where people might lean out over the rushing waters of the Arno. Filled with the bustle of humanity over many centuries.

Now the quarter is a maze of no-man's-land, where thirsty, overheated residents make desperate, frantic expeditions to find fresh water amid random bursts of machine-gun and rifle fire from upper windows. If I squinted, I could probably make out the rooftop above my old room at the Palazzo Guadagni, just alongside Santo Spirito, but if I were brave enough to try, I might not reach it. The streets south of the bridge are lost to us. It might as well be the other side of the world. I feel small. Impotent. Powerless against the relentless advance of a tide of events so large it threatens to wash over us and pull us under.

Below the bridge, most of the doors are hanging loose from the hinges or have broken into pieces. Two German soldiers appear in the street below. They walk up to an old wooden door with an iron padlock. The two soldiers bang on the door until the wood splits, opening a large, ragged hole in the ancient boards. Then, the younger, skinny soldier pulls the key on a hand grenade and forces it through the hole. In that moment, I realize the truth: they have already taken everything of value from the houses along the river. I feel a raw lump in the bottom of my stomach. One of the soldiers looks up and I press my back against the wall.

Enzo grasps my hand and pulls me back across the corridor. "We can't stay here," he says. "Come with me."

"Do you know about Paloma?"

Enzo and I sit on the floor in his family's old apartment along the northern edge of the river. The terracotta tiles are cool under the backs of my legs, a welcome respite from the oppressive heat. The building was once a grand, fine residence, I think. Above our heads are a series of beams once brightly painted. The red, green, and gold has faded to a pleasant, dull patina. Once there were rosettes and *putti* flitting among the small, painstakingly painted details.

But the dust-filled apartment looks as if it was abandoned long ago. The only piece of furniture is a narrow cot with a thin mattress, alongside a pile of dusty black clothing and a clutter of Fascist newspapers and pamphlets stacked on the floor. A pair of framed pictures, an unlikely combination of Il Duce and a stern-looking Italian grandmother dressed in black. Along one wall is a stash of German-issue rifles and ammunition that look as if they've been pilfered, collected over weeks. The room smells of must and gun oil.

A sniper's nest.

I push the thought away.

"You know your sister and your cousin Corrado are . . . *partigiani*?"

He shrugs, then gives me the same dimpled smile that pulled at my heartstrings all those months ago. "You have someone in your family who has different ideas than you?" he asks. "Sometimes we don't agree. Doesn't mean we don't love them all the same."

I think back to my Papa and his desire to send Gerhard into battle. "And what about you?" I hesitate, not able to find the words, the question that nothing is as I thought before. "What do you believe?"

"I believe they are wrong to trust the Amer—"

A burst of intense shelling erupts outside. It echoes across the river, seeming to come from the Oltrarno. I move closer to Enzo, our legs touching, our backs against the cool stucco wall. He emanates heat where our legs touch. The back of my neck feels sticky. Another blast. Outside, the Golden Hour begins its dramatic show of color, eternal and relentless in the face of machine gun fire. Yellow light floods the room, making brilliant plays of light and shadow on the faded stucco walls.

"I believe it's not safe for you to be in the streets by yourself," he says, his expression calm and unfazed. "You'll have to stay here." Then I feel his rough hand take mine and he grins.

As darkness falls, Enzo rummages through his pack and produces a stale hunk of bread. He tears it in two and hands it to me. He grabs one of the automatic rifles from his stash and lays it across his lap. We sit in the gathering darkness, eat the stale bread, and listen to the cascading sound of gunfire.

The rattling guns pause for a second, an echoing silence that is palpable and long enough for me to speak. "This is where you've been living?"

He shrugs. "My home. But I haven't spent much time here. I've been out there chasing you instead." A sly grin. The gunfire takes up again, a loud *pop-pop-pop* that fills the night. Enzo lights a candle.

On the floor is a stack of the *Nazione*, the Italian-language news-paper controlled by the German government. I pick up the copy sitting on the top of the stack. There is an article about the ordinance for the evacuation of the area around the bridges. In the flicker of candlelight, I struggle to make my way through the Italian.

The German headquarters wishes to confirm its respon-
sibility for the initiative in having declared Florence an
open city according to international standards, but
although the German side has entirely fulfilled the
agreements of the international conventions, a confir-
mation on the part of the Anglo-Saxons is still lacking.
In other words the enemy has not expressly declared
that he intends on his part to respect Florence as an
open city. Therefore it is not surprising if the German
headquarters suspects a possible enemy action against
the six Florentine bridges, which constitute so many
objectives within the reach of Anglo-Saxon offensive
means. But it is purely a suspicion, and thus a form
of precaution which does not in the least change the
determination of the German headquarters to abide
by the standards of the international conventions up
to now scrupulously respected . . . Evacuation of the
strip of habitations bordering on the Arno means only
the prevention of possible injury to the population in
case the enemy attempts to damage the bridges across
the river.

"Surely the Americans wouldn't really bomb the bridges?" I say
out loud. I can't imagine the Ponte Vecchio or the others crumbling
into the Arno. But Enzo remains silent, watching the windows.

As the shelling stops, Enzo stands and peers down to the deserted
streets below. I stand and join him at the windowsill. I see the advantage of the location now. From here, there is a vista down a long
stretch of the Arno. At the entrance to each bridge, German soldiers
have piled enormous hills of concrete, stone, and rubble to prevent
anyone from crossing.

I look down at a lone man and woman dart across the street.
They don't know we're looking down at them. Still, the woman keeps

looking backward as if she senses she is being watched. There is something spine-tingling about looking down at pedestrians from above, the backs of their necks open to the sky. Is this what Enzo sees when he closes one eye and peers through the scope of his rifle? He could kill them in an instant, I think. Would he do such a thing? Is he so convinced that the Germans will hold Florence that he will take matters into his own hands to help us win? If they cross the bridges, it wouldn't take long for the Allied troops to figure out where the shots came from, to pull us from the nest.

I yank on his sleeve and try to pull him down to the terracotta tiles. "If they see us . . ."

"Come on," he says, pulling me toward the door instead. "Let's go to the roof. We'll be able to see more there."

In the dark corridor, I follow Enzo up a steep metal staircase. He unlatches a hatch in the roof and offers a hand to pull me up to a small, flat area among the lichen-covered tiles. The golden evening light is gone now, and no electricity anywhere in the city. When darkness falls, the night descends like a great predatory bird, covering us with black wings. I can hardly see my hand before my face. Then, the dark cover parts and the southern sky beyond the Palazzo Guadagni flickers with distant bombardments, red and orange flares backlighting the hills of San Miniato and Poggio Imperiale.

When the darkness returns, I feel Enzo's breath at my neck. I close my eyes as a tingle runs through the length of my body. My senses are overcome with a heady mixture of hair cream, cigarettes, and gun oil. I reach for his waist, my hands along the rim of his leather belt.

"You know I have to leave . . . to go north with them . . ." I start, but I hardly know how to finish. For how could we begin to imagine a future together, Enzo and me? I know almost nothing about him. And even if we were not in the middle of a war, what could our life be together? And yet, if there had been no war, I would never have come to Florence, would never have fallen in love with this city, would never have lost my heart to this beautiful, complicated man.

"Come with us" is all that comes out. I run my hand lightly across his jaw, down the side of his neck where a vein pulses. For a moment, I remember how he picked me up like a child and carried me to the Red Cross clinic, whispering to me while I tucked my head into his neck.

But he only inhales and shakes his head. "I will stay and protect my city. Anyone who tries to stop me . . . American. Italian. Whomever. I will shoot them dead."

For a long moment, the heavy truth stretches out between us in the silence. "I have to go," I say finally. I stand brush the dust from my skirt.

"*Lo so. Quando e finito, ritorni cui.* I know," he says, and he looks sadder than ever. "After this is over, you will come back." But for the first time, he doesn't sound so sure of himself.

"I will. I have to. I rubbed the *porcellino*'s snout." I try to smile but I'm afraid it might look like I'm going to cry instead.

I don't have a way to imagine the war being over, or a way back to Florence for me when I leave here. I no longer know the difference between good and bad, black and white. Who is on the right side of history. Who is the enemy. And if it might be me.

All I can do is show Enzo what's in my heart. I put my palms on either side of his stubbled cheeks and kiss him with all the fear and fire within me.

Across the Arno, the sky explodes in a spray of orange flares behind the hills, then blackness envelops it all.

I turn the corner into the square in front of the Hotel Excelsior to find Horst pacing back and forth in front of the door.

"Good Lord, Eva!" He grasps my shoulders with his wide hands as if he will shake some sense into me. "Where have you been? I was about to have to leave this godforsaken place without you."

But I am speechless, still filled with the smell and taste of Enzo, the gun oil, cigarette smoke, and hair cream.

"Never mind. Get in!" he says, pressing a too-large helmet on my head and hurrying toward the Kübelwagen parked in front of the hotel.

I pull myself into the passenger seat with one hand. With the other, I raise my camera on its strap and squint into the viewfinder as the lights of the vehicle cast twin dirty beams through the stark, gray rubble. Horst steers around the debris in the narrow street, heading northward out of the maze of the historic center.

As we move into the wider streets beyond the rail yards, the air is full of fierce bombardment. Whereas the shelling we heard in Enzo's apartment was isolated bursts, now there is shelling without ceasing. It sounds like the whole world is imploding. There is fire, uninterrupted and in increasing intensity. We can hear the whistle and bursts, followed by the night sky lit up like fireworks.

I think of the terrified Italians clustered together in the courtyard of the Pitti Palace. I think of Paloma, her brother Corrado, and the rest of their family shuttered inside their tailor shop.

Horst steers around a burning car on the corner of the street. I try to snap a picture but there is no way to capture the sight. And it is too dark. As we leave the warren of streets toward the hills leading out of the city, there are panzers and lines of military vehicles rushing out of Florence in a stream of grinding engines. All I can see in the flashing orange light is helmeted heads—and us, open to the night sky, the wind whipping my hair against my cheeks.

I turn and press my camera to my eye again, trying to steady my hand. A loud whistle and a streak of smoke. Behind us, smoke rises into the night sky. There is a great flash and flare of light backlighting the hills as we speed northward.

And then, the unthinkable. The thing men on all sides have been trying to prevent for months, the thing that no amount of paperwork and negotiation could stop. Great plumes of ash explode in a series of spectacular blasts, lighting up the night sky. Then, in the darkness that follows, we hear the terrible crash of the piers and bridges of Florence as they crumble and collapse into the Arno.

Part II

AFTER

SUMMER 1944–SUMMER 1945

. . . in the still feeble light of the early morning, I saw the massacre of my Florence.

—UGO PROCACCI, FLORENTINE ART HISTORIAN

18

JOSIE

❦

Dear Mother,

I am sorry for not writing more often. But it is difficult for me to put all of this into words. I have been lucky enough to see so many famous paintings and sculptures here in Italy. I have even touched them with my own hands.

The Italians see these masterpieces as symbols of their own heritage. They work so hard to preserve them because their sense of identity and culture is closely tied to these old paintings. If they were destroyed, they could never be replaced.

Hopefully we will get into Florence soon. I have heard so much about its beautiful monuments and bridges. I'm enclosing a booklet about it. Maybe it will help you see it—if only a little bit—in your mind.

I miss you.

Your Josephine

P.S. You won't believe it, but Dot Nichols is in love with a plumber's son from Buffalo. Keep it to yourself.

• • •

On the broad, high terrace at Santa Lucia, we welcome our latest string of visitors. The crisp morning air has given way to the kind of heat that prickles the skin. The cicadas are already broadcasting their heady vibrato as we spoon the froth from our coffee cups and Signora Donati hums a little tune to her cat, who follows her, tail high.

"This is what we've been waiting for—for months." Captain Foster is clean-shaven but his face is a picture of tired, drawn concentration. He hands me a sheaf of rumpled papers, and I recognize immediately that it's an inventory of works of art. Handwritten.

Across the table, two Tuscan superintendents stir sugar into their cappuccino, their tiny spoons dinging against the cups. "To the best of our ability, this is what we believe is in each of our repositories," one of the men says. I squint at the quick, slanted, looping handwriting marked up with red ink, circles, and abbreviations in another hand. *Raffaello. Tiziano. Murillo. Tintoretto . . .* The words blur and repeat, a mass of ink. A story of priceless treasure. Of fear. Of determination and desperate action. I'm certain it will be my job to transcribe everything, but I worry I won't be able to piece it all together.

The sun sends golden streaks over the view of distant hills and farms. It's no wonder the Germans wanted to requisition this villa. They could see the Allies coming from this high terrace overlooking the southern countryside. But now, from here, we see only beauty. Peace. We can't see the crumbled village bridges and walls, the buildings with their black windows as hollow as eye sockets in a skull. The roofs open to the blue sky. We can't see the aimless sheep or the desperate mothers and children, cranking the well in the lower level of this very villa, eking out another day until this is all over and they can go back to their own villages.

One of the Italian men gestures to the dozen or so rumpled pages in my hands, a long list of handwritten works of art. "That's the official inventory," he says. "We haven't listed out each piece from the Bargello. It's more important that we protect it as a collection, you understand. Not just as a list of individual objects."

For the two superintendents and the other Italians, of course, none of the masterpieces in the countryside repositories is a discovery. They've known where the works were from the start. They hid them themselves over the course of just a few, frantic weeks when it seemed the world was about to come apart at the seams. Now their precious belongings are scattered across a battered patchwork of cratered roads, abandoned villas, and long stretches of unknown. They're not sure anything is where it's supposed to be anymore, after four years of hiding, four years of shifting loyalties. They are a haggard, exhausted picture of what it's like to be stuck in the middle of an impossible situation.

As the weeks unfold at Santa Lucia, more military officers and art professionals come to the villa, lured by the story of the incredible sight of these priceless works—the whole history of Italian art, Captain Foster says—hidden away in its rooms. Several Monuments officers assigned to other regions come to stay for a week or longer. British and American expatriate artists come to see us, telling us how they've been evading the Fascist edicts by staying with partisan friends in the countryside. For so many months before his arrival in Tuscany, Captain Foster has worked alone, with no resources. He's admitted to me that he's flattered but a bit overwhelmed to have so much attention now.

To accommodate the string of visitors, two of the refugee women from the wine cellars are hired as housekeepers. They dust the shutters and shake out bedding from the upper windows. Dinners become huge affairs, with more women corralled to bring us simple yet delicious plates of pasta, small sausages, and countless Chianti bottles, promptly emptied. Little by little, I watch the introverted, reserved Captain Foster begin to relax into this role as esteemed host with special knowledge of Italian art and its wartime status. Over dinner, we share our discoveries.

"We found several giant altarpieces stored in a wine cellar," I tell them. "Piled against the damp and moldy casks. The Italian laborers worked all day to move everything upstairs to a safe room that could be locked."

"Yes, pictures from the Horne Foundation, and Filippo Lippi's *Annunciation* from San Lorenzo," Captain Foster says. "We found a crucifix by Cimabue leaning on a wine cask. But at least they were accounted for—and safe."

We tell our visitors about the ancient sculptures—once the prized possessions of the Medici—we found in a hiding place at Torre del Castellano. We tell them that at the sleepy Villa La Torre a Cona, among intense shellfire, we found Michelangelo's enormous sculptures for the Medici tombs in the church of San Lorenzo, and colossal prophets by Donatello from the *campanile* of the Duomo. How we unlatched cases of documents and small bronzes that came from Michelangelo's own house. Plus more than sixty paintings from the Uffizi, including the famed *Portinari Altarpiece* and Perugino's *Assumption*. All undamaged.

Our relief at finding these treasures safe is tempered by the recent news from Pisa. A telegram from Captain Thomas tells us that an Allied air raid there started a fire near the Leaning Tower in the historic Campsanto, which burned for three days, causing the timber and lead roof to collapse. The disaster destroyed most of the sculptures and sarcophagi, and melted important Renaissance frescoes beyond saving.

"We have posted one Allied official and one Italian official at each of the depots," Captain Foster tells the men at the table. But their concerned expressions lead me to believe they are as worried to have the Allies in charge of their precious heritage as the Germans.

The terrace double doors open and Signora Donati escorts Nigel, one of the BBC journalists I recognize from the press camp. His footsteps crunch over the gravel as he approaches our table. He is sweating in his shirt and tie.

"Sir," he says, removing his hat and shaking Captain Foster's hand.

"*Capuccio*?" Signora Donati asks, but he waves her away.

Captain Foster invites Nigel to sit but he is visibly agitated. He walks to the stone railing of the balcony and lights a cigarette instead, then squints at us as beads of moisture collect on his forehead. "The New Zealand units have entered the section of Florence on the south bank of the Arno," he says, running his palm over his forehead.

Captain Foster pushes back his chair and comes to stand next to Nigel at the balcony. I collect the pages of our inventories under our coffee cups so they don't blow away.

"They are in their positions," he continues, gesturing with his cigarette over the stone parapet, "looking across the river to the Huns on the other side. Fierce machine-gun fighting from bank to bank."

"At last!" Captain Foster huffs, and a grin breaks across his face. "Surely it won't be long now."

But I can see that there is more to the story. The Tuscan superintendents seem to sense it, too, each of them pushing back their chairs and standing.

"Nigel," I say. "What is it?"

He looks at me, taking a deep drag on his cigarette and then flicking the short butt over the railing as he lets out a stream of smoke. He then sets his sights on Captain Foster. "They did it, Captain. The Nazis. They destroyed all the bridges of Florence. Those bridges are gone, sir."

Foster's face turns as white as a sheet as a long moment stretches out, with only the sound of distant birdsong. "No." It comes out as a whisper.

"All but the Ponte Vecchio, sir. Those bridges, they are . . . in the river."

For what seems an eternity, Captain Foster stands there, silent, staring blankly over the ripple of green hills. Not seeing. Nigel strikes a match to light another cigarette, trying to steady his hand.

I watch Captain Foster's face turn in an instant; rage, despair,

confusion, all there at once. After a long moment, he makes an an-
guished cry, then leans over the parapet and retches dripping coffee
into the ravine below.

As our soldiers draw ever closer to liberating Florence, our WAC unit
moves to a camp in the hills just beyond view of the city. Captain
Foster and I remain silent as we drive out from Santa Lucia, winding
along a hilltop overlooking a deep and verdant Tuscan valley, with
views of lone farms with stone buildings stretching out toward the
horizon. The hot air smells of grass, dirt, and cooking apples. I don't
know what to say to Captain Foster, who steers Georgette along rutted roads, his face etched with grief as if he has lost beloved friends
rather than bridges.

I am filled with relief to reconvene with my friends at camp. In
contrast to the temporary bivouac camps we've set up all the way
from Naples, it feels like we may settle for a while. The men have set
up their tents in a neat line. The sound of clattering pots and pans
comes from the mess tent, and my mouth waters to think that today
I might taste one of Lollie Dee's delicious concoctions.

Captain Foster leaves Georgette parked sideways in the dirt, and
hurries off to brief the commanding officers about what we have
found, and no doubt to plead his case for us to go into Florence as
soon as possible. And for him to stand and accept the terrible reality
that the historic bridges are gone.

Outside the WAC tent, I find the familiar trench latrines and a
long line of drying laundry. The sun shines through an opening in
the canvas, creating a long streak of light across the women's cots.
The camp feels welcoming and safe, like a secure room away from the
heat of the battle. It feels like home.

I duck under the tent flat to find Dot and Big Nellie unpacking
their barracks bags under the ceiling of thick, green canvas. From behind, I embrace Big Nellie in all her glorious bulk. "Hello, stranger."

To my surprise, she hugs me back, her abrasive New England demeanor softening for a moment before she bristles again. "Your perverted Monuments Man is back," she says in a low voice.

In the distance, I see the cluster of armored trucks. I recognize Captain Thomas's stout frame emerging from the passenger side of a troop transport vehicle. He hikes up his canvas trousers and trudges up the hill, greeting each man, who treats him like a long-awaited Hollywood star with a witty turn of phrase, a vigorous handshake, and a slap on the back.

"I don't care if you're in charge." Captain Foster's voice rises to a higher pitch, agitated.

I peer around the tent flap to see Captain Foster with his arm protectively around a tin cup of coffee, as if he expects Captain Thomas to take it from him. On the table between the two men, a map of central Italy lies open. Lollie Dee, suntanned and healthy-looking in a soldier's shirt knotted at her waist, is handing improvised yet delicious homemade cookies to the men and women sitting in the tent.

"I understand that Florence has now reverted from the Eighth to the Fifth Army and comes under your jurisdiction. I accept that," Captain Foster says. "But no one can argue that one single MFAA officer could preside over a cultural heritage as immense as Florence and all of Tuscany. You know that better than anyone, Rand."

"Look. Don't snap your cap," Captain Thomas says, leaning forward over the table as if he would just as soon arm wrestle skinny Captain Foster as negotiate with him. No doubt he would win any physical contest. But Captain Thomas seems to sense he might lose a battle of wits. "So we work out an arrangement."

"Yes," Captain Foster says. "We work out an arrangement between the Eighth and Fifth Armies. You can be responsible for the western Tuscan provinces—Grosseto, Pisa, and Livorno." He taps his index finger on the map sitting in the middle of the table. "I'll take responsibility for the three eastern provinces—Florence, Siena, and Arezzo."

For a moment, Captain Thomas runs his thick palm over his razor stubble. Perhaps he's trying to discern whether he's missing something, or being tricked. I know from the hours poring over the guidebooks that the eastern provinces of Tuscany hold many times more masterpieces than the west, and that Captain Foster wants to be the first Monuments officer into Florence more than life itself.

Finally, Captain Thomas says, "I might be able to live with that, but—"

"Done!" Captain Foster says, spreading his arms wide. A stupid grin crosses his face.

Captain Thomas spies me standing in the shadows. "Evans!" I feel his eyes scan me from head to toe. "This brownnose hasn't run you off yet?"

"Sir." I salute him. He stands and grasps my arm, then puckers his lips and kisses my neck, cold and wet. "Been a long time, cheesecake." I recoil but he only returns to his seat. "There." He turns his attention back to Captain Foster. "You got your precious Florence and Tuscany. You happy? The rest of us will fan out across the peninsula," he says, waving his hand as if shooing a fly. "But you report to me." Then, he gestures in my direction. "And I want her."

I feel my heart plummet to my shoes. For the first time, I realize I want to go to Florence almost as badly as Captain Foster does. And I don't want to spend who knows how many more months with a man who feels entitled enough to kiss my neck without asking.

"Wait!" I cry. "Captain Foster and I have been working through the Tuscan depots for weeks now. We—"

Captain Foster raises his lean hand, interrupts me. "I'll make you a deal, Thomas," he says, setting his jaw and leaning across the table. "I'll agree to report to you. That's already a sacrifice on my part. But in return, Miss Evans stays with me."

Captain Thomas looks me up and down for a long minute. "Jeez, you want it all. Alright. You got yourself a deal." The men shake hands and Captain Foster smiles at last. Captain Foster seems to realize he got the better end of things, but still, he reports to Captain Thomas. I think they are both satisfied.

Lollie Dee walks up beside me and squeezes my hand.

"Thank you, Jesus," I whisper, and she stifles a laugh behind her hand as I wipe the sloppy, unbidden kiss from my neck.

Captain Thomas jabs me gently with his elbow as he passes by. "Thinks he's the biggest toad in the puddle, don't he?" he says.

Of course I am relieved to be able to stay with Captain Foster. And I am eager for the chance to be the first into Florence, to see the restitution of all the works of art we've uncovered in the countryside over the past weeks.

Crisis averted, I grasp Lollie Dee's hand and pull her through the tent flap and outside, into the hot air. "Are you alright?" I whisper.

She nods and squeezes my arm. "I'm not in a family way, if that's what you mean," she says. "Thank heavens. I might'a been, but I ain't now. Not anymore."

I give her a tight hug. "I'm sorry, Lollie Dee."

For a second, her eyes well with tears, but she shakes her head and collects herself. "It's for the best," she says. I know firsthand what life as an unwed mother is like, and I feel relief that Lollie Dee won't have to endure the same fate as my ma.

Then I see a group of partisans—including Corrado Innocenti, neat and beautiful in his black shirt and slacks, an American rifle slung over his back—walking up the hill.

"Look at that," Lollie Dee says, and my face turns hot in the blinding sun.

As much as I am happy to reconnect with my friends, I am happier to see that the partisans have returned. Our commander orders Lollie Dee to set aside some rations for the partisan men who have collected on the edge of camp, smoking hand-rolled cigarettes, looking elegant in their shabby clothes.

In the distance, I see Corrado sitting on the edge with his meal, looking out over the green hills beyond. In the far distance, we see a village constructed of brown bricks, a short jumble of rugged towers, as if they have clung to these hillsides forever and will again forevermore.

"Sit with us, Mouse!" Ruby waves me over from a temporary table.

"I'll join you later," I say.

I find Corrado picking over the metal tin as if he's never seen such a thing.

"*Posso?*" I say. May I? Such a useful Italian expression to have learned.

Corrado's cheeks are full of the bland rations and so he says nothing, only pats the ground beside him. I lower myself, careful to tuck my skirt under me as I sit on the hard-packed earth.

"*Cucina bruta*," he says, gesturing to the tin. But I see he's nearly finished it.

"Yes." I laugh. "Ugly food. I suppose it's *very* ugly compared with what you're accustomed to eating." I think about the wonderful homemade meals we've enjoyed on the terrace at Santa Lucia, and I feel sorry for my friends who have subsisted on this camp food in the bivouacs through the muddy, cold months.

For a moment, the two of us eat in silence, watching the shifting shadows of the thin cypresses and the silvery, shimmering olive trees.

"Tell me. How did you get involved with . . . this?" I gesture to the cluster of men, somehow ragged and elegant at the same time in their dark clothes, seated on a nearby rise. "With them."

"A long story," he says. He shakes his head and abandons the ugly food box to a patch of grass beside him. Then he stares out over the cypresses. "I was in France when the Germans came," he says. "I had my business there, repairing machines in the garment district of Paris. My parents followed me there. There were a lot of jobs for Italians back then, in the factories. But things changed quickly," he says, his face darkening. "One day, they wanted us for cheap labor, but the next day, it seemed, we became their enemies. At first, they just treated us badly but then, the French government made all the Italians leave the country. We came back home. Didn't have much of a choice. I had to walk away from my business there. My parents, too. Lost their livelihoods. We all left France and came back to Florence."

"That's terrible."

He shrugs. "We do what we have to, to get by, no, *Topolina*?"

A tingle, a series of sparks, reaches from the base of my spine to the top of my head to hear my mother's words spoken in Italian.

"I suppose being in France changed the way I looked at things," he continues. "Not long before I left, the Louvre Museum hired me—well, they hired my truck, and therefore me—to drive it. I even saw *La Gioconda* with my own eyes," he says, pointing to his eyes with two fingers in the shape of a V.

"You saw what?"

"A famous portrait of a lady by Leonardo da Vinci," he says. "In the Louvre. I'm sure you've seen a picture of it."

"You mean the *Mona Lisa*?" My eyebrows rise. "You saw the *Mona Lisa*."

"Lisa. *Si. La Gioconda*. She traveled in my truck."

"The *Mona Lisa* traveled in your truck . . ." Surely I've lost the thread of the conversation and have not understood the Italian correctly.

"*Vero*. It's the truth," he says, reading my doubtful expression. "And many other pictures, too." A shadow passes over his face, a fleeting darkness, as if he's watching an old film behind his eyelids. "The people from the Louvre . . . They took everything out of the museum. Enormous pictures. Sculptures. Packed everything up and took it out into the countryside. Just like they did from the Uffizi." He gestures to the hillside, as if we could see the famous Florentine museum all the way from camp.

"Will you go back to France, then, after this is all over?"

He shrugs. "As soon as I got back to Florence, I returned to my family's tailor shop. And then my friends got me involved with the *partigiani*," he says, gesturing to the cluster of men picking curiously at their own metal tins a dozen feet away. "It wasn't hard to convince me, after everything I saw in France. Anyway, they couldn't do without me," he jokes. "*Bene*. I suppose my life is here now."

"And you wanted to help return the famous masterpieces to Florence," I say. All at once, I realize I've been carrying on a perfectly reasonable conversation in Italian.

"Well, some say that a human life is more important to save than some dusty old painting," he says. "But in France, I saw men and women risk their lives so that those works could return for everyone. That's when I realized what it meant. It's more than just saving one picture from damage or destruction. It's about . . . It's about protecting the entirety . . . The integrity of the whole. It means something to people. I don't know. *L'arte* . . . It's not just some dusty object. Somehow it's a living force. It helps us remember who we are."

He catches me staring at him and he smiles. "At least that's what I learned there."

"And so you found us."

He nods. "When I heard about your Capitano Foster, I decided to bring my *ragazzi* out here. I knew the work was important."

I smile back. "Our commander is letting me go to Florence with Captain Foster. There are still several hundred pictures unaccounted for," I say. "We don't know if they are hiding somewhere in another depot, or if they've been stolen or destroyed. And there are probably still a lot of repositories out there full of works of art that we can't get to yet. It's not safe to travel there."

The mess tent flap opens and Captain Foster emerges, along with several other high-ranking officers. He approaches the wall where Corrado and I are sitting.

"News at last!" Captain Foster raises his fists in triumph. "They've given us authorization to drive into Florence in the morning. The commander gave permission for you to come with us, Miss Evans. We leave at Zero Six Hundred."

"I'll be ready."

"*Allora!*" Corrado stands and squeezes Captain Foster's shoulders, as if welcoming an old friend into his home. "*Vi faccio conoscere la mia bella città.*" He will show us his beautiful city. At last, I understand.

From Georgette's hard back seat, I hold on for dear life and admire the undulating landscape of green and gold. The jeep shudders over the scarred roads toward Florence. I watch Corrado's beautiful profile, his broad shoulders, his thick curls blowing in the breeze. Captain Foster chatters away to Corrado in his fluid Italian, filled with nervous energy and anticipation for the long-awaited moment of our arrival in his beloved city. I catch snippets of his conversation at the same time that I inhale Corrado's scent on the air—a combination of shave cream, Tuscan earth, and gun oil.

"Our work is to support the Italian superintendencies," Foster says as he wrangles the steering wheel. "We help them figure out how to repair monuments and works of art that have been damaged, and to return all the works of art from the repositories back to their original places when it's safe. It's very challenging, but we've been doing this all the way up from Sicily."

Before we left camp, our commanders gave us permission to go directly to the Pitti Palace to locate the Italian superintendents of art and historical monuments. Nowhere else. We are expressly forbidden to cross to the north side of the Ponte Vecchio, even if it were physically possible. That area, they tell us, could be retaken by the Germans at any moment. The city is still under heavy bombardment from German positions around Fiesole and shells are still falling on the city. I tighten the strap on my helmet.

"You will see," Corrado says, "once we get to the Pitti Palace. It is not as you may remember, *capitano*. The whole building is a city of refugees, even of the most destitute of Florence's residents," Corrado tells us. "And more people flow in from the countryside every day. They believe they will be protected inside the palace walls. But ever since the night the bridges were destroyed . . . Well, people don't have so much hope anymore."

We enter the outskirts of the city, through the cypresses on the hill at Bellosguardo. All at once, the terracotta cathedral dome—the great Duomo of Florence—appears in the distance. I gasp. As many times as I've read about it, I am not prepared for the sight of the giant dome towering over a city of tiled roofs, with the violet and azure hills beyond. We also catch a glimpse of the dark waters of the Arno snaking through the charred, ruined quaysides. At the sight of this indescribable beauty and brutality, Captain Foster falls silent.

He remains silent as we descend into the edges of the city and enter a section of town that is little more than a warren of streets with wooden doors, either battened shut or busted open to reveal hollow, burned-out homes. The jeep squeezes into a dark cleft of a street.

"The Oltrarno." Corrado turns in his seat toward me. "There are many of us *partigiani* here." The streets are so narrow and the roofs overhang that it's like being in a tunnel, as if you could reach out and touch both sides at once. Above our heads, the sky is barely visible. Through a shredded door or a bombed hole in the wall, we can see what might otherwise be hidden from view: abandoned rooms choked with debris; beloved belongings half-buried in roof tiles; furniture, mirrors, other cherished things shattered beyond repair— everything left behind in a moment of desperate flight.

With a series of vigorous hand gestures and Italian commands, Corrado directs Captain Foster through the complicated web of streets. From behind, I watch him, his elegant profile. His slick, dark curls. His broad shoulders. An innate confidence that commands attention. I feel an immense pull to him, like the ocean tides to the moon.

At last, the dark misery of the Oltrarno's alleys falls away and we emerge into the blazing sun. Before us can only be the Pitti Palace, a vast, stone palace like a mountain face in the middle of the jumbled city. In the half circle in front of its small, arched door, Captain Foster is forced to bring the jeep to a crawl. Already, there are hordes of people. A woman spies the flag on the hood and she cries, "*Americani!*" Everyone cheers and comes running toward us.

We can no longer move forward. We step down from the vehicle into the swarm. A crush of ragged families greets us with such joy as if we were the second coming of Christ. Corrado is swept up in this mass of humanity and I lose sight of him. Captain Foster grasps my hand so we are not separated in this confusion of misery and joy. I feel his lean, bony hand pull mine toward the tiny door in the otherwise impenetrable wall of stone.

The tide of cheering Italians washes us into the vast, open courtyard of the palace. Under the arcades, hundreds of refugees mill around. In a flash, my mind returns to the slums of Naples. They swarm and surge around us like a river around a rock. Children, babies, women, men huddle together with all their belongings in miserable clusters. Sheets and clothing hang from balconies and windows. Tables and small charcoal stoves are set up for pathetic meals. The smell of sweat, excrement, and desperation is overwhelming in the heat. They move to the shadows, away from the punishing sunlight in the center of the courtyard.

"Capitano Foster!" An elegant man in a suit appears from the dark chasm of a stairwell. "We've been waiting for you." Captain Foster gives the man a heartfelt embrace, then I follow them up the staircase.

We follow the man to the upper floors of the palace, where at last we escape the pressing crowds. Captain Foster introduces me to Giovanni Poggi, the director of the Uffizi Galleries, and a mild-mannered Florentine art historian named Ugo Procacci. For the rest of the afternoon, Captain Foster and I are treated like visiting dignitaries. At a conference table in a hall covered in gilded and painted surfaces, the Italians review their full lists of the still-occupied depots. I struggle to keep track on my steno pad as I listen to the fast-moving Italian and long litanies of un-familiar locations.

In turn, the Italians tell us about the challenges in the city. For weeks, they say, there has been no water and no electricity. The hotels have no glass in the windows. The mosquitoes come in clouds from the stagnant Arno. The heat is intense and the air suffocating. The sewer mains and gas mains are all broken. No toilet in the city can be flushed. And there are corpses rotting under the rubble along the Arno.

Worst of all, they tell us, there are Fascist snipers in the windows all over town, who, knowing their time is up, pick off civilians at random. And German batteries continue to shell the town sporadically from the hills of Fiesole to the north.

"Only this side of the Arno has been liberated," Procacci says. "Thankfully, it's in the hands of the partisans at last." I am proud to think that Corrado is one of these *partigiani*. But he has disappeared now and I don't know when he will materialize again.

"I have not seen anything in the city . . . or the bridges," Captain Foster says with some trepidation. Signor Procacci offers to take us on foot. "The best view is from the Vasari Corridor."

Captain Foster gasps. "You can get us into it?"

He nods. "Follow me."

Captain Foster and I follow Procacci back through the misery of the palace courtyard. We continue up a set of terraced steps into the Boboli Gardens behind the complex. I am left to wonder at this paradox of desperate people living on the grounds of the most luxurious palace I've seen since Caserta.

We find Corrado waiting for us under the shade of an arbor, hav-ing reappeared as if by magic, like a prescient tour guide ready to take us to our next stop. "*Signorina Topolina*," he says in a singsong rhyme, breaking into a smile. I feel something like sparks fire inside my chest.

From the rise of the garden, an unobstructed vista of Brunelleschi's gigantic terracotta and stone dome opens up for us. Signor Procacci, Captain Foster, Corrado, and I pause to catch our breath from the climb into the gardens, and to marvel at the view of the cathedral, which, so far, still stands. In the gardens, too, hundreds of refugees have collected, seeking shade from the infernal heat under rows of neatly planted trees and flowering shrubs.

"I've been staying in a few rooms of the Pitti with my wife and children for weeks," Procacci tells us, as we walk across the gardens and toward the river. "Our house is close to the Campo di Marte freight yards and there has been so much shelling there. We had a terrible bombing last year that leveled several buildings and the neighborhood hasn't yet recovered. I feel fortunate that we have a little space compared to the desperate refugees in the courtyard. Every day, we have seen more and more people as the Germans have evacuated more streets around the river."

"You were in the palace the night of the bombing of the bridges?" I ask, struggling to imagine what it must have been like to live through the horror.

"*Si*," he says, his face darkening. "It happened in the middle of the night. All of us in the Palazzo Pitti were huddled together but the bombardments were so loud you could not hear the person next to you." I hang on every word, grasping what I can in Italian. He speaks beautifully and clearly, and I find I can understand him better than the villagers I have encountered south of here. "There in the darkness," he continues, " I felt nothing but desperation, but then, the sound of all that firing brought me hope for the first time. That's because I knew you—the Allies—were coming to help us. And for a moment, I even thought maybe our bridges would be spared. But I was wrong about that."

We fall silent as we continue toward the Ponte Vecchio. We glimpse the other side of the Arno, where the Germans are holding the northern half of the city. As we follow Procacci's hunched shoulders down to the riverside, I catch a glimpse of a building, perhaps a home, just a wall with a window and a balcony, little more than a stage set in a pile of rubble. My heart sinks to imagine that there might have been families hiding inside when the bombs fell.

We emerge into a small piazza with an avalanche of stone, plaster, glass, metal, and brick under the ruin of centuries-old houses, and a toppled ancient column in the center of the square. Corrado opens a small wooden door and we climb a staircase into a second-floor corridor lined with windows whose glass panes are shattered, little more than jagged razors.

Gray dust hangs in the air like a veil. The corridor continues in a long, narrow span over the top of the Ponte Vecchio. Through the busted windows left and right, we begin to get a fuller picture of the wreckage on either side of the bridge. Captain Foster stands before one of the open windows, his arms around his narrow midsection as if he's hugging himself. "There were towers and medieval houses all along the riverside," Captain Foster says, looking out to what appears like a gigantic trash pile spilling into the riverbed. "They used to overhang the river. Balconies, windows. Buildings that dated to the time of Dante." But at once, I see these historic buildings are now a giant sand pile slipping into the slow trickle of green water.

"And surely people, too," I say. One block back from the water's edge, the next row of buildings is little more than a complicated network of ragged, open walls, the remains of rooms, the remains of lives. If anyone was living in these houses along the river, I think, surely they are dead, their bodies floating down the river all the way to Pisa and the sea beyond.

An enormous mountain of rubble, several stories high, has been amassed—probably with tanks—at both the north and south entrances of the Ponte Vecchio, making it impossible to access. I recognize the work of the German soldiers. It's the same pattern they've created as we have battled our way north through the countryside thick with rivers, streams, and ancient thoroughfares. Bridges, exploded and blocked, one by one.

"They destroyed all of this just to block the Ponte Vecchio," Captain Foster says bitterly, looking past the jags of broken glass in the windowpanes. "Just to keep us from crossing it."

"Several dozen medieval houses, a dozen towers. All destroyed," Corrado says. "And even with all this clumsy destruction, they didn't even block the entrance to the bridge completely. Already some of the New Zealanders have moved parts of the avalanche enough for your jeeps to cross."

I look down into the river to see that several ragged-looking Florentines are clambering over the dams of rubble into the riverbed, perhaps desperate to get to the other side, where they may have homes, family members. Desperate to see if any of it remains. The stench is overwhelming, broken sewer lines reeking in the August sun.

I scan buildings left standing and try to imagine the barrel of a shotgun sliding over the top of a windowsill. Are Fascists watching us now from these snipers' nests? The men in the riverbed must certainly be risking their lives.

But Procacci and Foster are looking beyond to the ruins of the other bridges. "You see," Procacci says, "the state of the Ponte Santa Trinità." He gestures toward smashed, stumped piers and fragments of sculpted stone in the muddy riverbed. "The Ammannati bridge was one of the most beautiful and one of the finest examples of an Italian Renaissance bridge." There is no trace of it left.

"Everyone has been stuck in their houses—or wherever they are— for nine days. And no one wants to leave. They might be shot."

"I imagine," Foster says, "they can't get any food. Any water. Or medicine. Must be like living in hell."

"Surely," I say, "we can try to help bring some food or water, or medications, into the city?"

"Yes, we will communicate all this back to our commanders. There will be much to do here. For now," says Captain Foster, "we just need to find the people who can help us figure out where everything from the Florentine museums has been taken."

"I know someone who might be able to give you the information you want," Corrado says. "My sister Paloma has been working for the German art history institute here for years."

Captain Foster's eyebrows fly up in surprise. Then, his grave expression transforms into a wide grin and for the first time since our arrival in the devastation of Florence, I feel a glimmer of hope.

19

EVA

AS DAWN BREAKS OVER THE TUSCAN HILLS, HORST slows the Kübelwagen around a bend in the road. The landscape is still. Quiet. The overnight explosions that shook the city, that collapsed the bridges, have stopped.

During the ride out of Florence and into the black countryside, Horst and I have remained silent. For what words could we possibly find to say to each other? We only keep our eyes forward, tracing the twin beams of the Kübelwagen's headlamps as we move over the hills.

But as the faint light breaks over a hillside, Horst clears his throat and speaks. "The Kunstschutz wants us to inspect the depots we can get to," he says. "Major Reidemeister will be waiting for us at Poggio a Caiano."

"Major Reidemeister . . ."

"He reports to Colonel Langsdorff."

Horst turns into the long gravel lane that leads to the repository of Villa Bossi-Pucci at Montagnana. Everything is still. Quiet. The engine mingles with the first sounds of birdsong. Up ahead, the villa appears as a stark, light yellow stucco box at the top of a slope.

Just weeks ago, I handed my camera to a snaggletoothed girl in this very spot. We hid in the underground cellar with dozens of refugees while bombs rained on the countryside. I framed paintings in my viewfinder and snapped dozens of pictures, while laborers

brought them out into the sunlight one by one. Masterpieces from
the Uffizi, and the Palatine Gallery at the Pitti. Botticelli's *Minerva
and the Centaur*. Giovanni Bellini's *Pietà*. Caravaggio's *Sleeping Amor*.
Nearly three hundred paintings.

As we draw closer, it's clear that things are not the same as they
were that day. The front door of the villa has been pried off its hinges,
and lies in the grass. The opening is a gaping hole. All the glass in
the windows is shattered, and the villa stands like an empty skull.
Dozens of old books from the villa's library are scattered across the
red dirt, marred with boot marks, their pages ragged and fluttering.

Horst rolls up to the slope where the wine cellar stands, its wooden
doors open and gaping. From the vehicle, we can see that the cellar
has been pillaged. There are empty and broken wine bottles spilling
out of the doors.

On an empty space on the wall, someone has scrawled a message.
Chi entra dopo di noi non troverà nulla.

The words are Italian but the script the same angular, gothic script
that I and every other German child learns at school. *Whoever enters
after us will find nothing.*

Horst turns the key and the engine stalls. But we don't get out of
the vehicle right away. We sit there in stunned silence, watching the
wine flow out of the busted cellar like a river of blood soaking into
the ground.

Horst and I return to silence as we make our way over the next hour to
the Villa Medici at Poggio a Caiano. We've received word that artillery
shelling in the area has died down enough for us to go in and evacuate
the treasures. The sun turns brilliant and hot as we rumble across the
dusty roads, increasingly worried about what we will find next.

But in contrast to the deserted, savagely raped villa at Montagnana, at Poggio a Caiano, there are several armored vehicles, a half
dozen open-bed trucks, and two Mercedes sedans parked in front of

a grand stucco residence. The late morning sun turns the massive, rectangular façade of this former Medici countryside residence into a brilliant shade of burnished yellow.

We approach the main stairs to a wide loggia. A dozen armed SS officers stand before the door, shifting their eyes at us as we enter. We move from the heat into the dark, cool interior of the great entrance hall, where we find a German officer talking to the Italian caretaker with the help of an interpreter.

In the shadows, the caretaker, rumpled in his frayed suit, looks defiantly at a German officer who can only be Leopold Reidemeister. Reidemeister is sleek in his decorated field jacket, his light red hair slicked back from his forehead. "We had agreements," the caretaker says in Italian as the interpreter speaks German quietly in Reidemeister's ear. "There are more than fifty-eight cases of sculpture stored here. Everything is fragile. And we are under strict instructions from our superintendents that nothing be moved. It's too risky."

"And we have our own orders, *signore*. It is for your own protection. And the protection of the works. It's for the best," Reidemeister says, reading the caretaker's determined stance. "We have blown all the bridges to slow down the Allies but they are still coming. The British and Americans are only a few kilometers from here. They will take everything to America. You should see what destruction they have wrought. And you are unarmed. Unprotected."

"Then why aren't you providing us with some protection?!" The man can't help it. He gestures wildly toward the soldiers standing outside the front door. "And anyway, the works are not to leave the confines of Tuscany for any reason. It was written in the Medici documents. That's what they told us. They assured us they would either stay here or return to Florence."

"Things are not as they were," Reidemeister says. "We must take extraordinary precautions under extraordinary circumstances."

The caretaker's expression sours. "Some of the works are too large to move. We have the equestrian statue of Cosimo I from the Piazza della Signoria," he says. "It's enormous and fragile. You can't possibly move it without damaging it."

"We will determine what is portable," Reidemeister says.

"Then at a minimum," the custodian says through the interpreter, "you must leave me with a list of the cases removed. It's the least you can do."

Reidemeister hesitates. "Very well," he says at last. He glances toward Horst and me. "My assistants will take care of compiling a receipt for you."

"And our bishop and the Vatican authorities must be notified." The caretaker's eyes stay steadfast, defiant, even though he must know he has no credible means to resist the many SS soldiers lined up at the door, nor the armored vehicles and cargo trucks parked at. He is outnumbered. "We are under papal protection—as are the works of art," he says.

Reidemeister sets his square jaw into a hard line. "You have *our* protection, Signor di Luca. There is nothing more for you to worry about."

It's Enzo who fills the voids in my mind as we fall into a strange dance of nerve-racking monotony. We begin to compile a list of the contents at Poggio a Caiano. Donatello's life-sized *Saint George*. Michelangelo's life-sized *Bacchus*. Another fifty-eight cases of sculpture. We work under the watchful eyes of Major Reidemeister, the haggard custodian, armed SS guards, and the occasional refugee who straggles into the villa from the cellars and outbuildings, searching for food or water.

When the men break for cigarettes and coffee, I step out on the villa's gravel terrace. The late afternoon sun turns the thin cypresses into long shadows and the sky turns brilliant gold. Is Enzo still crouching in his Florentine sniper's nest, I wonder, going days without eating? Is he fishing in his shirt pocket for a cigarette, sweltering in his bare, top-floor apartment, waiting and watching for American jeeps to come rumbling down the riverside streets? Will he slide the barrel of his weapon over the windowsill and take a shot? Will he watch for partisans among his own countrymen—even his own family—men, women, and children who are helping the Allies? Will he look through the sight and contemplate putting a hole in the back of their necks?

A chill runs down my spine, for as hard as I try, I cannot reconcile this cold-hearted killer with the warm-blooded, handsome man who pinned me with his body under a bridge. Who put his own life at risk to protect mine. I breathe in the country air, which smells of garlic and parched, red dirt. A seemingly normal moment. In the long grass, red poppies sway in the hot breeze. A flock of swifts wheels in frantic unison overhead.

But when my mind conjures an image of those bridges falling into the Arno, I feel my chest tighten all the way up to my throat until I can hardly breathe. The images try to unspool in my head like a dream, a nightmarish film reel, but I push them away. Only the Ponte Vecchio is left, I've heard the SS soldiers say, talking among themselves while we work. Every other bridge has been blown to rubble, along with the many medieval towers and buildings along the Arno that populate my photographs.

My heart breaks for Poggi and the other Italian superintendents. We made them believe we were on their side. For all the Florentines who love their city. And even for Paloma, who is as puzzling and obscure to me as her cousin Enzo. For them, the destruction of their bridges must seem the end of civilization. I wish I could go back and somehow make it different.

Just a few months ago, Enzo and I sat on a wall and looked out at this same beautiful Tuscan landscape. It seems like a lifetime ago, back when we were under the illusion that the Germans and Italians were working together for a common future. Back when everything was black and white. Before everything blurred together like a

ruined, overexposed photograph in a developing bath, where everything is fuzzy and nothing turns out like you originally planned.
Before it was too late to go back to where you started.

I awake to the sound of a bomb.

In an instant, I go from sleeping on my back, hands over my
chest, like a fallen statue, to throwing off the sheet and standing,
sweating, heart racing in my chest. For a few long moments, I don't
know where I am. Eventually, I remember. The Italian custodian has
let us stay in some of the villa's bedrooms. What choice does he have?
He has no means to turn us away.

There it is again. A great rumble, then a flash. No. Not a bomb.
Only thunder. A summer storm.

I arise from the narrow bed and go to the window. Another
flash of lightning brightens the sky in a brilliant instant. I feel as
if an electric current is going through my veins. The rain flushes
through the cracks of the courtyard below the window. I open the
latch and feel the rush of warm wind, the vapor of the rain as it
splashes down like bullets on the terracotta bricks. How could any
of us sleep? Eventually, the pelting moves off, leaving behind loud
drips from the copper drain spouts. Somewhere in the villa, a pipe
shudders, then goes silent.

I return to bed. I turn on my side and try to resettle. But I only
drift along a tide of images like a flickering black-and-white newsreel playing in my head. I see a great cross from a Tuscan church
lying on its side, askew, inside a four-hundred-year-old villa. I see
Enzo's dimples, his brown eyes, his smile as he takes a cigarette and
places it between my lips. I see the intersecting tram lines across a
Florentine piazza and the shattered, dark rings under the eyes of a
mother holding a baby in the arcades of the Pitti Palace. I see stacks
of Renaissance masterpieces in a dusty Tuscan depot, hundreds of
invaluable paintings tottering in the back of an open truck bed. The

kaleidoscopic swirl of my shutter and the loud click of its release. The crash of the bridges as they fall into the Arno. *Whoever enters after us will find nothing.*

There is no falling asleep again. As the storm rolls away and the wan dawn light appears, I pull myself up and slip on my gray dress. I walk down the dark corridor, feeling the fabric paper along the wall of the stairwell. I make my way toward the villa's kitchen on the lower level to see if there is anything to eat.

I arrive in the dark kitchen to find a little girl rummaging through the old wooden cupboard where yesterday, there sat a bowl of apricots with woody stems and green leaves, picked from a tree in the villa's garden. No doubt she's snuck in here from one of the outbuildings or the wine cellar, which are overflowing with forlorn-looking families.

"*Non c'è più,*" she laments, running her small hand across the inside of the wooden bowl, as if I need convincing that there are none left.

"Let's check the storage room," I tell her in my broken Italian. I turn the doorknob of a small door near the sink. There are a few glass jars with canned fruit left on the very bottom shelf, where they might be easily overlooked. "Look!" I say, but when I turn around, the little girl is standing with her back against the wall, her eyes wide. Perhaps she thought I was Italian, but as soon as I open my mouth, it's clear that I'm a German speaker instead. She slinks along the wall to the doorway, then I hear her small footsteps slapping down the corridor.

We were helping them. We were once their friends, but now . . . Am I the enemy? In the little girl's eyes, it's clear that I am.

Without the armed SS vehicles as escorts, we wouldn't be able to make our way through this beautiful, desecrated countryside. To our north and east, the soldiers tell us, there are bomb-cratered roads and streams where the bridges have been destroyed and are now impassable. Only they know the way through this maze as we make our slow trek to the depots that are, for the moment, free of shelling. The air smells of rotting haystacks and the remains of artillery fire.

Over recent days, we've followed Major Reidemeister and the armored trucks around the Tuscan countryside, to privately owned villas, outbuildings, and country churches. We find more paintings, sculptures, and crates, hiding in the darkness. In the places where the Italian superintendents thought it best to hide them just a few years ago before any Americans were here.

When a custodian is present, they do what they can, their faces grim, hands clasped. But they can't stop us from picking up these six-hundred-year-old paintings that once hung on the walls of the Uffizi and the Bargello, and loading them in the back of our trucks. Reidemeister gets a tip that there's a stash of pictures belonging to a prominent Florentine art dealer at another villa nearby. We fill the trucks.

Over days, we've established a rhythm. Horst stands by with his inventories. One of the soldiers calls out the name of the artist and subject and museum. Horst checks it off on the inventory. I take a photograph, maybe a few, to make sure we have at least one good one. Then brutish soldiers haul them into the trucks.

"Where are we going with all of this . . . this stuff?" I ask Horst, as we trail an open truck full of pictures. They are teetering in the truck bed, with no crates, tarps, or protection. Open to the hot August sun. The works are stacked side by side tightly with a few blankets and handfuls of straw that blow out of the back as we rattle over rutted roads.

"Reidemeister said Langsdorff wants us to take everything either to Venice or the Borromean Islands. They'll be safe there."

"I thought the mission of the Kunstschutz was to *protect* works of art, not *steal* them." I watch Horst's square profile, which remains like a brick wall. Unreadable. "Horst?"

He keeps his eyes forward. "Italians are disorganized. You should know that by now, Eva. They probably don't even know what they have in all these depots, much less what's missing. Langsdorff says even General Wolff doesn't trust them. And he knows this country better than anyone." He glances at me briefly before turning his gaze back to the flimsy windshield, covered in dust from the trucks in front of us. "So . . . we *are* protecting them. We're taking them to a safer place."

"But . . . What we saw at Montagnana . . ."

Horst heaves a heavy sigh. "That wasn't the Kunstchutz. I suspect that was SS troops operating on their own."

But the rationale feels slippery, elusive. "Anyway, I thought there were agreements with the Italian government. Poggi said that, by law, everything was supposed to stay in Tuscany. You've seen the inventories. They are little scraps of paper with handwritten notes. How is anyone going to keep this all straight? It's impossible now."

"It's too late for that," Horst says. "They are better off north of the Alps. You said it yourself. Besides, there are works from all over Europe going to the salt mines now. France, Belgium, the Netherlands . . . It's all going to Germany anyway."

I imagine my father organizing thousands of the world's greatest masterpieces, deep inside the bowels of the earth at Altaussee. Surely they will be safer there than here, in a rattling, open truck, or in an unoccupied villa that might be destroyed at any moment? I always thought so.

But as I watch the Tuscan countryside roll by, I am overcome with remorse by the realization that I had a chance to tell Mr. Poggi and the others that the Cranachs had left Florence in the back of an ambulance. That Colonel Langsdorff lied to all of them. I was too afraid to speak up.

I think there must be a way at least to get the inventories and pictures to Paloma and her friends so they know where the works are heading. And that we will protect them. To tell Mr. Poggi, Mr. Fasola, Mr. Rossi, all of whom must be worried sick. But now, our channels of communication to Florence have all been cut off. There is no Kunstschutz staff left in the city. No one to contact and no way to contact them. Florence belongs to the Allies now.

As much as I try to rationalize all of this, I know in my heart that the works belong in Tuscany. But soon enough, we leave Tuscany behind. As I watch the cypress and olive trees recede and the countryside go flat and barren, I know we've done more than take a bunch of old paintings. We have stripped the people of their heritage, their right to hold on to their own patrimony. We have taken away their soul. What is the price to pay for that?

20

JOSIE

CORRADO BRINGS US TO MEET HIS SISTER PALOMA in the Piazza Santo Spirito.

I seek out the shade of a leafy tree while I admire the perfect symmetry of the church façade that dominates the square—a beautifully simple composition of yellow stucco with a couple of scrolls and a round window emerging from a mountain of sagging sandbags. For a moment, I have a fleeting vision of Florence as a living, vibrant community, not a shelled, shuttered city that has been brought to its knees.

In the square, a sign above a door reads CAFFÈ FIRENZE. The place isn't really open, at least not yet. But the owners are attempting to clean up the overwhelming mess. They seem to recognize Paloma. They wave us over, run a rag over a small table, and assemble chairs around it. We take our seats. Inside, the barman is wiping fine dust from a cappuccino machine, a seemingly impossible task. As soon as the dust is wiped away, a new layer of grit settles there. He stacks the espresso cups upside down on top of the machine and presses its giant plug into the socket as if by habit, but there is no electricity. The man, in his starched white shirt, runs the rag across it again. He rearranges the bottles on a glass shelf, his furrowed brow reflected in the cracked, crizzled glass behind the bar. At the doorway, a tiny woman in an apron runs a rush broom across the floor in short, staccato strokes, gathering up shards of broken glass. Then she gathers them into a dustpan and stands with her hand on the small of her back.

"The problem is that, for the past year, all our superintendents across Italy have had to rely on the German Kunstschutz," Paloma is saying to Captain Foster. She is tidy and petite in a flowered dress, her hair gathered into a neat bun. Corrado has explained to her that we are here to help. But she looks as if she might be as wary of us as she is of the Germans. She bites her lip and waits for us to respond.

"And what did they do for you?" he asks.

"Well, nearly everything. We've depended on them for fuel, trucks, material, photography, permissions to travel. And for protection," she continues. "In the short term, I suppose that has been good for works of art hidden in the countryside. But you must understand that by collaborating with them and getting their help, it also means that they know where everything is. And they have all the resources to put their fingers on it at a moment's notice."

"They were working right there." Corrado gestures to a building facing the *caffè*, a beautiful stone box with symmetrical arcades and a kind of open porch on the upper floor. "The Kunsthistorisches Institut," he says. "It's been the headquarters for any German working with art in Florence over the past few years. They've all left now."

"Palazzo Guadagni," Captain Foster says, pushing back his chair to admire the large, well-proportioned building across the square. "A perfect example of a Renaissance palazzo."

"Yes," Paloma says. "But you won't find anything left inside. We packed up all their photographs, archives, everything. It all went on a train to a salt mine in Heilbronn months ago."

"Our cousin Enzo was also working with them," Corrado says. Then he and Paloma exchange a fleeting, troubled look I can't interpret.

"Hmm." Captain Foster runs his palm over his jaw. "And all those Germans were right here, right in the middle of this hotbed of the neighborhood's partisan activities. Incredible."

Paloma and Corrado exchange another glance. I can see there is more to the story, but their interaction remains difficult to decipher.

The more we talk, the more Paloma begins to open up as Captain Foster explains the mission of the American and British Monuments officers. "At least we can inventory and document everything we can on the south side of the river," he says. "For now, we can't cross to the north side in any case."

"We can't go home for now, either," she says. "Until we can get back to the other side, we're staying with our cousins on this side of the river." At last, she agrees to walk with us through the Oltrarno.

We stand, say goodbye to the *caffè* proprietors, and cross the square. We make our way through the wall of sandbags into the dim, cool interior of the Santo Spirito church. Corrado removes his hat. "Michelangelo carved a wooden crucifix for this church when he was still a teenager," he tells me, looking up to an empty dome in a chapel off the main sanctuary.

"It was moved to safety a few years ago, of course," Paloma says.

We make our way through streets where scores of men, women, and children are picking up crumbled stones and bricks, one by one, to make them passable. The troop commanders have already told us the Germans have sown the rubble with mines. They haven't slowed down the progress of our troops for more than a day or two. And yet, they have paralyzed the city to a point where people won't be able to get their lives back for months, if ever. The effort to clean up feels overwhelming.

Captain Foster says he is eager to check on some famous frescoes by Masaccio. But inside the church of Santa Maria del Carmine, we find only a massive brick wall where the Italian superintendents have sought to protect it and we cannot see Masaccio's frescoes at all. The afternoon proceeds like this, a waxing and waning rhythm of promise and disappointment. Of relief at finding a historic building intact. Of worry, when we find its treasures missing or hidden away.

As the sky turns burnished, Captain Foster says the situation in

Florence being what it is, he is not eager to leave his idyllic quarters at Santa Lucia, an hour or so down the dusty roads to the southwest.

"Drop me off at the WAC camp, Captain?"

We say goodbye to our new friends, climb wearily into Georgette, and we head out of the city in a cloud of dust. "You sure you prefer a tent to your big bed at Santa Lucia?"

"I'm sure." I smile.

I know he's eager to return to his pictures in the countryside villa, but I only want to return to my friends.

At night, from our camp in the hills south of Florence, there is relentless, echoing German shelling and the night sky lights up with flashes of orange. We do our best to rest, all of us women sweating on our cots, surrounded by drapes of mosquito netting as if we are surviving in a tropical jungle. We sleep in our slips, in our undergarments, many of us lying with eyes wide open and watching flashes of orange through the veil of mosquito netting and green tarps.

At seven o'clock every morning, like clockwork, Captain Foster rushes into the camp, driving Georgette in a cloud of dust. The two of us return to the southern edge of Florence along the rutted roads. We move as quickly as we can through the hot streets, sweating, to check to make sure the sandbags are still in front of frescoes. We patrol the southern bank of the Arno to see what church vaults have fallen during the night. What church façades have new bullet holes. We pick up a sculpted hand or head that's toppled from a façade or a pedestal. I struggle to mark up our growing pages of notes and inventories. My forehead is wet and Captain Foster has large sweat stains in the underarms of his uniform.

Day by day, the Italian superintendents and their staff begin to find us, buoyed by Captain Foster's relentless commitment to show up each morning. When they go home at night, they have no lights, no plumbing in their homes. But in the morning, they put on a tie and hat, a dress, and come out to the streets, each to do his or her part. If my commitment to this cause should waver, all I have to do is look at what our Italian friends have endured, and yet how they continue to show up each time the sun rises. Together, we patrol the streets and report to one another on the state of monuments in the Oltrarno. We pick up fragments that German shells have knocked down during the night. We are all hot, filthy, exhausted, but utterly dedicated to our cause.

It seems that we may never emerge from this hellish, hot state of alternating night and day, alternating damage and retrieval. And then one afternoon, our commanders tell us that at last, our troops have pushed the Germans beyond the northern outskirts of Florence. And that the mountain of rubble blocking the Ponte Vecchio has been cleared to allow a path to cross to the north side.

Captain Foster and I step through the slim passage opened in the mountain of stone and walk up the slope of the city's oldest bridge. The Ponte Vecchio is deserted, the windows of its historic jewelry shops battened shut with their ancient wooden shutters and complicated metal locking mechanisms. He does his best to mask his emotion, but as we reach the center of the bridge, Captain Foster removes his wire-rimmed glasses and presses the back of his hand to his eyes. Seeing his reaction, I can't help but feel a lump rise in my throat. We look out to the water, snaking slowly toward Pisa and the sea beyond.

"Look at that, sir," I say. He sniffs loudly and comes to stand beside me, hands on his hips.

On the Ponte Santa Trinità, Allied troops are busy slinging a Bailey bridge over the stumped, ruined piers. Soon enough, I imagine, people will rush across it to embrace their loved ones on the other side of the river that separates friends and families as if they are in different worlds. This small measure will begin to make life possible for Florentines—like Corrado and Paloma—desperate to go home, to bring the two halves of their city back into a whole. To bring people together again who have been cleaved apart by this brutal conflict.

On the north side of the bridge, the streets are quiet and still. I follow Captain Foster into the courtyard of the Uffizi, the great museum I've read and heard about for so long. The building where all the masterpieces of Tuscan art should be proudly displayed instead of hiding in innumerable countryside repositories. The immense courtyard of the museum is a sea of broken glass, its windows standing dark and vacant. If the treasures had stayed here in this museum near the Arno, everything inside would have been destroyed.

Someone has scrawled some words in chalk, what seems a little poem in ugly graffiti underneath a statue of Dante, inside a niche of the Uffizi colonnade. I read the words but struggle to understand them:

In sul passo dell'Arno
I tedeschi hanno lasciato
Il ricordo della loro civiltà

Captain Foster translates for me. "In their pass over the Arno," he says, "the Germans have left the memory of their civility."

At last, the northern bank of the Arno, which has seemed as far away as another country, is safe enough for us to establish an office. Captain Foster and I walk across the new Bailey bridge on the Ponte Santa Trinità and follow the American tanks, soldiers perched on the tops, as they crawl through the streets. After weeks of being holed up in their cellars, Florentines emerge from their homes. They stand on the sidewalks and watch us pass, cheering and waving.

From the shadow of a doorway, Corrado steps down to the narrow sidewalk to greet us. He appears as if by magic, as if he knows where we are at all times. Is he watching us from somewhere unseen? It seems he and his partisan comrades have figured out how to navigate the city without their presence being known.

In contrast to our elegant Florentine partisan guide, Captain Foster and I stand out like sore thumbs. As the lean American captain and I follow our Italian friends, for the first time I feel conspicuous in my United States Army uniform. For months, all of us American army personnel have worn our uniforms in a sea of others just like us. Now Captain Foster and I are the only ones on the streets of Florence in these uniforms. As we move through the city, an occasional ripple of applause fills the air. They assume we have done something brave. A twinge of embarrassment fills my stomach in the face of this unwarranted praise. Judging by Captain Foster's sheepish expression, he feels the same way.

"We will need help to put everything back in its place," Captain Foster says. "Will you and Paloma work with us?"

"I will help you as much as I can," Corrado says, with a quick glance in my direction that makes my heart swell. "As for my sister, well, I don't know if I will convince her. You know, she worked for years for the Germans and . . . as things changed, it was difficult for her to hide her loyalties. To be honest, *capitano*, it took a toll on her."

"We won't ask her to do anything compromising. But having someone who has worked with the Germans, who knows where the works are. Well, it will be invaluable."

"I'll talk to her," he says, and then he smiles at me.

Corrado walks down a street where a store owner has opened the battens of his shop. "The Por Santa Maria," he tells us. "It's the place where my ancestors wove silk and wool. You know that cloth was the main reason why Florence became the capital of the Renaissance, right?" I don't grasp every single word, but inherently, I understand. He is passionate about his family's old trade. It may not be much: just a humble tailor shop with cramped spaces and battered shutters, but it has a long, centuries-old history. He is part of something bigger than himself, an unbroken chain across generations. And now I know that means something. To think about it crumbling away, I feel it hurt deep in my gut. I've begun to understand what it's like to be part of something bigger than myself. Something bigger than anyone in my family has ever done. I feel the hard pit of guilt inside me begin to crack and chip, like a fragile sculpture. For surely what we are doing here is enough to justify our being so far away from those who want us back home, who need us most.

One morning, a mist rises off the Arno and settles in the air, lifting the oppressive heat with it. At the same time, our troops drive the Germans beyond the northern reaches of the city.

"The superintendents have made room for us on the first floor of the Uffizi, near their offices," Captain Foster tells me as we make our way into the city, rumbling along in Georgette. "It'll be good to have them close."

Corrado's powers of persuasion have paid off, because we find Paloma waiting for us at the museum entrance. In a small office on the ground floor, we push two hulking desks together, facing each other.

Within a few days, we establish a routine. I type up correspondence in English for our Allied commanders, while Paloma does the same in Italian. The stacks of paper grow higher and our working hours grow long. But returning Florence's historic buildings to some semblance of normal feels impossible, when so many workers are needed to repair sewers, bridges, and water mains. "It's overwhelming," I admit to Captain Foster after another twelve-hour day. We have worked together long enough that I know he won't judge me poorly. "How can we possibly make a dent?"

"All I know is we can't sit here and watch these buildings fall to pieces while we wait for the paperwork to run the gauntlet of the government," he says. "The superintendents have to hire workmen and buy materials today. No doubt the superintendency will go into debt. But the list of repaired monuments justifies the immediate action. We have no choice if we want to save any historic buildings."

Our reports of the damaged monuments in the city grow long. I type memos for the Allied command describing how German fire has landed on Santa Croce, along the flank of the cathedral, on Giotto's campanile, on the roof of the Baptistery, on the central section of the Uffizi, in the middle of the Palazzo Strozzi.

Meanwhile, our office is besieged with helpless refugees and missing persons desperate to talk to any Allied officer. Paloma patiently listens to each ragged person who appears at our door. In the end, we can do nothing to help them.

We keep records, answer letters, write reports, prepare construction estimates, the many *preventivi* that take up untold hours of our time. Each estimate must be signed by Captain Foster and one of the Italian superintendents, then multiple copies are sent to various levels of the Allied and Italian hierarchy. Paloma seems the only person capable of understanding all the steps required to navigate this daunting bureaucracy. By the time we get our approvals, the Italian lira falls so far that the approved funds aren't enough. All day long, Allied officers apply to our office to requisition a building; on the other side, we respond to requests for OFF LIMITS signs from frantic proprietors who don't want their buildings requisitioned. There is not enough time to investigate before a new application arrives.

In the midst of this administrative chaos, Captain Foster says he is most anxious about the empty galleries upstairs, all the rooms of the Uffizi awaiting the return of their beloved masterpieces. The Italian superintendents begin to bring us pieces of a complicated puzzle. Dozens of hiding places across Italy, perhaps forty in Tuscany alone. Privately owned villas. Barns and outbuildings. Places no one would expect. There are priceless works by Michelangelo, Botticelli, Duccio, Giotto, Bronzino, many others, far-flung and dispersed around the countryside, tracked with little more than handwritten inventories edited in red pen. But most of the place names on our list—many of which even Captain Foster has never heard of—are still covered in Germans and we couldn't get to them anyway.

Paloma unfolds a Florentine newspaper that has just started print-ing again. "They are saying the Germans have stolen paintings from Montagnana and the other depots nearby," she says, her brow furrow-ing. "I went out there with them—the *tedeschi*—months ago. Every-thing was intact then." But Captain Foster hardly looks reassured.

One evening, when the sky turns golden outside our office win-dow, Corrado appears, leaning against the doorjamb. "Join me for a museum tour?" he says. I stand for the first time in hours, feeling the blood rushing back into my legs. We climb the staircase into the empty museum's upper floors. The doors of the Gabinetti dei Disegni are bolted; the superintendents have told us that a few masterpieces were returned here from the countryside before it became too dangerous to travel there—crated altarpieces and paintings by the Lorenzetti, Fra Angelico, Piero della Francesca, and many other pictures of great im-portance. Otherwise, the museum stands empty. We walk through the deserted galleries, a sad conglomeration of walls with empty hooks and nails, gray dust, and broken glass. We gaze up at the skylights, which I imagine must have let the beautiful light of Florence spill across the surfaces of every masterpiece. Surely it was right to have taken all the beautiful, priceless treasures out to the countryside, but no one seems to know when or how we will get them back.

I follow Corrado into the Vasari Corridor, the long, narrow pas-sage on the upper level of the Ponte Vecchio. In the glow of sunset, we watch the crush of foot and bicycle traffic over the Bailey bridge opened on the ruined piers of the Ponte Santa Trinità. In recent days, people have discovered fragments of the bridge's sculptures of *Spring*, *Summer*, and *Winter* on the banks of the Arno. A large chunk of Giovanni Caccini's *Autumn* is pulled from the riverbed and all the chunks are brought to a restoration studio in handcarts and barrows. A buoy of hope in an effort that seems overwhelming.

"Finally the two sides of the city are connected," I say, filled with a momentary grasp of hope. But when I turn to Corrado, I find him standing at the broken window, looking out over the quayside of the

Arno, where once there were medieval towers but now there is only a great pile of stones and rubble sliding down into the rushing waters.

"I believe my cousin is gone," he says.

"Your cousin . . ."

"Enzo. He was called Enzo. He was working for the Germans; Paloma got him a job at the German Art History Institute. God knows he needed gainful employment . . ." Corrado says, pressing the palms of his hands on the window jambs. "But we haven't had word from him since the night before the bridges were bombed. He liked to stay in our *nonna*'s old apartment along the river. Just there," he says. When I follow his pointed finger, all I see is a mountain of debris. "The building is gone of course. He wasn't stupid. He was savvy, you know. I kept thinking one day, he would appear from his hiding place. But . . ." He just shakes his head.

I touch his arm. "*Mi dispiace.*" I'm sorry. I'm not sure it's the right thing to say in this type of circumstance. "I am sad for you. And for Paloma. Did he have a wife or children?"

He leans out a window where the glass has shattered and looks toward the ruined bank of the Arno. "No. He wasn't a bad person," he says. "It's just . . . his ideas led him astray. He was passionate, but I would say misled. He got mixed up with the Black Brigades."

He huffs and turns toward me and in the evening glow, I explore the depths of his brown eyes. I don't see resentment or hate for someone who might have turned to the other side. I see nothing there but tenderness, and the sad resolve of someone who's seen the bittersweet turn of people's hearts, the brutal rupture of generations, during this long conflict. Someone who loves his family in spite of the deep-seated loyalties that have fractured them, and the tide of war that has brought these differences boiling to the surface.

When I return to the WAC camp after dark, I sit on my cot and try to write a letter to my mother, to try at last to explain all of this to her. How easily families can be fractured, but how love and commitment can last, how it can close a chasm of irreconcilable differences.

For all the years before I naïvely boarded a ship for North Africa, my mother and I were a team. But I see now that, if I acknowledged her sickness, it meant I also had to accept being all alone. And I haven't been ready to do that. Haven't believed I could bear to be all by myself in the world. But now I see that I've been selfish. Instead, it's my mother who's been all alone. Not me. I feel remorse for leaving her there by herself to deal with an illness that seems as barbaric and daunting as a war. Its own kind of battle.

I pull out a sheet of V-mail and try to find the words to explain everything I've been doing here. I hope it makes her proud to know that I can stand on my own, and that I haven't been alone at all; instead, I've been part of something greater, part of a group that has done something meaningful, important. Something bigger than myself.

As soon as our commanders give us the all clear to travel along one of the roads northwest of Florence, Captain Foster pulls Georgette into the courtyard of the Uffizi. Along with a stack of paperwork, in my hand, I hold the telegram that arrived from the ACC headquarters in Rome weeks ago:

SWISS GOVERNMENT INFORMED BY
GERMAN LEGATION AT BERNE THAT
GERMAN AUTHORITIES HAVE STORED
IN VILLA REALE POGGIO A CAIANO FIVE
KILOMETERS NORTHWEST OF SIGNA
VALUABLE ARTISTIC COLLECTIONS
AND ARCHIVES CONCERNING TUSCAN
RENAISSANCE WORKS. STATED BY
GERMAN GOVERNMENT THAT THERE

*ARE IN NEIGHBORHOOD VILLA REALE NO
REPEAT NO GERMAN TROOPS AND VILLA
REALE ITSELF NOT USED FOR MILITARY
PURPOSES. GERMAN GOVERNMENT DESIRES
TO INFORM BRITISH AND AMERICAN
GOVERNMENTS OF ITS DESIRE TO AVOID
BOMBARDMENT OR DESTRUCTION VILLA
REALE. GRATEFUL YOU INFORM ARMY AMG
OF CONTENTS OF THIS MESSAGE.*

"Poggio a Caiano was one of the Medici family country villas," Captain Foster tells me. "The AMG office confirmed that there has been no direct Allied bombardment in the area. Hopefully we will find everything intact."

"Paloma says they reported the same message on the Fascist radio," I say.

Paloma stays back at the office to deal with our never-ending onslaught of paperwork. But Filippo Rossi, the placid, middle-aged head of the Florentine Galleries, loads into the jeep with us. "*Andiamo*," he says, pulling a formal-looking, felted hat over his balding head. We head out of Florence into the early morning light.

I know Captain Foster is anxious to get back out to the other repositories. For an hour, we travel through a quiet landscape. Except for a few bombed-out farm buildings, you might believe the battle is far away instead of just a few miles from this idyllic panorama of golden and green hills.

"That's it," Captain Foster says at last, pointing to a tile roof visible over the treetops. We come to a halt before a shallow creek where a bridge has crumbled into the water, another victim of German explosives. "We'll have to go on foot from here," he says.

We leave the jeep and wade into the cold creek water. I hold my steno notebooks and my shoes high in the air as my feet sink into the slime of the creek bed. Ahead of me, Signor Rossi—a picture of

Italian elegance in his dark suit, tie, and hat—wades through the
shallow water with his marked-up inventory. We climb up the opposite bank, where a few locals are standing under the trees, clapping
and cheering for us. "We have to be the first Americans they've seen,"
Captain Foster says as we shake the water from our legs and make
our way through the trees. Signor Rossi stops and explains to the
curious locals what we are doing.

We find the custodian, Signor de Luca, standing outside the villa,
alerted by the sound of the locals cheering our climb up the creek
bed. At first, the villa seems just another beautiful, peaceful mansion
in the Tuscan countryside, but as we draw closer, we see that the roof
and façade of the building are riddled with pockmarks. The haggard
custodian motions for us to follow him up a steep stairwell to the
portico.

"I did everything I could," he tells us as we step into the cool, dim,
empty interior. "But I was here alone and what could I do? It was
me against dozens of armed Germans." He shrugs. "We appealed to
the local priests and the bishop, but no one could stop them. They
loaded up everything and left. Fifty-eight cases of sculpture."

I watch Captain Foster's face drain of color, then slowly turn
beet-red. "Fifty-eight cases!"

Signor de Luca consults his list and reads off some of them. Three
works by Donatello: the *Marzocco*, the marble *David* from the Bargello, and an Annunciation relief from Santa Croce. Michelangelo's
Bacchus. Two Madonna reliefs by Michelozzo, a *Madonna* and a *Res-
urrection* by Leonardo's teacher, Verrocchio. He lists out a litany of
additional ancient and Renaissance sculptures from Florentine collections.

"And Donatello's *Saint George*," Signor Rossi adds.

During the reading of this list of masterpieces, Captain Foster has
been pacing back and forth across the room. At the mention of the
Saint George, he slides his back down a stucco wall and sits on the
tiles. He is speechless.

"How long ago was this?" I ask. When Signor de Luca calculates the date, I realize it was the same date when we received the appeals for the Allies not to bomb the building. "So they weren't trying to save the place from bombing," I say. "They were making sure the coast was clear enough for them to come and clean out the place."

"What could we do?" Signor de Luca pleads with us as if we will accuse him for the wholesale theft. "We are unarmed. Powerless. It feels as if we ourselves have been violated." He pats his open palm to his chest.

Signor de Luca goes on to tell us he convinced the Germans to sign a document assuming responsibility for having taken these works. Signor Rossi and I review the elaborate German script on the crumpled paper, acknowledging General Kesselring's order of protection. "It's signed by someone called Reidemeister," I say to Captain Foster, who is still sitting on the floor. The custodian then produces a cardinal's letter stating that everything is under the protection of the Vatican. But it's dated two days after the theft.

After a while, when Captain Foster has recovered enough to stand upright again, Signor de Luca walks us through the nearly empty rooms of the villa. Some of the works, at least, remain, notably Giambologna's equestrian statue of Cosimo I de Medici that once stood in the center of the Piazza della Signoria. "I convinced them it was too large to fit in their trucks," he tells us. Giovanni and Nicola Pisano's pulpits from Pisa, and the entire contents of the Museo Civico of Prato. All safe.

But it is a small assurance in the face of such pillage.

"Where did they take everything?" I ask the haggard custodian.

He only shrugs. "I fear they are in Germany by now."

21

EVA

❧

AT LAST, WE LEAVE THE ROLLING HILLS OF TUS-
cany behind and late on a moonless night, our trucks enter the outskirts of Bologna. When we come to a stop at a rear entrance to
the Academy of Fine Arts, our group of exhausted workers descends
from the trucks and begins to unload the great wooden boxes and
uncrated pictures into a vast, shadowy series of galleries. I worry that
we haven't accurately accounted for everything. And in addition to
what we've brought on our own trucks, I see there are many, many
more works of art stored here already. More here than I ever expected.

Major Reidemeister steps out from behind the hulking shadows
of a large crate containing a sculpture. "Fräulein Brunner," he says.
"How was your trip from Tuscany?"

I consider. Should I tell him that I would give anything to return
to the city I have come to love? That I would go back even with the
rumble and whine of the bombs, the constant worry that I might
die? Should I tell him about the evening I spent under the bridge
with Enzo, or in his stark sniper's nest? That as much as I have endured the horrors of this conflict, I would turn back the clock to do
it all over again, if only I could change the course of events?

"It was fine," I say, gathering my camera bags. "Have you been in
touch with the superintendents to let them know where their works
of art are being stored?"

Reidemeister shakes his head and makes a tsking sound. "There are no lines of communication. A shame. Anyway, it's too late now. Florence and most of Tuscany are already in the hands of the Anglo-Americans."

Horst adds, "Good thing we moved everything out of Palazzo Guadagni when we did. We'd never be able to retrieve anything now." I think about my little room on the top floor and the loggia that overlooked Santo Spirito. How naïve I had been when I arrived in Florence just a year ago, thinking I was there to take some pictures, that I—that none of this—would be put in harm's way.

"For now, we simply guard and track everything that's in our care," Reidemeister continues. "That's where you come in. All your pictures. They will be invaluable."

After the trucks are unloaded, we settle in a dingy hotel in the center of Bologna. In the dim room, I open my camera bag and pull out a small stack of photographs. They are all pictures that didn't turn out exactly right in the old wine cellar darkroom in Palazzo Guadagni. Over- or underexposed. Smudged. I shuffle through the stack and stop on a picture I took in front of the Carmine church in the Oltrarno. There is Horst, with his wide grin, Paloma prim in her dress and bun. And Enzo. Next, I pull out the photo I took of Enzo on the hill at San Miniato al Monte, overlooking the city. I prop the picture up on the windowsill. He is smiling, sort of, a half smile that reveals both his dimples and the shadows around his eyes.

He was earnest about his work, about his vision for what Italy could be. He believed in a better future with all his heart. He thought that we—Germans and Austrians and Italians—could work together to make that happen. We were both so wrong.

I move to the narrow bed and curl up on my side. I'm tough; I haven't cried since I was a little girl, but I can't stop the tears now. They run down my temple and I feel them pool in my ear and stain the pillow. I shut my eyes and see us sitting with our legs dangling over a wall, speaking in our strange Italo-German. Enzo leaning in the doorway of the Kunsthistorisches Institut photo archive, watching me. Stirring sugar into an inch of bitter espresso. Struggling to communicate the insides of his heart with words and the expansive gestures of the broad, stained hands of a laborer.

I press the heels of my hands into my eye sockets. Somehow, I know in the pit of my soul that I won't see him again. He is no longer fighting, striving for a better future. I feel in my heart that he is no longer there at all. And if he is gone, really gone, will his own self-sacrifice have been warranted? Worth it? It is hard to see it as anything other than a waste of a perfectly good human life.

A soft rap on the door.

"Eva." Horst's muffled voice on the other side.

I swipe my tears away on my sleeve. The last thing I want is for Horst to see me crying.

"What is it?" I clear my throat. I don't open the locked door. For a moment, there is silence. Perhaps he is waiting, hoping I will open the door. But I lie still and say nothing.

Another hesitation. Then I hear Horst's voice again. "Major Reidemeister has found a place for the pictures farther north, in the mountains. But first we're going to Bolzano . . . He says to be ready early tomorrow." He waits. When I don't stir, he continues talking through the door. "Eva, will you open the door?"

I clear my throat again, hoping he won't hear the tears in my voice. "Leave me alone." I stay put in the long void of silence.

"Good night then . . ." Silence. "Eva." Finally, his heavy footsteps recede in the dark hallway.

I wake with the resolve that I won't allow my own life to be sacrificed for nothing. I won't be like Enzo. I won't be like my mother. I won't put my life on the line for something that was all a misunderstanding or a fruitless search for what seemed at the time like the truth.

Now that I understand the scope of this looting campaign, this

Kunstraub, then what could I do to right such a wrong? I have no money or power. I have no way to reach Paloma or Mr. Poggi or any of the Florentines who now find themselves bereft of their greatest treasures, the embodiment of their history and spirit, and must be sick to death. I'm just a woman with a camera. The only thing I can think to do—the only thing that might make a difference at this point—is to take a picture of every single painting, every sculpture, every crate that passes before my eyes. To preserve a record, the trace of where everything is. The best—perhaps the only—action I can take is this.

Our convoy arrives in Bolzano as the afternoon light turns to bronze. The city, which has become General Wolff's headquarters, lies along a stretch of valley at the foot of the towering Dolomite mountain range. In the distance, I see the craggy peaks and I feel a punch in my gut. It's been more than a year since I have laid eyes on this familiar landscape. Still Italy, yet so close to home.

The trucks come to a squeaking halt in the courtyard of a stately city mansion. Major Reidemeister and our own trucks are there, but we are not alone. Many more vehicles are parked on the street surrounding the building. There are more SS officers directing the grim-looking Italian laborers to unload things from the trucks. More paintings. More crates. It's evident that Tuscany is not the only region that has been robbed of its greatest treasures. I take note of the place names written hastily on some of the crates. Venice. Modena. Verona. Forlì. Hundreds of paintings and sculpture. Many crates, cases, and loose canvases from all parts of Italy. I snap a series of quick pictures of labels that read Tiziano. Canaletto. Bronzino.

"Where is Colonel Langsdorff?" I hear Horst ask Major Reidemeister. Horst is so enamored with our prickly, art-historian-turned-colonel that it has become annoying.

"He's been detained in his office in Bergamo," Reidemeister says, slamming one of the truck doors closed. "We've had telegrams flying back and forth between the Fascist ministries in Padua and he couldn't be here."

"The Fascist ministers are coming here?"

Reidemeister shakes his head vigorously. "No. I have apprised them of our work and reminded them that we are responsible for holding the works in trust for them—for the Italian nation. We will do our own inspections here. We'll account for everything." I feel relief that at last, we might show some backbone. Some reason. Some responsibility.

"And how did they respond?" I ask, but Reidemeister ignores me. Soon enough, we get our answer.

With all the treasures tucked away inside the building's rooms, Horst steps out to the courtyard, where I am cleaning my camera lenses at a small table. "Südtirol," he tells me. "Major Reidemeister says he's located two safe places where we can bring the paintings. Higher up in the mountains from here. Gauleiter Hofer is in charge of that area. Neither Germany nor Italy . . . The Italians call it Alto Adige."

"But I thought they weren't allowing Italians to cross into that region anymore," I say. Südtirol is a zone neither Germanic nor Italian, but somewhere in between. Just a heartbeat away from the steep mountain passes leading to Austria. To home.

"They aren't," Horst says as we hear another vehicle engine approach just outside the building. The daylight begins to wane and deep shadows turn the now-empty mansion courtyard into a cold, stark space. We move to the doorway. At once, I recognize the vehicle outside. It's the same Red Cross ambulance that I saw parked in front of the Hotel Excelsior in Florence just a few weeks ago. A carefully disguised getaway car that allowed Colonel Langsdorff to steal the handpicked paintings he wanted. The vehicle is now covered in mud from the battered roads, but there's no mistaking it.

The men open the back doors and remove two large pictures. The wrapping is gone and at once, I recognize the hand of one of

Germany's greatest Renaissance painters. Lucas Cranach the Elder. I recognize Eve's sinewy, nude body; the coils of her light red hair; the round, red apple in her hand; the serpent, unfurling from the tree with his deceiving tongue. And then the bewildered Adam, scratching the crown of his head as if he can't fathom that the two of them will set off the whole unspooling of human history with such a simple action as taking a bite of fruit. He takes a step toward Eve, looking as if, in that moment, he realizes they are making a grave mistake that will put the future of humanity in peril.

"Look at that," Horst says.

I hold up my Leica and press the shutter release in a series of rapid-fire clicks that echo through the empty space.

A gaggle of honking geese bustles out of the way as the first of two dozen rattling trucks arrive at the Alpine depot. It's a clear afternoon with a taste of autumn in the air. The trucks are splattered with mud from the battlefield, and I wonder how the drivers can see through the windshields. They come to a stop before the front door of a building on the edge of the modest village. Children press their curious faces to the windows.

I wait outside a three-story building that looks like many others in this little village: San Leonardo in Passiria—or St. Leonhard in Passeier, depending on who you ask. Either way, it looks as if it could have been lifted straight from the Austrian countryside. A world away from Tuscany. There are stucco homes with broad, wooden porches and gently sloping slate roofs to let the snowmelt drain into the green ravines. At the windows, there are decorative wooden railings overflowing with red blossoms that will soon wilt in the cold nights. The village is nestled at the base of a dramatic mountain slope with craggy peaks towering above. Along the main street are shops selling copper cookware. Wooden clogs. Fur coats. Cuckoo clocks. All things that can be made in the winter months when snow blankets the region and people are stuck inside. Shop and street signs are written in both German and Italian. And as long as I have been in Italy, home has never felt so close.

A little boy with black hair and light blue eyes steps out from the house across the street. "*Tedeschi!*" he cries. A stooped old woman dressed in black pulls him back through the doorway. He jumps up and down and points at the convoy of trucks grinding slowly up the mountain pass.

I would recognize the trucks anywhere now, with their cargo of teetering canvases and wooden crates. The dozen or so trucks screech to a halt and the drivers emerge, slamming doors. Suddenly, a man rushes up from a nearby street with a set of keys. His hair is white and wild, held off his face by a pair of thick, smudged spectacles pushed on top of his head.

"*Scusate, signori!*" he calls to the big men in helmets and long coats as they descend from the trucks and collect around the door. He fumbles with a large iron ring of ancient-looking keys. At last, he opens the door to the stucco building. The inside is dim and smells of mildew and abandon. My eyes adjust to the darkness. To my amazement, I realize we're inside an old prison. Before us, lined up in neat rows, are a series of dark, damp, and narrow cells locked with iron bars. Small windows let in wan light from the street. Beyond these small squares of light high up on the walls, you can see a small sliver of mountains with their rugged, jagged peaks.

The Italian man dumps a pile of bursting folders on a nearby old desk. "*Luce, luce,*" he mumbles in the dark, then at last locates the light switch that turns on a harsh beam of light from a bare bulb. "*O Dio, Dio.* This won't do," he mutters to himself, trying and failing to find the right keys to all the cells. He pats his open coat and runs his hands futilely through the empty pockets of his baggy pants.

One of the drivers yells, "Hurry up!" They are playing on the poor man's fear.

"*Ecco, bene! Bene!*" The man nearly falls down with relief as he produces the correct key from his coat pocket.

Soon enough, the men begin unloading the trucks. I stand outside and photograph everything that comes off the truck beds—all the wooden crates, hastily tarped frames, and centuries-old paintings with no protection at all. Behind the trucks, at the end of the line, the Red Cross ambulance carrying the pair of Cranach's *Adam* and *Eve* putters to a stop. The men bring the pictures inside and stack them against the walls in the dank cells. Horst paces back and forth with his tattered inventory pages. I load new canisters of film into my camera, and collect those full of pictures in a separate compartment of my camera bag.

I walk up and down the corridor between the dank cells. It's the first time I've seen everything all together at once. Hundreds of paintings. A museum in Florence might dedicate an entire wall to a single one of these pictures, yet they are hastily stored away here like abandoned goods in a warehouse. I recognize Caravaggio's *Bacchus*, a handsome youth with a laurel of grape leaves, a clear glass of red wine, and a mischievous expression. Botticelli's *Minerva and the Centaur*, with its placid-faced woman and her strange, hybrid creature. Signorelli's *Crucifixion*, Lorenzo Monaco's tremendous *Adoration of the Magi*. Paintings by Rubens, Titian, and Dosso Dossi. And of course the *Adam* and *Eve* that I've seen at Oliveto, at the doorway to Colonel Langsdorff's hotel room in Florence, in Bolzano, and finally here, in this desolate Alpine jail. Some of the greatest masterpieces of the Italian nation, collected here in three floors of abandoned cells. Hundreds of treasures that have survived being transported over bombed-out roads in open-bed trucks, plus a Red Cross ambulance.

Of course, these pictures don't belong here in this abandoned Alpine jail. I know now they don't belong at Altaussee either. They belong back home in Tuscany instead. But I am powerless to make that happen.

I wander into the modest jail kitchen, its cabinet doors open, only a few old dusty cans left. Wandering into a hallway off the kitchen, I find a caretaker's bedroom with an adjacent water closet. It's not much, but it's a step up from the upper-floor jail cells where Horst and a half dozen of the men who will stay on as guards will be lodged. I lug my modest suitcase and camera equipment into the room.

I dust off a deep windowsill that frames a square view of the cragged peaks. I unpack the drawing that Gerhard made of Michelangelo's *Bruges Madonna*, and prop it up next to the photograph I took of Enzo, sitting on the wall near San Miniato al Monte, with the panorama of Florence behind him.

I pick up the roll of film that is labeled FLORENTINISCHE BRÜCKEN. Florentine bridges. I rotate the metal canister between my fingers, seeing my distorted reflection wavering back at me in the cold light. If I had a darkroom, I could open it and place the negatives into the metal pans. The tangy smell of the developing bath would, as always, be the smell of a world that no longer exists, a moment lost in time. That's because photography can make the dead live. That is the power of a picture. It endures, it is a testament of life. A three-dimensional thing in two dimensions. Magic.

But it is only an illusion, a life captured on a flat surface, not truly resurrected. I can only pray that Gerhard won't disappear into a figment of black and white, just like Enzo did. And I pray this will all be over soon.

But instead, we spend weeks stuck. Jailed along with hundreds of the world's masterpieces. Holding our breath. Thirteen kilometers from the Austrian border as the crow flies. Yet it seems as far removed as if it were on the other side of the ocean.

22

JOSIE

AFTER WITNESSING THE EXTENT OF THE GERMANS'
deception firsthand, all of us in the Uffizi offices are anxious to reach
the other countryside deposits as soon as possible. But early September brings relentless rains. The swollen river engulfs the detritus
of the medieval tower houses along its banks. The level of the Arno
is frightening to behold, its angry waters swift-moving, swirling to
overflowing. It threatens to demolish the temporary Bailey bridge
and the stumped piers of the ruined Ponte Santa Trinità. Pedestrians
cross under threat of being washed away with the debris.

In the ground floor of the Uffizi, we wade in water up to our ankles. Paloma and I move all the files out of the bottom drawers of our
filing cabinets. We take as much paper as we can to the second floor.
From our offices, we can hear the rushing waters of the Arno. We
pull boxes from the shelves in the archives, holding them up while
we climb the narrow stone treads of the stairwells that have worn
down under centuries of foot traffic. Around the city, rain flows into
the churches with no roofs and turns the tiled floors into ponds. We
could sail rafts in the squares bordering the river if we wanted to.
Driving Georgette out of the city is unthinkable, as every stream bed
is a river, every river awash with mud. The roads leading to the WAC
camp are washed out and I worry about my friends.

Captain Foster, having bid a sad farewell to his lodgings at Santa

Lucia, shifts from one requisitioned Florentine hotel to another until an Italian countess who is an avid art collector takes pity on him and offers him an apartment in her palazzo near San Lorenzo.

From across our communal desk, Paloma says, "I would offer you lodging, Josie, but our home is bursting with people. But I know a place where you can stay."

We dash over the Ponte Vecchio under Paloma's flimsy umbrella. And she leads me to the humble Pensione Sorelle Bandini in Santo Spirito, now requisitioned by the Fifth Army.

The Pensione Sorelle Bandini occupies the upper floor of the Palazzo Guadagni, the beautiful Renaissance palazzo we admired upon our arrival in Florence, in the Piazza Santo Spirito. One of the three ancient sisters tells me the whole building housed Germans until recent weeks. Near the reception desk, there is a peaceful loggia that overlooks the Piazza Santo Spirito and its butter-colored church façade. She leads me out onto the terrace, where I can see the gray clouds collect low like a blanket over the domes and tile roofs. "If you come at seven," she tells me, "I'll bring you a glass of prosecco."

In the breakfast room, there are a couple of haggard-looking women with a gathering of children sitting at the tables, eating crusty bread and cheese. Around them, colorful modern paintings are displayed on easels and propped on the buffet cabinet that holds bread and jam. The children look hollow-eyed and haunted, as if they have witnessed a tragedy. The oldest sister, a petite, scrappy woman who is permanently stooped, shows me to my room. I follow her up a narrow, stone staircase to the top floor, where the rooms are small and dark. At the top of the stairs, there is a large wooden armoire that has been pushed away from the wall. One of the other sisters is dusting the empty shelves.

On the wall where it seems the armoire fits, there is a tiny wooden door tall enough for a child, with a lock. The door is open. Inside, there is a vast, dark attic space. Thin mattresses and the smell of sweat and excrement.

When I recoil, the sister turns to me. Hesitates. "Those Jewish people in the breakfast room . . ." she says finally. "The mothers and their children." She gestures to the recesses of the dark attic. "They've been living in there for the past year."

"But . . . I thought there were Nazis staying in this building."

"*Si.*" She nods once, then she turns and motions for me to follow her to my room.

"What's cooking, Mouse?"

Over the crackling telephone line, Dot's voice sounds like home and I can't help it. I break into a smile that brings tears with it.

"The usual," I say. "Figuring out how to find enough trucks and gasoline to bring every picture in Tuscany back to the Uffizi."

"What do you think this is, some kind of army logistics headquarters? Oh yeah. OK, I'll see what I can do."

"You're the best, Dot."

Now that a line of communication has been established from the Uffizi offices, Dot races her friends at the switchboard to plug in any call coming from Florence. Thanks to Dot and her friends in the mobile trailers, along with Captain Foster's swift approval, we manage to arrange trucks and gasoline for the superintendents. We know the Fifth Army Freight Section is doing everything in its power to help us, even though its primary job is to carry supplies to the front-line troops. With these precious resources at our disposal, Captain Foster is able to arrange to move supplies and construction materials around Florence, and to prepare to evacuate the treasures from the countryside repositories, as soon as we can reach them.

Ever since our desperate trek to Poggio a Caiano, Captain Foster has made several more forays into the countryside, but he hasn't been able to reach any of the other depots. The roads are still covered in

German panzer and paratrooper units, and he has had no choice but to return to Florence. In his absence, Paloma picks up an agitated telegram from Signor de Luca, the beleaguered custodian at Poggio a Caiano. In spite of our OFF LIMITS signs, a South African unit had requisitioned the villa as a field hospital, where, he says, the sick and dying men lie in bed and contemplate Pontormo's frescoes. Captain Foster writes a letter to our commanders in protest, but I can see from his expression that his faith in this gargantuan project has begun to waver.

In the evenings, I walk across the Ponte Vecchio and into the maze of streets in the Oltrarno, making my way to the *pensione*. My eyes scan the doorways and street corners for Corrado to appear magically and walk with me. To my delight, he does.

After two weeks that seem a lifetime, the rains stop and the clouds make way for a brilliant blue sky. Every evening, Florentine sunsets turn a shade of gold and copper I've never witnessed before. I catch a ride on a Fifth Army transport vehicle to the WAC camp on the edge of the city. I find the girls cleaning up from what looks like a natural disaster.

The sun flares hot and bright, but the tents lie in great puddles. It's obvious that any efforts to keep them dry have been a lost cause. Equally futile, I see, is any attempt to maintain the dress code. It seems the rules of women's uniforms were left behind on the coast of Algeria all those months ago. The girls have exchanged their work dresses, skirts, and pantyhose for makeshift garments. Sergeant Barnes is wearing men's coveralls that make her look as if she belongs in an auto mechanic shop rather than a women's army tent. I find Dot wearing an oversized man's wool shirt cut off like some kind of battle jacket, her pin curls brushed out to a frizzy mess in the humid air. But somehow she seems strong, and still beautiful. Lollie Dee brings me a cup of watery coffee and a slice of crumbly cake.

They crowd around me, hug me, as if I am a long-lost relative or visiting dignitary. They haven't been into Florence yet and they want to know what I've seen.

In the soggy mess tent, I sit in the center of a crowd of men and women hungry for information. "Well, according to Captain Foster's estimates, about a third of the medieval city is destroyed," I tell them. "There were lots of historic tower houses along the Arno, and those are lost. But we are worried about the repositories in the countryside that we haven't been able to get to yet. We're afraid the Germans may have taken a lot of the artwork from the Uffizi Galleries and Pitti Palace. But enough about me . . ."

"You haven't missed anything except this damned flood," Ruby says. "Otherwise, it's the same as always. The men are still complaining about the local women. Apparently they can't get any Italian girls to go out with them." Lieutenant Hamm gives her a goofy grin and she swats his shoulder. "Ha! I wonder why."

"Yep," Dot says. "And the Red Cross workers and nurses aren't allowed to go out with enlisted men. That leaves us. So if we don't go out and show them a good time, we feel like a heel. And anyway, we're the only American girls around, so what else are we to do?"

Later, I find Lollie Dee alone in the mess tent, washing cups. "How are you, Mouse—really?" she asks. "Are you as—solid—as you seem to be?"

I nod. "I'm doing alright. And I might be in love."

Lollie Dee slaps me on the arm with a faded dishrag. "Beat me daddy eight to the bar!" she cries in a loud whisper. "See? I told you you could do better than eating Dot's leftovers. Your Monuments officer!"

"No, no." I can't help but cackle. "Not Captain Foster. He's married, and anyway, he's not my type. No. An *Italian*."

Lollie Dee's smile collapses. She shakes her head. "Oh, no, Mouse. It cannot end well. That man will break your heart. I guarantee it." She squeezes my hands and looks in my eyes.

I can only believe she's right, but I'm too starstruck to accept it. And I don't want to think too far ahead.

In my sagging WAC tent, I find my abandoned cot with a small stack of V-mail, dots of water staining the thin papers.

I tear open one of the nearly weightless slips. I recognize my home address, our old apartment near the oak tree and the crumpled sidewalk. But it's not my mother's handwriting. I feel my heart drop to my shoes even before I read my aunt Betty's first words: *I'm sorry, Josephine*, the letter begins. *She didn't suffer too long. You know how much she loved you.*

But I can't read the rest. I press the letter to my chest, where it feels my heart will thump right out of it.

After all I did to make my mother proud, I wasn't there for the most important thing. I just wasn't there at all.

"Mouse, what is it?" I hear Ruby's voice from across the tent.

But how could I begin to explain? For the long span of years, I took for granted the unshakable rock of my mother's love and pride in me. Now I float alone in my grief, as if a stone crumbled and dislodged from a great building, washed away like a piece of rubble in an angry torrent.

By the middle of September, my friends on the switchboards have helped arrange a Fifth Army convoy for a trip to Poppiano and Montagnana, areas now free of direct fighting.

"Hey, Mouse, I managed to get four trucks." Dot's voice on the other end of the scratchy line.

"No packing material? No crates?"

"Don't press your luck, dolly. Count your blessings that you got any trucks at all. You're not the only one asking for them."

I know Dot's only trying to cheer me with her familiar banter. She's sent me messages every week, saying nice things about my ma, sharing her memories of our time together in New Haven. I know she's trying to help but I remain alone in my loss.

We set off from the Uffizi offices at dawn, the rattling trucks empty except for a few metal rollers and ropes provided by the superintendency. Captain Foster says that in the absence of packaging, crates, or boxes, we will have to make do with whatever we can find.

Along with the drivers and a few hired laborers, Filippo Rossi, Paloma, and I ride with the motorcade through the rugged hills. I recognize the familiar way to Santa Lucia, up and down through the hills. On the way, we pass the charred remains of German trucks that line the road, bringing visions of what a fighter plane might do to a convoy of works of art.

We pass through a village that seems untouched by war. You would never know that utter destruction lies just a few miles away and a bitter battle rages just over the next range of hills. Captain Foster points out houses dating back to the twelfth and thirteenth centuries, historic churches and structures of sandstone and ruddy roof tiles. These hulking structures look like they will last forever, will endure any injustice that may be thrust upon them. Here and there, there is scarring or bullet holes, but it is unclear, to me at least, whether this is the result of last week's fighting or some ancient battle between warring hilltops. A few brave people poke their heads out of doors, or open their shutters and wave as we pass.

Beyond the village, olive trees and cypresses stand peacefully alongside the perfection of the landscape and architecture. A blue-green valley lies behind a town that rises to a series of brown, ruddy towers. In some places, roofs have collapsed. A disemboweled German tank has been abandoned in a grove of olive trees.

At last, we arrive at the old castle of Poppiano. Little has changed since our last visit other than the placement of guards. Inside the castle, we greet the men and head off to locate the giant Mannerist altarpieces. Through the hours, the laborers groan, push, lift, ease, and haul these precious works into the trucks, interspersed with a few words I don't recognize, but that make Captain Foster howl with laughter.

By late afternoon, we return to the trucks, where Paloma and I cross-check my typed inventory pages with her Italian paperwork from the superintendency:

Pontormo's *Deposition* from Santa Felicita
Visitation from Carmignano
Vecchietta *Madonna Enthroned*
Ambrogio Lorenzetti, *Presentation in the Temple*
Rosso Fiorentino's *Depositions* from Volterra and Sansepolcro
Detached frescoes by Paolo Uccello from Chiostro Verde

I also check off a series of altarpieces by Vasari, Saviati, Pomarancio, Cigoli, Santi di Tito, Passignano, and others. Our pages match, and we squeeze each other's hands for a job well done.

Heading on to the Villa Bossi-Pucci at Montagnana, we pass a handful of hollow, burned-up tanks abandoned to the forest. In places, trees are charred brown by artillery fire. We haven't been able to reach this villa before now, even though it's just a stone's throw from Santa Lucia. At last, the fighting has died down long enough for us to get there. Captain Foster turns Georgette down a country lane. Even from afar, we are filled with a new sense of trepidation; the old villa and its grounds are a scene of utter devastation. The windows are broken, no more than open, gaping holes. Captain Foster rolls to a stop and cuts the engine at the base of a slope, where the villa's lower level wine cellar doors are broken open, the weeds covered in broken wine bottles.

Entering the busted front door of the villa, we find no one; no custodian, no guards. We walk through empty rooms, sitting still under layers of dust, filth, and rubble revealed from the dust-filled beams of sunlight streaking through the shutters. We drag ourselves up the old staircase with trepidation, only to find the old rooms of the house full of smashed furniture. Not a single chair or table leg remains in one piece. Piles of human excrement in each room have drawn scores of flies. The stench in the summer heat is overwhelming.

"There is nothing here," I say.

Rossi flips furiously through his lists as if he will rip them apart. "Bellini," he reports. "Piero di Cosimo. Signorelli."

Leaning over his shoulder to review the pages, I see:

Giovanni Bellini, *Pietà*
Botticelli, *Minerva and the Centaur*
Five paintings by Piero di Cosimo
Four altarpieces by Filippo Lippi
Pollaiuolo, two small *Labors of Hercules*
Signorelli, *Crucifixion*
Roger van der Weyden, *Entombment*
Pontormo, *Martyrdom* and *St. Maurice and the Theban Legion*
Tintoretto, *Venus, Mars, and Vulcan*

Captain Foster opens a window and leans over the sill, looking out to the quiet olive grove beyond. "A large portion of the treasures of the Uffizi and the Pitti," he says.

"There's something here!" I say, walking into an adjacent room, where there is an elaborate panel painting, some eight feet tall, that looks like it might have been detached from an altarpiece.

"Ambrogio Lorenzetti's *Presentation in the Temple*," Foster says, coming up behind me.

"At least they left behind one important picture," I say.

Captain Foster only shakes his head. "It means the men who stole the rest don't know what they have. Brutes who have no understanding or knowledge of what they have taken—or how to handle or care for it."

With nothing more to load, we prepare to return to the city. Workmen pile into the back of the open trucks and secure the few pictures with whatever we can muster—cushions, blankets, tarps, quilts. They tie them down with ropes so nothing moves. In perfect Italian, Captain Foster gives each driver a lesson about the incalculable value of the treasures in their possession. "No truck is to exceed six kilometers per hour," he tells them.

The trucks crawl back toward Florence with their meager cargo. We roll through an olive orchard, where we come across an encampment of American GIs. A few men, their uniforms dirty and ragged, sit around a makeshift campfire. The air is thick with laughter, cigarette smoke, and roasting meat. When they see us, they stand and gawk, then start to cheer us on. The ruckus lures more men out of their tents. A few of them clamber onto the trucks, hanging on the edges of the towering altarpieces to hitch a free ride to Florence.

"Get down from there!" I yell from the window.

"You an American girl?" one of the men yells. "Come on! Stay with us! We'll show you a good time!" A burst of cheering.

Captain Foster jumps down from the passenger seat of his truck, and peels the men off the gilded frames. The men shout and laugh at one another. At last, they give up their game as we roll out of the orchard. The Italian workmen also hang on the backs of the trucks, moving overhanging tree limbs and downed, dangling wires so nothing catches on the pictures. What should take us forty minutes takes hours along the cratered roads.

We make our way into the southern outskirts of Florence as the sun makes its dramatic descent over the distant hills. The trucks crawl toward the Pitti Palace, as more and more Florentines lean out of their upper-floor windows or step out into the street to gawk at the sight of the towering pictures on the trucks.

In the dark, one of the British commanders is waiting for us at the back doors of the Pitti Palace. He tells us that new fighting has broken out north and west of the city. We watch the men unload the paintings in the gathering dark.

"I know you have every intention of returning the other master-pieces to Florence," he tells Captain Foster, "but we can't risk it. The rest will have to stay in the deposits for now."

If we can't undertake another rescue mission, for now, we try to put together pieces of the giant puzzle from our offices in Florence. Our ledger books grow long and marked up as ragged bits of information come in. The superintendents climb through the boxes in the dark storage rooms of the Uffizi, cross-checking their pages with the works that the Germans and Italians returned to Florence before the final days leading up to the blowing up of the bridges. They report that the works from the hiding spots at Santomato, Striano, Incisa, and Scarperia match their inventories. Nothing is missing.

A patchwork of complicated messages reaches us from custodians in the countryside. They report that the stained glass of the Duomo of Florence has been located safely inside a villa near Maiano. A deposit of important works from the Pitti and Uffizi has been located at Poggio Imperiale, on the outskirts of the city.

But a significant number of works in our inventories remain unaccounted for. After what Captain Foster and I witnessed at Poggio a Caiano and Montagnana, we grow increasingly worried about the fate of the remaining masterpieces. I come into the office early and he's been there for hours; he stays late into the night, sending telegrams, making calls, checking and double-checking the lists. Paloma and I observe Captain Foster's pacing, his nervous rummaging over and over, through the same files and stacks of papers.

One morning, we receive word that the German paratrooper units in the vicinity of Poppi have moved far enough off to the north for us to reach an important deposit there. Captain Foster, Rossi, and I head out of the city along an ancient, winding road toward the Umbrian border. Against a clear blue sky, Captain Foster points out the distant white peaks of the Apuan Alps to the west. "Where Michelangelo quarried his own marble," he tells me, and Rossi nods. But to the north and east, the hills appear as a succession of grim ridge lines that turn ocher and blue in the distance. The stench of gunfire and rot grows heavy in the air.

Near the edge of a chestnut forest, the road is nearly demolished. Captain Foster is forced to pull Georgette off the roadside. We rumble alongside streambeds or over open, fallow fields for a long way before we can rejoin the road. Along the way, rain clouds gather over a vista of gutted villages. After more than two hours, my body is exhausted and wrung out from rambling through the cratered countryside.

At last, Rossi points out a tall, skinny watchtower in the distance. "The counts of Guidi dominated this whole area in the Middle Ages," he tells us. The jeep struggles up the steep hill to the ruins of a medieval gate that has been blown to rubble. We circumnavigate the village to find a rear town gate still intact. We make our way through narrow lanes and to a small square before an imposing medieval castle that looks like it could be a little replica of the Palazzo della Signoria in Florence.

Inside, the custodian, a small man with streaks of white through his dark hair, brings us into a large hall full of hulking wooden crates, strung together with ropes and cleats. "The Germans took as much as would fit in their trucks," he says. "I was here. And Father Luca, too. I will bring him to tell you everything." The custodian heads off into the shadows.

We light candles and begin to go through the boxes. Some of them have labels. Botticelli, *Birth of Venus*. Leonardo da Vinci, *Adoration of the Magi*. Filippo Lippi, *Madonna and Child with Angels*.

After a while, the custodian returns with a skinny, bedraggled-looking priest and the strapping, white-haired local mayor.

"They came in the middle of the night," the priest tells us. "We heard their trucks and their loud voices, but they ordered everyone in the village to stay in their homes. Everyone was terrified, hiding in their cellars with the shutters and doors closed. But we heard the trucks leave as soon as the sun rose . . ."

"We were worried they might have left mines in the castle," the mayor says. "Or that there might still be soldiers about. But after a while, everything was quiet and we came into the courtyard. We found doors forced open, smashed bricks all over the place, and then . . . the empty boxes. Then there were two German officers with an interpreter."

The priest says, "They claimed they had orders from their High Command, that the entire operation was official and was designed to protect the works from the Anglo-Americans. They apologized for not having enough trucks to remove everything. Then they told us we would have to be responsible for protecting what is left."

"They also ordered a bunch of men to clean up the rubble so it looked like nothing happened. When they left, they exploded our medieval gate."

We find many smashed cases, some empty, some hastily closed up. These contain dismantled ceramic reliefs by della Robbia.

"The rest are missing," Rossi declares, slapping his inventory pages with the back of his hand. We are surrounded by opened boxes, beautiful paintings. Gold frames glowing in the candlelight. "About thirty cases. Two hundred works of art."

Rossi reads out the list. Three paintings by Raphael—an early self-portrait, a portrait of Cardinal Bibbiena, and the *Donna Velata*. Two Madonnas by Botticelli, Titian's *Concert*, three pictures by Andrea del Sarto, Dürer's *Calvary*, a *Madonna and Child* by Correggio, a late Rembrandt portrait of an old man, Rubens's *Holy Family*, Watteau's *Flute Player*. Cranach's portraits of Martin Luther and his wife. Many more.

"You notice something," Foster says. "They left behind major works like Michelangelo's *Doni Madonna* and Mantegna's *Adoration of the Magi*. And what they took are mostly German pictures. And Dutch and Flemish. Five Dürers, seven Cranachs. A Bruegel, a Holbein, four Memlings. Works by Ruysdael, Steen, Joos van Cleve, Terborch, Teniers, and other northern painters."

"They want as many of their own pictures as they can get away with," I say.

We post OFF LIMITS signs, say goodbye to the men, and prepare to return to Florence.

In the back of the jeep, rumbling back toward Florence, I check our inventories to see that the works of art stolen by the Germans have more than doubled.

I find Corrado sitting at a small table at the *caffè* across from Palazzo Guadagni. It's been a few weeks since I've seen him, mostly because we've been working outside the city. If I am honest, I've swallowed what must be the truth of Lollie Dee's assessment. *That man will break your heart.* But at the sight of him, I can't wipe the stupid grin off my face.

"Paloma told me you were back in the city," he says, standing and pulling out a chair for me. "I thought if I hung out here long enough, I would run into you." My heart lifts to think that he might be thinking of me while I've been out at the countryside depots. That he might have been hoping for my return.

Around the city, I see the first signs of normal life. At the *caffè*, a cluster of elderly men sit in wrought iron chairs, shooting small cups of espresso and talking with loud voices and animated gestures. One old man is so passionate that he keeps getting up from his seat to argue his points with hand gestures in front of his friends' faces. Two young women sit together at a table, talking softly.

"We've been to so many places, I can hardly keep track," I say. "We've counted more than seven hundred works of art missing so far," I tell Corrado as he brings me a small cup of thick chocolate gelato, the most delicious ice cream I've ever tasted.

"*Dimmi tutto,*" he says, resting his elbows on the table. Tell me everything.

I know he means tell him about what we've found in the repositories. But the mere words *dimmi tutto* seem to unlock, then unleash, what I really need to say instead, and *my mother died of lung cancer* comes tumbling out of my mouth.

In my best effort, a mangled patchwork of Italian and English, I talk about my mother. About how I was so quick to leave home. So quick to leave her behind, where she suffered alone in her last days. At a certain point, he places his elbows on his knees and hangs his head while I talk, as if he, too, has fallen grief-stricken even though he never knew Darla Evans.

Eventually, I do tell Corrado about works of art we've found from all over Tuscany—from Siena, Arezzo, Pistoia, Livorno, Pisa, Lucca, and Grosseto—mostly intact. About the places, like Poppi and Montagnana, that have been savagely raped. And about the complicated puzzle of figuring out which works have been brought back to Florence, which have been stolen, and which are yet to be found. I tell him about the Villa Bocci at Soci, which the Germans requisitioned as a field hospital and where sixty-nine cases of art have gone missing. About how we've driven through blinding rain and across minefields at Camaldoli, and where we found some of the Uffizi's most prized possessions. Works by Botticelli, Titian, and Leonardo da Vinci. Piero della Francesca's portraits of the Duke and Duchess of Urbino that brought Captain Foster to tears.

While I tell Corrado these stories, he watches me carefully. But the way he watches me is different than other men. He doesn't ogle me like Captain Thomas did. He doesn't expect me to entertain him in the same way that some of our boys do in the camp. He doesn't look past me, like so many men do when Dot or other women more beautiful than I are present. Instead, he looks at me, into me, seeming to see what's inside. No one's ever looked at me like that before.

"But it's hard on the American side, too," I say. "We rely on our boys to respect what's inside and to post guard. But many of our soldiers don't recognize the importance or value of what's inside these depots. We don't have the kind of cultural heritage in the United States that you do in Italy."

But even though I never understood art before coming to Italy, and even though my homeland doesn't have this kind of cultural history, I realize now that I've begun to feel that my own fate is somehow tied up with these masterpieces and I want nothing more than to save them, to protect them. I understand now why so many people have put their lives on the line to save them. I celebrate what has been recovered, mourn for what has been destroyed, and I worry what the Germans will do with those treasures still in their hands.

I wish my Italian was good enough to explain all of this, but I am struck mute with the enormity of it. Somehow, Corrado seems to understand. He reaches for my hand, which feels warm and secure between his palms.

Every day in our offices in the Uffizi, we listen to the daily German and Italian Fascist broadcasts. Paloma translates for me. They call us "American art Jews" and they accuse us of pillaging all of Italy. In one broadcast, they describe Italian works of art being spread out in a line for Allied generals to take their pick. They describe works of art being loaded onto ships and sent across the ocean to Britain and America. One broadcast reports that a special fleet of ships is poised in the Bay of Salerno to spirit off Italy's masterpieces across the ocean. Another claims the Allies have dismantled the cathedral of Monreale stone by stone, so that it can be reconstructed on the other side of the Atlantic Ocean. We hear of a New York art auction house selling off the finest treasures of Sicily to the American public; the Germans claim they even have an auction catalog in their possession. Another broadcast claims that our Buffalo soldiers have stolen the greatest treasures of Italy; another that a ceremony at the National Gallery in Washington, D.C., celebrated the arrival of newly acquired Italian paintings into their collection.

Not one of these stories is true, of course. We have seen with our own eyes the destruction of the Florentine bridges and have witnessed the missing crates in the countryside depots.

"You think the Americans have taken nothing from Italy?" Paloma asks me.

I consider her question before answering. I pick up a small photograph on my desk. I found it on the floor under my narrow bed at Palazzo Guadagni. It shows a bombed-out wall alongside a church, a skeleton in stone. Testimony to some unlabeled, horrific event, snapped by an unknown photographer who might have stayed in my own room before me.

"I wish I could say no," I say at last. The truth is, of course, the temptations are great and we have heard stories of Allied soldiers picking up souvenirs along the way. "But you've seen the Germans' propaganda. Nothing we have done measures up to their portrayal of us as ravagers of the Italian countryside."

Paloma sits quietly for a moment, and I wonder if she is thinking about the Allied bombings I've heard so much about—terror dropped from the sky around Florence for the better part of a year. I wasn't here to witness it. But she was.

On a cool evening, Captain Thomas pays us a visit. We assemble around a table in an impressive dining room, thanks to the hospitality of the countess who is lodging Captain Foster near San Lorenzo. Countess Lucrezia Rotondi di Grillo is a severe-looking older woman in a silk dress the color of champagne, a dash of effortless elegance. She seems to have taken it on as a personal project to support the

Allied Monuments officers. And when she gets word that Captain Thomas is coming up from Pisa, she throws an impromptu dinner party.

But there is no celebration. Captain Thomas is a diminished shell of himself. He's lost weight in the few months since we've seen him. Over several emptied bottles of Chianti, he tells us of the devastation of Pisa, how forty days of continuous shelling have left the historic city little more than a smoking pile of gutted buildings, resulting in an entire city's worth of roving refugees. Over dinner, we hear the story of how blazing beams in the Camposanto fell on Roman-era sarcophagi and centuries-old tombs. How the lead roof melted and ran down the walls decorated with medieval frescoes. How Benozzo Gozzoli's masterpiece, the *Triumph of Death* series, cooked in the searing heat. It's a miracle that the famous leaning tower is still standing, he tells us. And how lucky we are to find any work of art still in existence after such hell.

When we get up from the table late into the night, Captain Foster and Captain Thomas stagger toward the door, their arms around each other's shoulders, snickering together in drunken unison. The once-rivals are staking each other up to face another day. For who else could understand all that we have seen and been through?

The next morning, there is a telegram from someone working in an office of the Patriarch of Venice. "It says that some Tuscan artwork is being hidden somewhere in Alto Adige," Paloma says, holding the thin paper between both hands. "In a place called Neumelans in Sand." The words come out with some hesitation.

But none of us can find such a place on any map or in any guidebook. None of the Italians have ever heard of it. And anyway, Alto Adige is practically Austria and there is no hope of reaching it now.

23

EVA

MAJOR REIDEMEISTER HAS LOCATED A SECOND HID-ing place higher in the Dolomites, a two-hour journey from San Leonardo in the lumbering trucks. From the passenger seat, I watch the open truck bed in front of us wind ever so slowly along the switchback mountain passes, the trucks tottering with pictures. Along the mountainsides, the leaves have turned burnt scarlet and orange, their edges curling and furling, quivering, preparing to drop.

The Kunstschutz is paying a handful of local men to drive and load the trucks. Beside me, a lean man with a hardened face, his mouth a thin line of concentration, maneuvers the swaying truck around the switchback roads, their crumbled pavement edges giving way to deep ravines and cold mountain streams.

Beyond San Leonardo, the landscape rises to staggering, steep peaks that form the spine of the Italo-Austrian border. Our father always told us stories of the secret, winding paths that cross these mountains, well-worn trails for smugglers and black-market traders moving unseen between Italy and Austria with packs on their backs. I search the rocky peaks for any sign of those secret little paths. But all I see are chapels with gilded onion domes sitting alone on hilltops. And on the highest craggy peaks, there is the first dusting of snow.

"Did they find another jail?" I ask the driver in Italian.

"No," he says. "A noble house. *Il Capo* told us it's better if the treasures are spread out. Not all in one place." Horst—the boss he refers to—has gone ahead with Major Reidemeister to sort out the details.

We roll into a green valley standing quiet amid stark, steep peaks. The truck comes to a stop before a grand manor house with four turrets standing in the shadow of the rugged landscape. On the grounds, there are a variety of smaller residences and outbuildings. On a mountain above us stands an ancient castle, its towers looming above the village in the valley below.

"*Heil!*" An officer in a greatcoat extends his arm, then directs us to park the truck alongside the others in front of the manor house.

"*Ecco,*" the driver says. "*Siamo arrivati.* We call it Campo Tures. But you might know it as Sand in Taufers. Or Neumelans."

I find Major Reidemeister, Horst, and several other German officers inside. They seem to have made themselves at home in the grand residence. The smell of something delicious wafts from the ground-floor kitchens. There are roaring fires in the enormous hearths.

Immediately, I see that this building is more ideal for storing paintings than the jail at San Leonardo. There are dry, high-ceilinged rooms on the upper floors. Several German officers and the Italian laborers collect in the rooms around wooden crates, enormous paintings, ceramics and tapestries, and small bronzes of the type Professor Kriegbaum and I were off to photograph near the Campo di Marte all those months ago, back when I was so naïve.

In an adjacent carriage house, two soldiers in helmets and greatcoats roll back the doors. Their boots make muddy footprints through the leaves. As my eyes adjust to the dark interior, I recognize the stout Florentine boxes containing Donatello's statue of *Saint George*, Michelangelo's *Bacchus* from Poggio a Caiano, and Raphael's portrait of *Donna Velata*. In the shadows, I find Major Reidemeister and Horst surveying the boxes stacked from floor to ceiling. "We have seven additional cases from the Florence museums," Horst tells me. "They were in a depot in Verona but Major Reidemeister thought it best to bring them all here. We can't risk that the Italians might have access to them. You know how they are."

All morning, I take pictures of the Italian workers unloading the trucks into the manor house and its outbuildings, my toes turning numb in the cold. At noon, the sun turns brilliant but the air stays cold, inhospitable. Major Reidemeister hands me a grainy photograph. "Our intelligence got this to us," he tells me. At first, I see nothing but rubble, misshapen outlines of stones and water. "We managed to hold them for a while on the southern bank, at least," he says. "I thought you might want to see it." Now I begin to recognize the line of the northern bank of the Arno, once lined with medieval towers and wide stone parapets. I recognize the stumped piers of the Ponte Santa Trinità, one of Michelangelo's contributions to the Florentine cityscape. Now there is only destruction. Once there were stone towers, centuries-old buildings. People's homes. Enzo's home. The very sniper's nest where I spent my last night in Florence.

In the depths of my gut, I have felt the gaping hole of his absence, even so many kilometers away. But now my fears are confirmed. And I know for sure he's gone.

In the end, Enzo was wrong to trust us. He was wrong to assume we wouldn't consider him collateral damage. All justifiable in the name of war. It's exactly the same thing I tried to protect Gerhard from. And now I wonder if it is too late for him, too.

At midday, the soldiers and laborers file into the manor house's dining hall. Some of the soldiers remove their muddy boots on the stone floor and thaw themselves by the roaring fire in the hearth. Others rifle through the carved armoires and cabinets. Open doors to other rooms. See what might be yet undiscovered, ripe for pilfering.

Several unhappy-looking local women have been corralled into the effort of feeding the dozens of Kunstschutz staff, soldiers, and officers who collect in the dining room. A stout woman ladles a serving of stew into a bowl and hands it to me. I find a spot at the table near the fire. My numb toes begin to thaw as I inhale the steam. I look around. I am the only woman at the table. The men chatter on about the best place to find cigarettes and flour, about their luck—or lack thereof—with the local women. One man comments on the relative merits of a woman in a village south of here, and the other men roar with laughter.

After a while, the soldiers stand, retrieve their gloves, and return to the cold. Through the window, the air turns pink and still. It looks as if we might have an early snow.

I feel the back of my neck prickle. I turn to find Major Reidemeister watching me with interest from the other end of the table. Before I can excuse myself, he slides his coffee cup across the wooden tabletop to the spot across from me. Reidemeister presses back in his chair and makes a tent of hands under his thin lips. "Fräulein Brunner, there's something I'd like to discuss with you."

I don't try to imagine what is on his mind.

"You are doing good work, Fräulein. Important work. I would like to give you a new assignment," he says. "A promotion."

"Oh? What is that, sir?"

"As of today," he says, "I'm assigning you and Horst to create a catalog." A smug smile.

"A catalog? What for?" I feel unease rise in my throat.

"A catalog of all the important works we have brought to safety . . . It's for our Führer. The treasures of Italy. Everything we have safeguarded—to be celebrated. Think of it, Fräulein," he says. "Our Führer will be able to hold the book in his hands, see your pictures. We will show him everything we have done here." Now his face opens into a wide, self-satisfied grin. "You should consider it an honor."

Unable to find the words to respond to such a directive, I rise instead and stand for a moment before the fire. Then I go to the window, where my cameras are sitting on a heavy, carved wooden table. I loop two camera straps around my neck. My thumb taps on the shutter release. I take a deep breath.

I feel his presence before he comes to stand beside me at the window. Through the glass panes, I see that a new truck has pulled up in the gravel before the carriage house, and several soldiers in greatcoats are moving the crates out of the truck.

I turn to face him now. "What would be an honor, sir, is if all of these works could return to Tuscany, where they belong."

In the light of the window, his face is clenched, unreadable. He seems to think about this carefully, then he says, "For now, they will stay here. Südtirol is an in-between land. Gauleiter Hofer has given us the troops to guard the works, the facilities." He gestures to the warm room around us, with its carved ceiling, long dining table, and roaring fire. "He assures us they will not allow any Italians into the region. Anyway, we're not really in Italy anymore, are we?" A sly grin. He touches the back of his leather-gloved fingers to my elbow and I flinch.

"And then?" I steady myself and look at him again.

He purses his lips at my recoiling, then says, "And then, when the time is right, they will go to the salt mines in Austria for safekeeping, and ultimately, to the Führer's museum in Linz."

If ever I thought we were going back to Tuscany, I was wrong. Everything here—from the Cranachs to the Italian treasures and everything in between—has been pilfered. The men have no intention of returning them.

Behind us, the fire spits several glowing embers beyond the hearth and onto the stone floor. And a new truck pulls up to the carriage house outside the window. A group of men in greatcoats opens the truck doors and begins to unload the crates.

In one of the jail cells at San Leonardo, Horst and I are moving a large panel painting when I see two armored vehicles pull up outside through the narrow, barred window.

Horst has just begun to outline a catalog entry: a beautiful portrait attributed to Andrea del Sarto. The Kunstschutz has provided
rolls of film, a fine new box camera, and has promised to have the
pictures developed at a reputable photo processor in Bolzano when it
comes time to produce the Führer's catalog in its final form.

"It's Professor Heydenreich!" I say. Horst tucks his pages under
the crook of his elbow and pushes his bulk next to me to peer out
the jail cell window.

Beyond the narrow silhouette of craggy peaks, the sky is the color
of steel. The trees on the steep mountainsides have turned golden.
They seem to whisper to one another to be as brilliant as they can.
Soon, the leaves will darken, curl, and fall to the ground in a crispy
carpet. I see Professor Heydenreich walking toward the prison, his
long wool coat flapping, the wind sending his slicked hair into a
peak. Behind him, the driver slams shut the car doors. It's the first
time we've seen our old director since he left Florence for Milan.
Seems a lifetime ago. My first reaction is relief—I have come to see
Heydenreich as a friend—but after all that has happened in recent
days, I no longer trust my own judgment about the motives of the
men around me. Still, there is an excitement in greeting as we reunite
with our former director.

"I've been waiting at the Deutsches Institut in Milan," Heydenreich tells us as he introduces the two staff members he's brought
with him from the German Institute there. "I've been appealing to
Major Reidemeister and Colonel Langsdorff to let me come here to
check on everything."

In the kitchen, we offer the men bitter coffee and the remains of a
strudel we bought from a baker farther up the steep street. Professor
Heydenreich tells us the Deutsches Institut has suffered much the
same fate as the art history institute in Florence, that most of its offices, contents, and staff have returned to Germany. Only a handful
of German scholars remain. He tells us that the damage in Florence
pales in the face of what the Allies have done in Milan. The cathedral

and the Castello Sforsezco have suffered damage. City blocks have been razed to the ground; many citizens have fled their homes in Milan and may never return. Leonardo da Vinci's famous fresco of the *Last Supper* in Santa Maria della Grazie has been shored up with sandbags but its building is open to the sky. "I have no idea how it is still standing," he tells us. "Nothing short of a miracle."

We spend the afternoon inspecting the condition of the paintings locked in the jail cells. Heydenreich files through the tightly stacked frames, running his eyes over the priceless works pilfered from the countryside depots. Horst has prepared a press release, which he shares excitedly with Heydenreich. A story about how we—a special team of German and Austrian custodians—are caring for and safe-guarding the cultural patrimony of the Italian nation.

"Have you been in touch with Poggi, or Rossi, Fasola . . . any of the other superintendents?" I ask. "Do they know where we are? And where we have taken the works?"

His face turns dark. "I'm afraid not. We have no channels of communication with them. You must understand that Florence, Tuscany . . . They are no longer ours. They're in the hands of the Anglo-Americans now."

"But . . . we have to do something!" I insist. "They must be worried sick. All the agreements, those assurances from Colonel Langs-dorff . . ."

At the mention of the minacious colonel, Professor Heydenreich bristles. "The German consul and I have written a formal letter to Colonel Langsdorff. He must remember, firstly, that in our role as Kunstschutz, we are following the Führer's orders to hold the works in trust for the Italian nation. It is our mandate to keep them safe and secure. That is the reason the Kunstschutz officers were called to Italy in the first place."

"Exactly!" I feel my shoulders fall with relief. "They must realize we have the best interest of the works in mind. And they must know that our friends—the superintendents—are desperate to get their treasures back. After all, they belong in Tuscany. Don't you agree, Professor?"

Heydenreich leans against the bars of the cell and crosses his arms. Looks trapped. "We have requested permission from Langsdorff to hand over the inventories you and Horst have made—as well as the photographs—to the Italian superintendents so at least they know where everything is, that they have some peace of mind that everything is safe."

"Yes!" I say. "Then surely they will send trucks to take the works back to Tuscany—now that the battle has died down?"

Horst scoffs.

"No, I don't see that for now," Heydenreich says. "Not for the foreseeable future, at least. Now that the pictures are well known in the highest circles . . . Even Mussolini and his closest advisors know about them. Not to mention our own highest-ranking officers. I'm afraid things very quickly have become . . . political."

"Then what do we do?"

He shrugs. "We wait. In the meantime, our office has proposed a series of formal inspections—with a team of both German and Fascist art experts present. There are of course Italian experts in the territories under German control—in Milan, Genoa, and elsewhere. We have proposed to invite them to inspect the depots at San Leonardo and Campo Tures so that they may see everything is in order. In that way, I'm sure those working for the Fascist government may get word to the Tuscan authorities."

"Then they would at least have some assurance that we intend to return everything," I say.

"Yes," Heydenreich says. "What we need to communicate is that we declare the works of art held in trust for the Italian nation, with a complete inventory delivered to the Italians."

"Probably a good way to deal with the press," Horst says.

"Yes, but until we get confirmation from Colonel Langsdorff and

General Wolff about our plan, you are not to send any written releases or pictures to the press."

Horst scoffs. "Then what do we do for now, Professor?"

Heydenreich shrugs. "We have no choice but to wait. I hope it won't take long for them to see reason. Hopefully this will all be over soon. Hopefully our troops will stop the Allies in Tuscany and they won't go any farther north."

For a moment, I feel hopeful that the Italians, poor men like Poggi, at least will know where their things are. That they will have hope they are safe and will be returned after this is all over. I think about Paloma. Even though she wasn't as she appeared—even though, deep down, she considered me an enemy—with some distance, I understand. She had the same mission: to protect these treasures and preserve them for the future. I can't blame her actions.

But now, neither Paloma nor any of our Florentine friends know where the works are. I know now that Paloma considers me her sworn adversary, but if there was any way for me to get word to her, I would do it.

And while Reidemeister and Langsdorff may believe I'm creating a catalog for our Führer, I am creating it for my friends in Florence who have been stripped of everything they love, of everything that means something and makes them remember who they are.

Weeks pass by in a blur of quiet. With a loud, relentless tick, an ancient clock in the jail office measures the rise and fall of days. It turns cold, the wind biting through my layers of wool. I cut the ends off my mittens so I can still manipulate my F-stops and lenses, but now I regret it. The tips of my fingers go red and numb. I have found some flimsy wool blankets in a cupboard off the warden's rooms, and have piled them on the thin mattress. We boil water for tea and weak coffee, and do our best to be as comfortable as possible inside our prison home.

In the quiet, I fill my ever-fresh supply of film canisters with images of snow drifts that begin to collect on the sloping rooftops. Of the old woman in the house facing the jail, throwing a bucket of dirty mop water over her wilted plants in the window box. Of geese and stray cats meandering along the main street, pecking and scratching at the cracks. With my camera, I capture the distant, lone figure of a man trying to make his way along a footpath high up on one of the craggy mountainsides—perhaps a path to the Austrian network of trails on the other side of the peak. How easy it would be, I think, to put something precious in a pack and walk over the mountain to another world. I snap pictures of the stray cat who has taken up residence with us. Admiring her gray and white markings, I feed her food scraps and speak to her in my now-familiar mixture of German and Italian. I don't know if she understands.

Every moment, I listen for the sound of a car engine or the familiar rumble of a Kübelwagen. With the arrival of each vehicle on the street, my chest fills with hope that Poggi or another one of the Tuscan superintendents will arrive, frantically seeking their treasures. That we will open the jail cells and fill them with relief and hope that everything that was theirs is safe. And that this is all over.

But there is no evidence that Colonel Langsdorff has responded to any of Professor Heydenreich's proposals. And no Italian inspectors come to the depots.

Instead, there are only Germans. And only high-ranking ones.

They arrive in motorcades of long, sleek vehicles with fluttering flags, with metal jangling on the front of their field tunics and long coats. In the tight circles of these officers and their close civilian friends, word has spread—whispers over a tumbler of brandy and cigar smoke. The Tuscan collection is suddenly the center of attention inside a circle of well-connected men.

As each car arrives, it falls to Horst and me to welcome them, to show them the Florentine treasures while one of the SS guards struggles with the jangling keys to open each cell. The men ogle Cranach's *Eve*, the landscapes of Rubens, Caravaggio's *Bacchus*, running their fingers over the pictures.

It is a relief when the men leave, continuing on to Campo Tures, climbing higher in the mountains. There, the guards will slide open the barn doors and pry open the crates. Soon enough, the men will come face-to-face with the work of Michelangelo, of Raphael, of the most famous artists of history.

One gray afternoon, Gauleiter Franz Hofer, the governor of the Tyrol region, totters into the jail, grinning. He is olive-skinned and stout, in a long wool coat and a short tie that looks like it has turned his face fat and red. We have heard small bits about Hofer—that he sees the Tyrol region as the southernmost bastion of the Reich. That he is planning the construction of a vast Alpine fortress to lock up English and American prisoners of war. That holding a huge number of prisoners might help fend off Allied bombing in the area. We stand at each barred doorway and watch the gauleiter run his wide fingers over the masterpieces of the Uffizi Galleries and Pitti Palace.

And then, to my surprise, art dealers come from Berlin and Vienna. They don't introduce themselves by name but they are accompanied by a German officer full of metal on his field coat. Their intentions are clear. In each dusty cell, the men touch the pictures, examine their backsides. They whisper among themselves and make notes in their notebooks. They make quick photographs with a small, cheap Contax camera. Then they tip their hats as they return to their cars and leave in a cloud of dirty snow and car exhaust.

They don't allow me to take pictures of any of these visits.

The weeks at the mountain depots slide into winter. A string of high-ranking visitors come to see the works of art. They remove their leather gloves and put their hands on them. They run their eyes over them, commenting, assessing, whispering to one another. Their leering, calculating way of looking feels somehow violating. These continued visits have made me prickly, difficult. I don't care if the men think so. I've become leaner. I smoke more than before. I keep going. I only answer their questions in the most curt way. I keep pressing the shutter, keep snapping pictures, keep bankrolling the film canisters in my bag.

One quiet afternoon when it seems that winter has set in for good and we may never see the spring again, General Wolff himself—the Supreme SS and Police Leader in Italy—comes up from Bolzano. I am giving the cat a saucer of milk when the armored motorcade comes to a halt in front of the jail. The village falls into a sudden silence. The old lady across the street slams her shutter closed. Outside the window, I recognize the tall, angular general by the cascade of metal on his field jacket, visible under a thick, long coat. There are a dozen additional officers and drivers, and to my relief, I see Professor Heydenreich at the back of the group. The door to the prison opens and I change into a clean wool dress and arrange my hair. Then I grab my Leica and pull the strap over my head.

I find the men at the entrance to the jail. Horst is showing the general his pages, a draft of the catalog we are preparing—the one everybody but me hopes will be presented to the Führer. "His birthday is on April twentieth," Horst says. "Our plan is to have it complete by then." All the men except for Professor Heydenreich—who looks as grim and haggard as any Italian superintendent I've seen—nods as they listen to Horst's description of the catalog.

Horst seems to be powered with a rush of enthusiasm as he walks the men through the cells, pointing out what will be earmarked for Linz. As the men continue their tour, I touch Professor Heydenreich's sleeve and he follows me into the corridor.

"Have you been able to reach our friends in Florence?" I whisper. He looks at me with ringed eyes. "We have a constant onslaught of messages from Poggi and the Fascist authorities—even the Holy See. They want to know where the works are. They want to come and inspect. But we have not been allowed to share any information or invite them here. I'm afraid my hands are tied," Professor Heydenreich says. "Gauleiter Hofer will not allow Italian visitors in the region at all."

"And Colonel Langsdorff? Didn't he respond to your proposals?"

But I already know the answer. Langsdorff has duped Poggi and the other Italians once, and will do it again in an instant.

"He only says we should be satisfied we have saved the works of art from inevitable destruction at the hands of Anglo-American barbarians." He shrugs.

"But we have heard the new prime minister in Rome on the radio broadcasts," I say. "He is complaining about *Kunstraub*. Looting. Surely that cannot be good for our efforts."

I see the veins stick out of Professor Heydenreich's temples. "I know, but it's too late for me to do anything now. General Wolff will have the final word. Only he and our Führer will decide the fate of the works of art. At least the general denied Gauleiter Hofer his request to take a few pictures into his personal collection," he whispers. "We should be glad of that."

Professor Heydenreich and I step out of the hallway as the men conclude their tour. Horst's face is still flushed with excitement at the prospect of touring the general through the cells.

"I'm satisfied," General Wolff says, bowing slightly toward Horst. "Il Duce has also confirmed receipt of your lists," he says. "He sends his regards and deepest appreciation for the work you are doing here."

Professor Heydenreich gestures to me, my camera weighing down my neck into a slump. "General," he says, "allow me to introduce Fräulein Eva Brunner. She has done good work photographing the efforts of the Kunstschutz. Her father is in charge of our preservation project at Altaussee."

For a long moment, there is only silence. Then, to my surprise,

General Wolff reaches out one of his long, lean arms and lifts my chin with one leather-gloved knuckle. He examines my face and his thin lips spread into a grin. "Very good," he says. "I'm sure your father will be happy to have his daughter home soon enough."

A gust of wind makes the door slap against the wall as the men exit the jail, and they return to their motorcade in a swirl of snow.

It doesn't take long for word to travel. The next week, there is a letter from my father. How it reaches me in this far-flung mountain jail is a mystery. I hold the envelope in my hand and look at the familiar, neat, jagged script. Our home address. The Austrian stamp.

I hear you may be coming home. And that you may have many beautiful things with you. He's being obscure so the censors don't rip up the letter or throw it in the fire. I run my eyes over the looping script familiar from so long ago. *I am proud of you, Eva. You are working for our glory, for the future of the Reich.*

I think of all the things I might write in response, but I know it will never pass the censor, will never reach him. And the last thing I want to do is put my father or the works in the mine at risk. I know that bringing the Italian works to Altaussee is the thing that's going to make my Papa the most proud of me than anything else in the world. He expects me to do everything to make the right choice; I've earned his pride, his blessing in a way I've never earned it before. I think about how much I used to think sending the works to the salt mines was the unequivocal right choice. And how much has changed.

A little boy is standing outside, watching me. I have seen him before. He is about five years old and beautiful, with an arresting combination of hair as black as coal and eyes as blue as an Alpine lake.

The boy waves at me, his little hand in the air. I'm making my way from the jail, up the cobbled hill toward a restaurant where a few German officers and our SS guards have collected. The boy wears only a thin white shirt and worn trousers. His feet are bare. For days, a light dusting of snow has fallen, creating a slick surface across the street. I have been out with my Leica, capturing the reflections.

"My *nonna* is sick," he tells me without preamble, in South-Tyrolian German.

"Oh." I hardly know what to say. "I'm sorry to hear it."

"And she's hungry," he says, then presses his thumb to his lips, considering. It's clear to me that he's hungry, too. "There's no wheat," he continues. "And no sugar." No doubt he's repeating something overheard from the adults.

"I see."

He's silent then, but he doesn't move. He continues to stare at me with that arresting, clear blue gaze.

"You want something to eat?" I feel stupid for asking such an obvious question.

He nods.

"Wait inside," I say. "It's cold."

He backs up behind the door and peers out through the open crack.

I return to the jail and make my way to the dark kitchen. The building is empty, all the staff having taken themselves down to the local restaurant to celebrate Christmas. In the shadows, the cat crouches under the table and watches me with round, reflective eyes, like an owl. I rummage through the supplies for a bag of flour and a piece of stale cake.

I step out of the jail to find fresh snow cascading from the black sky. The air is still, windless. There is only the endless sifting of white flakes. They accumulate on doorsteps, windowsills, in the crevices of the cobblestones. I find the little boy still peeking through the crack in the door. His toes must be blue by now.

I hand him the supplies and he nods. "What's your name?"

"Daniele."

"Daniele. Don't tell your grandma where you got this. If she asks, tell her Babo Natale brought it. Understood?"

He nods, then turns away from the open door. "*Nonna! Guarda!*" I hear him say into the dark reaches of the house. I hear his grandma's voice echo from some distant room in the house, and an image of my Oma bubbles up in my mind. I would give anything to be sitting in front of her hearth right now, breaking into a hot apple pastry.

"*Buon natale,*" I whisper, then close the door shut behind him.

I pass shop windows where proprietors have arranged small, hand-carved nativities of the type we have in Austria. They have put up wreaths and candles, a meager and subdued Christmas, my second such holiday in Italy. For a moment, my heart is back home, in the snow-covered mountains far from this country of musical language and golden light, in the alleys of Salzburg with its Christmas markets, its carved wooden toys, its honey cakes. I think about Gerhard, and wonder where he is on this night. If he has found any bit of Christmas cheer or whether, instead, he is crouching in a foxhole on the Russian border, red-cheeked and cold to the bone.

From the street, I overhear loud voices and cheering in the nearby restaurant. The Kunstschutz has made sure that this particular restaurant is supplied with enough flour and other supplies to feed us well. The proprietor is a lady from an Austrian village just over the mountains who married a Südtirolean man. Their home is neat and their coffers full, while many others in town seem to have very little. I've heard that no one in town talks to them anymore, but they must consider it a small price to pay for their good fortune.

I step down a narrow staircase and into the restaurant below street level, careful not to slip on the fresh snow. There, the men are hunched over tables crowded close together. Candles drip wax down empty, fat-bellied wine jugs coated in straw and wax. Loud conversations fill the room. They greet me with raised glasses and shouts of recognition. I pull up a chair.

One of the men grasps a jug of wine from the middle of the table. "Salute!" he cries, then slops the red liquid into my glass. "To Eva! Our own resident photojournalist."

The Austrian lady delivers several plates of noodles and a beef roast with meat falling off the bones. I think of last year, when I tried my best to make myself part of Paloma's family Christmas celebration. Back when I was blind to the truth and I still thought she was on our side.

Horst slides a small glass down the table to me. It's filled with a shot of clear liquid, so sharp it's like drinking gasoline. I turn it up and swallow it in a single gulp. It burns the inside of my throat as it goes down. They refill my glass and I shoot down a second, plugging my nose this time. My colleagues cheer.

"Trying to get me drunk, are you, Horst?"

The other men hoot and revel in this provocation.

At last, I think, bitter as the clear liquid that burns the lining of my throat. I belong.

It turns out I do get drunk.

It isn't completely Horst's fault. I did it to myself. The whole of Christmas Eve tips sideways as I stagger back in the cold blackness to the jail, my breath a cloud of vapor fueled by grappa. The guards walking behind me have broken into a round of a loud German Christmas carol. Horst falls into step next to me, perhaps emboldened by my slightly drunken state. I've pushed him away so many times that surely he has given up by now.

"Eva . . ." He hikes up his pants over his broad midsection. "You have seen Professor Heydenreich's telegram? The British and American newspapers are claiming the Germans have stolen famous artworks from the Florentine museums." The word "museums" comes out with a slur. "Don't know how it got out to the press. Wasn't supposed to."

"And?"

"And they want me to write something countering the claims of *Kunstraub*."

"And what will you say, then?"

"I don't know." His lower lip projects in a pout. "I was hoping you would help me think of something."

"Why don't you just say that SS troops *did* steal everything?"

"Maybe I should do that." His voice sounds sad. "Hmm. Maybe you're right." For a minute, I'm certain this is an apology.

But then, I feel remorse in the pit of my roiling stomach and I think I might vomit, from too much wine and grappa, or from the regret that goes along with a gross failure in judgment. I'm not sure. If only I could have seen things for what they were, and had the courage to stand up to it, perhaps I could have done something about it. I should be the one to apologize.

"I don't know," he says again. Then he takes my arm presumptively. "Maybe if we just wait long enough, this will all be over and we can go home."

I pat his arm. "I don't think so, Horst."

We arrive at the door to the jail, a great wooden contraption faced with iron studs and bars. I fumble for the key and we step into the dank entry. Horst heaves himself up the stairwell and I return to my room off the kitchen. Together and apart, we incarcerate ourselves in the silence of the dark night.

24

JOSIE

ONE AFTERNOON, CORRADO APPEARS AT THE DOOR to our offices in the Uffizi. With him is a ragged-looking man dressed in black.

"He's from one of our groups in Bologna," Corrado says. "Says he has some important information for Captain Foster." But I'm the only one in the office.

"You can tell me," I say, opening my steno pad. "*Ma piano, per favore,*" I tell him. Slowly.

The man sits down and looks nervously at Corrado, but Corrado nods.

"At the end of July," he tells me, "I was in a safe hideout in a small village called Marano sul Panaro, south of Modena. Two German trucks pulled up with trailers full of a strange cargo. We realized soon enough they were paintings. The Germans said they came from the Pitti Palace and Uffizi Galleries."

I think of our inventories from Montagnana, Monte Oliveto, Poggio a Caiano, and the other depots whose inventories have large holes.

The man rubs his rough-looking palm across his stubbled chin. "We watched them unload the pictures into a private villa there. But some of them were left outside under the portico. Later," he continues, "there was a big party with lots of drinking. Must have been hundreds of German officers and soldiers. It seemed like they were using the paintings as . . . party decorations. Then a few weeks later, we watched them leave the villa with the pictures loaded again."

That was more than three months ago now.

"And where were they taking them?" I ask.

He only shrugs.

I arrive at the WAC camp excited to present my friends with their Christmas gifts, small trinkets I've collected in Florence. A sheet of handmade, marbled paper for Lollie Dee. A tiny leather box for Dot. And I can't wait to share my stories. All about the incredible masterpieces we have brought back to Florence from the countryside depots. About famous Italian paintings being used for decorations at a German drinking party. About the Jewish families hidden in the attic of Palazzo Guadagni, right under the noses of the Nazi-appointed offices of the Art History Institute. About Corrado and his bravery, his beautiful smile.

But as soon as I see their worn faces, their stooped shoulders, I know that none of my stories can compare with theirs. Their stories are about the ambulances that arrive at the nurses' tent in a constant stream. About the blood banks that run dry. About the men—our friends— there one day, gone the next. It's been a long, difficult year, and the nurses are particularly battle-weary. It's hard to keep faith when the muddy road to the WAC camp outside Florence is covered in a light, frozen crust. Beyond, the abandoned fields have fallen fallow. More of the men's tents go empty. And the winter stretches out before us.

In the tents, my friends tell me they sleep fully clothed in their bedraggled uniforms, layering their girdles, wool sweaters, pantyhose, and flannel shirts under their modified men's uniform trousers and field jackets. They've procured every woolen army blanket they can find. Outside the mess tent, a cluster of men huddle around a fire improvised with a few logs.

In the mess tent, a few of the women are opening boxes from home.

"Oh my goodness," Lollie Dee says. Her little nephew from Mississippi has drawn a picture of her in her green uniform, standing next to a Christmas tree decorated with colored circles. She laughs and wipes her eyes.

Dot opens a package from her mother and pulls out a pair of leather gloves. "Look at that!" she exclaims, plopping the gloves in my hand. They are beautiful, brown, and soft as butter. "Wouldn't you know, they're from Bloomingdale's. Perfect gift for camp living."

"Smashing," I say.

"One for you, Mouse," one of the men says, and to my surprise, he hands me a small box. I recognize my home address, but it's not my mother's handwriting. I run the blade of my pocketknife under the flaps and string around the tattered cardboard.

Inside, there is a tangle of small things from New Haven. I recognize them immediately. A delicate silver necklace from my mother's top drawer that I've never seen her wear; two of her handkerchiefs edged with tattered lace; a few pictures. I hold one of the handkerchiefs to my nose and inhale the familiar scent of my mother. I'm pretty sure my childhood memories will always smell of this strange combination of cigarette smoke, floor polish, and my mother's favorite rosewater spray.

I know it's not much, my aunt's letter says, *but it's what I could fit in the box. And I thought you might like to have something of hers while you're over there.*

She's also included a few photographs of my mother. I recognize the first one. She's sitting on a bench on the edge of campus, smiling. There's another of her as a young woman, from before I was born. I recognize the curve of Shell Beach, down near the lighthouse. In the picture, she's about the same age as I am now. She's wearing a bathing costume and standing next to a handsome young man. Is this man my father? I'll never know. At this point, I realize, it doesn't matter.

Even if he was responsible for my birth, he wasn't there for either my mother or me. Ma was the one there for me. Every moment my biggest supporter, no matter what kind of path I took. Even if I decided to do more with my life than just get by.

I hold the picture closer to my face and squint, as if this level of scrutiny might help me see something new, something important about my ma that I didn't see before. She and her friend look young and in love. But this version of Darla Evans is a stranger to me.

Looking back, the signs were clear. Her hacking cough. Her sunken eyes. Her wan face. A spray of blood on a handkerchief. *It's nothing*, she had said. *Don't worry about me*. I wasn't brave enough to stay and face it. And now there's nothing I can do to go back and change the course of things.

All those years, I considered Ma my closest friend. And yet there is so much I don't know about her. I suppose the only things we never talked about were the things that really mattered. Before, I was lonely. Now I'm just alone.

Dante Ruggero leans over from his chair. "Merry Christmas, doll," he says. He grasps my hand and pecks me on the cheek. Last Christmas, such an act of affection would have made my hopes soar. A glimmer of what the future could be. So much has changed since then.

"You too." I stand quickly and leave the tent, trying to catch my breath. I watch it swirl into the frozen air.

"Come with us and have some hot cider, Mouse," Dot says, poking her head through the tent flap. Then she gives me a firm squeeze, seeming to sense my disquiet. She's the only one here who knows the whole span of my story, who might begin to understand or sympathize. The closest thing to family I have here in Italy. Maybe.

"Thanks, darling." I give her a quick squeeze in return. "But I'm going back into Florence. I have an invitation for Christmas dinner."

• • •

Standing on a sidewalk no wider than my hips, I knock on the metal battens of Paloma's family tailor shop. For a few long moments, I stand and watch my breath swirl in the air. Then, there is a loud rattle and the metal shutters open. Inside, there is a warm glow.

Paloma walks me through a closet-sized space, filled with two ancient sewing machines and shelves stacked high with dark fabrics. Then she leads me through a door at the back of the shop, which opens to a tight living space with a tiny kitchen, a large table crammed into the living area, and a dark hallway beyond. As much the kind of apartment that any cleaning lady back in New Haven might inhabit. On a small table is a basket holding a few glass Christmas ornaments.

"This is my *nonna*," Paloma says, leading me into the tight, warm space. Paloma's stooped grandmother hunches over the narrow stove, stirring something in a pot that makes saliva rush to my cheeks. With her meaty, arthritic hand, she has pinched out small lines of fresh dough onto a floured board. Steam swirls up from a large pot too big for the narrow cooking range.

Paloma sits me down at the head of their table, placing her hands on my shoulders. Her sister's son and daughter watch me warily from their spots at the table. Paloma brings over a bottle of red wine with no label, as if she's produced something from their own cellar. This simple apartment, warm, crammed with people who love one another—family—for a moment it overwhelms me.

The little boy asks his mother something, something about *americani*. But the boy's high-pitched, rapid form of Italian escapes my understanding. His mother shushes him, then gives me an apologetic smile. I remove my little triangular uniform hat and place it in my lap.

"He wants to know if you have been into battle," Paloma's sister says. "Fighting Germans."

"*Opa! Opa!*" the little boy says, flopping over the table, squinting one eye and aiming his little finger at me as if shooting me with a gun.

"War isn't only about people shooting other people," I say in

English. "Men or women, either." Paloma smiles and translates for her nephew.

Then Corrado emerges from the dark hallway and I feel my heart lighten. He looks as if he has just had a bath, his face shining, his hair still damp and slicked back from his forehead. He wears a black sweater that hangs on his lean frame, the sleeves pushed up to reveal his muscular forearms. For a moment, he looks at me as if we are the only two people in the room.

"She's not a killer," he says in Italian, smiling at me and rustling his nephew's hair while the boy's mother grabs his shoulders and pulls him to a straight sitting position. "She's helping to bring our famous pictures back to the Uffizi," he says. "The Pitti. The Bargello."

The little boy asks his mother something, speaking so rapidly that I catch nothing.

Paloma laughs. "He asked why you are called *topolina* when you are so beautiful."

I feel heat rise to my cheeks.

"*Ecco ci.*" Paloma and Corrado's *nonna* waddles over, huffing as she manages a large plate of homemade pasta. She places it in the middle of the table and freshens up the shivering noodles with a large spoon. "*Buon natale at tutti.*" She takes her place at the table across from Corrado.

"*Buon natale,*" Corrado says, then winks at me.

Paloma catches it, this little unspoken exchange between us, like a flame leaping from one side of the table to the other.

It can't end well, Mouse. That man will break your heart.

But Paloma pretends not to notice. "*Buon appetito,*" she says. Then she reaches into the basket and tears a piece of unsalted bread in two.

EVA

ALL MY LIFE, I BELIEVED MY CAMERA TOLD THE truth. Now I know it only tells a story.

In this story, I'm telling what happened when the Americans came. I hold the photograph in my hand, looking at the great cloud caused by an explosion, and I remember a day when American planes dropped their fury on the rail yards outside Florence. They flew overhead, dropping a projectile that whistled through the air, then exploded in a spectacular blast, taking down the vaults of a church that has stood for eight hundred years.

Other pictures tell stories of possession. Of obsession. Of pictures hidden away for all but the highest-ranking, most privileged gazes. Of us holed up for months in the most unlikely place.

Other rolls of film have not been developed at all. I label each of my metal film canisters with tape, then put them in my bag. They line up: Montagnana, Oliveto, Poggio a Caiano. These have not been developed. No one wants to see the irrefutable evidence collected there.

Over months, I realize, I've told a story as rich and persuasive as my mother ever told in words. I stack up my rolls of film and estimate their number. Some of these will be published in booklets to show what damage the Allies have done. Others will be sterile illustrations in a catalog presented to our Führer on his birthday. The

Kunstschutz will use some of my own photographs to paint a different picture, a picture that counteracts the now overwhelming looting claims in the international press.

Lies. End game unknown.

What will be the next chapter in this ragged story? I expect it will be how we load the trucks, travel over the steep Brenner Pass, and tuck the Italian treasures deep in the bowels of the salt mine at Altaussee.

But that's not what happens.

In a thin, two-line telegram, Colonel Langsdorff calls us to Venice. A group of Kunstschutz officials is convening there, he says, and my photographic skills are needed. They send a fine vehicle to fetch Horst and me, along with an Italian driver and a fresh supply of film cartridges.

We descend along slippery, curving mountain roads. From the car window, I watch a swollen mountain stream, filled with snow-melt. Along a hairpin turn on the mountainside, we catch a glimpse of Bolzano, spread across a wide, flat valley ringed by mountains. "Professor Heydenreich is traveling from Milan to meet us," Horst tells me, while from the back seat, I reorganize the contents of my camera bag.

On the outskirts of Bolzano, there are dozens of SS soldiers walking along the winding streets. Their uniforms and weapons flash by in a blur of *caffè* windows and restaurants. There are dozens of them, then hundreds. In the center of town, it is as if there is some kind of disorganized parade of idle soldiers forming. As if every German soldier from Sicily to the north has been squeezed into the city and has no idea what to do next.

Outside a splendid Renaissance palace in the center of town, the driver stops. Professor Heydenreich pushes his way through a cluster of SS soldiers and tucks himself into the car, his long coat still cold and smelling of a smoldering fireplace. The palace contains General Wolff's headquarters, along with the high-ranking men who report to him. Other Wehrmacht officers, I'm told, are operating from a network of caves and mines in the mountain faces nearby.

"The Italians are continuing to pester us about the location of the artworks," Heydenreich says as we move eastward toward Verona, where the landscape flattens out and the driver picks up speed. "The Italian ambassador in Berlin is getting involved. Even Il Duce has complained to General Wolff about it."

"Couldn't some of the Italian superintendents just come to live at San Leonardo and Campo Tures for a while?" I ask. "Give the idea that they are caring for the paintings, at least?"

"We proposed that; I think it's a good idea. We also suggested that the works might be transferred to Venice. But so far, General Wolff has not responded to our requests."

Somehow, the treasures of Florence have become pawns in a political chess game with the highest stakes. Even so much that men who ought to be concerned with the outcome of nations, with the future of humanity, are instead concerned with old panels and canvases collecting dust in a jail and a carriage house in the remotest mountain passes.

I push back into the plush seat of the sedan and wonder how I got here. I came to Italy to prevent my brother from getting killed. To do a small part in documenting, in saving important historic works of art. Eventually, I came to see that I could have a role in preserving the heritage of the Italian people for them. For all of us. By trying to show the world that the Aryan nation could be the custodian of the world's masterpieces.

I used to think my photographs would be used to tell this truth. Just like my mother thought her role was to tell the truth, too.

But now I know a photograph, just like words, can show something that's not real instead. My pictures will only be used to perpetuate lies.

As long as I have been in Italy, I think, I have been hiding behind my camera. Hiding the truth from everyone, and especially myself. But now it's time to come out from behind it.

As it turns out, composing a photograph—a meaningful photograph—seems impossible in Venice. How to select one view, a focus that will accurately convey the complex, jumbled beauty of this city? No single photograph, perhaps not even a full album of photos, could begin to convey it.

Bracing myself on the white leather bench of the passenger motorboat, I turn my back to Professor Heydenreich, Horst, the old priest, and the two SS officers riding in the boat. I frame an image of the fanciful domes and brick tower of San Marco. The lighting is perfect—a cloud-covered afternoon that creates an even, diffused light reflecting off the shimmering canal waters. But the boat is moving too swiftly to capture it. I focus instead on the stone quatrefoil decoration of the Doge's Palace, a great monolith alongside the wide expanse of the Grand Canal.

"Magnificent," Professor Heydenreich says, admiring the vista.

"Yes," I say, but then realize Heydenreich isn't talking to me. He's addressing Padre Vanucci, a stooped, elderly Italian priest who is just one of the Church authorities Heydenreich and several SS officers have been meeting with. I've spent the day photographing the men—soldiers in SS uniforms and clergy in their variously colored vestments—at a meeting inside the old monastery of San Giorgio Maggiore. The pictures will be sent to the international press, to tell the story of our efforts to work through ecclesiastical channels to safeguard historical monuments as the Anglo-Americans make their relentless, violent advance up the Italian peninsula. In this story, we will tell how the Germans have done everything we can to spare Venice and its unique waterscape.

"It is," the priest responds. A frog-like little man in black robes, he gives the professor an innocent-looking smile that belies shrewdness in his eyes. "And blessed to have avoided any damages. So far."

Heydenreich turns to Horst and me as we admire the colorful façade of a noble palace while the boat glides past. "You see how the Church authorities have been important in supporting this mission. Of course, no one knows what might happen from here, with the violence heading northward."

Padre Vanucci listens to Heydenreich's explanation but he remains silent, placid, the wispy strands of his hair rising like spiderwebs from his lined forehead. Other parts of the Veneto have not been so lucky. Padua has trembled with the thunder of falling bombs just as much as Milan and Genoa.

The Venetian boat captain expertly steers the vessel around a bend in the canal. As a girl, I saw pictures of Venice in books and always dreamed of visiting one day. But apart from its overall extravagance, I see that the city is as sandbagged and shuttered as every other Italian town I've seen so far. Most of the buildings are locked, empty, and grain sacks are stacked before every important building, a desperate bid to protect its buildings from the chaos that has turned our world upside down.

I raise the camera to my face again, struggling to capture the crumbling, pastel-colored beauty of this place in black and white. I've underestimated the challenge. And capturing *this*—churches of inestimable beauty covered in sandbags—is a thousand times more difficult.

"That may be," the priest says at last, "but I can tell you the Americans, the English, their friends . . . They have many people with the same mission as you do. To save our historic structures. Not only here in Venice but all over Italy. As in my own home region of Tuscany," he says. "There, our superintendents have moved our greatest artistic treasures out of harm's way."

I turn to look at the old priest, startled that he would be so bold as to say this in front of a German professor—even though I know

Heydenreich's motives—and even more, the SS officers in the boat. There's no fear in his eyes, but neither is there anger. Can I trust him with the heavy truth sitting on my chest, squeezing the air from my lungs?

"You are from Tuscany?" I ask.

Professor Heydenreich raises his chin, sharpness in his eyes. He looks nervously at the officers sitting in the back of the boat.

"From Siena originally, yes," he says. To Heydenreich, he says, "You have no need to question my loyalties, professor. I volunteered for this task."

The boat draws closer to the quayside, where the ornate façade of a Baroque church has been constructed right along the water's edge. I attempt to capture the striped gondola moorings, the magnificent footbridges that have been here for hundreds of years. Almost every building I've seen as we move down the Grand Canal has stood for half a millennium or more. These buildings have seen revolts and revolutions, peace and violence. But none has ever seen such destruction dropped from the air.

I press the shutter release and advance the film. Snap. Snap. The shutter clicks over the church itself, the straight lines of its spires jutting out from among the sandbags. The façade is nearly covered, but at least I catch a heart-lifting glimpse of the long pale curve of the archway over the door, its ornate carvings half-hidden by the dull bags.

Finally, I put my camera on my lap and look out, feeling the wind in my hair as the boat captain throws a rope over a mooring pole.

"Come," the old priest says. "I will show you my church." The captain steps out of his boat effortlessly, then reaches his hand down to help Padre Vanucci, who moves more fluidly than I expect. While the other men alight from the boat, I snap a few more pictures of the ornate church façade rising out of the sandbags. I wonder if the film will be able to capture the desolate feeling I have looking at that church with its sagging bags along the waterside. Will a world ever exist where it can stand tall and proud in the sunlight again, where crowds of people from all over the world can walk its hallowed space without fear? It's been a long six years of conflict and we are weary; sometimes it's hard to imagine that world can ever return.

From the beginning, I have had it all wrong in thinking that the pictures needed to go to the mines, that they would be better hidden below the earth at Altaussee. I have made a terrible miscalculation. I have even helped make a catalog for Hitler himself, the hard truth of which makes me shudder. I don't have the power to undo all these German troops, these powerful men, have done already. I don't hold the power to return the pictures to Florence. But the least I can do is to accept responsibility for my own actions. For months, I've looked for some way to get word to the Florentines. Some way to let them know their masterpieces are safe. Some way to return these works where they belong. And now, just maybe, an opportunity has presented itself. In spite of the high risk, I know what I need to do. I think of Paloma, a woman prepared to do whatever she had to do to make things right.

Padre Vanucci leads us through a narrow gap in the sandbags and into his church. Professor Heydenreich looks haggard and worn as we step into the cool, ornate interior. I can't help but gasp in awe the moment we step inside. The building rises around us, stately and magnificent, a perfect dome towering over our heads, pillars and columns intricately decorated on either side of us. It's empty, nothing but a quiet splendor. I feel my shoulders relax.

After a stroll through the ornate church, the two SS officers seem to have forgotten about my existence. They speak with Professor Heydenreich, and I wander off a little way, seeking a better angle for my photographs. When I turn around to see if I can get a picture of the dome, Padre Vanucci is suddenly behind me and I see my opportunity.

"Padre," I say in a low voice. "I would be honored if you would take a moment to pray with me. And to hear my confession."

Padre Vanucci's eyes glitter with understanding. He glances, almost imperceptibly, at the soldiers kicking up dust from the tiles, now bored. "I can spare a few moments."

We walk across the vast floor of colored marble. I keep glancing back, but Professor Heydenreich seems consumed with chatting with Horst as they walk through the church, regarding the high vaults and the old paintings gathering dust in the shadowed chapels.

We slip inside the small, wooden confessional, taking our places on either side. It is warm and claustrophobic. Through the mesh screen, Padre Vanucci's profile looks like an old toad. He folds his arms and waits, as though knowing that this is not about prayer.

"You understand why we are here, Padre?" I ask quietly. I ought to be afraid, but I feel only peace.

The priest nods. "You're here to assist us in preserving art and monuments in case of bombing by the Allies." His face is a blank slate, surely practiced. A careful look of calculated neutrality.

"That's the official mission." I bite my lip. "We're supposed to be keeping Italian art safe, but instead, I am certain that some high-ranking Nazis have . . . other plans for it."

"Oh?" Padre Vanucci's voice stays calm, but his eyebrows shoot up.

"We are hiding two large troves of paintings and sculptures in the Dolomites," I whisper. "Masterpieces from Tuscany—mostly from Florence. The Uffizi, the Pitti, the Bargello. But also elsewhere." I shift on the hard wooden bench. "But no one—not the German officers, SS troops, not even our highest-ranking men—has any intention of returning it. There are plans to take everything over the Alps and put them in a salt mine in Altaussee. Then—after this is all over—they will go into the Führer's art museum in Linz. Austria."

Padre Vanucci cocks his head to one side. His enigmatic smile is gone, and his eyes are suddenly bright and glittering, like a frozen lake. I feel as though I've stepped out onto the ice and found it slippery beneath my feet.

"I'm sorry," I whisper. A pathetic thing, this apology, in the face of what my people have done. I steady my hands around the camera in my lap.

He turns his face close to the metal screen, and when he speaks, his voice is unexpectedly broken. "You are certain about this . . ."

"More certain than anything in my life," I say. "I know the mine like the back of my hand. These works . . . They have become pawns in a political chess game. Only the highest-ranking men hold the power to decide where they go. I have been asked to make a catalog of the works myself. It will all be presented to the Führer for his birthday. Next month. Unless we do something to stop it."

Padre Vanucci is still and silent for what seems a very long time. I watch his stooped shoulders and for a moment, I wonder if he's fallen asleep. "I'd hoped they would leave our treasures alone," he murmurs at last. "They have always been our legacy to this world." Then he takes a deep breath and turns back to me. "Where are they exactly?"

Outside the confessional, there are echoing footsteps. Through a narrow part in the curtain, I see the uniforms of the SS officers, their coats flapping, their shining boots on the tiles.

I lower my voice and speak quickly. "They are in a prison in the village of San Leonardo in Passeir, above Bolzano. And farther to the east, in a privately owned house called Castello Neumelans in Campo Tures. Pictures from the Uffizi, the Bargello. All taken from repositories in the Tuscan countryside. Everything is in good condition right now. But things could change at any moment."

He nods. "Thank you for what you've told me, signorina. It took courage, and for that, you have my respect."

"Please, Father. Can you get the word to Signor Poggi at the Uffizi? To any of the Florentine superintendents? Even to the Americans . . . ?"

Padre Vanucci's *Mona Lisa* smile returns to his face, and it's answer enough.

In a loud voice, the priest says, "*Io ti assolvo dai tuo peccati nel nome del Padre e del Figlio e dello Spirito Santo!*" He opens the curtain of the confessional and makes a show of gesturing toward me with the large sign of the cross.

I can't help but smile now, too. I've been absolved. "Amen," I say, and step out of the stifling wooden box.

Outside, the boat captain offers his hand for me to step into the gently rocking watercraft. As the men follow, I press the camera to my face and take a few more pictures of the church façade, trying with every ounce of concentration to steady my shaking hands.

We leave the old priest on the quayside, standing next to his church as still as a statue, watching the boat glide away in the wake of its own wavering reflection.

We don't return to the mountains right away. Instead, we travel with Professor Heydenreich across the devastation of the Veneto and eastern Lombardy, until we reach the German Institute in Milan.

As long as I don't look out the window at the wasteland of the cratered Milanese buildings, for a moment, this suite of rooms on the upper floor of an elegant building feels like home. I imagine myself transported back to Florence, the way things were months ago, when I first arrived in Italy. The institute feels like a safe haven, with German speakers who care about culture and history. With a quiet library and a small archive, with a kitchen where a German woman is baking something that smells like something my Oma would make. Apart from Professor Heydenreich, there are a handful of other German scholars who have fled Rome, Florence, and other points south of here for the relative safety of northern Italy. And what I'm most happy about: a proper darkroom where I can begin to develop my rolls of film at last.

The darkroom is a converted bath, with an old, stained sink, a floor of cracked tiles, and a claw-footed tub that looks like it hasn't been used in years. In a small storage cabinet next to a wooden dressing table, I find a stash of developer solution, acetic acid, and fixing bath along with a few battered metal trays.

I remove the first print from the fixing bath and gently pin it on the wire strung above the dressing table. Cold water drips into the pan. But as I hang each new print, a sense of uneasy disappointment seats itself in my gut. As I imagined, my black-and-white shots of Venice don't begin to convey the experience of gliding down the Grand Canal. I scrutinize the negatives again in the raking light. I make out the sandbagged churches; the fussy, Gothic tracery of the Doge's Palace; the domes and tower of San Marco; the canals' shimmering surfaces, now frozen in black and white. And I replay that conversation with Padre Vanucci again in my head. *Nel nome del Padre e del Figlio e dello Spirito Santo.* A strange, incongruous absolution, over and over, like respooling a film reel back to its clattering, flickering start.

I lean in close to examine the façade of Padre Vanucci's church, with its fanciful, Baroque window decorations jutting up among its drab sackcloth. Was that brief confession enough? Will the frog-like old priest be able to convey the information about the location of the looted paintings? My body clenches at the thought. I'm not sure there's anything that can be done about it, but I knew I couldn't keep the secret any longer. I've spent days wondering, dying to know if my impromptu confession to old Padre Vanucci has gotten to the right people, if it's made any difference to anyone at all.

I turn off the yellow lights in the improvised darkroom and wipe my hands on a rag. I don't believe the assessment that the Allies might bomb the historic heart of Venice. If that had been their plan, they would have done it long ago. Just look at what they've done here in Milan. I have to believe that the Allies have more respect for the cultures that are being trampled underfoot by the juggernauts of this war—and that they might be able to help get those artworks back where they belong. If I stop believing that, I feel I will lose all hope.

There's little more to do now other than to wait for the pictures to dry. I let the curtain fall behind me as I slip out of the bathroom. I head through the dark hallways of the institute, listening to the echo of German voices filling the air.

At a large table nestled among the archives, I find Horst, Professor Heydenreich, two Milanese superintendents. And to my surprise, Colonel Langsdorff. He sits at the head of the table, deep in conversation with the other men. I shrink back into the shelves, but it's too late. They've seen me.

"Eva," Heydenreich says, "join us." Horst stands and pulls out a chair for me.

I slink into the chair while Professor Heydenreich says, "You must understand that this is not about art anymore. It's about much more than that—"

But one of the Milanese men interrupts him. "We're talking about the works of Michelangelo, of Leonardo da Vinci, of Botticelli. Bronzino. Pontormo. Some of the greatest masters Italy has ever known. Of course it's about art!"

"I understand," Heydenreich says. "But at this point, the fate of the works in the Alpine repositories has everything to do with politics. There is too much scrutiny on it from the highest levels for us to have any leverage."

I wonder what Donatello and Botticelli and Ghiberti would think of this. Their priceless artworks, torn from their people, smuggled off into the mountains by foreign invaders, and now in danger of being blown to pieces. Pawns in a political chess game that is much larger than us.

Aggrieved, the older superintendent has no response, but his younger colleague tries again. "Political leaders will rise and fall, professor. But these works of art are timeless. Long after . . . our leaders . . . are gone, art will remain." His eyes shift nervously to Colonel Langsdorff, who sits eerily placid, his hand over his mouth, looking at old photographs of the Pantheon and the Colosseum hanging on the wall.

I watch a dangerous glitter creep into Horst's eyes. "The Führer may leave us someday, but the Third Reich is forever. And the art will be moved only on the orders of Il Duce or the Führer himself. General Wolff has made that clear." Horst's eyes also shift to Colonel Langsdorff, who remains worryingly silent.

"But none of that matters if the art is destroyed," says the younger Italian man bluntly. "We have to face facts. The Allies are moving farther north. Those repositories could be in danger very soon. Carlo Anti, who is the director general of fine arts from the Fascist ministry, has recommended that the works be moved to Switzerland. It's neutral. They could be moved easily over the roads to Saint Moritz—"

"Or they could be sent to the salt mines in Austria," Horst says. "It's not so far from where the works are now . . ." Just a few months ago, I would have suggested this solution myself. But now, all I feel like doing is slumping down lower in my chair.

"No," Langsdorff interjects and the heated banter at the table comes to a halt. "I'm afraid they would be more at risk there than anywhere else."

Now I sit up straight in my seat. "Why do you say that, sir?"

In the silence that follows my question, a terrible suspicion grows in the pit of my stomach.

"Because," Langsdorff says, "Hitler has ordered that all the mines be wired with explosives."

"What?!" Suddenly I am standing as my chair topples to the floor. And everyone else at the table is shifting, murmuring in shock.

Even Horst is standing now, his bulk towering over the table. "What do you mean, sir—'wired with explosives'?"

Langsdorff looks profoundly exhausted. As if he has given up. "If the Anglo-Americans get close enough, our officers have been commanded to execute the Nero Order. That means if these works are not destined for the Reich, then the Allies won't get them, either."

Silence falls over the room as the truth of this revelation settles in the minds of all of us sitting around the table. I feel as if the air has become as scarce and thin as an Alpine mountaintop. Does my father know about this? Is there some way for me to contact him? I think about how proud my father was to have overseen the construction of all the wooden scaffolding, of the special rooms and spaces made to protect some of the world's most precious treasures. About how we started out trying to save the greatest examples of western civilization. Would they—and the human beings tasked with storing and guarding them—disappear in a single, blazing instant? We began by trying to save everything for a glorious future. But now, our highest leaders have lost sight of the future. Lost sight of life. They have chosen death instead.

26

JOSIE

IN THE POCKET OF MY FIELD JACKET, I KEEP A LETter from my mother. My aunt sent it to me weeks after she died.

I'm alright, my ma writes. *Really, I am. Death is part of life, Josephine. The only thing that pains me is to see my sister's distress, and to realize that you may feel it, too, so far away from here. But I want you to know that I am at peace. And I want you to be, too. You go on and do what you were meant to do in this life. Don't you worry about me.*

In my mind, I hold a picture of my ma sitting at our linoleum kitchen table, smoking a cigarette and writing me a letter on discarded university stationery she must have picked out of one of the garbage bins at Yale. She was always picking things from the rubbish cans across campus. At the time, this habit made me feel deeply ashamed. Now I realize it was ingenious, her way of making something out of nothing, a treasure from trash. And if there's one thing I hope I learned from my mother, it's how to make something out of a terrible situation.

I hold on to the part about doing what I'm supposed to do in this life. The problem is, I don't know what that is exactly. I only know there's no longer anything pulling me back to Connecticut. And somehow, Florence now feels more like home to me than anyplace else in the world.

Being here, working with Captain Thomas and Captain Foster, seeing how Corrado and Paloma live—all of it has given me pause, has made me realize that there is more to life than just getting by. From their humble family tailor shop, Corrado's family gets by, yes. But they do much more than that. They reach for the things that matter. Things bigger than themselves. The things—like great masterpieces of art—that stand for something more than ourselves, that remain as a testament to human achievement long after we are gone. That is, if we have anything to do with it.

In the evenings, Captain Foster, Paloma, a few Italian superintendents and laborers in the Uffizi, and I cluster around the wireless in our office. Paloma tunes into the German broadcasts and translates for us.

"They are saying that 'Allied invaders' have torn a path of destruction across Italy," she says. "That you are desecrating sacred monuments and pilfering priceless artwork owned and beloved by the Italian people. That you are taking our national treasures to America and that they will never be recovered."

"Allied invaders!" I repeat, shaking my head as the broadcast concludes.

"You think the German people believe this?" one of the skinny Italian laborers asks.

"*Zito*," Paloma shushes him and turns the dial to the Fascist version, broadcast from their new headquarters in Padua. "Listen."

Captain Foster leans forward toward the radio, his angular face a focused grimace as the static clears and the sound of a deep Italian voice fills the airwaves. I begin to catch the news broadcaster's words, and then the gist of the message. "Officials blame American soldiers in particular for the pillaging," they say. "In the countryside of Tuscany, they have stolen crateful of masterpieces by Donatello, Michelangelo, and other masters. The price of these and other objects, collectively, is reported by experts to be beyond estimation."

"They are blaming us!" I say. "But it's a flat-out lie! We can't even get to the countryside depots, much less take anything from them, even if that were our intention in the first place."

Captain Foster says, "They aren't blaming us specifically."

"No," Mr. Poggi says. "You have more than proven your intentions."

But that's cold comfort. The people listening to this report from their homes across Italy have no idea of the truth. They have no idea how hard Paloma and I have worked from our little office to coordinate a thousand details of helping to get building materials, appropriation of Italian government funds, gasoline for superintendents' trucks so they can travel to distant monuments in the countryside. It is a slap in the face of all of us who are working as one to vanquish one of history's great evils, the scope of the horror and brutality only now becoming known, leaking in as rumors from Germany, reports of genocide beyond imagining.

And of course, our own broadcasts and newspaper articles describe colossal looting on the part of the German troops. Now I see the two faces to the reports—the two sides of the coin—each spinning opposite stories from the same set of facts.

From our view, it seems that good is triumphing over evil. Though nothing is yet certain, the prevailing feeling is that the tide is turning for the better. That it will take a miracle for the remaining Axis powers to prevail, and those are in desperately short supply. But the greatest casualty of this war seems to be the truth, and I know it's no better on the Allied side. Each side is swimming in misinformation and supposition. Some lies are more deliberate than others, and more destructive.

"Listen!" Paloma insists. "It's Signor Anti."

The broadcaster changes, and we recognize the voice of Carlo Anti, from the Fascist Ministry of Fine Arts, appointed by Mussolini himself. Anti seems to be reading from a press release. He says that he has received word that the deposits of works of art removed from the Florence region are, "except for slight damage, all intact."

As soon as the words are spoken, Captain Foster shoves back his chair and begins pacing the room. "He doesn't say where they are," he says.

"Or if they are in the care of Italians or Germans," one of the superintendents says, standing and cupping his hands around a newly lit cigarette.

Another day of information, misinformation, and working to find the truth when so much is hidden, so much unknown.

In the wake of the continued mysteries and uncertainty, there is one consolation: the equestrian statue of Cosimo de Medici we discovered at Poggio a Caiano—the one the Germans left behind only because it was too large to transport—returns to Florence.

In the middle of the crowded Piazza della Signoria, I shield my eyes from the sun and wait for an enormous drape to be removed from the public statue. A platform has been erected so that government officials can properly celebrate the statue's triumphant return to public display.

For all the unknowns, for all the misinformation, and for all that is still missing, at least we have some consolation that a few things are being put back where they belong. The tall, narrow tower of the medieval Palazzo Vecchio makes a long, streaking shadow across the cobblestones. Before its intimidating, crenellated façade, the mayor of Florence—a stern-looking gray-haired man in his tricolor sash—makes a speech, surrounded by men in British and American military uniforms. Captain Foster sits on the podium, where I feel relieved to see he's getting credit for his role in returning the beloved statue to its rightful place in the middle of the square.

The space is packed with Italians, Allied soldiers, and a gaggle of wayward and displaced refugees. From the camp outside the city, many of the WACs have come into town for the ceremony. For a moment, the vision of the group of American women in uniform striding across the hot Piazza della Signoria takes my breath away. I realize the adventure I've been on, and I know I was right to come. If I ever thought I didn't belong here among these hardworking girls, I was wrong about that.

Dot presses against me and takes my hand. "You understand any of this?" she asks me as I listen to the mayor's words and try to make them out. His beautiful Italian voice on the microphone rings out in the square. "It is in the sunlight of a new dawn that we return our beloved statue to its pedestal. It has escaped the Axis aggressions, like *Italia* herself, and emerged ready to move forward into the future."

"Mostly, yes," I say.

The crowd applauds. I look around with a certain satisfaction I don't try to resist. Just a year and a half ago, I sat in a Chapel Street diner with Dot and professed to not see any way I could make a difference in a war. Now my efforts have helped the recovery of many valuable and beautiful treasures, and the preservation of such cultural treasures as the very statue they are about to see restored to its proper place. In spite of all that's missing, I celebrate a small, silent victory.

"It will be a long time before things are back as they were before," I say to Dot. "For now, we just try to prevent further deterioration. Later, they can replaster and repaint; they can fix broken sculptures, restore paintings. In the meantime, we just repair roofs so rain won't come in. We consolidate masonry. We replace shattered timbers. We find building materials. We bring back works of art to the city when we can."

"The future is great," the mayor continues, "but so is our glorious past. And whatever has happened, nothing can wipe away the magnificence and independent spirit that is Florence, the cradle of the Renaissance. We will never abandon our love of this city, its past, present, and future, the love of nation and humanity which keep us together for all times!"

The crowd applauds again and the drape pulls away from the statue with a dramatic flurry. The statue stands where it belongs, horse's foreleg raised. It is magnificent, and I feel a rush running through my body, the now-familiar thrill of being in the presence of a great work of art. It's a feeling I've only experienced since I came to Italy. Everyone in the square cheers and their eyes smile at the statue and everything it represents. It's more than a fanciful hunk of bronze. It's a symbol of the life they missed, the life they've almost lost, the life and sense of normalcy they long to live again.

In the midst of this communal joy, Corrado appears from an alley alongside the Loggia dei Lanzi.

"It's him!" I say, squeezing Dot's arm. "The man I've been telling you about."

Corrado walks across the square toward our cluster of women in American army uniforms. I see his brown eyes scanning the crowd. From this distance, I admire how handsome he is, his dark hair, his big, soulful brown eyes, and a face that looks as if it might have been crafted by a master sculptor. Our lines of sight finally find each other and he smiles. Waves his hand.

"Corrado Innocenti, meet Dorothea Nichols. My closest friend." But as I say the words, I feel a cold shock streak through me as these two halves of my life come together—my old life in the U.S. and my new one in Italy. Two halves of me I thought might never come together. Have I just made a terrible mistake? Will Corrado—like so many men—lay eyes on Dot Nichols and feel her inexorable pull? Will I be lost to the shadows of Dot's bright light?

"Pleased to meet you," Dot says, smiling. I am struck with white fear that he will abandon me on the spot. Lollie Dee has predicted it will not end well.

But he only takes Dot's hand and says, "*Piacere*." Then he looks at me and winks.

"Well, my goodness, I see why you have been staying in Florence, Mouse," Dot says.

"Type of fella you'll want to wear lipstick for, Dot," I say. A few other WACs crowd around us now, the sight of this handsome Italian man squeezing my shoulders drawing them into a curious circle.

I recognize Sergeant Barnes's stout frame as she approaches the crowd. She's changed back into her skirt, blouse, and stockings. It's been a long time since I've seen her in anything other than men's coveralls or field jackets. I smile and salute. "Sergeant Barnes."

"At ease, Evans." She salutes me back. "I'm glad we finally made it into Florence after waiting so long. Ladies, enjoy it while it lasts."

I feel my smile waver. "What does that mean?"

Dot's face falls. "I didn't want to tell you, Mouse."

"Tell me what?" I feel my throat tighten.

"We're off to Bologna," Sergeant Barnes says.

"Bologna!" I turn to see Corrado's reaction, but he's walked off to shake Captain Foster's hand as he steps down from the platform.

"I'm sorry, Mouse," Sergeant Barnes says. "We're pushing back the Germans, the front line is heading north, and we've already started packing up the WAC camp. We'll need you back as soon as you can arrange it." When I prove myself speechless, she squeezes my arm and says, "This is what we all signed up for, remember?"

My heart sinks as she walks away. Of course I know war rages on, and so do its consequences. Many have made sacrifices much worse than this. Families have been torn apart. Men have gone into battle and not returned. We've seen enough to have no more illusions about this. My time of trial isn't over, and it seems only to be getting more dire, the sacrifices more painful. I've left the United States, never to see my mother again. I know that to leave Florence will mean to leave Corrado, too. Another heartbreaking separation.

Also, there are many more works of art north of here. Surely Captain Foster will be called north as well. He, too, will be torn away from his beloved Florence.

What possible reason could we invent to refuse? Duty calls, and I know I have come too far to resist it, whatever the price. To fall short would be to sacrifice every victory, every life saved, and that's more than I can bring myself to do. Instead, I will fight on to the end. Liberty is at stake. And surely liberty is more important than love.

But that's my head talking, not my heart.

We set up camp in a field beyond Modena in a torrent of rain.

I am numb from the cold and wet, but mostly from having been ripped from Florence—from my Italian colleagues at the Uffizi, from my comfortable room in the Palazzo Guadagni, from Corrado—so abruptly. Before leaving, Captain Foster, too, was a shadow of himself, knowing it was time to turn our operations over to the capable hands of the Florentine superintendents and to their greatest asset, Paloma. "See you in Bologna, Evans," he said as he pulled away in Georgette to head to Arezzo to check on things one last time before heading north. I wondered if he sped away so quickly so I wouldn't see his tears.

Between Florence and Bologna, the countryside is a panorama of cold mud and Germans. We travel under an armed convoy, settling finally in a vast field that couldn't feel farther away from the sun-kissed hills of Tuscany. The landscape becomes flat and bleak, a vista of gutted farm buildings and fallow fields as far as the eye can see. Gone is the gold and green beauty of the Tuscan landscape.

Rain pours down on us as we erect our tents and the men dig trenches and latrines out of the thick mud. The hooded rain gear helps limit the soakage, but water drips into my collar nevertheless, my field jacket sticking to my back, armpits binding. My boots are heavy with caked dirt, collecting fast despite my periodically shaking it off in heavy slabs. But the journey is no worse than the departure from Florence, and I have more weighing on my mind and heart than is pulling at my clothes and boots. The rain seems appropriate, under the circumstances.

When I left the United States, it was the hardest thing I'd ever done. I didn't know it would be the first in a series of painful separations that pull at my heart—from my mother, from Corrado, from Florence, from my frustrating and satisfying work with Paloma and Captain Foster.

Inside the tent, I remove my slicker and hang it to drip-dry. I have to stop feeling sorry for myself. I'm not the first or only woman to fall in love overseas and have her heart broken. Europe is strewn with women raising the children of Allied and Axis soldiers, products of fleeting love or fleeting violence. Others suffer the loss of their men to far-flung assignments, men asked to lay down their lives in the cause of freedom. Little solace even when their sacrifice has a noble purpose.

With this latest march north, we also lose some of our women. Some of the switchboard operators and nurses are reassigned to England and France. Others left behind here in Italy have become disenchanted with the whole enterprise, grumbling about pointless effort and wasted time and blood. Even Lollie Dee, with her usual sunny disposition, huffs down on her cot and curses under her breath as she removes her boots. It has been a long winter. We hang inside the mess tent, grim-faced, shoulders sagging, drinking weak coffee, trying to keep our shoes out of the puddles that collect under the portable tables and chairs in the ceaseless din of pelting rain. Despite the turning tide of war, everyone seems torn between eagerness to end our journey and despair at what we'll find north of here.

"I don't understand why the Germans continue to behave as if they will win," Sergeant Barnes complains, her face lined, weary.

"The more they feel squeezed," Lieutenant Hamm says, "the more they sense loss, the more they will pillage and destroy. It's as if they want to go down in some kind of . . . nihilistic flame of fury. A man like that will sooner burn the entire planet than accept that he's lost."

"Exactly," says Staff Sergeant Pierce. "Who's to say they won't blow everything to smithereens in some kind of burst of rage just to spite us? We might be winning but if you ask me, it's the most dangerous moment of all."

Our commander paces back and forth as Lollie Dee hands out ration kits. "Don't y'all think about getting soft," he says, his voice snapping with a commanding baritone. "The Jerrys know we're coming. The closer we get, the more desperate they'll get. And we already know what a desperate Kraut is capable of. I don't have to tell you how vulnerable our troops will be in these conditions."

I worry about our troops, of course. But now all I can think about is where the art treasures may be, and if they, too, might be just as vulnerable as our men.

At last, the day comes when the rain stops and the sun reappears. There is the first glimpse of spring in the warm sun. And my Monuments officers—both Captain Foster and Captain Thomas—convene on our camp.

"Evans!" Captain Foster breaks into a smile as he steps out of the jeep. I feel as happy to see Georgette as I do Captain Foster.

Captain Thomas steps down from the passenger seat. "You still here, doll? We heard you might'a run off with some Casanova back in Florence."

My face flushes red. Have they been gossiping about me behind my back? My infatuation with Corrado Innocenti must be impossible to hide.

"I have news!" Captain Foster looks as if he is about to burst. "There's been a large cache of Italian paintings located in the Dolomiti."

"The Dolomiti. Here in Italy?"

He nods. "Somewhere in Alto Adige. Makes sense. That's an independent region, but let's face it. It's essentially Austria. We're trying to get the specific location." The men and women collect around the two Monuments officers to hear the incredible news.

"How did you find out about it?"

He scratches his head and sits in a seat as Lollie Dee brings him a tin of coffee and more of us collect around them. "The information came from Venice," he says. "Apparently a German informant leaked the location to a priest there. We don't know much more than that. Only that the information traveled through the ecclesiastical channels to one of our double agents, then to the superintendent of monuments and galleries in Venice. Since it had to do with works of art of the utmost value from Florence, they knew to contact us about it."

I think it out, about all the ragged clues and misinformation that have been traded over the past months, on the radio, in newspapers, among art specialists, in telegrams, even via German informants, double agents, and priests. "You think it's true? If it came through a web of spies, diplomats, partisans, informants . . . things get scrambled up. You know that."

"Yes, and I'm sure they will claim they are saving the works, not looting them."

With a growing audience, Captains Foster and Thomas go on to recount to everyone in the circle about the works looted from Poggio al Caiano, from Montagnana, and the other depots. Some of the treasures of the Uffizi and the Pitti Palace, altarpieces from some of Florence's most beautiful churches. The entire collection from the Museo San Marco and the picture gallery of the Accademia. "About one-fifth of all the paintings in Florence," Captain Foster says.

I think about all the priceless pictures we have seen that were never crated or boxed. That were exposed to the elements and whatever danger might befall them. They traveled over mountain roads that are under shellfire day and night.

"What do they want with them?" one of the men asks. "Don't the Jerrys have enough to worry about without spending all their time looking at some damned pictures?"

"Without a doubt, Hitler wants those works for his Führermuseum in Linz," Captain Thomas says. "The works of art stolen from the Tuscan depots represent the most important treasures of Italy, for that matter more important than works from any German-occupied country. Maybe even all the German-occupied countries put together."

We're interrupted by a cry of anguish. Sergeant Barnes bursts into the tent. "Oh no!" We women gather around her, rigid in our posture despite the weariness of our bodies and bones. I'm immediately alarmed, as I've never seen Sergeant Barnes show any kind of emotion like this. "We've lost our commander in chief," she says. "Just got a telegram from Washington." A palpable gasp rises up out of the women. "Our president is dead!"

Immediately, the telegram passes from hand to hand inside the tent.

FRANKLIN DELANO ROOSEVELT PASSED YESTERDAY, RESULT OF A MASSIVE STROKE.

Nausea swells in my belly and my mouth goes dry. There have been rumors of his ill health, but no one expected this.

In the shadows of the tent, two of the women scramble to find and plug in the wireless.

Captain Thomas dips his head and everyone in the tent follows suit, a moment of silence for the passing of a great man. And we wonder what will happen next, what it means for all of us, and for the outcome of this war. Who knows what will happen now, especially now that we might be on the cusp of victory—or of that "nihilistic flame of fury" that Lieutenant Hamm talked about. But none of us in the soggy tent has an answer.

27

EVA

I CLUTCH THE HEAVY BLACK TELEPHONE RECEIVER close to my face. My hands are sweaty where they grip it, trembling with the force of fear. For days, from this phone in the German Institute, I've tried to reach my father, my Oma—anyone in Altaussee. But there is no answer, only a stretch of scratchy static silence or series of distant, tinny rings. I slam the receiver down again in frustration.

"Eva, what is it?" Horst comes around the corner.

When I first became Professor Kriegbaum's photographer all those months ago, it was easy to talk to Horst. Even to rely on his knowledge and experience. That was when, like him, I believed in our cause. I believed in the premise—the promise, even—of the Third Reich. But as my belief waned, his only seemed to grow stronger. It feels as though we've drifted to opposite sides of the conflict, but in this place—in this little slice of Germany inside Italian borders—he's still one of the only people I can lean on, even a little.

"It's my Papa," I say at last, swallowing the threat of tears. "He works in those salt mines. The ones that could be blown up at any minute."

Horst's broad face falls. "Can't he get away?"

I shake my head. "He's in charge of the whole thing. If this goes wrong—"

"Things won't go wrong." Horst's voice rings with certainty. "The Führer will make sure of that."

I stare at him, wondering if he still believes as firmly as he seems to. Doesn't he feel any doubt? Hasn't he wondered, just a few times, witnessing everything we've seen, whether we really are doing the right thing?

"Can't you admit that the Allies are creeping closer and closer? Horst?" He looks at me for a long, wordless moment. "What's going to happen if Germany falls?" I whisper urgently. "They'll consider us thieves for hiding all that art in the mountains. They could take us as prisoners of war. Or worse."

"The Führer won't fall," says Horst, but he doesn't sound so sure anymore.

"Come on. You must see this is wrong. How could they rig those mines to explode, even though they're filled with irreplaceable artworks and innocent people?" A tear escapes down my cheek; I dash it away. "What kind of country would do that to its own people? My Papa has never done anything wrong in his life. But he could be killed in a second. And why would the Führer go to so much trouble to collect all the masterpieces of Europe, only to explode everything in one big blast?"

"It won't come to that," says Horst, hesitating. "Don't worry about your papa. Everything will be fine." He reaches out his arm as if he will touch me, but then he thinks better of it and scratches the back of his neck instead.

"I wish I could believe that." I shake my head. "But look how quickly they're advancing. Italy is on its knees, and they're closing in on Germany itself . . ." Horst's face looks twisted in confusion. "What gave us the right to take those paintings from Tuscany?"

"We did it for safekeeping," he says. "You know that."

"But where did they end up? In a prison? In a carriage house where they keep horses? What makes you think they won't blow that all up, too?" Horst is silent. He's been holding my gaze all this time, but now he drops his eyes, as though a shudder of doubt is creeping over him.

"Horst." I get up, reach out, wrap my fingers around his wrist. It's the first time I've ever touched him. "I don't want us both to end up on the wrong side of history."

He looks at me, his eyes unreadable, and opens his mouth to speak. Then, there's a distant roar, a chaotic sound echoing up from the street. He says nothing, but his eyes widen. I'm suddenly trembling, as though I have summoned the Allies to our doorstep.

Horst rushes to the window. "Eva—it's . . . a mob!"

I hurry to join him, and we look down to see a crowd of people surging through the streets below, yelling, shoving aside the same military police officers that the Italians have feared for so long. There's chanting, shouting; someone throws a brick, and glass tinkles as it breaks in a downstairs window.

"What's happening?" I cry out, terror lancing through me.

Professor Heydenreich bursts into the room, breathless. "Right now," he barks. "We have to go."

"Where, sir?"

"Südtirol."

"To the prison?" I say, confused.

"Yes. Hurry!" he says.

"What's happened?" Horst asks.

Professor Heydenreich seems unable to find the words for a moment. "Mussolini is dead. Shot by partisans. They've hung his body—" He glances at me, then stops, repeating the words that seem to have left him so shell shocked. "We have to leave here now."

From the window, I catch sight of several German armored vehicles racing northward out of Milan.

We drop Professor Heydenreich in Bolzano. By the time Horst and I arrive in San Leonardo in Passiria, it's after midnight. I make my way to my room through the prison's dank, dark kitchen, where the striped cat sits placidly on the counter, licking the underside of his paw.

There are small pieces of the story emerging. That Benito Mussolini traveled undercover to Como to say goodbye to his wife. That he attempted to conceal himself under a German greatcoat and helmet, but that a group of partisans recognized him and pulled him from the car. That in a nearby lakeside town, he was shot along with his lover, Clara. That partisans have now dragged his body to Milan and hung it upside down from steel girders across town in the Piazzale Loreto. In the streets of Milan, there is chaos.

"Best if we stay here for now," Professor Heydenreich told us on the way to Alto Adige. Outside the jail, the SS guards pace back and forth. But two days later, we're still waiting. Still holding our breath, wondering who will come for the treasures in our possession. Not wanting to leave them. And wondering if we will be held accountable.

And then, the news comes on the wireless. Adolf Hitler is dead. And General Wolff has ordered German soldiers in Italy to surrender.

The next day, the normally vacant streets of San Leonardo fill with SS troops. Some of them whoop and sing. Others drink big bottles of wine and take shots of the gasoline-like local spirit. Others look like they have been through hell. They heave themselves up the smugglers' trails into the peaks, where the snow is melting at last. And they disappear to the other side.

On the table is the remains of our Führer's catalog. Horst's handwritten pages. My own pictures—some developed, some still in the metal canisters, waiting for access to a darkroom. I pick up one of the pages and scan Horst's latest catalog entry. Number 276. Lucas Cranach the Elder's pair of panels. *Adam* and *Eve*.

Cranach captures the moment when Eve holds the fate of humanity in a single bite of forbidden fruit. When evil separates from good. The moment of an irreversible decision that will set humanity on its destructive course. The moment when a woman who has seen something beautiful—irresistible—gives in to the terrible beauty of temptation.

Should we, too, leave these paintings behind and head over the mountain pass? What would become of them if we did? There is no longer anyone to tell us what to do with the pictures in our care. What would happen if we took them. Or what will become of us now.

On the third day after our arrival, the four SS guards outside the jail disappear up the mountain trails and Horst and I are left alone together in the jail.

28

JOSIE

ONE MORNING, WE AWAKE TO NEWS THAT MUSSOLINI has been executed by his own people. The partisans strung his body up on a steel girder along with that of his mistress. Neither were to be martyred, not by the Fascists who followed him nor by the resistance who thwarted him, nor by those who captured and murdered him. He tried to be at once a father and a dictator, a man of the people and of the State, but I suppose his failure stood as a beacon for those with too much ambition and too little humanity.

And then, the tide turns again. Days later, Adolf Hitler, too, is dead. Filled with excited energy, our men and women begin packing up the camp. By the time we get it dismantled, we learn that General Karl Wolff has handed over Italy to the Allies.

The women are giddy. "We're going home!" Ruby cries. Immediately, dancing and cheering break out but I feel as desolate and flat as the now-emptied field where our trucks are loaded with supplies. It feels far from over for me.

"Look at her!" Ruby cries, twirling around in the stunted wheat. "She's still wishing she was out there looking for her treasures."

"Let it go, Mouse," Lollie Dee says. "It's been a long two years. Don't you want to go home?"

"Nope. She wants to go back to Florence," Dot says. "Right, Mouse?"

Of course Dot knows my heart. But the truth is that I want to locate the Florentine treasures almost as badly as I want to return to Florence. "I will stay with Captain Foster until we can find the works we've been searching for all these months." At the edge of the field, Georgette stands, her muddy wheels askew. I watch Captain Foster extend his hand to Captain Thomas. But Captain Thomas responds by pulling Foster's lean frame to his bulk, then giving him a bear hug and a slap on the back so vigorous it looks like it hurts.

"Well, then where is the stuff?" Sergeant Barnes asks.

I shrug. "Maybe in the mountains, north of here. Captain Foster says there's a bilingual region on the Austrian border where they might be hiding."

"You can't be serious, Mouse," Ruby says. "What's the point of going all the way up there? So what if they make off with some pictures in their bags? What's it got to do with you?"

"I for one would rather see my husband than any musty old painting!" Margaret Olson says. "I'm pretty sure everyone just wants to go home."

Lollie Dee squeezes my hand. She knows I don't have anyone to go home to.

"Because . . ." I struggle for words I've never explained before. "Look, none of us, nobody, is going to live forever. But we're here for the things that *will* live forever. We're here for the idea of family, not just our own families. We're here for freedom, and not just our own. And these . . . these musty old paintings as you call them, they're the living embodiment of that idea. They're not just for the Italians. They're for all of us."

In the distance, some of the women begin to load into the troop transport vehicles. Next stop, Bologna.

Next to me, I feel Lollie Dee squeeze my hand again and then her skinny hip bumps mine. "I know why you want to stay," she whispers. "It's that Italian man."

"Stop." But then I laugh.

Corrado.

Amid the chaotic tangle of Bologna, I think of him. In the crowded street, I press next to Private Ruggero and loop my hand around the hardness of his arm. Dot hangs on to the other arm while we move through the mass of revelers. Ahead of us, impromptu celebrations break out, men and women kissing and drinking in the streets, Italian flags waving from the windows. The smell of fresh bread and grilled meats clings to the air, the promise of bounty after six years of relentless deprivation. Children run through the crowd, weaving in and out of people's legs. In front of us, I see a man and woman pass a bottle of wine back and forth, drinking straight from the bottle. Then they kiss, a long, slow, sloppy mess.

But all I can think about is sitting with Corrado in the red dirt under the olive trees, its silvery leaves dancing in shimmering patterns above our heads. I think about standing next to him in the quiet ruin of the Vasari Corridor, looking out to the stumped piers of the Ponte Santa Trinità and the unrelenting swirl of the Arno.

"You're brave to stay here, Mouse," Dot says.

I shrug. "What do you mean? Things should be just swell from here," I say. For a moment, we watch a couple staggering ahead of us, drunk on wine or love, or the simple idea that all of this hell is over.

She tsks me. "Well, I expect to see you in New Haven very soon."

"Maybe."

"What do you mean, 'maybe'? You have a wedding to come to, you know."

"I know," I say, smiling at her. Part of me can't envision a wedding between Dorothea Nichols and an Italian-American plumber from

Buffalo. Even less, Dot's mother heading up such a celebration. As much as I want to see it with my own eyes, I'm not ready to return to New Haven. "This isn't over yet for me," I say. "Or Captain Foster. Especially not for the people of Florence." On the outside, I think, it sounds like I hold the power of my conviction. And I can't help but cling to the notion that the worst is behind me, behind us all, and that somehow, I will make it back to Florence, even as a future with Corrado and me in it seems as murky as a river filled with rubble.

But the bitter tang of separation stays on my tongue. And as much as I imagine Florence will be a place we can move to and from freely, if I return, I don't know what I will find. *It can't end well, Mouse.* We've been swept up in a flurry of fresh infatuation, a beautiful, colorful bloom among the muck. But even if I get back there, we have realities to face upon our reunion. Things have been so uncertain, we haven't given a thought to any kind future. In the back of my mind, separation and heartbreak still loom, their shadows inescapable.

As much as my heart pulls me south to Florence, instead we move ever north. Georgette has never promised a smooth ride, but the rigors of the shell-pocked roads and rough trails have made the rusted jeep run like it's on its last legs. It bounces with every bump, shocks completely worn. Its engine growls and groans, and it stinks of leaking fuel. For miles, Captain Foster and I ride in silence, covering countryside riddled with shell holes and farmhouses reduced to sand heaps silhouetted in the fog. Many of the roads have been torn apart by mines, reeking of death and sewage.

The farther north we go, the more Germans we encounter. By the time we reach the outskirts of Bolzano, we begin to wonder which side has surrendered. Ahead of us on the cratered roads, Germans rush ahead in trucks, cars, and armored vehicles. Heading north with us. An armored German truck rushes around us, just inches from the side of the open jeep. One of the soldiers whistles at me and his friends cheer him on.

"Go home!" I yell, but I don't know if he understands or even hears me. But it feels good to yell back all the same.

Captain Foster doesn't comment. His mouth is a thin line of concentration, his knuckles white on the bucking steering wheel. He coaxes his beloved jeep into Bolzano, a city stretching out in a flat, snug valley at the base of a ring of mountains. The mountainsides are carpeted in lush green trees and white stucco houses with flower boxes and sloping roofs. The stones and tiles of Tuscany, and the giant craters our Flying Fortresses have made across the desolate expanse of the Po River Valley—all of it seems a world away.

As we enter Bolzano, we find a maze of streets blocked with piles of debris and half-blown buildings, and all of it crawling with so many German soldiers I couldn't begin to count them. I glance nervously at Captain Foster. He's not pleased to see so many Jerrys walking around like they hadn't put their hand to the most grotesque campaign in modern history. There are no Allied uniforms to be seen. Only ours. I feel exposed, vulnerable, a woman in an American uniform, in an open vehicle. I search the upper-floor windows of the still-standing buildings.

We watch the soldiers stroll through the streets, laughing, drinking, celebrating as much as our American friends in Bologna. It isn't an easy thing to accept, given how bitter the fighting has been, and how great the stakes. They seem to outnumber the locals by almost ten to one, the crowds of their ranks becoming denser as the jeep crawls closer to a fine Renaissance palace at the city's center. Several inns and a fine hotel have armed German guards at their doors. At sidewalk *caffès*, the soldiers, now aimless and leaderless, drink from wine bottles and bite into whole loaves of bread like sloppy drunks. One of them turns to us and cheers, as if we have been on the same team all along.

"They seem comfortable enough," Captain Foster says as we pass a cluster of soldiers staggering down a sidewalk, their arms around one another's shoulders. "Miserable bastards," he grumbles. "They'd as soon shoot us all through the back of the head right now if word for it came down."

I give it some thought. "Wouldn't our boys do the same?"

The captain doesn't seem able to disagree. We don't try to stop or get out of the jeep. We don't see a single Allied soldier or vehicle. For the first time, I see bitterness in the captain's face, the sense of loss. Throughout the months of almost inconceivable obstacles, I've only seen him as a picture of the dedicated serviceman. A man who puts duty and dedication to his mission above everything. A man who never talks of his wife, of his home, or work in the U.S., of anything back in America at all. But now, I catch a fleeting glimpse of the life the captain has left behind. A whiff of nostalgia. Just like the rest of us.

"You wish you were going home?" I ask as we pull away from the city and begin to make our way up a lonely mountain road. Below us, I watch Bolzano spread out like a mottled carpet at the base of the undulating green mountains.

"Part of me, yes," Captain Foster says. "How about you? A lot of your WAC unit's leaving. Your friend Dot is headed back to Massachusetts."

"Connecticut," I say. I think about the fall in New England, the leaves that, just a few months from now, will display their incredible show of annual color. Our apartment, still and quiet, just two months left of rent from my mother's final paychecks. I have to decide what to do with it—return to it or let it go. But I don't feel ready to face it.

The jeep groans as we wind around a hairpin turn, rising higher as the city of Bolzano grows ever distant below us. The roads become narrow and meandering, the trees clinging to the vertical mountainsides, reaching for the streaks of sun that flash between their branches. Here, everything seems peaceful.

But in the thick forest, we continue to see clusters of wayward

German soldiers on foot. "Maybe they're walking home," I say to Captain Foster. "I guess they're not waiting around for orders—or transportation." They are just people, I think, who have made a decision. Who have taken their fate into their own hands. Every German soldier is still armed but they don't try to threaten us. They taste defeat and seem relieved by it, resolved only to return home, just over the craggy peaks. Still, a man and a woman—in American uniforms, in a jeep, in an isolated stretch of twisting mountain road—can come across any number of misfortunes, and being shot by a retreating German is only one of them, I think, as I contemplate the yawning ravines at the road's edge.

Up ahead, we catch up to an armored truck heaving its way up the winding roads. On the back of it are several German soldiers, their helmet straps loose and flapping in the breeze. One of them has a bottle of beer in his hand. I press my own helmet to my head as the wind picks up.

I study the men's faces as they rattle on in the truck bed, looking back at us. Two of them appear to be sleeping. Another hunches over, a picture of defeat. But the young man with the beer breaks into a wide smile and raises his bottle to me in a silent toast. Then he takes a deep swig as the truck picks up sudden speed and covers us in a cloud of dust.

29

EVA

❧⟡❧

THROUGH THE BARRED GROUND-FLOOR PRISON WIN-
dow at San Leonardo, I see white blooms emerging among the tender grass on the mountainsides. The snow has melted, swelling the
streams, a din of relentless rushing. The sky has turned as blue as a
robin's egg. I watch Daniele's hunched grandma pour water on the
bare dirt in her window boxes, using an empty tomato can repurposed as a pitcher. I imagine the old woman has endured years of war
and hunger. For her, this is just another day.

But for Horst and myself, it's not just another day at all. It's the
day when we've been ordered to stay and wait at the prison. When
the SS guards fled into the mountains, they left the cells unlocked.
One of the guards has left his rifle sitting on a wooden table in the
kitchen. Horst is pacing outside among the chittering geese.

In the end, Professor Heydenreich told us, General Wolff supplied
Colonel Langsdorff with a demobilization order and instructed him
to hand over Campo Tures not to the Italians, but to the Allied authorities instead. And he instructed Major Reidemeister to travel to
San Leonardo for the same purpose. Reidemeister hasn't arrived yet,
but I expect to hear his escort vehicle arriving in the muddy street at
any time.

We will surrender and the Americans will get the paintings after
all. As much as I should feel trepidation—maybe even a flash of

white fear at the thought of our enemies arriving at the door—the realization that the Anglo-Americans will prevail washes me with a surprising wave of relief. Of acceptance. A strange feeling of solace to arrive at a resolution after so many months of fear and uncertainty about what will happen to the pictures—and to us.

I raise my Leica and point it at the window. I turn the aperture. For a moment, it brings the black bars into focus, and the world outside the window turns into a bright blur. When I turn it again, the black bars blur and instead, it is Horst who comes into focus. He is pacing up and down the street outside the jail, smoking with erratic flicks of his arm, kicking up puffs of dirt with his enormous shoes while the geese amble around him and one of them beats its great, white wings, sending up a flurry of dander.

I feel my hands tremble slightly as I bring my camera back down and hold it against my chest. They've been shaking ever since we rushed out of the crowded streets of Milan and arrived back at the quiet mountainside. In my head, I still hear the shrieking Milanese mob, still taste the air, thick and sour with wild rage. It was as though the discontent that had been rising to a boil throughout Mussolini's reign suddenly exploded. So much yelling and chanting in the streets. So many faces filled with rage and exuberance all at once.

I didn't see Mussolini's ruined, beaten corpse myself, nor that of his young lover. But the harrowing cries in the street made me visualize something that was perhaps even worse than reality. Papa always admired Mussolini. He said that it was a good thing we Germans had a real leader on our side, someone with the courage to stand up against the faltering West and usher in a new age of glory. I grew up admiring him, if for no reason other than that he was one of my Papa's heroes.

Trying to calm myself, I raise the camera to my face again, looking for a good angle. The subject matter is glorious. It seems that no one has told Mother Nature that we're in the death throes of the bloodiest war in history; she has brought a perfect spring to the flanks of the Alps that cup this tiny village so securely in a bowl of pure green. The lane meanders below, dotted with sleepy homes and wildflowers strewn across the mountainside like stars.

Suddenly, there is movement in the edge of the frame. I remove the camera from my face and see a line of soldiers, hiking up the steep mountain pass like a herd of goats. The minutes tick by and there are more of them. More and more men in uniform, walking to Austria with their packs on their backs. Leaving Italy behind for good. I think of all the SS troops across this land, their mission forfeited, their heroes slain. They have been squeezed like a tube of paint all the way up the boot of Italy. All the way from Sicily to the Alps, where some fed-up souls have decided not to wait for their next orders but simply to walk home over this narrow mountain pass.

I lower the camera and turn away from the window. Behind me is the broad table where Horst and I have been preparing the Führer's catalog. There are stacks of Horst's drafted words. Hundreds of catalog entries for the glorious museum over the mountains that will now remain only a perverted dream. There are also small, uneven stacks of my own black-and-white pictures of many of the paintings in these jail cells. Not only an exercise in colossal greed, but now one of futility.

The door opens at the far end of the hallway, and I hear Horst's heavy footsteps. He says nothing, only marches up the narrow stairwell to his cell on the second floor.

I step into the nearby cell and look at all the pictures there. Tremendous landscapes by Peter Paul Rubens. The enigmatic figure of Saint John the Baptist in the desert by Raphael. A few altarpieces by unknown Tuscan masters. A beautiful portrait by Bronzino. All packed so tightly I can barely pull them apart. What will happen when the Allies come? After all I have seen and heard, I have to believe they will want to return the works to Florence, as they should. Won't they?

After a few moments, Horst returns. I am surprised to see that he has changed into old clothes and boots. He carries a pack on his back.

"You're leaving!"

Horst sets his pack down on the table alongside our catalog notes.

"I'm not the only one," he says. He's seen the line of defeated men heading over the mountain pass. "And you should, too. Come with me, Eva." His face is putty-gray and full of shadows, but his eyes are hardened, more serious than I have ever seen him.

"I . . . I'm staying."

"You don't know what the Americans will do to us!" he exclaims, and for the first time, I feel his fear, heavy and palpable in the space between us. "They could take us as prisoners of war, Eva. They could shoot us dead! Give me one reason they wouldn't!"

"Because . . . because we know everything! Because they need us to give them the information to piece this all back together."

He scoffs. "You believe that's what they're going to do? Piece everything back together? Send it all back to Tuscany?" He flings his big arm toward the door, as if we could open it and see the green and gold hills of central Italy, the ruined bridges of Florence, just outside the door. "Well, I don't. I believe they're going to pack all of this up and send it to America instead. And that we'll be lucky to leave this god-forsaken jail with our lives."

"You're going to leave this place. Leave some of the greatest masterpieces of the world, all here by themselves, with no protection? Our so-called custodians and our guards have already run off. Who else will stay and protect these works of art now? It's just you and me."

"Major Reidemeister should be here any day now," Horst says. "Let him take responsibility for"—he gestures grandiosely to the dank cells—"for all this. But I'm not waiting for them to tell me what to do. I'm going home to get married. She's been waiting long enough." He rustles the stack of his catalog drafts with his hands. I notice they are trembling, just like mine. When he speaks again, the hysteria is gone from his voice. Now he looks into my eyes. "Eva. For the sake of everything we have been through together in Italy. I care for you. I don't want to see anything bad happen to you. Come with me. Please." He reaches for my hand. It feels small and soft in his huge, meaty palm.

"I will not leave these works of art like this," I say. "Someone has to guard them. *We* —we Germans—looted these works, Horst. But I don't believe the Allies intend to."

He lets go of my hand. "Then you are a fool."

He picks up his pack from the table and turns away. Even after all the times I felt he wanted to touch me, every time he tried to be tender or at least friendly, now he doesn't say goodbye, doesn't try to embrace me. Doesn't talk to me at all. He simply hoists the bag on his back and walks out the door, leaving it hanging open to the blue sky.

For a long few moments, I stand there, alone in the prison, and listen to the loud, ticking clock. Then, I walk into the kitchen and pour myself a glass of water. I try hard to steady my shaking hand long enough to slake my thirst, to coat my dry tongue.

I walk slowly to the table, where a guard has left his rifle along-side the large iron ring full of complicated keys that open each one of the cells. I unfurl the camera strap from my neck and set my Leica on the table. Then I pick up the gun. It feels heavy and awkward in my hands. I stretch my arm out and look through the sight. Peer through it to the end of the barrel at the tattered lace curtain blowing in the mild breeze. I lay the weapon on the table again, then turn and slide back the steel bolt. I pull out the clip and touch my fingertips to the cold tip of each of the shiny bullets inside. One. Two. Three. Four. Five.

I pace back and forth down the corridor between the jail cells, with the rifle hanging heavy from its strap across my shoulder. I'm used to carrying a heavy camera around my neck for hours at a time. The gun feels foreign. Unwieldy. Like I might topple under its strange, one-sided heft.

I step into the cell where there are dozens of pictures, including Cranach's *Adam* and *Eve*. In the shadows, the pair look sad and neglected, partly covered with an old bedspread that's slipped off the frames. But something in the cell is not as it was. One of the small, allegorical pictures by Piero Pollaiuolo. It's missing. Just small enough to fit inside a soldier's pack.

I hurry back to the barred window, the rifle shifting awkwardly on my hip. Through the square opening, I can see Horst, just a tiny figure in the distance now, walking swiftly toward the trailhead. It will be a long, arduous vertical hike for a big man like him, especially with a big pack on his back. A pack just large enough for a little picture. I stand at the window for a long time, watching his silhouette grow smaller, then it disappears over the mountain pass.

Sometimes, people aren't who you thought. I learned that lesson in Florence. But maybe Horst was right. Perhaps the Allies will come here and want to take something—some of the greatest masterpieces of history—for themselves. Maybe I had it all wrong. And at the last minute, in the face of imminent defeat, things could go badly.

I return to the kitchen. I sit down at the table, turn the bolt of the rifle, and count the bullets in the clip again. The jail falls quiet now. Just me and the loudly ticking clock. I take a deep breath and sit in a chair. Then I hold the rifle in my lap and wait for Leopold Reidemeister or the Americans, whoever comes first.

30

JOSIE

❧❧❧

THE MOUNTAIN VILLAGE OF SAN LEONARDO IN PAS-
siria is a cluster of neat Tirolean houses with stone chimneys, pale
walls, and sloping rooftops. The sky is clear blue and a stream
rushes by in a torrent of snowmelt. Two children are running
down a footpath among a herd of goats grazing on the wildflowers.
Nearby, wooden carts are piled with freshly shorn sheep's wool.
In the distance, German soldiers are hiking up steep trails along
the mountainside. They are barely recognizable, tiny silhouettes in
their uniforms and packs, threading up the mountain trails like an
army of ants.

"It's supposed to be a jail," Captain Foster says as he slows the
jeep and we scan the buildings along either side of the narrow road
winding through the village. We soon reach the woods on the other
side of the settlement, and have to turn around to retrace our path
down the main road through town.

"There!" I say, noticing that one of the nondescript buildings—
one that looks like every other one in town—has small, iron bars on
its windows. We pull up to the building and Captain Foster cuts the
engine. The door to the old prison gapes open like a yawning black
mouth.

Behind us, an armored truck comes to a stop and several armed
American GIs hop down from the vehicle, rifles at the ready.

"This can't be it," Captain Foster says, but we get out of the vehicle and step into the shadows of the gaping prison doorway.

At first, the dark, dank prison feels empty. Our footsteps slide over dirt dislodged from the cracks of the floor. As our eyes adjust to the light, we find ourselves in a long, sad corridor lined with the iron bars of jail cells. The GIs enter the building and press ahead of us, guns drawn.

"U.S. Army," one of the GIs calls into the dark. "Hello? Anybody home?"

"*C'è qualcuno?*" Captain Foster echoes.

"Captain." I wrap my hands around the bars of the nearest cell. "Look at this."

He comes to stand next to me and we press our faces between the bars. There, in the dank, are paintings stacked against the wall, several dozen deep. "Caravaggio," he says. "Titian. Bellini."

"This is it," I whisper into the darkness.

"Captain Foster." We turn to see two of the GIs standing on either side of a young woman dressed neatly in a gray dress, holding each one of her elbows. "She seems to be the only one here. I can't understand German. She had a rifle but we disarmed her."

"And we found these," one of the GIs says. The skinny man steps forward and holds up a huge iron ring full of skeleton keys.

"Swell," Captain Foster says. "Figure out how to unlock all this for us? And then hold her here until we can understand what we're dealing with."

With a clang of metal, the GI opens one of the cells and pushes the woman inside with the end of his rifle.

"*Aspetta!*" she calls. "I will tell you everything," she continues in heavily accented Italian. Captain Foster and I approach the cell. "But only if you let me out of here. And only if you assure me that you intend to return these things to Florence."

· · ·

Until we can find an interpreter, Captain Foster and I communicate with the woman in Italian with a few German and English words thrown in. We have made out that her name is Eva Brunner. The captain's Italian is much better than hers or mine, but we make ourselves understood. Notwithstanding the relative language barrier, she seems to understand that we have every intention of returning the works to the Uffizi.

Slowly, the GIs figure out which key matches each prison cell. In some of the cells, the pictures are stacked so tightly that there's no room for us inside. With only the wan light from the small, barred windows—framing a view of lofty pines and narrow streaks of snow on the bald peaks—Captain Foster pulls out individual pictures and brings them into the corridor. With each picture uncovered, his excitement grows.

"This one is from . . ."

"Montagnana," Eva Brunner says. Several GIs stand behind her, shifting their weight back and forth. They look ready to spring into action in case she makes an unexpected move.

"Yes!" he says. "Montagnana." It comes out in quiet disbelief. My mind floods with images of the desolated villa, with its smashed windows and wine bottles, its empty rooms, its piles of German feces, drawing flies.

In damp, narrow cells, we find the other paintings that our Italian friends told us they hid at the Villa Bossi-Pucci at Montagnana five years ago. In one of the rooms, we find Caravaggio's *Bacchus*, which Captain Foster tells me is a very famous picture indeed, and Titian's *Philip the Second*. There is also the *Saint Sebastian* by Ercole da Ferrara. Botticelli's *Minerva and the Centaur*. And two beautiful landscapes by Peter Paul Rubens propped against the wall.

I step into a cell and remove a dusty, cheap bed covering from a pair of framed wooden panels. I hear Captain Foster emit a cry of glee. "Lucas Cranach's *Adam* and *Eve*!"

In the entry to the jail, there is a large wooden table with stacks of pages and photographs scattered across its surface. The pages are handwritten in precise, meticulous German writing. I can't read it but it consists of numbered entries, like an inventory, or maybe a catalog. I pick up one of the black-and-white photographs. It shows men in SS uniforms standing alongside a truck bed. Inside, there are paintings stacked tightly together. They are uncrated, uncovered, open to the elements. They only have a little straw between them; some have blankets hastily thrown over the top. I try to imagine these priceless masterpieces traveling all the way up from Tuscany across the battle-scarred roads like this. Near the jail's kitchen, we find a bedroom filled with old cameras, tripods, and metal film cartridges.

"You have to tell us how all this got here," Captain Foster says to Eva Brunner.

"And we have to find the second depot," I say, unfolding the paper with the name of the place on it. *Neumelans in Sand*.

"No," she says. "Sand in Taufers. The Italians call it Campo Tures. There's a Castello Neumelans there."

"No wonder we couldn't find it. That's where the rest of the pictures are?"

"Yes. In a manor house. About an hour's drive from here," she says. "I can show you how to get there."

"Alright. No time like the present," Captain Foster says. "When her commanding officers show up," he says to one of the GIs standing guard at the door, "lock them up in one of the emptied cells until we can get Captain Thomas up here to help me with interrogations. Until then, post guards at the door. Do not let anyone else in here. And for God's sake, keep those pictures locked up and don't open the cells for any reason until we get back."

31

EVA

⤠⤠

THE SKINNY, INTELLIGENT-LOOKING AMERICAN captain drives his assistant and me to Campo Tures in his battered vehicle. The car looks similar to the Kübelwagen Horst and I have driven all the way here from Florence, but the American vehicle is rusted and dented, powered by a trail of black smoke. But it brings us all the way to the manor house that holds the rest of the Florentine treasures.

Unlike our deserted jail at San Leonardo, at Campo Tures, there are already a dozen American soldiers, sweating in their tan uniforms. Alongside, there are also German SS guards, and even a group of Italian partisans. They shift nervously around the doorways to the manor and carriage house. Waiting. I twist my hands around the straps of my camera bag, my fingers slippery with sweat. The American vehicle quakes and coughs to a halt in front of the carriage house. The captain leaps from the driver's seat. I step down to the ground under the watchful eyes of Americans, Germans, and Italians alike. All of us have a stake in the fate of the masterpieces inside this unassuming place.

As we approach the main entrance to the manor, to my surprise, Colonel Langsdorff fills the doorway, straight-backed, as if he is the distinguished proprietor of this fine house, waiting to welcome his guests. But his face is not one of a welcoming host. Instead, his mouth works like he's chewing something bitter. When he recognizes me alongside the Americans, our eyes meet for a long second that seems suspended in time. I watch one side of his mouth twitch.

Finally, he acknowledges the American captain and nods, reaching for the belt that holds his pistol to his waist. He unbuckles it and hands it wordlessly to an American GI standing guard by the door.

"Your men, too," says the American captain. Captain Foster. "Tell them to surrender all of their weapons." The captain's eyes stay cool. "Your weapons," he repeats.

The SS soldiers watch Colonel Langsdorff warily. For a moment, my stomach clenches. Then the colonel waves a hand. "Do as he says," he spits in German.

One by one, the German soldiers begin to hand over their pistols to the American GIs and ragged-looking Italian men. I loosen my fingers where they've locked around one another, rubbing the feeling back into my hands. When all the Germans are disarmed, the American woman steps out of the jeep, clutching several spiral-bound pads of paper, a bundle of pens, and a metal case with a handle. It's disconcerting to watch this neat, pretty woman about my own age who looks like she's on her way to a regular day at the office. She gives me a tight nod as she walks past, and it feels strangely reassuring. I follow suit, pulling my camera bag from the back of the vehicle.

Colonel Langsdorff, still bitter-faced, walks to the carriage house and gestures for the SS soldiers to roll back the heavy door. All of us—like an unlikely tour group of strangers—follow his lead. Moments later, we're all standing in front of the dozens of crates stacked from floor to ceiling. Some of the American soldiers don't seem to understand the fuss; they look around, their eyes still wild, seeking danger. But the American captain stands very still for a long few moments, staring into the dark storage area, his hands clasped behind his back. When he turns around, I think I see the glimmer of a tear in his eye. But he blinks, then appears cold and hard again, clearing his throat.

"We will set up an interrogation room inside the house," he says coolly. "You—young man." He points at one of the Italian partisans, standing with his arms crossed. "Find a suitable room inside the house with thick walls. One where we will not be overheard. Johnson speaks good German," he says, gesturing to one of the GIs. "He can translate for us." His eyes flash. "We will find out how all these Tuscan masterpieces came to be locked up in a storehouse full of Germans in the Dolomites."

Langsdorff shrugs off the American GIs who stand at his elbows. "You will find that we have taken all these works in trust for the Italian nation," the colonel says in fluent Italian, still defiant even though he is now unarmed. "We have many years of experience and agreements with them. If it weren't for our significant efforts over years, these works would not have survived to this point."

There is a brief exchange of glances between the American captain and one of the Italian partisans, whose mouth has turned into a deep frown.

Captain Foster matches the colonel's fluent Italian. "*Questo lo vedremo.*" We'll see about that.

Langsdorff is the first to be led away. He goes, his back very straight, a muscle popping in his jaw. I am left to wonder which version of our story he will tell.

32

JOSIE

THE TIROLEAN MANOR HOUSE AND ITS OUTBUILD-
ings sit on a green slope, the rugged mountain peaks magnificent
behind it. The mansion stands like a monolith, a five-story square
building with turrets on each corner. Outside, the disarmed SS soldiers mill around aimlessly, some with an air of disdain, others with
relief written on their faces.

I suppress a lump in my throat as we watch two hulking German
soldiers roll the large wooden door of the carriage house open and
their bitter-looking colonel steps into the dark space. I know whatever is on the other side of that door can only be everything else we've
been desperately seeking for months.

In contrast to the bare canvases and panels in the jail at San Leonardo, here, in the cavernous space of the carriage house, wooden
crates are stacked floor to ceiling, all the way from the front to the
back wall of the building. My mind reels to think what treasures lie
inside, and how much work is ahead of us to record everything we've
discovered at last.

"You will find everything here in order, thanks to our efforts,"
Colonel Langsdorff says in perfect Italian to Captain Foster.

I recognize Signor Rossi from the Florentine Galleries exit the
door of the main house. He and Captain Foster greet each other

warmly. "I see you've made the acquaintance of the lady photographer," he says, gesturing toward Eva Brunner, who is standing near the door of the carriage house, her small camera raised to her face.

"You know her?" Captain Foster says.

Rossi nods. "She will be able to tell you some important things."

33

EVA

WHEN MY TURN IN THE INTERROGATION ROOM COMES at last, an American GI leads me into one of the great halls of the Renaissance manor house. It is empty except for a wooden table and several ornately carved chairs set before a gaping fireplace. Two American guards stand by the door, while Captain Foster and his stenographer sit on the other side of the table. Two British officers join us at the table.

"My name is Johnson," one of the guards says in German as I take a seat. "I will translate for you."

"Let's start from the beginning with your name and your job title," Captain Foster says.

"As you already know, I am Eva Brunner," I say. "For the past eighteen months, I have been documenting works of art and damage to historic monuments."

I watch the stenographer move her fingers swiftly across the metal keys of her gray machine. Evans, the tag on her shirt says. She looks relaxed, like she's done this many times before. She is an attractive woman. Not in a flashy, glamorous way. She is natural-looking, with even features and brown hair in waves around her face. She looks like she doesn't know how pretty she is. I feel a tinge of envy for these Americans with their loud voices, their easy smiles, their confidence that seems at the same time overblown and naïve. They haven't endured the same things we have.

Captain Foster asks, "And you said you've been working for the Kunstschutz . . ."

"Yes, for Colonel Langsdorff and the Kunstschutz, but that wasn't how it started. Initially, I came to Italy as a photographer for the Kunsthistorisches Institut in Florence."

The stenographer stops typing. "Florence?" she says. "You were in Florence?"

I nod. "Up until August of last year . . ." But I don't know what to say next. How could I find the words to describe that fateful night when I left Enzo in his desolate sniper's nest, much less everything that's happened in the meantime? The Americans, too, seem to be rendered silent for a long moment. I take advantage of the momentary silence to ask a question of my own. "How did you find this place? And San Leonardo?"

Captain Foster gives me a long look. "Apparently, a German informant conveyed it to a priest in Venice who was acting as a double agent. Then it was put to good use. You know anything about that?"

My heart leaps. *Padre Vanucci.* "No, sir."

Captain Foster says, "Alright, let's go back. You say you were living in Austria."

My mind has been made up for a long time. I nod, and as the stenographer begins to capture my words with swift, sure strokes of the keys, I begin to tell them everything. About the salt mine at Altaussee. About my father and how the thousands of treasures hidden there narrowly escaped being blown to dust. About my brother, whose whereabouts are still unknown. I even tell them about my mother, how she dedicated herself to uncovering the truth, and how that pursuit didn't end any better for her than it has for me.

"OK," the American captain says. "Tell me about Montagnana."

"We got there after the troops had already . . . gone through the place," I say, thinking of the river of wine soaking through the grass and the busted door hinges. "At that point, I wanted more than anything to get word back to our friends in Florence, but it was too late. Your troops had moved into the city and we didn't have any lines of communication. There was no way to tell them what happened, or where to look." The more I talk, the more the story widens, unfolds. And as I talk them through these past two years, the weight of my country's guilt—and then my own—begins to lift from my shoulders.

While I talk, Captain Foster stands and paces the room, listening to Johnson's translation of my story, his arms crossed.

"But Signor Rossi will vouch for the rest of my story," I say. "He will tell you about the work we did to preserve things in Florence. Me. A few others from the German art history institute. Even some Italians. Especially one of the Italian workers there named Paloma."

At the mention of Paloma's name, the woman stops typing and she stands. "Paloma?" she says. "Paloma Innocenti?"

"Yes."

Captain Foster only says, "Dear God!"

34

JOSIE

꿍

"THIS HAS GOT TO BE THE SINGLE GREATEST ART-looting operation in recorded history," Captain Foster says, standing at the window of the interrogation room with his hands in his pockets. From the third floor, we watch more Allied vehicles collect in the gravel outside the manor house at Campo Tures. I smile as I see Captain Rand Thomas hop down from an army jeep and hike up the waist of his drab pants.

"Well, look who's here," I say.

"Rand Thomas," he says, shaking his head. "Always looking for a piece of the action." In recent days, two British Monuments officers and several more Italian superintendents have arrived, all lured by the discovery of close to seven hundred treasures spirited away from Tuscany to the border of Austria.

A truck full of GIs has gone back to the prison at San Leonardo to collect Leopold Reidemeister. We've heard enough about him in the interrogation room to know that, along with the petulant Colonel Langsdorff, Reidemeister will have little excuse for his actions when it comes his time to sit with us at the table.

"Want to know what I think is the strangest part of this whole thing?" I say to Captain Foster. "Everyone who has sat with us at this table has spent their career in some way dedicated to the creation, study, or preservation of art. And yet, look how many men let greed overpower their actions which were initially altruistic."

"You're right," says Captain Foster. "Plus, several dozen things are still missing. I'll bet money that some of these so-called 'art lovers' have these treasures stuffed in their bag or in the back of a truck."

In the afternoon, Captain Foster and I take the newly arrived Monuments officers and Italian superintendents through the manor house and its outbuildings. Around the dry, airy halls of the house—so much better of a refuge than those dank prison cells at San Leonardo—we show them the incredible finds. "Some of them weren't even packed," I tell Captain Thomas, pointing out some of the damage done to the surfaces and frames.

"Looks like you're a bona fide art expert now, sweetheart," Captain Thomas says to me as we descend the grand staircase toward the ground floor. "I guess old Foster is good for something after all."

"Well, I learned a lot in Florence," I say. "But I plan to use all this new knowledge for good, not evil." I smile.

"You mean like Langsdorff?"

I nod. "During the interrogation, he actually told us we have not fulfilled our duty to the future of art because it took us so long to get here."

Thomas shakes his head. "Probably just looking for you to recognize his superior rank. Unfortunately there are men like him in every army."

"Yes. He told us he was awarded a silver cross just a few days before Italy surrendered. But he also wanted us to give him credit for protecting all of these artistic treasures for the future of civilization. Captain Foster did his best to disillusion him on that count but I'm not sure it sank in."

Captain Thomas gives me a tight grin. "He'll have plenty of time to think about it when he gets to the POW camp. Within a few weeks, I expect he will have lost a little of his swagger."

We file out to the carriage house. When the doors are unlocked, we look into the dark interior full of the dry and beautifully packed crates stacked to the ceiling. Captain Foster describes a little of what's inside the stout boxes: Donatello's *Saint George*, Michelangelo's *Bacchus*, Raphael's beautiful *Donna Velata*. Boxes containing the treasures from the Tuscan depots at Poggio a Caiano, Poppi, Dicomano, and Soci. The cases are jammed so closely together that we can hardly count their number. But on each box is a clear label for our benefit: Kunstwerke aus Italienischen Staatsbesitz.

Lieutenant Johnson translates for all of us. "Works of art from the Italian State."

35

EVA

OVER THE NEXT FEW DAYS, THE ALLIED OFFICERS
continue their questioning. I've told them everything I know except
for the small part I played in Venice. I don't want to get that poor
priest in trouble or targeted as a spy, especially after everything he
must have done to help.

The Americans and Italians also begin to make detailed inventories of everything in the deposits at San Leonardo and Campo Tures.
I hand over the photographs and entries that Horst drafted for the
Führer's catalog. That American captain looks like he might burst an
artery when I explain to him what it is.

They find other paintings missing, too. Lorenzo de Credi's self-
portrait, Bronzino's *Deposition* from the Uffizi, a rash of smaller
pictures. Again and again, they ask me what I know about them,
but the truth is I have no idea. They might have been stashed in a
soldier's bag. Dropped in a ravine to lighten an overloaded truck.
Trampled or burned. I do not know and perhaps never shall. I
think about Horst lumbering over the mountain pass with his
pack.

I feel sad now that Horst was so quick to abandon San Leonardo. Things might have worked out better for him if only he had
stayed. But the big man's fear led his actions. I might decide to tell
the Americans about Horst and his stolen painting. But I have a

feeling no one will be able to find him now, even if they had the time and resources to go looking for him.

One evening, as the local women being paid to cook for us dish thick soup into our bowls, the American stenographer—Miss Evans—comes to sit with me at the table. I speak no English and she no German, and we soon discover that her Italian is as rudimentary as mine. We exchange a few benign comments about the delicious food and the beautiful landscape of Italy. I ask her what part of the United States she comes from and she tells me a place whose name is too complicated for me to say.

"You will return to America," I ask her, "when this is finished?"

My question seems to trouble her. Her brow wrinkles when she responds. "I don't know," she says. "My mother died while I have been here in Italy. So perhaps I need to go home and sort out her affairs. But if you want to know the truth, more than anything, I would like to return to Florence. Maybe for a while. Maybe forever." I watch her face flush red.

"If you go to Florence," I say, "maybe you will take a letter for me? For so many months I have been trying to reach our friend. Paloma." I stop, realizing I've just asked for something I haven't really thought through properly. And I'm not sure Paloma wants to hear from me at all.

"*Con piacere*," she says. With pleasure. "And you, Eva? You are anxious to return home to your family in Austria?"

I take a deep breath and consider her question. In that instant, it comes rushing back to me. The blue sky and tender grass of a summer's day, when the underground passages are a cool respite from the heat; the pink glow and the briny smell of the salt mine; the sweet, flaky crust of my Oma's apple tarts; the twinkling lights and hot, mulled wine in the cold Christmas markets of Salzburg and Innsbruck.

For the better part of a year, I've been living in a prison. A prison filled with the world's greatest examples of beauty and human achievement. And in the prison of my own mind, my own choices. But now, even though the Americans are holding me, posting guards at my door every night, I don't feel like a prisoner anymore. Instead, I feel I have broken free.

In my heart, as much as I felt lured by all the temptations of Florence, I know there is nothing left for me there anymore. And I want to go back to Austria more than anything else in the world.

"Yes," I tell her. "I'll go home."

JOSIE

THE DAYS PASS SLOWLY AS WE DISCUSS WHAT TO DO with the two huge deposits at San Leonardo and Campo Tures, containing some of the most significant artistic heritage of Italy and the world.

"I think everything should be left here. Right where they are," one of the British Monuments officers says. "The Italians can do with them as they wish, whenever they are able."

"I don't recommend it," Captain Foster says. "It would mean the Allies would have to provide a prolonged commitment to guard everything. And just look how many SS troops there are wandering the mountains here. It's a setup for sabotage."

Eventually, Captain Foster's argument that the works should be returned to Florence wins the Fifth Army's approval and financial support, but things are not so simple. Outside the jail at San Leonardo, a superintendent from Milan supervises the construction of more than a hundred wooden crates. We coordinate local Italian workers to pack the fragile works. We make detailed inventories so that they can be unpacked upon their return to Florence. Guards are posted twenty-four hours a day at both depots.

But the biggest problem is that it's not clear how to transport all these works safely back to Florence. Most of the train lines between Florence and northern Italy have been shattered. And traveling the ruined roads from the Alps to Florence seems only a way to damage these fragile goods. The Fifth Army can't spare the more than fifty trucks it might take to transport everything. They have more pressing needs for them.

So we wait.

We settle into the comfortable bedchambers at Campo Tures. Langsdorff, Reidemeister, and a few of the other Germans are guarded night and day, undoubtedly the most luxurious of POW situations in all of Europe. Some of the SS soldiers on-site, now unarmed and unimportant, have simply wandered off to the north, along the mountain foot trails. Whatever wrongs they have done over the course of this war, I have little doubt that they will escape justice.

"What about that photographer?" I ask Captain Foster one afternoon. "Eva Brunner? I know they are guarding her room at night, but I don't see how she poses any threat to us. Right?"

Along a lone train track near Campo Tures, a line of cargo trucks stands ready to load the contents of the carriage house into a train of freight cars. Rossi and a few other Florentine officials are there to supervise the loading with us. They double-check their case-by-case inventories, sweating under the July sun in their suits and ties.

In the weeks since we began strategizing a way to return the works to Florence, the Fifth Army has been busy repairing the train lines to Florence. The Monuments officers have devised a complicated series of train switches down from Campo Tures to Brunico, then to Bolzano. From there, the Campo Tures train cars will be loaded with the contents of the jail at San Leonardo, where all the bare canvases and panels are now safely packed in crates. Meanwhile, the Florentines say they have arranged for truck transport from Santa Maria Novella to the Pitti Palace, once everything has arrived safely home in Florence.

In the evening, when we return to the quiet manor house from the train track, we find that Colonel Langsdorff and Major Reidemeister have simply slipped out of our grasp. Decorated uniforms, cigarette butts, and dirty dishes left behind in their rooms. Curtains undulating in the hot breeze.

We check Eva Brunner's room to find her sitting at a small writing desk, her hair twisted away from her neck and secured with a pencil. She stands, crosses the room, and hands me a letter. "Perhaps you could deliver this for me, Signorina Evans," she says in Italian, "when you get back to Florence."

EVA

Dear Paloma,

If eighteen months in Italy have taught me anything, it's that war is full of unexplainable twists of fate. That the truth is elusive. And that sometimes, someone you think you know well turns out to be the opposite of what you thought.

Maybe you still see me as your enemy, even now. But I like to think that you and I mostly saw eye to eye, that we had the same purpose, after all.

MY PEN STOPS IN MID-AIR. I WANT TO TELL PALOMA how I have helped the Americans, how I have only tried to return the treasures home to Florence, how I have worked to redeem myself here, while I've been a prisoner in this desolation of the mountain depots. But I only end up sounding as arrogant and presumptive as Colonel Langsdorff. So I crumple the page and start again.

Josephine Evans is a good woman, I write instead.

Yes, that's better. Josephine Evans *is* a good woman. And brave. I wish I could be as brave as she. I wish that I could have made a contribution half as large as hers. A woman in a uniform, with a job to do. A *real* woman at war. A woman who left her country, her home, everything she loved, for a chance to do something that mattered. It's evident to me and everyone else that she's succeeded in her mission. She has made a contribution in a way that I never have. And besides that, she stands so well on her own.

I return to my letter.

I hope Miss Evans finds a way to stay in Florence, which is deserving of her.

> *Cordiali saluti,*
> *Eva Brunner*

In the afternoon, I find a ragged group of retreating Austrian soldiers in an armored truck. They've stopped in the shade of towering fir trees on the edge of the grounds, a short respite from the blinding sun. In exchange for an unlabeled bottle of amber-colored wine and a pack of American cigarettes I found discarded or forgotten in the old carriage house, they agree to give me a ride to Innsbruck.

Before I sling my camera bags over my shoulders, I pick out my best photograph of the church of Santo Spirito. I took that picture on the day I arrived in Florence, from the top-floor loggia of Palazzo Guadagni, Horst looking over my shoulder. It's a unique view of the square and I hope Miss Evans likes it. I place it in a piece of folded paper with her name on it, then tuck one corner of the paper under the metal case of her steno machine.

Later, rumbling along over the pass, one of the men extends the red pack of American cigarettes toward me. Little white tubes poking out of the opening. I whisk out a cigarette and run it under my nose, inhaling the rich, sun-burnished smell of an American tobacco field. I catch a last glimpse of the round turrets on the manor house of Campo Tures before it disappears in the thick green forest. Ahead of us, there are only bald, craggy peaks.

38

JOSIE

WHEN CAPTAIN FOSTER AND I RATTLE DOWN THE
mountainside in the empty jeep, I can only wonder if it has any tread
left on the tires. Just weeks ago, we traveled up this same mountain road. Filled with trepidation about what we would find. In
the back, I've loaded my stenography machine and supplies, spare
carbon paper, our interrogation reports in progress, the confiscated
Kunstschutz documents, and the photographs and film cartridges
handed over by Eva Brunner. A letter for Paloma. And a beautiful
photograph of Santo Spirito that Eva herself must have taken from
the loggia at Palazzo Guadagni.

Foster brakes for the several armored trucks ahead of us, moving at a snail's pace down the mountain, filled with carefully crated
works of art. "Are you surprised at what's gone missing, sir?"

Captain Foster thinks about this for a long while. "It's incredible
that the vast majority of the paintings and sculptures survived that
trip up here under combat conditions. So many unwrapped, all the
way up to the Dolomites from Tuscany. So, I think I'm more surprised at what *has* been found rather than what hasn't."

By the afternoon, the train is ready to depart Bolzano. Thanks to
the help of dozens of local laborers hired for the job, the loading of
hundreds of wooden crates into the thirteen train cars goes smoothly.
There are six additional cars for the guards arranged throughout the

train, a kitchen car, a passenger and office car, and a flat car carrying a few jeeps. But not Georgette.

"I'll go right on to Florence. Someone will need to arrange the details of the unloading," he says. "Might as well be me. And I guess I'll need to organize a ceremony of some sort."

"I'll bet Paloma can help you with that."

He nods and smiles. "And we need to get those interrogation documents typed up so we can send everything to our commanders."

"Yes, sir. I'll have plenty of time to type them up on the train."

At last, the loaded train cranks and groans as it gathers itself to momentum. When the breeze wafts through the open windows and heads south, the train carries nearly seven hundred masterpieces. Dozens of fire extinguishers. More than sixty Allied officers and enlisted soldiers.

And one girl from New Haven.

Captured Documents of the German Kunstschutz

Dear Sirs,

You will find attached a full report of our recent activities in Italy along with original documents we confiscated from German Kunstschutz officials over the course of our interrogations. These have been compiled with the help of my fellow Monuments officers and my trusted assistant who has been working with me all the way from Tuscany to the Dolomites.

What is important to note up front is that the Germans have offered three different justifications of their action, namely:

a. *That the works of art were in danger of destruction by bombing or shellfire in the deposits.*
b. *That the masterpieces of Italian art had to be protected from seizure by the Anglo-American barbarians. (Incidentally they*

spread the story that British and American art dealers had been
brought to Italy to "acquire" what they could.)

c. *That they were preserving the masterpieces both for Italy and for*
the world. These stories are scarcely reconcilable with any of the
facts, and if (b) were true one must ask why in the end it was
to these same Anglo-American barbarians that the deposits were
handed over.

The next time I see Captain Foster, he's standing in the shade of a cypress tree in the Boboli Gardens, admiring the vista of Brunelleschi's hulking cathedral dome over the tiled rooftops of Florence. For a moment, I stand there and contemplate the wonder of the view, along with the wonder of our safe return to Florence along with the trainloads of artworks. And the wonder that I've gotten the chance to return here at all, when all my friends are picking up their old lives back home in the States, crying grateful tears to return to their loved ones.

Below us, in the Pitti Palace, the trucks arrive from the Campo di Marte, where a single track has been reconstructed among the twisted metal carnage to welcome our train. The conductor tells us we're the first freight train to pull into the station since the Germans blew up the bridges. Now the trucks fly Italian and American flags on their hoods, and people hang out of their windows and cheer as the trucks make slow progress through the streets and cross the Ponte Vecchio. In the courtyard of the Pitti, there are only a few straggling refugees left, seeking shade from the searing heat. Those left perhaps have nothing to return home to and figure they might as well stay put. I empathize with them to the pit of my stomach.

Across the city, the scars of war are everywhere, from shell-pocked streets to bombed-out buildings. But since we left two months ago for Alto Adige, more debris has been cleared and new structures erected. Florence is a city of architectural and inventive wonder, so it's not surprising to see the Florentines so resilient and ready to put their city together again.

"You ever think you'd be a war hero, Evans?" Captain Foster asks, his voice teasing.

"Not once."

"Me neither. I'm just an art historian."

"You plan to stay in Florence, Captain?" I say as we look out over the river to the cathedral dome.

"I wish I could," Captain Foster says wistfully. "My favorite spot in the world is right here," he says, taking a deep breath as if he's inhaling the entire vista of Florence. "But it's not in the cards for me."

"Then you're headed back home to New York? To your wife?"

"Not yet," he says, removing his thin glasses and wiping his brow. "First I'm going to the mountains. Over to the other side this time. As you know, there are still a few more things to track down, restitution agreements to settle. They have established a Collecting Point in Munich where everything is being amassed so we can figure out what to do with it," he says. He shakes his head. "It's going to be a mess. I'll probably be needed there. But first I'm going up to those salt mines in Austria that photographer told us about . . ."

For a moment, I feel my heart seize. Will Captain Foster want me to go with him? Part of me is dying to go, to see those salt mines Eva Brunner told us about, the one where her father stands guard, the one containing thousands and thousands of art treasures seized from every corner of Europe. And to continue on this grand adventure. But now that I'm back in Florence, I don't want to leave.

"Don't worry," he says as if reading my mind. "I won't ask you to take another ride in that poor jeep. Georgette's going out to pasture soon enough." He smiles. "Besides, you've outstayed your welcome. You're the last man—woman—standing."

"I'm just glad I could play a small role, sir."

He nods. "We did a good thing here, Evans. I couldn't have done it without you. More women like you, and things at home are definitely going to change, maybe sooner than you think." I crack a little smile and take a deep breath. The garden air is ripe with the scent of orange and lemon trees. "And how about you?" he asks. "All your WAC friends are Stateside by now. You probably have some things to deal with in Connecticut, I imagine, your mother having passed since you left."

I shrug. "She didn't have much to settle, I'm afraid. My ma's sister saw to her in those last days, and she settled the small matter of what my mother left behind. If you want to know the truth, sir, I would do anything to stay in Florence." There. The truth. I'm surprised I blurted it out so carelessly, but it's all I could think about on the train.

Captain Foster's eyebrows fly up. "Ah! Yes, I do understand that sentiment, better than you might expect. Well, perhaps you could continue your education here, like I did before I had to settle down to more . . . responsibilities."

"I never really started my education, so . . ." I begin, but I stop myself. "You really think I could study here?" It's hard to imagine it, when any kind of education beyond high school seemed out of reach for me not so long ago. An opportunity reserved only for men like Captain Foster and privileged girls like Dot.

"Why not?" He shrugs. "You've seen more important works of art up close than just about anyone. Maybe you'll become an art historian. A curator? I could make some introductions for you. Whatever you choose, I'm sure you'll do splendidly."

My mind expands with this new possibility, as if a gust of fresh air has blown in all at once. But as I look down toward the wide stretch of the Arno, at the buildings along the riversides about to rise from the ashes, my own future remains a mystery. I see in the city my own life, laid to waste by loss, violence, and uncertainty. But now, I also see a glimmer of hope for Florence. And for myself. I know I will have to rebuild my life from the ground up, too. It will not be a carefree undertaking, nor one without risk. But I sense a certain hum in my body and brain, a new strength and confidence that I will, in fact, do splendidly.

"It's been an honor, Evans. Mouse." Instead of a salute, the captain extends his hand to me, denoting my civilian status, my dismissal from his service. But for me, it's also a gesture of goodwill, of admiration and respect.

"Thank you, Captain Foster . . . Wallace."

His face breaks into a wide grin. "Well," he says, "we have a celebration to get to."

Before noon, the procession forms. I stand in the Piazza della Signoria and listen to the grinding engines as the convoy makes its slow progress down the dark ravine of the via Calziauoli. When it emerges in the square, there is a burst of cheering and applause. The tall, skinny tower of the medieval Palazzo Vecchio stands proud against a blue sky.

The trucks make a loud grinding noise when they pull into the piazza. First is a jeep loaded with MPs, then Georgette, carrying Captain Foster, Mr. Poggi, and two American officers, neat in their uniforms. Then at last, six open trucks with wooden slats along their beds, each loaded with a few crates, forming a symbolic convoy around the city. They roll at a snail's pace between the cathedral and the Piazza della Signoria, as crowds of cheering, weeping Florentines stand by on the narrow sidewalks. By the time the simple procession reaches us in the hot square, bells from towers around the city are clanging in a wonderful cacophony.

Allied and Italian dignitaries sit in rows under the arches of the Loggia dei Lanzi, shielded from the blinding sun. I spot the mayor of Florence, a handful of museum officials from the Uffizi and the Pitti, an American brigadier general, and several other Fifth Army officers. In the back row, I spot Captain Thomas, squinting up at the tall tower of the Palazzo Vecchio, his hand over his brow. At the front are two lines of men dressed in brightly colored medieval Florentine costumes, under flapping banners decorated with the red *giglio*, the lily of Florence. When the trucks approach, they blow into long, elaborate trumpets decorated with colorful silk cords, but their triumphant melodies are drowned in cheering and church bells. The huge trucks maneuver around their positions near the bulk of the Palazzo Vecchio.

I move to the front of the crowd, near the wooden speakers' platform. There, standing in front, is Paloma.

Paloma stands near the stage that's been erected before the Loggia dei Lanzi, alongside those men with their floppy medieval hats and trumpets as tall as their bodies. She is neat and beautiful as always in a dress, her dark brown hair pulled back from her face.

"Ciao, Paloma," I say.

She startles, then her face breaks into a big smile and she squeezes my neck. "*Topolina*! I thought we had lost you forever."

We watch Captain Foster walk up the stairs to the stage. He is a picture of exhausted contentment as he takes a seat next to Captain Thomas, who shakes his hand in greeting. Two large microphones are set up at a wide podium. The tall, gray-haired mayor of Florence, elegant with his tricolor sash, stands and approaches the podium while an interpreter speaks through a second microphone.

"This city, this nation, has given the world so much." The mayor surveys the crowd, his voice echoing in the square. "At one time the capital of the Kingdom of Italy, and widely regarded as the most beautiful city in the world, the home of Medici, the cradle of the Renaissance, Florence has given us countless monuments and museums. She has given us the writings of Dante Alighieri, of Niccolò Machiavelli, of Galileo Galilei, of Petrarch and Boccaccio."

I take in the sight of Captain Foster, sitting on the stage before this sea of Florentine men, women, and children. He is received as a liberator, a quiet hero. I've come to see him in that light more and more. He is inspirational and impressive in his self-deprecating manner. The warm summer sun beats down on my face, warming me from within.

"Today," the mayor goes on, "the Allies are here to give back to this beautiful city, to return to *bell'Italia* the priceless artworks which are rightfully hers." The crowd applauds, but they quiet to allow him to resume. "Now future generations will be free to enjoy them, among so many other treasures once thought lost."

The Allied officers' speeches focus more on themes of liberty. "Just like these precious works of art," one colonel says, "freedom and democracy must be valued and safeguarded. They can always be stolen again by another, and we will not always be able to count on victory. The price of war is great for all sides, in victory and in defeat. So let diligence be our campaign, standing guard against those who would rob us of the things which are vital, which are central symbols of our culture and humanity." The Italian interpreter's melodic voice sounds out through the microphone as the colonel says, "So we all swear to pay the price of eternal vigilance, necessary for the preservation of freedom and democracy. Long may they bring peace and good fortune to the people of Florence and all of Italy, to the people of Europe and all the world."

When it's Mr. Poggi's turn to speak he says, "This is the second time in my career that I've had to evacuate my museum. This time was in many ways more challenging than in the Great War. What I've learned through these experiences is that it's more than about just the material conservation of individual works. It's about protecting the integrity of Italy's artistic patrimony as a whole, as an expression of the historical and cultural traditions of this nation—they are different and distinct from anywhere else. And any Italian work of art, even privately owned, could be considered part of the 'spiritual patrimony' of our nation. And I am gratified—and grateful—to the men on this stage, who have helped return the spiritual patrimony of Florence to us at last."

When they call Captain Foster's name, he seems surprised to have been invited to the microphone. For a fleeting moment, his eyes meet mine, then he begins to address the crowd in Italian, which flows easily from his lips. "I am humbled to be standing before you," he begins. "Humbled not only to have played some small part in this worthy endeavor, but also to have had such able assistants. None of this would be possible without two women who are standing here in the front row. Their contributions have been as important as my own. Would you please join me in recognizing my invaluable assistants, Miss Josephine Evans and Signorina Paloma Innocenti?"

The burst of applause thunders around me, detached and surreal, and I feel as if my feet have lifted from the cobblestone and I'm floating in the square above the crowd. But then Paloma squeezes my hand, I come back to my senses, and release the breath I didn't even know I was holding.

Sometimes, I think, you have to figure out what you're not before you can become who you are. Now with some distance, I see this whole adventure of joining the Women's Army Corps wasn't really about biding my time until I could find a husband. It wasn't about doing whatever I had to do to avoid turning into my mother. It wasn't even about not having the strength to resist Dot's overwhelming powers of persuasion, or even about following her to the enlistment center in New Haven on a whim.

These are the thoughts that cycle through my mind after the ceremony ends and the crowd disbands from the Piazza della Signoria. Paloma and I walk past the tinkling boar fountain, near the Por Santa Maria district and her family's tailor shop.

If I had committed to any one of those directions, I see now that I would have sold myself short. I would have been walking the wrong path. Working with my brave yet flawed Monuments Men helped me see that there were more opportunities out there than I ever knew were possible. That there is wonder and power in small things—both in the world around us and also inside us. That the broken parts of me are just part of a journey that's brought me back to a place that lives like a flame within my heart.

I wish my Italian was good enough to share these revelations with Paloma, who walks with me through the old *porcellino* market. Maybe one day I'll be competent enough in Italian, but right now, it all seems too deep, too difficult to explain, and so instead, I just say, "Good thing I rubbed the pig's nose." In the shallow fountain at the base of the bronze *porcellino*, with his tusky grin, his bronze nose scrubbed shiny and reflective in the sun, two little boys are slapping their hands in the water. "It brought me back here to Florence, after all."

"It always works," she says, smiling, reaching her hand out to touch the well-rubbed end of the pig's snout.

We continue to the river, where the Ponte Vecchio stands defiant and eternal over the sparkling Arno. People are strolling back and forth across the bridge like they have for hundreds of years. From the edge of the bridge, we catch a view of Ponte Santa Trinità, where people are walking and pushing their bicycles over the temporary Bailey bridge. I hope it won't be long before the bridge can be recon-structed, as beautiful as when Ammannati and Michelangelo envi-sioned it all those centuries ago. And more than anything, it will be a momentous day when all the bridges are reconstructed and things can go back to the way they were before the war. Back when people on both sides of the river were just two halves of a united whole.

But my train of thought is interrupted with the sight of a familiar face at the crest of the Ponte Vecchio.

Corrado.

"I was wondering when my brother was going to honor us with his presence," Paloma jokes.

His strong arms are slack at his sides, curls loose over his face. I freeze, unable to think of anything else. I am struck by the moment of rediscovery, doubt obliterated along with all thought. He is just as handsome as I remember, even more so. He raises his hand in greeting to us. And his smile tells me that our reunion is as striking to him as to me, perhaps even more so still.

There is so much to say. That life is short and fragile. That we have to reach for things—like art—that seem out of reach. Things bigger than ourselves. That we must do the things that make life worth living. And say the things that matter before it's too late.

But for now, I'm speechless.

39

EVA

I COME OUT OF THE MINE TO FIND THE NOON SKY bright and blue behind the familiar peaks of Altaussee. In the valleys below, fields are ripening to gold in small patches amid the emerald mountainside, striped and dotted with stands of pine, fir, and birch. Along the lakeside, every line of small homes and sleepy farms finds its perfect mirror image in the glass-smooth surface of the water.

Against the beauty of the summer morning, the diesel trucks that rumble toward the salt mine's entrance seem like brutish impostors. Brown and blockish, coughing fumes, their engines echoing across the pass. I stand in the entrance to the mine, my arms wrapped around myself against the dark rush of cold air, watching them come.

When the next truck comes to a heaving, huffing stop, I step into the sun. I remove my coat, still damp and infused with the briny smell of the salt mine, and set it on a wooden table the miners use for their lunch break. I sling my camera strap around my shoulder and climb the grassy hillside that affords a view unlike any other in the village. It's the same place where I found Gerhard in tears on his sixteenth birthday.

When I reach the top and turn back, the whole area is abuzz with activity. The men are opening the backs of the trucks, ready to receive the treasures. A pair of Allied soldiers emerge from the mine entrance, carrying a carefully labeled wooden crate. I wonder how

many months this effort will take. Now there are many more priceless treasures in the mine than when I left. More than six thousand
objects, my father has told me. Deep inside the earth, new scaffolds,
shelves, and storage areas have been constructed for works by some
of the greatest masters the world has ever known. Michelangelo, Ver-
meer, Rubens. So many others. The men have even constructed a
specially designed room to house the *Ghent Altarpiece*, one of the
mine's greatest treasures of all. One of the interpreters has told me
the Americans complain that many hundreds of the things pulled
out of the mine are worthless German nineteenth- and twentieth-
century paintings. I think they are biased, but I admit that the works
we kept at San Leonardo and Campo Tures far outstripped anything
held here.

I lift my old box camera and frame a grainy view of a half a dozen
Allied armored trucks. The men in their drab olive uniforms, their
dusty helmets. For a while, I watch them heft the pictures out of the
darkness, bringing them into the light of a new era. I lift my camera and take a picture of a skinny American soldier who looks even
younger than Gerhard.

Amid all of this, I recognize Captain Foster's rusted, battered jeep.
A group of American GIs loiter around Georgette, laughing. Their
sparkling white teeth, their swaggering, loud chatter, their joking—
all of it seems incongruous in this place that, for so long, has been
dark and quiet. Hidden away. But we are living in a new world now.

At the entrance to the mine, I watch Gerhard emerge. Remove his
coat and helmet. Adjust his small, round spectacles. Father emerges
from the door behind my brother, speaking animatedly with the
American interpreter, who is listening carefully, his helmet crooked
on his head. Now I can see my little brother has grown a head taller
than our father since I left Austria. I press the shutter release and capture the three of them like that: serious, earnest, deep in conversation
among the trucks. The aperture swirls to black and just like that, they
are frozen in time.

• • •

I pick up my camera bag and the last piece of Oma's apple cake, then walk out to the broad stretch of garden behind the house. At the edge of the property, Gerhard is building a fire in an earthen pit while our German shepherd patrols the edges of the weeds. The dog jogs to where Gerhard is bent over, placing logs in a careful arrangement. Presses his ears flat, lowers his head, offers his soft belly. By instinct, he knows Gerhard is a grown man now. Gerhard ruffles the dog's scruffy undercarriage and continues his work.

When the flames are blue and crackling, I sit in a low chair and break my piece of cake in two, handing Gerhard the other half. The dog settles at our feet, his bushy eyebrows alive, his brown eyes flickering, observing the flames, the cake, our conversation.

"When I first got my orders," Gerhard says, poking one of the logs with a long, crooked stick, "I felt sure I would be on the next train to Russia. I guess by that point, I was prepared to go." He shrugs his broad shoulders. "But the day before I was to leave, we got the telegram. All of us working in the mine—and there were many more men here then—would be exempted from military service elsewhere."

"That's because stashing paintings and sculptures away for the Führer's museum became more important than any other priority," I say bitterly. "I can tell you that from firsthand experience." I think back to the dozens of high-ranking officers who stepped over the threshold of the prison at San Leonardo to lay eyes on the treasures they thought would soon live within the confines of the Reich.

Gerhard nods. "All that time, Papa was just trying to find someone who could override the Nero Order. Anyone who was authorized to remove the charges from the mine. We were all desperate."

Over weeks, the story has emerged. How Hitler was adamant that the masterpieces inside the mines not fall into enemy hands, even at the cost of destroying all of them in a single, violent blast. How the gauleiter of our own region set the charges in order to win the Führer's favor, bringing in dozens of crates labeled MARBLE, full of powerful explosives and placed among the underground chambers. It seemed no one could stop him.

But it was Gerhard—my sensitive, reticent soldier—who rose to the challenge. His eyes dancing with pride, our father told Oma and me how Gerhard devised a plan to reset the charges, and convinced all the other miners to join in the effort. To do it, they risked their lives—both at the hands of the explosives as well as the consequences of defying our gauleiter's orders.

"Then we reset the charges," Gerhard explains. "One of the old men knew how to rewire them. We only set a few, less powerful ones around the entrance to the mine. We defused all the ones in the underground rooms. After everyone was safely outside, we just . . ." He makes a gesture like pushing down a lever to activate an explosive. "The entrance was sealed off and everything inside was safe."

Gerhard. A war hero. Imagine that. I can't help but smile. In any other circumstance, he might have been taken prisoner. Instead, he is a savior. He was more brave, more cut out for war, than I was all along.

For a long time, we sit together in comfortable silence and I think about how Gerhard decided to save everything by resetting the charges so that they blasted only the entrance to the mine but none of the tunnels—and none of the art—inside. How this served to seal off the masterpieces inside, waiting in the pitch dark until they could be rescued. Now a special group of American GIs has removed all the explosives and made an entrance in the rubble so they can safely evacuate the treasures from the depths of the earth.

Gerhard pokes at the logs, the flames dancing and flickering in his eyes as the sun falls behind the green mountain peaks. The air turns cool. I pull my sweater closer across my chest, then reach into my camera bag. There are several stacks of small pictures I developed in Florence. Little shots of Palazzo Guadagni, of Horst, of Paloma and

Enzo, of all the famous paintings and half-blasted buildings I documented over months.

But I don't want to revisit those pictures now. Maybe in time, I'll feel ready to bring them out and scatter them across Oma's little dining table. Maybe in time, I'll feel ready to talk about them, to tell my family what I've seen and done. But not now.

Deeper inside the bag are dozens of small metal film canisters. Undeveloped, unrealized memories of my time in Italy. I pick up each silver cylinder and look at my own dull, distorted reflection in the flickering firelight. I know what's inside each one. Pictures that show the shadowed faces of caretakers at the countryside depots. The patterned marble of Florence's baptistery and cathedral. Enzo's haggard, beautiful face. Medieval tower houses along the Arno that exist now only as figments. Wavering reflections of church façades on the Grand Canal. Caravaggio's languid face of Bacchus. Duccio's gigantic, flat Madonna, floating in a sea of glistening gold. Adam, bewildered, scratching the crown of his head. And Eve, in her moment of decision that will cast the die of human fate for all eternity. Inside each cartridge is the record of every hiding place from Tuscany to Südtirol. A record of our tracks. Every trace that put us on the wrong side of history.

Gerhard stands and places another log on the fire. It ignites, a tiny flame flaring, wisps of smoke rising into the darkening sky. He adds another and the sparks leap high and golden, spitting and twirling upward. I turn a canister over between my fingers, consider my reflection in all its distortions. In each roll, every last masterpiece in black, white, and every shade of gray.

Then, one by one, I cast each roll of film into the fire, watching them char and melt in the searing, unrelenting heat. Eventually, the flames consume them.

ACKNOWLEDGMENTS

It's thanks to my readers that I get to spend my days doing what I love most: researching, writing, and sharing my passion for the ever-fascinating history of art. Reading a novel requires an investment of many hours. I am profoundly grateful to each one of you who chooses to spend some of your own precious hours reading my words.

Many helpers assisted me in assembling the haphazard pieces of research that I gathered together for this project. Bits of critical information seemed to fall from the sky like scattered leaflets dropped from a plane. I ran to snatch them up before they blew away.

Curator Tracy Bradford and the volunteer archivists at the Women's Army Museum at Fort Lee, Virginia, pinpointed firsthand testimonies and remarkable photographs of WACs serving in the Fifth Army division in Italy. Perusing the museum's archival boxes and their wonderfully presented museum of women's roles in the army has been one of the highlights of my research.

Franklin Burton in the archives of the National Gallery of Art in Washington, D.C., gathered the cartons containing art historian and Monuments Man Frederick Hartt's personal papers and photographs, and pointed out things he thought I would be interested in reviewing. Kathleen Williams helped me assemble a mountain of boxes related to the history of the Monuments Men and Women, and their incredible work. Tracing the story of the Florentine treasures from Tuscany to Alto Adige kept me on the edge of my seat for the better part of a year.

In Florence, the staff of the Kunsthistorisches Institut helped me piece together the complex history of the German art history institute's activities during the war years. I am grateful to archivist Silvia Garinei for her enthusiastic help via email and Zoom, and to the institute's director, Professor Gerhard Wolff, for supporting my project and for access to their collection. Dr. Ute Diercks shared her valuable time and incomparable knowledge of German wartime photography in Florence. She pulled archival boxes for me in the Phototek and pointed me to fascinating resources about Hilde Lotz-Bauer, a rare female photographer who worked for the ill-fated Professor Kriegbaum and whose life bore strange, real-life parallels to the fictional Eva I'd already drafted on the page.

Special thanks to Simona Pasquinucci in the archives of the Uffizi Galleries for sharing the unbelievable handwritten, marked-up, and hastily typed inventories of priceless works of art spirited away to countryside depots in a historic moment of desperate action. Thanks to the lively and knowledgeable Attilio Tori at the Casa Siviero for sharing his deep knowledge of the Florentine art collections and the people whose brave, individual decisions helped bring these treasures back home. Francesca Bozzetto and Corinna Maria Carrara helped me experience World War II Florence through their eyes, pointing out things I'd never seen on my many trips to the city. Learning about the important activities of the *partigiani* in the Oltrarno was particularly fascinating.

While in Florence, I had the pleasure of lodging at the Palazzo Guadagni, which used to house the Kunsthistorisches Institut and whose top-floor *pensione* is now a hotel. It was thrilling to peruse the corridors and rooms of the former Pensione Sorelle Bandini, where Eva and Josie stayed. Special thanks to proprietors for offering me a prosecco on the loggia and sharing their knowledge of the building's history. When they surprised me by opening a tiny door behind an armoire—a dark attic where the Bandini sisters hid Jewish families, just above the heads of Nazi-appointed German scholars on the floors below them—it took my breath away. I also stayed at the Excelsior Hotel in a room I imagined might be the one where Colonel Langsdorff held Lucas Cranach's *Adam* and *Eve*. I thank Noemi Chiara for sharing otherwise inaccessible parts of the hotel that helped bring its 1940s atmosphere to life for me.

My generous art history colleagues, Paola Vojnovic and Alexandra Korey, connected me to more helpful people in Florence. Elena Fulceri was my eyes, ears, and feet in Florence during the global pandemic, when I couldn't be there myself. She got me into those hidden repositories in the Tuscan countryside and arranged important resources for me in advance of my arrival. I couldn't have asked for a more dedicated, resourceful assistant. Thanks to everyone at the various privately owned Tuscan depots who opened access for me. Of this group, my special thanks goes to Andrea Pestelli for sharing his incredible family history at Montegufoni (the inspiration for Santa Lucia in this story). *Grazie mille* to Marco Paoletti for getting me to the Tuscan depots and back to the Oltrarno in one piece.

Many thanks to Harald Pernkopf in Altaussee for sharing important resources related to the singular history of the salt mines. Thanks to Lana Praprotnik, who helped me track down Austrian and German historical sources—everything from 1940s-era train schedules between Salzburg and Florence, to military draft documents for Austrian boys in the district of Altaussee. Readers love to point out when I've gotten a historical detail like these wrong. I don't know a historical novelist who makes such errors intentionally, but I take responsibility for any that may remain.

On the home front, I am grateful to Jordyn Sava for her cheerful support in even the most unglamorous parts of an author's job. Profound gratitude to editor extraordinaire Jessica Hatch for her tough love on my earliest, ugliest drafts; she always helps me make them better. And to my online art history students for never failing to ask the thought-provoking, sometimes surprising, questions that keep me engaged.

At HarperCollins, I am grateful to my editor, Tessa Woodward, for her enthusiastic support of this project; and to Mary Interdonati, Eliza Rosenberry, and Amelia Wood, whose passion for sharing books with the world shines through. And thanks to my wonderful literary agent, Jenny Bent, for her sound advice and for helping me keep everything in order.

Continued gratitude to my husband and children for their patience with my 4:00 a.m. wakeup calls, plus many hours spent at my desk and in my own head. And to my mother, who, after five decades, remains my fastest and most enthusiastic reader. She speed-reads stories that take me years to pull together, then smiles and asks the most important question: What's next?

AUTHOR'S NOTE

In 2003, Ralf Peters, a staff member at the Central Art History Institute in Munich, discovered a set of mysterious boxes in the photo library. The boxes contained photographs cataloging Italian monuments damaged by Allied attacks during World War II. Who took these pictures, why did they take them, and what were they used for? The boxes made for a fascinating research project and exhibition titled "Archives of the Destroyed Artworks of Italy." It opened a door to a little-known German story against the backdrop of World War II Italy—a story about how photography could be used to persuade and propagandize. To illustrate what Eva realizes in *The Last Masterpiece*: that she always assumed photographs told the truth, but now she sees they only tell a story.

My job as a historical novelist, of course, is also to tell a story. But telling a story about art protection in World War II Italy means facing ironies, contrasts, concealments, and complications that are as puzzling to untangle as any box of mysterious photos. In contrast to France, Poland, and other European countries on Germany's radar, Italy was an "occupied ally." That means the Germans were initially intent on documenting buildings that should be protected. But as the Italians switched allegiances, the line between "protection" and "looting," just like a blurry or confusing photograph, became fuzzy at best.

I've written several historical novels about the intersection of art and war. The more research I do on the topic of World War II plunder, the more I realize that those who loved and understood art the most were sometimes the ones tasked with stealing it, or at least with hiding what they knew. They were art historians. Curators. Art critics. Dealers. Collectors. Preservationists. Conservators. Professionals like me. I cannot imagine being put in a situation where my livelihood, maybe even my life, hinged on stealing or hiding something I was trained to save. This paradox continues to fascinate me, as both an art historian and a historical novelist. The staggering scale of art pilfering in Europe between 1938 and 1945 contrasts with the reality that, except in the case of the highest-ranking officials, the specific activities of individual art professionals are sparsely documented. Mostly, these art workers flew under the radar and went back to their lives after the war. I imagine that many must have felt shame over their wartime activities and never passed on their stories. It's left me with a lot to ponder about what this experience was like, and to imagine it on the pages of historical fiction.

Both in history and historical fiction, I think the most interesting characters are bad guys who aren't completely bad, and good guys who aren't completely good. This is how human beings really behave. *The Last Masterpiece* has given me the chance to explore the same set of wartime circumstances from opposing sides—with characters who grapple with how their actions might impact the fate of an irreplaceable treasure, and if their decisions will turn them up on the right side of history or not.

In a similar way, today in our culture, we experience deep divisions within our communities and even inside our own families; we read the news and struggle to know what is real and how opposing stories are spun from the same set of facts. We struggle to decide what actions to take, when things are rarely black and white. This stark reality made this project feel relevant and contemporary as I picked my way through the complicated historical research.

In addition to the art historical research, assembling the cast of characters for *The Last Masterpiece* proved an unwieldy task. As a historical novelist, I like to develop fictional characters set against a historical backdrop that is as authentic as I can make it. *The Last Masterpiece* casts fictional protagonists acting alongside characters who represent real historical figures, as well as others loosely based on real people.

On the Axis side, Eva is a fictional character, which makes it possible for her to navigate everything from the bowels of the Altaussee salt mines to the looted art repositories in the Tuscan countryside to the snipers' nests along the Arno on the eve of the explosion of the Florentine bridges. Other characters in her chapters—including the Bandini sisters in the Palazzo Guadagni, Italian art officials like Giovanni Poggi and Cesare Fasola, the German art history institute personnel like Friedrich Kriegbaum and Ludwig Heydenreich, and Nazi military leaders like Leopold Reidemeister and Alexander Langsdorff—are all based on real historical figures. I have done my best to ascribe specific characteristics and actions that are true to the historical record. Eva's father and brother are loosely based on the real-life miners whose decision to defy orders and disarm the explosives placed inside the Altaussee salt mines saved some of the world's most valuable and beloved masterpieces.

Among the most chilling research sources for this side of the conflict are interrogation reports and German documents that the Monuments Men confiscated as the war ended. The Captured Documents of the German Kunstschutz, now in the archives of the National Gallery in Washington, D.C., helped shape my understanding of how the Allies interpreted the complicated information the Germans gave them about their efforts to safeguard art collections. Another set of fascinating sources are the leather-bound art catalogs prepared for Adolf Hitler, as a showcase for the works of art he intended for his supermuseum in Linz, Austria. Nearly a dozen of the original thirty-one catalogs remain missing, and the Monuments Men and Women Foundation is offering a reward for their return. Who created these catalogs? Surely people who knew about art, who were intimately familiar with these works. People like Eva and Horst. In my research, I found an incidental mention of an unnamed German female photographer taking pictures of paintings in the snow outside the jail at San Leonardo—another elusive historical detail that is the perfect fodder for the historical novelist.

Deciding that Eva would be a photographer gave me the chance to take a deep dive into the history of 1940s photography. After completing the first draft of Eva's story, I discovered the photographer Hilde Lotz-Bauer, a real-life version of Eva who worked at the Kunsthistorisches Institut in Florence; whose photographs documented Allied damage to Florentine monuments under the direction of Friedrich Kriegbaum; and who took up temporary residence at Palazzo Guadagni. While Eva is not intentionally based on Hilde, what a surprise it was to find that Eva's story so closely mirrored this groundbreaking female photographer working in Florence at the time.

On the Allied side, Josie is also a figment of my imagination. I based her childhood on my own few years of living in New Haven, Connecticut, a city of stark contrasts between its haves and have-nots. Josie's wartime experience is based on firsthand accounts I researched of the Fifth Army WACs, the first American women on foreign soil who were not considered auxiliary but were officially embedded with male troops. General Douglas MacArthur called them "my best soldiers."

Nothing compares with traversing the past alongside a person who lived in the time period and experienced things firsthand. I pored over archival photographs, letters, diaries, and oral histories to imagine Josie's incredible experience in Italy. I stand in awe of these women who did something no American woman had done before, but whose stories are, by contrast, self-deprecating and often humorous. Their eyewitness accounts gave me details like undergarments hanging from tent flaps, tuna crackers and poker games, impromptu Christmas dances, and wedding dresses sewn from parachutes that failed to open (you can see one on display at the Women's Army Museum at Fort Lee, Virginia). Josie's fellow WACs and American soldiers—including Dot, Dante, and others—are fictional but pinned on these delicious testimonies.

The two Monuments officers in this story—Rand Thomas and Wallace Foster—are loosely based on the real Allied officers who contributed so much to the return of the Italian art treasures at the end of the war. Real-life Monuments Men Frederick Hartt and Deane Keller cut a path across war-torn Italy in a dogged pursuit to save monuments and works of art. These men experienced the immediate aftermath of horrors I cannot imagine, like the inferno that decimated the Camposanto in Pisa and the bombing of Santa Maria delle Grazie in Milan, which left Leonardo da Vinci's *Last Supper* exposed to the elements as the last wall standing. They worked tirelessly alongside their Italian colleagues, and if it weren't for their efforts to ensure the safety of these works, we would be much poorer as a world culture. To appreciate the full scope of the work of these Monuments officers, check out the publicly available resources of the Monuments Men and Women Foundation and read the wonderful books by Robert Edsel, Lynn Nichols, and Ilaria Dagnini Brey.

To be clear, in this book I have ascribed personality traits and quirks to Captains Thomas and Foster that their real-life inspirations may not have had. So much has been documented about the important role of the Monuments Men in the restitution of works of art across Europe during World War II that it would be difficult to improve on the real-life history in a fictionalized account. There's no way I could do justice to Monuments Man Frederick Hartt's beautifully written memoir, *Florentine Art Under Fire,* and I did not attempt to do so. All the same, Josie's chapters closely follow the itineraries and efforts of the Monuments officers in Italy. My ultimate aim is to preserve the spirit of their adventures and contributions. I hope my story has served to honor the efforts and sacrifices of Captain Thomas's and Captain Foster's real-life alter egos.

Across Italy, fifty or so secret repositories housed hidden works of art during the war. Thirty-eight of these hiding places were located in Tuscany alone, a testament to the incredible cultural wealth of the region. Each one—whether a privately owned villa, a remote castle, a quiet wine cellar—was under constant threat from the ground and the air. The security of the priceless artworks depended on regular people who risked everything to keep them safe. According to the Monuments Men and Women Foundation, across Europe, some 1,400 repositories—churches, tunnels, mines, barns, and so on—held millions of artworks displaced in some way by the war. Even though thousands of cultural objects are still missing today, what's more amazing is that most of these treasures returned to their original collections unscathed. To me, that seems like a miracle.

And now, the elephant in the room. The most unsung heroes of the real history behind *The Last Masterpiece* are the Italian art officials and partisans whose individual actions helped save Italian patrimony for future generations. English-language accounts of this period often use the word "discovery" to describe the Allied role in the restitution of Italian art. But the truth is that these works were never lost. The Italian art officials hid their most precious masterpieces themselves—thousands of works of art in a matter of weeks. Then they documented their ever-shifting locations, and tracked them in a convoluted, complicated game of cat and mouse. Understandably, they kept things secret, and their work and contributions remain little known to an English-speaking audience.

The reality is that the Italian superintendents and art officials played an enormous role. They risked their lives to protect the works of art that they saw as symbols of their history and culture, the very embodiment of their own identity. The characters of Paloma, Corrado (who you may remember from my novel *The Stolen Lady*), and Enzo are all fictional, but gave me the chance to explore the complicated allegiances that tore apart many Italian families during this tumultuous chapter in history, while they risked everything to save these centuries-old masterpieces that helped them remember who they were.

During the course of research on this book, the generous Italians I interviewed in person opened my eyes to the incredible bounty of stories on the Italian side of the war. As I researched, written and oral firsthand accounts began to stack up on my shelves. Stories of individual bravery and heroism. Of heartbreaking hardship and loss. So much untold. Often, the end of one historical novel leads to the beginning of the next. I'm deep down the research rabbit hole, collecting tales so incredible you can't make them up. Still, I endeavor to do so, for the historical novelist always finds holes in the ragged tapestry of the historical record that beg to be filled in.

ABOUT THE AUTHOR

Laura Morelli is an art historian and a *USA Today* bestselling historical novelist. She holds a Ph.D. in art history from Yale University and is the author of fiction and nonfiction inspired by the history of art. She has taught college students in the U.S. and Italy, and has developed lessons for TED-Ed. Her flagship guidebook, *Made in Italy*, has led travelers off the beaten track for more than two decades. Her award-winning historical novels include *The Painter's Apprentice, The Gondola Maker, The Giant, The Night Portrait,* and *The Stolen Lady*. Learn more at lauramorelli.com.

For more historical background, videos, images, maps, research, interviews, reading recommendations, and further resources related to *The Last Masterpiece,* visit lauramorelli.com/masterpiece.